W9-BNN-816

New York Times **bestselling author**

ELIZABETH LOWELL

**Winner of the Romance Writers of America
Lifetime Achievement Award**

"Lowell is great!"
Johanna Lindsey

"I'll buy any book with
Elizabeth Lowell's name on it."
Jayne Ann Krentz

"There is no finer guarantee of outstanding romance
than the name of Elizabeth Lowell."
Romantic Times

"Hers are frequently the books you pick up
to read again and again."
The State (Columbia, MD)

"Lowell's keen ear for dialogue and intuitive
characterizations consistently place her a cut above
most writers in this genre."
Raleigh News & Observer

"No one can stir the passions, no one can keep
tension at such a sizzling high, no one can give you
more memorable characters."
Rendezvous

By Elizabeth Lowell

THE SECRET SISTER • ALWAYS TIME TO DIE
DEATH IS FOREVER • THE COLOR OF DEATH
DIE IN PLAIN SIGHT • RUNNING SCARED
MOVING TARGET • MIDNIGHT IN RUBY BAYOU
PEARL COVE • JADE ISLAND • AMBER BEACH

WINTER FIRE • AUTUMN LOVER
ENCHANTED • FORBIDDEN • UNTAMED
ONLY LOVE • ONLY YOU
ONLY MINE • ONLY HIS

EDEN BURNING • THIS TIME LOVE
BEAUTIFUL DREAMER • REMEMBER SUMMER
DESERT RAIN • WHERE THE HEART IS
TO THE ENDS OF THE EARTH • LOVER IN THE ROUGH
A WOMAN WITHOUT LIES • FORGET ME NOT

Don't miss the next book by your favorite author.
Sign up now for AuthorTracker by visiting
www.AuthorTracker.com.

Forget Me Not

ELIZABETH LOWELL

Beautiful Dreamer

(Originally published as *Valley of the Sun*)

AVON BOOKS

An Imprint of HarperCollinsPublishers

Forget Me Not and *Beautiful Dreamer* were originally published in mass market by Avon Books in 1994 and 2001 respectively, and *Beautiful Dreamer* was originally published in hardcover in January 2001 by William Morrow.

Forget Me Not was previously published in an altered form by Silhouette Books in 1984.

Beautiful Dreamer was previously published in an altered form entitled *Valley of the Sun* by Silhouette Books.

FORGET ME NOT/BEAUTIFUL DREAMER. Copyright © 2005 by Two of a Kind, Inc. *Forget Me Not* copyright © 1984, 1994 by Two of a Kind, Inc. *Beautiful Dreamer* copyright © 2001 by Two of a Kind, Inc. All rights reserved. Printed in the United States of America. No part of this book may be used or reproduced in any manner whatsoever without written permission except in the case of brief quotations embodied in critical articles and reviews. For information address HarperCollins Publishers Inc., 10 East 53rd Street, New York, NY 10022.

HarperCollins books may be purchased for educational, business, or sales promotional use. For information please write: Special Markets Department, HarperCollins Publishers Inc., 10 East 53rd Street, New York, NY 10022.

FIRST EDITION

ISBN 0-06-084771-9

05 06 07 08 09 JTC/RRD 10 9 8 7 6 5 4 3 2 1

Forget Me Not

for my sister
Susan Mills
port in many storms

1

When the phone rang, Alana was almost relieved. Though it was before dawn, she was wide awake. Since she had come back from Broken Mountain, she had slept very little, and never peacefully.

Kicking aside the tangled sheets, Alana turned toward the phone. It was too early for anyone she knew on the West Coast to be up and about. That meant it was probably her brother in Wyoming calling to see how she was.

Calling to see if she remembered what had happened on Broken Mountain.

"Hello," Alana said, keeping her voice steady with an effort.

"Sis? Is that you?"

"Hi, Bob. How's Merry?"

"Counting the weeks until February," said Bob, laughing. "If she gets much bigger, we'll have to put her in a stall with the brood mares."

Alana smiled at the thought of petite, blond Merry tucked into one of the heated stalls Bob kept for his prize mares.

"Better not let Merry hear you say that," Alana warned.

"Hell, it was her idea." Bob paused, then said, "Sis?"

Alana's hand tightened on the phone. She had heard that tone before, little brother to big sister, a smile and affectionate wheedling.

He wanted something from her.

"When are you coming home?" Bob asked bluntly.

Alana's heart began to beat too fast. She didn't know how to tell her brother that she was frightened by the thought of returning to the ranch where Broken Mountain rose steeply, mantled in ice and darkness.

Before her last trip to Broken Mountain, Alana had loved the ranch, the mountains, the silence, the heights, and the clouds swirling overhead. She had loved the memories of Rafael Winter—Rafe reflected in every lake, every fragrant forest, sunsets and sunrises sweeping across the land like fire, the wind's keening harmonies echoing the music Rafe had made on his harmonica.

Alana had come to love the land even more

because she and Rafe had been part of it, lovers suspended between sky and mountains, more beautiful than either, timeless, burning with the sun.

But now those mountains terrified Alana.

Now the memories of Rafe were a brittle, cutting armor that she pulled around her like the colors of dawn, hoping to drive away the horror and darkness that crawled up out of the abyss of those six missing days.

"I don't—" Alana began.

Her brother interrupted before she could refuse.

"I've already talked to your agent," Bob said cheerfully. "He told me you've refused to accept any concerts and won't even look at the songs he sends to you."

"Yes, but— "

Bob kept talking.

"So don't tell me how busy you are," he said. "If you're writing songs again, you can write them just as well here. Better. You always did your best work here."

With a conscious effort, Alana loosened her grip on the phone. She had no more excuses, so she said nothing.

"Sis? I need you here."

"Bob, I don't think—" Alana began.

Then her voice broke.

"Don't say no," Bob said urgently. "You don't even know what I want yet."

And you don't know what I want, Alana thought rebelliously. You've never even asked if I want something.

The words went no further than Alana's thoughts, a silent cry of need. Yet even as the cry echoed in her mind, she recognized its unfairness.

What she needed, Bob couldn't provide. She needed warmth and reassurance, safety and a man's hard strength standing between her and the abyss, protecting her until she knew what had happened and could protect herself once more.

She needed love waiting instead of terror. She needed a dream to banish a nightmare.

She needed Rafael Winter.

But Rafe was just a dream. The nightmare was real.

With a deep breath, Alana gathered herself and set about living in her new world just as she always had lived. Alone, depending only on herself.

She had done this many times before, the deep breath and the determination to do the best she could with what she had, no matter how little that seemed to be when the nightmare descended like a storm.

"What do you want?" Alana asked softly.

"You know cash has always been a problem with the ranch," Bob said quickly. "Land poor, as they say. Well, Merry and I had this idea for a classy—and I mean *classy*—dude operation. High-country fishing safaris for people who can pay high prices."

Alana made a neutral sound.

"We had it all planned, all lined up, all our

ducks in a row," Bob said. "Our first two cus-
tomers are very exclusive travel agents. Their
clientele list reads like *Who's Who*. Everything
was going great for us, and then . . ."

"And then?" Alana prompted.

"Merry got pregnant," Bob said simply. "I
mean, we're both happy, we've been trying for
two years, but . . ."

"But what?"

"Dr. Gene says Merry can't go on the pack
trip."

"Is that a problem?"

"Hell, yes. She was going to be our cook and
entertainer and general soother, take the rough
edges off. You know what I mean, sis."

"Yes. I know."

It was the same role Alana had played in
the family since she was thirteen and her
mother died, leaving behind three boys, a dev-
astated husband, and a daughter who had to
grow up very quickly. That was when Alana
had learned about reaching down into herself
for the smile and the touch and the comfort
that the people around her needed. She had
rebuilt the shattered family as best she could,
for she, too, needed the haven and the laughter and the warmth.

"It will really be more like time off than a
job," coaxed Bob.

Alana heard the coaxing, but it didn't move
her nearly as much as the disturbing thread of
urgency beneath the soft tone.

"Riding and fishing and hiking in the high
country just like we used to do. You'll love it,

sis! I just know it. A real vacation for you."

Alana throttled the harsh laugh that was clawing at her throat.

Vacation, she thought, shuddering. In the mountains that nearly killed me. In the mountains that still come to me in nightmares.

Oh, God, that's some vacation my little brother has planned for me!

"Sis," Bob coaxed, "I wouldn't ask if I didn't really need you. I don't have anywhere else to turn. The pack trip is all set and the two dudes are here. Please?"

Unexpectedly, a vivid memory of Rafe came to Alana. . . . Late summer, a narrow trail going up Broken Mountain, a lame horse, and a saddle that weighed nearly as much as she did. She had been leading the horse, dragging the saddle, and watching the silent violence of clouds billowing toward a storm. At fifteen, she knew the dangers of being caught on an exposed ridge in a high-country cloudburst.

Without warning, lightning had come down so close to her that she smelled the stink of scorched rock. Thunder came like the end of the world. Her horse had screamed and reared, tearing the reins from her hand. Then the horse's lameness had been overridden by terror. The animal had bolted down the mountainside, leaving her alone.

She, too, had been terrified, her nostrils filled with the smell of lightning and her ears deafened by thunder. Then she had heard someone calling her name.

Rafe had come to her across the talus slope,

riding his plunging, scrambling horse with the strength and grace she had always admired. He had lifted her into the saddle in front of him and spurred his horse back down the slope while lightning arced around the mountain.

Sheltered in a thick growth of spruce, she had waited out the storm with Rafe, wearing his jacket and watching him with the eyes of a child-woman who was more woman and less child with every breath.

On Broken Mountain Alana had found first fear, then love, and finally horror.

She wondered if there was another balance to be discovered on Broken Mountain, opposites joined in harmony, freeing her from nightmare.

The possibility shimmered through Alana like dawn through night, transforming everything.

"Sis? Say something."

Alana was appalled to hear herself take a deep breath and say calmly, "Of course I'll help you."

She didn't hear Bob's whoop of victory, his assurances that he wouldn't tell any of the dudes that she was the famous singer Jilly, his gratitude that she was helping him out. She didn't hear anything but the echoes of her own terrifying decision to go back to Broken Mountain.

As though Bob sensed how fragile Alana's agreement was, he began speaking quickly.

"I've got you booked on the afternoon flight

to Salt Lake. From there, you're booked on a little feeder flight into the airport here. Got a pencil?"

Bemused, Alana stared at the phone. The simple fact that Bob had thought to take care of the details of her transportation was so unusual as to be overwhelming. It wasn't that Bob was thoughtless; he was very considerate of Merry, to the point that he was almost too protective.

Alana, however, had always been taken for granted in the manner that parents and older siblings often are.

"Sis," Bob said patiently, "do you have a pencil? He'll skin me if I louse this up."

"He?" asked Alana as she went through the drawer in her bedside table looking for a pencil. "Who will skin you alive?"

There was a static-filled silence. Then Bob laughed abruptly.

"The travel agent who made the arrangements," he said. "Who else? Ready?"

"Hold your horses," Alana muttered.

She found a pencil, grabbed a credit card receipt, turned it over, and wrote down the flight numbers and times.

"But that's today!" she protested.

"Told you we needed you."

"That's not much warning, little brother."

"That's the whole idea," Bob muttered.

"What?"

"Nothing. Just be sure you're on that plane or my butt is potato salad."

"Bob," Alana began.

"Thanks, sis," he said quickly, talking over her. "You won't regret it. If anyone can pull it off, he can."

"Huh?"

Alana felt as though she was missing half the conversation, and the most important half at that.

"He who?" she asked.

"*Damn*," Bob said beneath his breath.

"The travel agent?" Alana guessed.

"Yeah, the travel agent. He's something else," said Bob dryly. "See you tonight, sis. 'Bye."

Before Alana could say good-bye, the line was dead.

She stood and stared at the receiver clenched in her hand. Silently she asked herself why she had agreed to do something that terrified her.

She was a fool to let warm memories of Rafe Winter lure her back to the icy source of nightmare. She didn't even know if Rafe was in Wyoming. In the past, Rafe's job had taken him all over the world. His time at the Winter ranch had been limited to a few weeks now and then.

It had been enough, though. Alana had learned to love Rafe and to accept his absences. She had learned to live for the day when he would come home and marry her and she would never cry for him at night again.

And then Rafe had died.

Or so the Pentagon had said.

The phone began to make whooping noises, telling Alana that the receiver had been off the hook too long. She hung up and stared at the phone.

It was deep red, like the flowers in the Spanish tile that covered the kitchen counters. Red, like the wildflowers that grew high on the mountain slopes.

Red. Like blood.

"Did I see Jack die on Broken Mountain?" Alana whispered. "Is that what my mind refuses to remember?"

With a shudder, she jerked away from the bright red telephone.

Rubbing her arms to chase away the chill that had been with her since Broken Mountain, Alana walked quickly to the closet. She pulled on jeans and an old cotton blouse. From habit, she buttoned the blouse completely, concealing the delicate gold chain that Rafe had given her years before.

As always, Alana's fingertip lingered on the tiny symbol of infinity that was part of the chain.

Love ever after, love without end.

A beautiful dream.

Reality was six days missing from her life and a nightmare whose end she was still trying to find.

Slowly Alana walked into the kitchen. With hands that wanted to tremble, she plugged in the coffeepot, scrambled two eggs, and buttered a piece of toast. She forced herself to eat and drink, to clean up after herself, to do all the things normal people did.

An untidy stack of papers on the kitchen counter caught Alana's eye. Unhappily she looked at them. She should read the song sheets her agent had sent over. New songs. Solo material for the sole survivor of the Jack 'n' Jilly duo.

Alana should read the music, but she wouldn't, for she no longer could sing.

That was the most bitter loss, the most unbearable pain. Before Broken Mountain, she had been able to draw songs around her like colors of love chasing away the gray of loneliness and the black of despair.

Alana had taken her love for a man she believed was dead and transformed that love into song. Singing had been her greatest pleasure, her reason for living after she was told that Rafe was dead.

Jack Reeves hadn't loved her, but she had always known that. Nor had Alana loved him. Theirs had been a business marriage, pure and simple. Jack loved fame and Jilly loved singing.

Now Jack was dead and Jilly could sing only in her dreams. And in her dreams it was Rafe's harmonica that accompanied her, not Jack's flawless tenor.

Awake, she had no music in her.

It wasn't stage fright. Even now, Alana wasn't afraid of being in front of people. Nor was she afraid of the savage doggerel that would be running through the fans' minds as they watched her.

Jack 'n' Jilly
Went up the hilly

To fetch a pail of vodka.
Jack fell down
And broke his crown,
And Jilly lost her mind.

Alana had listened to it all before, read it in print a hundred times, heard it whispered. She could face that.

But she couldn't face opening her lips and feeling her throat close with terrible finality, as though there were no more songs in her now and never would be again. Nothing but screams and the silence of death.

Uneasily Alana looked around, barely recognizing her surroundings. Even though she had lived in the Oregon apartment for three weeks, the place was neither comfortable nor familiar to her. It certainly wasn't as real to her as the nightmare about Broken Mountain.

But then, nothing was.

Abruptly Alana walked toward the wall of glass that opened onto a small patio. She stood near the glass, trying to shake off the residue of nightmare and death, fear and mistakes, and most of all a past that was beyond her ability to change.

Or even to understand.

"I'll remember what happened someday," Alana whispered. "Won't I?"

2

TAKING A RAGGED BREATH, Alana forced herself to look at the dawn that was etching the room in shades of rose and vermilion, gold and translucent pink. The September sun's radiant warmth was like a miracle after the endless hours of night.

Alana found herself staring at her reflection in the glass as she often had since Broken Mountain, searching for some outer sign of the six-day gap in her memory. Nothing showed on the outside. She looked the same as she had before she had gone up the mountain with the worst mistake of her life—her singing partner, Jack Reeves.

The singing hadn't been the mistake. The

13

marriage of convenience had. He had always pushed for more. She had always wished for less. He had wanted a reconciliation. She had wanted only an end to a marriage that never should have begun. So they had gone up Broken Mountain together.

Only one of them had come back.

No visible marks of the ordeal in the mountains remained on Alana's five-foot, five-inch body. Her ankle had healed. It ached only when it was cold. The bruises and welts and cuts were gone, leaving no scars. She no longer had to diet to fit into the slender image demanded by the public. Since Broken Mountain, her appetite was gone.

But it wasn't something that showed.

Alana leaned forward, staring intently at her nearly transparent reflection in the sliding glass door. Everything still looked the same. Long legs, strong from a childhood spent hiking and riding in Wyoming's high country. Breasts and waist and hips that were neither large nor small. Her skin was a golden brown. Nothing unusual. Nothing at all.

"Surely something must show on the outside," Alana told her reflection. "I can't just lose my singing partner and six days of my life and wonder about my sanity and not have any of it show."

Yet nothing did.

Though Alana's eyes were too dark, too large, too haunted, her mouth still looked as though it was curved around a secret inner smile. Her hair was still black and glossy, divided into two thick braids that fell to her waist.

Alana stared at her braids for a long moment, realizing for the first time that something about them made her . . . uneasy.

She had never particularly liked having long hair, but she had accepted it as she had accepted the nickname Jilly, both necessary parts of the childlike image that audiences loved to love. The image went with her voice, clear and innocent, as supple and pure as a mountain stream. . . .

Water rushing down, cold, and darkness waiting, lined with rocks, ice and darkness closing around, clouds seething overhead, lightning lancing down, soundless thunder.

Fear.

It was too cold, no warmth anywhere, only fear hammering on her, leaving her weak.

She tried to run, but her feet weighed as much as the mountains and were as deeply rooted in the earth. Each step took an eternity. Try harder, move faster, or get caught.

She must run!

But she could not.

She was broken and bleeding, screaming down the night, running, stumbling, sprawling, and then lifted high, she was falling, she spun and screamed, falling. . . .

Alana's heart beat wildly, responding to the fragment of nightmare turning in her mind.

"Stop it!" she told herself fiercely, seeing the

reflection of her terror in dawn-tinted glass
and sliding black shadows.

She took several deep breaths, bringing herself under control, telling herself that she had
to stop treating her nightmare as though it was
real. It wasn't.

The nightmare was simply a creation of her
mind as it dealt with the horror of Jack's death
in a mountain storm, and her own near death
from exposure and the fall that had left her
bruised and beaten.

That was what Dr. Gene had told Alana,
and she had trusted his gravelly voice and
gentle smile for as long as she could remember. He had said that her amnesia, while unusual, was not pathological. It was a survival
reflex. When her mind felt she was strong
enough to remember the details of her husband's death and her own suffering as she
clawed her way down Broken Mountain, then
she would remember.

And if she never remembered?

That, too, was all right, he had assured her.
Alana was young. She was healthy. She could
go out and make a new life for herself.

Alana's lips twisted bitterly as she remembered the conversation. It had been easy for
Dr. Gene to say. He wasn't the one whose
mind was turning six missing days into endless nightmares.

It wasn't that Alana missed her dead husband. She and Jack had been two very separate people bound together by the accident of
perfect harmony. That was enough for a suc-

cessful singing career. It wasn't enough for a successful marriage.

Yet sometimes Alana couldn't help feeling that maybe, just maybe, if she had done something different, Jack might have been different. If she had tried harder or not so hard. If she had been weaker or not quite as strong. If she had cared for Jack more or pitied him less . . .

Maybe it could have worked for the two of them.

But even as the thought came, Alana knew it was a lie. The only way she might have loved Jack was if she had never met Rafe Winter, never loved and lost him; Rafe, with his laughter and his passion and his gentle, knowing hands.

She had loved Rafe since she was fifteen, had been engaged to him when she was nineteen. And they had become lovers when she was twenty.

Rafael, dark hair and amber eyes glowing, watching her change as he touched her. Her fingers had looked so slender against the male planes of his face, the sliding sinew and muscle of his arms. His strength always surprised her, as did his quickness, but she had never been afraid with him. Rafe could hold her, could surround her softness with his power, and she felt no fear, only a consuming need to be closer still, to be held tighter, to give herself to him and to take him in return.

With Rafe there had only been beauty.

Then, four years ago, the Pentagon had told Alana that Rafael Winter had died. They had told her nothing more than that. Not where her fiancé had died. Not how. Certainly not why. Just the simple fact of his death.

It was a fact that had destroyed Alana. Never again would the lyric beauty of Rafe's harmonica call to her across the western night. Never again would her voice blend with that of the silver instrument that sang so superbly in Rafe's hands. She had sung with Rafe for pleasure and had known no greater beauty except making love with him, bodies and minds sharing an elemental harmony that surpassed everything, even song.

Alana had been empty after Rafe's death. She had cared for nothing. Even life. When the minutes and hours without Rafe had piled up one by one, dragging her down into darkness, she had turned instinctively to a singing career as her only salvation, her only way to hold on to the love she had lost.

Singing meant Jack Reeves, the man she had sung with in all the little cafés and fairs and roadhouses, the man for whom singing was a business rather than a pleasure. Jack had measured Alana's vulnerability, her desperation, and then he had calmly told her that there would be no more duets unless she married him and left the high plains for the high life in the city.

Alana had resisted marriage, wanting no man but the one who was dead.

Then the hours without Rafe had heaped into the hundreds, a thousand, fifteen hundred . . . and she had agreed to become Jack's wife because she must do something or go insane. Rafe was dead. There was nothing left but the singing career that Jack had badgered Alana for even while Rafe was alive.

So Alana had left the high plains and mountains of Wyoming, hoping that in another part of the world she wouldn't hear Rafe in every summer silence, sense him in every moonrise, feel his heat in the warmth of the sun.

She had married Jack, but it was a marriage in name only. With Jack Reeves there had been nothing but an emptiness Alana had tried to fill with songs.

Then, a year ago, she had been told that Rafael Winter was alive.

Rafe wasn't the one who told her. Rafe had never called her, never written, never in any way contacted the woman he once had said he loved.

Now it was Jack who was dead, killed four weeks ago by the wild country he had despised. Alana had been with Jack on Broken Mountain when he died. She didn't remember it. Those six days were a blank wall.

Behind that wall, fear seethed and rippled, trying to break free.

Alana closed her eyes, unable to face their dark reflection in the glass door. Rafe was dead and then not dead. Jack was dead now and forever.

Her love for Rafe, undying.

With a small sound, Alana closed her eyes, shutting out her reflection.

"Enough of that," she told herself sharply.

"Stop living in the past. Stop tearing yourself up over things you can't change."

She opened her eyes, confronting herself in yet another reflection, another window dawn hadn't yet made transparent. She looked like a mountain deer caught in the instant of stillness that precedes wild flight. Long brown limbs and brown eyes that were very dark, very wide, wild.

A black braid slid over Alana's shoulder and swung against the glass as she leaned forward. She brought the other braid forward over her shoulder, too. It was a gesture that had become automatic; when her braids hung down her back she pulled them forward.

That way if she had to run suddenly, the braids wouldn't fly out behind her, twin black ropes, perfect handles for something to grab and hold her and *lift her up, trapped, weightless, falling, she was falling—*

Alana choked off the scream clawing at her throat as she retreated to the kitchen. Her reflection looked back at her from the window over the kitchen sink.

Without looking away from her reflection, Alana groped in a nearby drawer. Her fingers closed around the handle of a long carving knife. The honed blade glittered as she pulled it out of the drawer.

She lifted the knife until the blunt side of the blade rested against her neck just below her chin. Calmly, deliberately, she began slicing through her left braid. The severed hair fell soundlessly to the floor. With no hesitation, she went to work on the right braid.

When Alana was finished she shook her head, making her hair fly. The loose, natural curls that had been imprisoned beneath the weight of the braids were suddenly set free. Wisps of hair curved around her face, framing it in soft, shiny black. Her brown eyes glowed darkly, haunted by dreams.

Abruptly Alana realized what she had done. She stared at the long black braids on the floor, the steel knife in her hand, the reflection in the window that no longer looked like Jilly.

The knife dropped to the floor with a metallic clatter.

Alana stared at herself and wondered if she had finally gone crazy.

She ran from the kitchen to the bedroom. There she pulled her few things out of drawers and off hangers, packing haphazardly. It didn't matter. Most of her clothes were still in L.A. or at the ranch, left there in anticipation of weeks spent with her brother and Merry.

Alana had been too frightened to go back to the ranch and pack after she had fled from the hospital. She had simply run to Portland, a city she had never lived in, hoping to leave the nightmare behind her.

It hadn't worked.

As Alana packed, she kept looking at the bedroom telephone. She wanted to call Bob, say that she had changed her mind, and then hang up before he could object.

Yet each time she reached for the phone, she

thought of Rafael Winter, a dream to balance her nightmare. She used memories of Rafe like a talisman to draw the terror from her six missing days.

The greatest pleasure and the greatest horror in Alana's life had both taken place on Broken Mountain. Perhaps they would simply cancel each other, leaving her free to go on with her life. Neutral, balanced.

No memories of the man she had loved, or of the husband she had not. No memories of the lover who had died and then come back, or of the husband who had died and would never come back.

Rafe, who came to her in dreams.

Jack, who came to her in nightmares.

When Alana finally picked up the phone, it was to call a nearby beauty salon and make an appointment to have her hair styled. The utterly normal activity reassured her.

By the time Alana got on the airplane, she felt more calm. Tonight she would be home. If nightmares stalked her, it would be down the familiar corridors of her childhood home rather than the strange hallways of a rented apartment.

She held to that thought as she switched planes in Salt Lake City and settled in for the flight to Wyoming. When the flight attendant offered her a newspaper, she took it automatically. As she flipped through the pages, a headline in the entertainment section caught her eye: *Jack 'n' Jilly's Last Song.*

Though Alana's stomach tightened just at

the headline, she knew she would read the article. She had read everything written about Jack's death, even the most sleazy imaginings of the yellow press. She would read this article too, because she could not help herself.

It had been a month since Jack's death. A month since the gap in Alana's memory had appeared. She kept hoping that someone, somewhere, would know more about Jack's death than she did, that a word or a phrase in an article would trigger something in her mind and the six days would spill through, freeing her from nightmare.

Or sending her into a more terrifying one.

There was always that possibility lurking in the twisting shadows of Alana's mind. Dr. Gene had suggested that there could be horrors Alana didn't imagine, *even in her nightmares.*

Amnesia could be looked at in many ways. Gift of a kind God. Survival reflex. Fountainhead of horror. All of them and none of them. But fear was always there, pooled in shadows, waiting for night.

Maybe Dr. Gene was right. Maybe she would be better off not remembering.

Impatiently Alana shoved the unwelcome thought away. Nothing could be worse than not trusting her own mind, her own courage, her own sanity.

Since her mother had died, Alana had always been the strong one, the one who saw what had to be done and did it. Then Rafe had died and Alana had been destroyed.

Music was her only solace after Rafe died.

With music she wove glowing dreams of warmth, of his laughter, and of a love that could only be sung, not spoken.

With song, Alana had survived even Rafe's death.

She could do whatever she had to. She had proved that in the past. Somehow, she would prove it again. She would survive.

Somehow.

Alana shook out the paper, folded it carefully, and began to read.

The first part of the story was a review of the Jack 'n' Jilly album that had just been released. The rest of the article was a simple recital of the facts of Jack's death.

A month ago, Jack and Jilly Reeves had gone on a pack trip in the Wyoming backcountry. An early winter storm had caught them. They had tried to get out, but only Jilly had made it. Jack had been killed in a fall. Somehow Jilly had managed to hobble down the mountain on a badly wrenched ankle until she had reached a fishing cabin and radioed for help.

Even so, she had nearly died of exposure. The experience had been so traumatic that she had no memory of the time she spent crawling down the mountain.

Hysterical amnesia, brought on by husband's accidental death, said the doctor. Apparently Sheriff Mitchell had agreed, for the autopsy listed the cause of Jack's death as a broken neck sustained in a fall.

Accidental.

Nothing new. Nothing unexpected. Nothing

to fill the horrifying gap six days had left in Alana's mind. Yet still she reread the article, searching for the key to her amnesia.

She didn't find it. She was neither surprised nor disappointed.

As the plane slid into its landing pattern, Alana sat up and nervously ran her fingers through her hair. Her head felt strange, light, no longer anchored by dense black braids. The stylist had transformed the remnants of her knife-cut hair into a gently curling cap that softened but didn't wholly conceal the taut lines of Alana's face. The result was arresting—glossy midnight silk framing an intelligent face that was haunted by loss and nightmare.

The small commercial plane touched down with a slight jerk. A few eager trout fishermen got off before Alana, trading stories of the past and bets for the first and biggest fish of the future.

Reluctantly she stood up and walked slowly down the narrow aisle. By the time she descended the metal stair, her baggage had already been unloaded and placed neatly beside the bottom step. She picked up her light suitcase and turned toward the small building that was the only sign of habitation for miles around.

Behind her the aircraft began retreating. It moved to the head of the runway, revved hard, and accelerated, gathering speed quickly, preparing itself for a leap into the brilliant high-plains sky.

Alana reached the building as the plane's engines gave a full-throated cry. She set down her bag and turned in time to see the aircraft's wheels lift. It climbed steeply, a powerful silver bird flying free. She listened until the engines were no more than a fading echo and the plane only a molten silver dot flying between the ragged grandeur of the Wind River and Green River mountain ranges.

For a moment, Alana closed her eyes. Her head tilted toward the sky, catching the surprising warmth of Wyoming's September sun. The wind was rich with scents of earth and sagebrush. Not the stunted, brittle sagebrush of the southwestern desert but the thick lavender-gray high-country sage, bushes as high as her head, higher, slender shapes weaving patterns against the empty sky.

A clean wind swept down from the granite heights, carrying sweetness and the promise of blue-green rivers curling lazily between rocky banks, of evergreens standing tall and fragrant against the summer moon, of coyotes calling from the ridge lines in harmonies older than man.

Home.

Alana breathed deeply, torn between pleasure and fear. She heard footsteps approaching across the cement. She spun around, her heart beating heavily. Since Broken Mountain, she was terrified if anything approached her unseen.

A man was walking toward Alana. The sun was at his back, reducing him to a black silhouette.

As he walked closer, he seemed to condense into three dimensions. He was about seven inches taller than she was. He had the easy stride of someone who spent as much time hiking as he did on horseback. His jeans were faded. His boots showed the scuff marks peculiar to riding. His shirt was the same pale blue as the sky.

Hair that was a thick, rich brown showed beneath the rim of his black Stetson. His eyes were the color of whiskey. His lips were a firm curve beneath a silky bar of mustache.

With a small sound, Alana closed her eyes. Her heart beat wildly, but it sent weakness rather than strength coursing through her. She was going crazy, hallucinating.

Storm and cold and terror, falling—

"Alana," he said.

His voice was gentle, deep, reaching out to her like an immaterial caress.

"Rafael?" She breathed raggedly, afraid to open her eyes, torn between hope and nightmare. "Oh, Rafe, is it really you?"

3

RAFE TOOK ALANA'S ARM, supporting her. Only then did she realize that she had been swaying as she stood. His warmth and strength went through her like a shock wave. For an instant she sagged against him.

Then she realized that she was being touched, *held*, and she wrenched away. Since Broken Mountain she was terrified of being touched.

"It's really me, Alana," said Rafe, watching her intently.

"Rafael—" Alana's voice broke as emotions overwhelmed her.

She extended her fingers as though she

would touch him, but did not. With an effort that left her aching, she fought down the tangle of emotions that was closing her throat. She was being torn apart by conflicting imperatives.

Run to him. Run from his male presence.

Be held by him. Fight not to be held by a man.

Love him. Feel nothing at all because the only safety lay in numbness.

Remember how it felt to be loved. Forget, forget everything, amnesia spreading outward like a black balm.

"Why are you here?" Alana asked in a ragged voice.

"I've come to take you home."

Inexplicably the words all but destroyed Alana.

With a small sound, she closed her eyes and struggled to control herself. Coming here had been a mistake. She had wanted a dream of love to balance a nightmare of terror. Yet Rafe was real, not a dream.

And so was terror.

Alana clung to the shreds of her control, wondering what had happened during those six missing days that had left a black legacy of fear. And most of all, she wondered if the nightmare would ever end, freeing her, letting her laugh and sing again . . . or if she would simply give up and let the black balm of amnesia claim all of her mind. All of *her*.

Rafe watched Alana, his eyes intent. When

he spoke, his voice was casual, soothing, utterly normal.

"We'd better get going," he said. "I'd like to beat the thundershower back to the ranch."

He bent to take Alana's suitcase from her nerveless fingers. With the easy movements of a mountain cat, he straightened and walked toward a Jeep parked a few hundred feet away.

Alana watched, her hand resting on the high neck of her burgundy silk blouse. She took a deep breath, still feeling the warmth of Rafe's hand on her arm as he had supported her. Just that. Support. Help. There was nothing to fear in that.

Was there?

Motionless, her heart beating rapidly, her dark eyes wide, Alana watched Rafe turn back toward her. The slanting, late-afternoon sun highlighted the strong bones of his face and made his amber eyes glow. As he turned, his shirt stretched across his shoulders, emphasizing the strength and masculine grace of him. His jeans fit the muscular outline of his legs like a faded blue shadow, moving as he moved.

Alana closed her eyes, but she could still see Rafe. He was burned into her awareness with a thoroughness that would have shocked her if she had any room left for new emotions. But she didn't.

She was still caught up in the moment when he had turned back to her, light brown eyes burning, mouth curved in a gentle male smile.

That was Rafe. Male. Totally. She had forgotten, even in her dreams.

Rafe hesitated as though he wanted to come back to Alana, to stand close to her again. But he didn't move. He simply watched her with whiskey-colored eyes that were both gentle and intent, consuming her softly, like a song.

"It's all right, Alana." Rafe's voice was as gentle as his smile. "I've come to take you home."

The words echoed and reechoed in Alana's mind, sending sensations sleeting through her. Cold and wind and snow, fear and screams clawing at her throat. Pain and terror and then . . .

It's all right, wildflower. I've come to take you home.

She had heard words like those before, and something more, other words, incredible words, dream and nightmare intertwined.

Without knowing it, Alana whimpered and swayed visibly, caught between hope and terror, dream and nightmare.

"What?" Alana demanded breathlessly, her heart beating faster, her voice urgent. "What did you say?"

Rafe watched Alana with a sudden intensity that was almost tangible.

"I said, 'I've come to take you home.' "

He waited, but Alana simply watched him with wide, very dark eyes. His expression shifted, gentle again.

"Bob threatened to have my hide for a saddle blanket if I didn't get home before Merry fell asleep. And," added Rafe with a smile, "since she falls asleep between coffee and dessert, we'd better hurry."

Alana watched Rafe with eyes that were dazed and more than a little wild.

"That wasn't what you said before." Alana's voice was as tight as the hand clutching her throat. Her eyes were blind, unfocused.

"Before?" asked Rafe, his voice intent, hard, his topaz eyes suddenly blazing like gems. "Before what, Alana?"

It was dark, so dark, black ice around her, a glacier grinding her down until she screamed and tried to run, but she couldn't run because she was frozen and it was so cold.

Alana shuddered and swayed, her face utterly pale, drained of life by the savage nightmare that came to her more and more often, stalking her even in the day, stealing what little sanity and peace remained.

Instantly Rafe came to her, supporting her, his hands warm and strong. Even as she turned toward his warmth, fear exploded in her. She wrenched away with all her strength.

Then she realized that it hadn't been necessary. Rafe hadn't tried to hold her. She was reacting to something that hadn't happened.

"I—" Alana watched Rafe with wild, dark eyes. "I don't—I'm—"

She held out her hands helplessly, wondering how to explain to Rafe that she was drawn to him yet terrified of being touched, and that above all she thought she was losing her mind.

"You're tired," Rafe said easily, as though Alana's actions were as normal as the slanting afternoon light. "It was a long flight. Come on. Bob and Merry are waiting for you like kids waiting for Christmas morning."

Rafe turned back to the suitcase, picked it up, and walked toward the Jeep. Before he arrived, a man got out of a Blazer and approached Rafe.

As Alana walked closer, she recognized Dr. Gene. He smiled and held out his arms to her. She hesitated, fighting against being held, even by the man who had delivered her, who had attended to all of her childhood ills, and who had cried in frustration at her mother's deathbed. Dr. Gene was as much a member of her family as her father or her brothers.

With an effort of will that made her tremble, Alana submitted to Dr. Gene's brief hug. Over her head, the doctor looked a question at Rafe, who answered with a tiny negative movement of his head.

"Well, it's good to have you back, " said Dr. Gene. "No limp, now. You look as pretty as ever, trout."

"And you lie very badly," said Alana.

But she smiled briefly at hearing the pet name from her childhood. Even so, she stepped back from the doctor's hug. Her haste was almost rude, but she couldn't help herself. That was the worst part of the nightmare, not being able to help herself.

"The only thing that was ever pretty about me was my voice," Alana said.

"No pain?" persisted the doctor. "How's your appetite?"

"No pain," she said evenly, ignoring the question about her appetite. "I don't even use the elastic bandage anymore."

And then Alana waited in fear for the doctor to ask her about her memory. She didn't want to talk about it in front of Rafe.

She didn't want to talk about her memory at all.

"You cut your hair," said Dr. Gene.

Alana raised her hand nervously, feeling the short, silky tendrils that were all that remained of her waist-length braids.

"Yes." And then, because the doctor seemed to expect something more, she added, "Today. I cut it today."

"Why?" asked Dr. Gene.

The doctor's voice was as gentle as the question was blunt.

"I . . ." Alana stopped. "I was . . . I wanted to."

"Yes, but why?" he asked.

The doctor's blue eyes were very pale, very watchful beneath the shock of gray hair and weathered forehead.

"The braids made me . . . uneasy," said Alana.

Her voice was tight, her eyes vague, frightened.

"Uneasy? How?" asked Dr. Gene.

"They kept . . . tangling in things." Alana

made a sudden motion with her hands, as though she were warding off something. "I..."

Her throat closed and she could say nothing more.

"Alana's tired," Rafe said, his voice quiet and very certain. "I'm going to take her home. Now. Excuse us, Dr. Gene."

Rafe and Dr. Gene exchanged a long look. Then the doctor sighed.

"All right," Dr. Gene said, his voice sharp with frustration. "Tell Bob I'm trying to get some time off to go fishing."

"Good. The Broken Mountain camp always has a cabin for you."

"Even now?"

"Especially now," said Rafe sardonically. "We may disagree on means, but our goal is identical."

Alana looked from one man to the other. "Goal?"

"Just a little fishing expedition in the high country," Rafe said, turning to her. "The good doctor prefers to drown worms. I, on the other hand, prefer to devise my own lures."

Dr. Gene smiled briefly. "Bet I catch more trout than you, Winter."

"I'm only after one trout. A very special one."

Alana wondered about the currents of emotion running between the two men, then decided she was being overly sensitive. Since Broken Mountain, she jumped at sighs and shadows and saw conspiracy and pursuit where there was nothing behind her but night and silence.

Dr. Gene turned to Alana. "If you need anything, trout, I'll come running."

"Thanks."

"I mean it, now," he added.

"I know," she said softly.

He nodded, got back in his Blazer, and drove off with a backward wave.

Rafe handed Alana into the Jeep truck and climbed in himself. She watched him covertly the whole time, matching memories with reality.

The Rafe Alana saw was older, much more controlled than in her memories. When he wasn't smiling, his face was hard, almost frightening in its planes and angles. Yet he still moved with the easy strength that had always fascinated her. His voice was still gentle, and his hands were . . . beautiful. It was an odd way to describe anything as strong and quick and callused as a man's hands, yet she could think of no better word.

Not all masculine hands affected Alana like that. Sometimes she saw hands and terror sleeted through her.

"We're lucky today," said Rafe as he guided the Jeep expertly over the rough field that passed as the parking lot.

"Lucky?" said Alana, hearing the thin thread of panic in her voice and hating it.

"No rain so far. It rained a lot the last few days."

Alana tried to conceal the shudder that went

through her at the thought of lightning and thunder, mountains and slippery black ice.

"Yes," she said in a low voice. "I'm glad there isn't a storm."

"You used to love storms," said Rafe quietly.

Alana went very still, remembering one wild September afternoon when a storm had caught her and Rafe while they were out riding. They had arrived at the fishing cabins, soaked and breathless. He had peeled her wet jacket off her, then her blouse, and his hands had trembled when he touched her.

Closing her eyes, Alana tried to forget. The thought of being touched like that by Rafe made her weak with desire—and all but crazy with fear, dream and nightmare tangled together in a way she could neither explain nor understand.

But if Rafe remembered the September storm when he had undressed and caressed Alana until there was only fire and the hushed urgency of their breathing, his memories didn't show in his face or in his words.

"We had a good frost above five thousand feet last week," continued Rafe. "The aspen leaves turned. Now they look like pieces of sunlight dancing in the wind."

He looked quickly at Alana, seeing the lines of inner conflict on her face.

"You still like aspen, don't you?" Rafe asked.

Alana nodded her head, afraid to trust her voice. Mountain aspen, with its white bark

and quivering, silver-backed leaves, was her
favorite tree. In fall, aspens turned a yellow as
pure as . . . *sunlight dancing in the wind.*

A sideways glance told her that Rafe was
watching her with intent, whiskey-colored
eyes.

"I still like aspen," said Alana.

She tried to keep her voice normal, grateful
for the safe topic. The present, not the past.
The past was more than she could handle. The
future was unthinkable. Just one day at a time.
One hour. A minute. She could handle anything, one minute at a time.

"Even in winter," Alana added, her voice
little more than a whisper, "when the branches
are black and the trunks are like ghosts in the
snow."

Rafe accelerated down the narrow, two-lane
blacktop road. He glanced for a moment at the
magnificent granite spine of the Wind River
Mountains, rising on his left.

"Be a while before there's real snow in the
high country," he said. "The frost put down
the insects, though. Then it turned warm
again. Trout ought to be hungry as hell. That
means good fishing for our dudes—guests,"
he corrected immediately, smiling to himself.
"Nobody likes being called a dude."

"*Our* dudes?" asked Alana slowly, watching Rafe with eyes so brown they were almost
black.

Sunlight slanted through the windshield, in-
tensifying the tan on Rafe's face and the richness of his dark brown mustache, making his

eyes almost gold. His teeth showed in a sudden gleam of humor, but his expression said the joke was on him. He answered her question with another question.

"Didn't Bob mention me?"

"No," said Alana, her voice ragged. "You were a complete surprise."

Rafe's expression changed.

For an instant Alana thought she saw pain, but it came and went so quickly that she decided she had been wrong. She was being too sensitive again. Overreacting. Yet she still wanted to touch Rafe, to erase the instant when she sensed that she had hurt him and didn't even know how.

The thought of touching Rafe didn't frighten Alana. Not like being touched did. For an instant she wondered why, but all that came to her was . . . nothing. Blank.

Like those six missing days.

"Looks like we'll have to do it the hard way," Rafe said softly.

His voice was an odd mixture of resignation and some much stronger emotion in his voice, something close to anger.

Before Alana could speak, Rafe did.

"Bob and I are partners."

"Partners in what?" Alana asked.

"The dude—*guest* ranch. The cottages and fishing water are on Lazy W land. My land. The horses and supplies belong to Bob. He's the wrangler, I'm the fishing guide, and you're the cook. When Dr. Gene shows up," added

Rafe with a crooked smile, "he'll be the chief worm dunker."

Stunned, Alana could think of nothing to say. She would be going up Broken Mountain with Rafael Winter. Dream and nightmare running together, pouring over her, drowning her in freezing water.

She sat without moving, letting the sunlight and the landscape blur around her, trying to gather her fragmenting thoughts.

No wonder Bob didn't say anything to me about Rafael Winter, Alana thought unhappily. If I'd known that Bob had a partner, I might have let the partner bail Bob out of the mess.

Especially if I knew that the partner was Rafael Winter.

It was all Alana could do to handle the recent past, amnesia and accident and death. Bob should have known that she couldn't handle a present that included Rafe.

A year ago Bob had told her that Rafe was still alive. Then Bob had taken her letter to Rafe's ranch. Bob had come back with the letter unopened, *Deceased* written across the envelope's face—written in Rafe's distinctive hand.

Bob had seen Alana's pain and anger, then her despair. And now he was asking her to go up Broken Mountain with Rafael Winter, to confront the past love and loss all over again. And the present nightmare.

Alana shuddered and tried to think of nothing at all.

"Alana," began Rafe.

Somehow she was certain that he was going to talk about the past, about dying but not quite, about surviving but not wholly, about her and Jack and an envelope with a "dead" man's handwriting across its face, tearing her apart.

She wasn't strong enough for that. Not for the past. Not for anything but this minute. Now.

"Bob and Tom Sawyer have a lot in common," Alana said quickly, her voice as strained as it was determined. "Don't go near either of them if a fence needs painting. Unless you like painting fences, of course."

Rafe hesitated, visibly reluctant to give up whatever he had wanted to say. But Alana's taut, pale face and haunted eyes persuaded him.

"Yes," Rafe said slowly. "Bob could charm the needles off a pine tree."

Relieved, Alana sat back in the seat again.

"The only thing that ever got even with Bob was the hen he poured jam on and then dumped in the middle of eight half-grown hounds," Alana said. "That hen pecked Bob's hands until she was too tired to lift her head."

Rafe's laughter was as rich as the slanting sunlight pouring over the land. Alana turned toward him involuntarily, drawn by his humor and strength, by the laugh that had haunted her dreams as thoroughly as the scent of evergreens haunted the high country.

"So that's how Bob got those scars on his

hands," Rafe said, still chuckling. "He told me it was chicken pox."

Alana's lips curved into a full smile, the first in a long time. "So it was, after a fashion."

She glanced up at Rafe through her thick black lashes and caught the amber flash of his eyes as he looked away from her to the road. For an instant her heart stopped, then beat more quickly. He had been watching her.

She wondered if he was comparing the past and present as she had. And remembering.

"How did Bob talk you into painting his fence?" Alana asked quickly, wanting to hear Rafe talk, his voice deep and smooth and confident, like his laughter.

"Easy. I'm a sucker for fishing. I spend a lot of my time in the high country chasing trout. Might as well make it pay."

"Land poor," murmured Alana. "Rancher's lament."

"I have it better than Bob," Rafe said, shrugging. "I'm not buying out two brothers."

Alana thought of Dave and Sam, her other brothers. Sam worked for a large corporation with branches around the world. Dave was a computer programmer in Texas. Neither brother had any intention of coming back to the ranch for anything other than occasional visits. Of the four Burdette children, only she and Bob had loved the ranching life.

Nor had Jack Reeves loved the ranching life he had been born into. He couldn't leave Wyoming fast enough. He had hungered for city streets and applauding crowds.

"Jack hated Wyoming."

Startled, Alana heard the words echoing in the Jeep and realized she had spoken aloud.

"He's dead," she added.

"I know."

Alana stared at Rafe.

"How—" she began.

Then she realized that of course Rafe knew. Bob must have told him. They were partners. But how much had Bob told Rafe? Did he know about her amnesia? Did he know about the nightmares that lapped over into day, triggered by a word or a smell or the quality of the light? Did he know she was afraid she was going crazy?

Did Rafe know that she clung to her memories and dreams of him as though they were a lifeline able to pull her beyond the reach of whatever terror stalked her?

As though Rafe sensed Alana's unease, he added quietly, "It was good of you to help Bob. It can't be easy for you so soon after your . . . husband's . . . death."

At the word *husband* Rafe's mouth turned down sourly, telling Alana that her marriage was not a subject that brought Rafe any pleasure.

But then, Rafe had never liked Jack. Even before Rafe had "died," Jack had always been urging Alana to pack up and leave Wyoming, to build a career where artificial lights drowned out the cascading stars of the western sky.

"Did Bob tell you how Jack died?" asked

Alana, her voice tight, her hands clenched in her lap.

"No."

Rafe's voice was hard and very certain.

Alana let out a long breath. Apparently Bob had told Rafe only the bare minimum: Jack had died recently. Nothing about the amnesia or the nightmares.

She was glad Bob had told Rafe something. It would explain anything odd she might do. Jack was dead. Recently. She was a widow.

And when she slept, she was a frightened child.

The Jeep jolted off the pavement onto a gravel road. The miles unwound easily, silently, through a land of gently rolling sagebrush and a distant river that was pale silver against the land. Nothing moved but the Jeep and jackrabbits flushed by the sound of the car.

There was neither fence nor sign to mark the beginning of the Broken Mountain Ranch. Like many western ranchers, Alana's grandfather, father, and brother had left the range open wherever possible. They fenced in the best of their breeding stock and let the beef cattle range freely.

Alana searched the land for signs of Broken Mountain steers grazing the high plains.

"Has Bob brought the cattle out of the high country yet?" asked Alana.

"Most of them. He's leaving them in the middle elevations until late September. Later if he can."

"Good."

The longer the cattle stayed in the high and middle elevations, the less money Bob would have to spend on winter feed. Every year was a gamble. If a rancher left his cattle too long in the high country, winter storms could close in, locking the cattle into certain starvation. But if the rancher brought his cattle down too soon, the cost of buying hay to carry them through winter could mean bankruptcy.

"Grass looks thick," Alana said.

She wanted to keep to the neutral conversational territory of ranching, afraid that if the silence went on too long, Rafe might bring up the recent past and Jack's death. Or, even worse, the far past. Rafe's death and resurrection, a bureaucratic error that had cost Alana . . . everything.

"I'll bet Indian Seep is still flowing," she said. "The hay crop must have been good."

Rafe nodded.

Alana's dark eyes cataloged every feature of the land—the texture of the soil in road cuts, the presence or absence of water in the ravines, the smoky lavender sheen of living growth on the snarled sagebrush, the signs of wildlife, all the indicators that told an educated eye whether the land was being used or abused, husbanded or squandered.

And in between, when Alana thought Rafe wouldn't notice, she watched his profile, the sensuous sheen of his hair and lips, the male lines of his nose and jaw. Rafe was too powerful and too hard to be called handsome. He was compelling—a man made for mountains, a man of strength and endurance, mystery and silence, and sudden laughter like a river curling lazily beneath the sun.

"Am I so different from your memories?" asked Rafe quietly.

Alana drew in her breath sharply.

"No," she said. "But there are times when I can't tell my memories of you from my dreams. Seeing you again, close enough to touch, *alive*..."

Alana looked away, unable to meet Rafe's eyes, regretting her honesty and at the same time knowing she had no choice. She had enough trouble sorting out truth from nightmare. She didn't have the energy to keep track of lies, too.

When the truck rounded the shoulder of a small ridge, Alana leaned forward intently, staring into the condensing twilight. A long, narrow valley opened up before her. A few evergreens grew in the long, low ridges where the land began to lift to the sky. The ridges soon became foothills and then finally pinnacles clothed in ice and distance.

But it wasn't the savage splendor of the peaks that held Alana's attention. She had eyes only for the valley. It was empty of cattle.

Alana sat back with an audible sigh of relief.

"Good for you, little brother," she murmured.

"Bob's a good rancher," said Rafe quietly. "There's not one inch of overgrazed land on Broken Mountain's range."

"I know. I was just afraid that—" Alana's hands moved, describing vague fears. "The beef market has been so bad and the price of feed is so high now and Bob has to pay Sam and Dave. I was afraid Bob would gamble on the land being able to carry more cattle than it should."

Rafe glanced sideways at Alana with the lightning intensity that she remembered from her dreams.

"Since when do people on the West Coast notice feed prices and the carrying capacity of Wyoming ranch land?" he asked.

"They don't. I do." Alana made a wry face. "People in cities think beef grows between Styrofoam and plastic wrap, like mushrooms in the cracks of a log."

Rafe laughed again, softly.

Alana watched him, feeling the pull of his laughter. Above his pale collar, sleek neck muscles moved.

She felt again the moment of warmth at the airport, the resilience of his muscles beneath her fingers before she had snatched back her arm. He was strong. It showed in his movements, in his laughter, in the clean male lines of his face. He was strong and she was not.

Distantly Alana knew she should be terrified of that difference in their bodies. Yet when Rafe laughed, it was all she could do to keep herself from crawling over and huddling next to him as though he were a fire burning in the midst of a freezing storm.

The thought of being close to Rafe both fas-

cinated and frightened Alana. The fascination
she understood; Rafe was the only man she
had ever loved. She had no reason to fear him.

Yet she did.

Rafe was a man, and she was terrified of
men.

The fear baffled Alana. At no time in her
life, not even during the most vicious arguments with Jack, had she ever been afraid.

Am I afraid of Rafe simply because he's
strong? Alana asked herself silently.

She turned the thought over in her mind,
testing it as she had tested so many things in
the weeks since she had awakened in the hospital, six days and a singing partner lost.

It can't be something as simple as physical
strength that frightens me, Alana decided. Jack
was six foot five, very thick in the shoulders
and neck and legs. He never used his strength,
though, or even seemed to notice it. He did
only what was needed to get by, and not one
bit more.

Jack had been born with a clear tenor voice
that he had accepted as casually as his size,
and he disliked working with his voice almost
as much as he had disliked physical labor.

Alana had been the one who had insisted
on rehearsing each song again and again,
searching for just the right combination of
phrasing and harmony that would bring out
the levels of meaning in the lyrics. Jack had
tolerated her "fanaticism" with the same easygoing indifference that he had tolerated
crummy motels and being on the road three

hundred and fifty-two nights a year.

Then Jack 'n' Jilly had become successful.

After that, Jack would rehearse a new country or folk song only as long as it took him to learn the words and melody. Anything beyond that was Jilly's problem.

A year ago Alana had left Jack and come to Broken Mountain Ranch to think about her life and her sad sham of a marriage. When word of their separation had leaked to the press, record and concert ticket sales had plummeted. Their agent had called Alana and quietly, cynically, suggested that she continue to present a happily married front to the world. Fame was transient. Obscurity was forever.

That same afternoon, Bob had come back from a trip to the high country babbling about seeing Rafe Winter. Alana had written the letter to Rafe, seen Rafe's rejection condensed into a single harsh word: *Deceased.*

She had wept until she felt nothing at all . . . and then she had gone back to L.A. to appear as half of Country's Perfect Couple.

Until six weeks ago, when Alana had told Jack that the sham was over. Country's Perfect Couple was an act she couldn't handle anymore. He had pleaded with her to think again, to take a trip with him to the high country she loved, and there they would work out something.

"Did you miss the ranch?" Rafe asked quietly.

Alana heard the question as though from a great distance, calling her out of a past that was another kind of nightmare waiting to drag her down. She reached for the question, pulling it eagerly around her.

"I missed the ranch more than . . . more than I knew."

And she had. It had been like having her eyes put out. She had hungered for the green and silver shimmer of aspens, but saw only dusty palm trees. She had searched for the primal blue of alpine lakes set among the chiseled spires of mountains older than man, but found only concrete freeways and the metallic flash of cars. She had always looked for the intense green silences of the wilderness forest, but discovered only tame squares of grass laid down amid hot stucco houses.

All that had saved Alana was singing. Working with a song. Tasting it, feeling it, seeing it grow and change as it became part of her and she of it.

Jack had never understood that. He had loved only the applause and worked just hard enough to get it. Alana loved the singing and would work to exhaustion until she and the song were one.

"If you missed the ranch that much, why did you leave after Jack died?"

Alana realized that she had heard the question before. Rafe had asked it at least twice and she hadn't answered, lost in her own thoughts.

"Jack died there," she whispered. "On Broken Mountain."

She looked to the right, where the Green

River Mountains lifted seamed granite faces toward the evening sky. High-flying clouds burned silver above the peaks, and over all arched an immense indigo bowl, twilight changing into night.

"You must have unhappy memories," said Rafe quietly.

"Yes, I suppose I must."

Alana heard her own words, heard their ambiguity, heard the fear tight in her voice. She looked up and saw that Rafe had been watching her.

But he turned away and said nothing, asked no more questions.

He simply drove her closer and closer to the ramparts of snow and ice where Jack had died and Jilly had lost her mind.

4

IT WAS DARK BY THE TIME RAFE
turned onto the fork of the road that led to the
Broken Mountain ranch house. An autumn
moon was up, huge and flat and ghostly, balanced on the edge of the world. Clouds raced
and seethed, veiled in moonlight and mystery,
veiling the moon in turn.

The mountains were invisible, yet Alana
could sense them rising black and massive in
front of her. They comforted and frightened
her at the same time as childhood memories
and recent fear set her on an emotional seesaw
that made her dizzy.

Alana knew she had been at the ranch just
four weeks ago.

She knew she and Jack had ridden into the high country.

She knew Jack was dead.

She knew—*but she didn't*.

Alana had awakened in the hospital, bruised and cut, ice-burned and aching. And frightened. Every shadow, every sound, had sent her heart racing.

It had taken a huge effort of will to allow Dr. Gene to examine her. He had tried to explain the inexplicable in ordinary words, telling Alana that her fear was normal, the overreaction of someone who had never known physical danger, much less death. In time, her mind and body would adjust to the presence of danger, the nearness of death in everyday life. Then she would be calm again. Until then, Dr. Gene could prescribe something to help her.

Alana had refused the tranquilizers. She had seen too many musicians dependent on drugs. For her, chemical solutions were no solution at all.

But it had been tempting, especially at first.

The presence of Dr. Gene had unnerved Alana to the point of tears. Even Bob, her favorite brother, had seen Alana withdraw from any kind of physical touch, any gesture of affection he made. Bob had been hurt and very worried about her, his brown eyes clouded with conflicting feelings.

Then, on the third morning after Alana had awakened, she had quietly walked out of the hospital, boarded a plane, and flown to Port-

land, a place where she had never lived. She
hadn't waited for Sheriff Mitchell to come
back down off the mountain with Jack's body.
She hadn't stopped to think, to consider, to
reason. She had simply run from the black gap
in her mind.

Portland was big enough for Alana to lose
herself in, but not big enough to remind her of
L.A. and her life with Jack. There were mountains in Portland, but only in the distance.

Yet fear had run with Alana anyway.
Though she had never before been afraid of
flying, or heights, there had been a horrible
moment of terror as the plane had left the
ground.

*Earth falling away and her body twisting,
weightless, she was falling, falling, black rushing
up to meet her and when it did she would be torn
from life like an aspen leaf from its stem, spinning
away helplessly over the void—*

"It's all right, Alana. You're safe. It's all
right. I've come to take you home."

Vaguely Alana realized that Rafe had
parked the Jeep at the side of the road. She
heard Rafe's soothing murmur, sensed the
warmth of his hand over her clenched fingers,
the gentle pressure of his other hand stroking
her hair. She felt the shudders wracking her
body, the ache of teeth clenched against a futile scream.

Rafe continued speaking quietly, repeating
his words. They warmed Alana, words as un-

demanding as sunlight, driving away the darkness that gripped her.

Suddenly she turned her head, pressing her cheek against the hard strength of Rafe's hand. But when he would have drawn her closer, she moved away with a jerk.

"I—" Alana stopped abruptly and drew a deep breath. "I'm sorry. Something—" Her hands moved jerkily. "Sometimes I—since Jack—"

Alana closed her eyes. She couldn't make Rafe understand what she herself had no words to describe.

"Seeing death is always hard," said Rafe quietly. "The more sheltered you've been, the harder it is."

Rafe's hand stroked Alana's hair, his touch as gentle as his words, as his presence, as his warmth.

After a few moments Alana let out a long sigh, feeling the tentacles of terror loosen, slide away, the nightmare withdrawing. She turned her head and looked at Rafe with eyes that were no longer black with fear.

"Thank you," she said simply.

Rafe's only answer was a light caress across Alana's cheek as his hand withdrew from her hair.

He started the Jeep again and pulled back onto the narrow gravel road that led to the Burdette family house. Beneath the truck, the country began to roll subtly, gathering itself for the sudden leap into mountain heights.

The ranch house was on the last piece of

land that could be described as high plains. Behind the ranch buildings, the country rose endlessly, becoming ranks of black peaks wearing brilliant crowns of stars.

Gradually, squares of yellow light condensed out of the blackness as the ranch house competed with and finally outshone the brightness of the stars. Dark fences paralleled the road, defining corrals and pastures where brood mares grazed and champion bulls moved with ponderous grace. A paved loop of road curved in front of the house before veering off toward the barns.

As Rafe braked to a stop by the walkway, the front door of the house opened, sending a thick rectangle of gold light into the yard like a soundless cry of welcome. Three quicksilver dogs bounded off the porch, barking and baying and dancing as though the dewy grass were made of icicles too sharp to stand on.

Rafe climbed out of the truck and waded into the hounds with good-natured curses, pummeling them gently until they had worked off the first exuberance of their greeting. Then they stood and watched him with bright eyes, nudging his hands with cold noses until each silky ear had been scratched at least once. In the moonlight the hounds' coats shone like liquid silver, rippling and changing with each movement of their muscular bodies.

Alana slid out of the Jeep with a smile on her lips and the hounds' welcoming song echoing in her ears. She stood quietly, watching the dogs greet Rafe, feeling the cool breeze tug at her hair.

One of the hounds lifted its head sharply, scenting Alana. It gave an eager whine and scrambled toward her. Automatically Alana bent over to greet the animal, rubbing its ears and thumping lightly on its muscular barrel, enjoying the warm rasp of a tongue over her hands.

"You're a beauty," Alana said, admiring the dog's lithe lines and strength.

The dog nosed her hand, then the pocket of her black slacks, then her hand again.

"What do you want?" asked Alana, her voice carrying clearly in the quiet air.

"Vamp wants the crackers you spoiled her with the last time you were here," called Bob as he stepped out onto the porch, laughter and resignation competing in his voice.

Alana looked up blankly.

"Crackers?" she repeated.

She looked down at the dog. The dog watched her, dancing from foot to foot, obviously waiting for something.

"Crackers," said Bob, holding one out to Alana as he walked toward her. "I figured that you'd forgotten—er, I mean I figured that you wouldn't have any crackers on you, so I brought one."

"Vamp?" asked Alana.

She took the cracker and looked at the pale square as though she'd never seen one before. She held it out.

The hound took the tidbit with the delicate mouth of a well-trained bird dog.

"Vampire," Bob said, gesturing to the dog at Alana's feet. "You know, for all the sharp teeth she had as a pup."

The look on Alana's face made it clear that she didn't know the story behind the dog's name. Yet it was equally clear that Bob had told her the story before.

"*Hell*," said Bob under his breath.

Then he hugged Alana and spoke so softly that only she could hear.

"Sorry, sis. It's hard for me to keep track of all the things you've forgotten."

Alana stiffened for an instant as her brother's arms held her. Then she forced herself to relax. She knew she must get over her irrational fear of human contact. The source of fear was only in her nightmares, a creation of her mind that had nothing to do with here, now, reality. Withdrawing would hurt Bob badly, just as she had hurt him at the hospital.

She returned the hug a little fiercely, holding on too tightly, releasing her brother too quickly. Bob gave her a troubled look but said nothing.

Until he saw her hair.

"What in God's name did you do to your hair?" Bob yelped.

"I cut it."

Alana shook her head, making moonlight run like ghostly fingers through the loose black curves of her hair.

"Why?" asked Bob.

"It seemed like a good idea at the time."

"But you've always had long hair."

His voice was surprisingly plaintive for a man who was just over six-and-a-half feet tall and nearly twenty-three years old.

"Things change, little brother," Alana said tightly.

"Not you, sis," Bob said, confidence in every word. "You're like the mountains. You never change."

Alana stood without moving, not knowing what to say. In that moment, she realized for the first time how much like a mother she was to Bob, how fixed in his mind as a port for every storm. Somehow she had given a continuity of love and caring to him that she had never found for herself after their mother died. And Rafe, who had died and then not died. But he had come back too late.

Like now. Too late, Alana thought. How can I tell Bob that there are no ports anymore, only storms?

"You're forgetting something, Bob," said Rafe, his voice easy yet somehow commanding.

"What? Oh. Yeah. Damn. I told you, Winter, I'm no—"

"Sisters are women, too," Rafe said, cutting across whatever Bob had been about to say. "Some sisters are even beautiful women."

Rafe's amber eyes flashed as he looked briefly at Alana. His smile reflected the light pouring out of the ranch house.

Bob cocked his head and looked at Alana as though she were a stranger.

"A matter of taste, I suppose," Bob said, deadpan. "She looks like a stray fence post to me. Didn't they have any food in Portland?"

Quietly Rafe looked from the graceful curve of Alana's neck to the feminine swell of breasts, the small waist, the firm curve of hips, the legs long and graceful.

"Burdette," Rafe said, "you're as blind as a stone rolling down a mountain."

Alana flushed under Rafe's frankly approving glance. Yet she was smiling, too. She was used to being told she had a beautiful voice. As for the rest, she had never felt especially attractive.

Except when she had been with Rafe and he had looked at her the way he was looking at her right now, smiling.

"I guess Rafe told *you*, baby brother," Alana said, glad that the words came out light, teasing. She smiled at Rafe. "I'll bet you ride a white horse and rescue maidens in distress, too."

Rafe's face changed, intent, watching Alana as though he was willing her to do . . . something.

The look passed so quickly that Alana thought she had imagined it.

"Wrong, sis," said Bob triumphantly, yanking her suitcase out of the back of the Jeep. "The horse Rafe rides is as spotted as his past."

Alana looked from Bob to Rafe, wondering what her brother meant.

What had Rafe done in the years before, and after, he was declared dead in Central America?

"Bob, you need a bridle for that tongue of yours," said Rafe.

His smile was narrow, his voice flat.

Bob winced. "Stepped in it again. Sorry. I'm not very good at forgetting. Or"—he looked apologetically at Alana again—"remembering, either."

She sighed. "You couldn't even keep secrets at Christmastime, could you?"

"Nope," Bob agreed cheerfully. "Not a one. In one ear and out the mouth."

Rafe made a sound that was halfway between disgust and amusement.

"There are times when I can't believe you're Sam's brother," Rafe said dryly.

Alana looked quickly at Rafe. Something in his voice told her that Rafe had seen Sam more recently than the times when Sam had hero-worshipped the older Rafe from afar.

"Have you seen Sam? I mean, lately?" Alana asked Rafe.

When Bob would have spoken, Rafe gave him a quelling look.

"We met in Central America," Rafe said, "when Sam was drilling a few dry holes. I haven't seen him in a while, though."

Alana's lips turned down.

"Neither have I," she said. "It's been years.

I was in Florida doing a concert the last time he came to the States."

"My brother the spook," said Bob. "Now you see him, now you don't."

"What?" asked Alana.

"Oops," said Bob.

What Rafe said was mercifully blurred by Merry's voice calling out threats to the husband who had let her sleep through Alana's homecoming.

"Honey," Bob said, dropping Alana's suitcase and racing toward the steps, "be careful!"

The dogs ran after Bob, yipping and yapping with excitement. Alana couldn't help laughing as Bob swept Merry off her tiny feet and carried her across the grass, swearing at the dogs every step of the way. Merry was laughing too, her face buried against Bob's neck as she squealed and ducked away from the long-tongued, leaping hounds.

Rafe put his fists on his hips and shook his head, smiling. He turned to Alana and held out his hand.

"Welcome to Broken Mountain Dude Ranch," he said wryly. "Peace and quiet await you. Somewhere. It says so in the fine print in the brochure."

"I'll hold you to that," murmured Alana.

Smiling, she rested her hand lightly on Rafe's, feeling the heat and texture of his palm as his fingers curled around hers. The touch sent both pleasure and fear coursing through her.

The instant before Alana would have withdrawn, Rafe released her hand and picked up her luggage. She went ahead quickly, opening the screen door for Rafe and for Bob, who was still carrying a giggling Merry.

The dogs stopped short at the threshold and begged silently, their amber wolf eyes pale and hopeful.

Alana looked toward Bob.

"No," he said firmly. "No weimaraners allowed."

"Not even Vamp?" Alana asked coaxingly.

"Sis," Bob said in an exasperated tone, "I told you the last time that I don't want to take a chance of Merry tripping over—"

Bob stopped abruptly, remembering too late that Alana had no memory of her last trip to the ranch.

"Sorry," said Alana tightly, closing the door. "I forgot."

"So did I. Again. *Damn.*"

Bob ran his fingers through his thick black hair in a gesture both sister and brother had learned from their father.

"Oh, Alana," Merry said softly, her pretty face stricken as she looked at her sister-in-law. "Bob didn't mean to hurt you."

"I know."

Alana closed her eyes and unclenched her hands.

"Where do you want the suitcase?" asked Rafe into the silence.

His voice was matter-of-fact, as though he hadn't sensed the undercurrents of emotion swirling through Alana. She knew better. With every instant she and Rafe spent together, Alana became more certain that he was intensely aware of everything about her.

"Alana is sleeping in the upstairs bedroom on the east corner," said Merry, wriggling in Bob's arms. "Put me down, you big moose. There's nothing wrong with my feet."

"Never mind," said Rafe. "I know where the room is. Don't climb any more stairs than you have to."

"Not you, too!" Merry rolled her blue eyes and pulled on her long blond hair in mock despair. "Why me, Lord? Why am I stuck with men who think pregnancy is an exotic kind of broken leg?"

Rafe smiled crookedly as he watched the tiny woman's halfhearted struggle in Bob's thick arms.

"Enjoy it, Merry," Rafe said. "Come diaper time, Bob will develop an exotic kind of broken arm."

"Slander," muttered Bob to Merry, nuzzling her cheek. "Don't believe a word of it."

"Believe it," said Alana. "Every time there were grubby chores to be done, Bob evaporated."

"Hey, not fair," he said, a wounded look on his face.

"Not fair or not true?" Alana asked wryly.

"I grew up after that carnivorous hen ate half my hands."

"Chicken pox," called Rafe just before he disappeared down the hall at the top of the stairway. "Remember?"

Bob groaned. "He's worse than Sam when it comes to keeping track of life's little lies. Mind like a steel trap. No fun at all."

Privately Alana thought it would be wonderful to have a mind that forgot nothing, held everything. If she knew about those six days, her nightmares would be gone.

Or maybe they would just move in and take over her days, too.

Maybe Dr. Gene was right. Maybe she wasn't ready to accept what had happened, at least not all of it, every little horrifying detail.

Height and ice and falling . . .

"You look tired, sis," said Bob.

He set Merry on her feet with exaggerated care and watched lovingly as she yawned, waved good night, and went back to the downstairs bedroom. He turned back to Alana.

"Want to go right to bed?" he asked.

Bob waited, but there was no answer.

"Sis?"

With a start, Alana came out of her thoughts. Her hand was against her neck, as though holding back a scream.

"Sis? What is it? Are you remembering?"

Alana forced herself not to flinch when Bob's big hand came down on her shoulder.

"No," she said, hearing the harshness of her voice but unable to make it softer. "I'm trying, but I'm not remembering anything."

"Where does your memory stop?" asked Bob hesitantly.

"California. I was packing to come here."

"Where does it begin again?"

"When I woke up in the hospital."

"Six days."

"Nice counting, baby brother," Alana said sardonically. Then, "I'm sorry. It's just . . . not easy. I don't know why I forgot, and I'm . . . afraid."

Bob patted Alana's shoulder clumsily, not knowing how to comfort the older sister who had always been the one to comfort him.

"I love you, sis."

Tears burned behind Alana's eyes. She looked up into the face that was as familiar to her as her own. Familiar, yet different. Bob was a man now, but in her memories he was so often a boy.

"Thanks," she whispered. "I love you, too."

Bob smiled almost shyly and squeezed Alana's shoulder. A frown passed over his face as he felt her slight body beneath his big hand.

"You're nearly as small as Merry," said Bob, surprise clear in his voice.

Alana almost laughed. "I'm three inches taller."

Bob dismissed the inches with a wave of his hand.

"That's not what I meant," he said. "I've always thought of you as . . . bigger. You know. Physically."

"And I've always thought of you as smaller. Guess we both have some new thinking to do."

"Yeah, guess so." Bob ran his thick fingers through his hair. "I've been thinking a lot

since Merry got pregnant. It's kind of scary."
Then he grinned. "It's kind of fantastic, too."

Alana smiled despite her trembling lips.

"You'll be a good father, Bob. Just like
you're a good rancher."

Bob's eyes widened slightly, showing clear
brown depths.

"You mean that, sis? About being a good
rancher, too?"

"You've been good to the land. It shows.
Rafe thinks so, too," she added.

Bob smiled with pleasure. "High marks
from both of you, huh? That means a lot to
me. I know how much you love the ranch.
And Rafe, well, he's a hard son of a bitch, but
he's working miracles with the Lazy W. It had
really gone to hell by the time his father had
that last stroke."

"How long has Rafe lived at the Lazy W?"

Bob looked uncomfortable, obviously remembering the time Alana had come for a
visit and he had told her that Rafael Winter
was alive.

"Bob?" Alana pressed.

"A couple of years," he admitted.

"All that time?" asked Alana.

Before, when she had known Rafe, loved
him, been engaged to him, his work had taken
him on long trips to unexpected places.

"He used to travel a lot," she added.

"Yeah. About four years ago he was . . . uh,
he had some kind of accident in some godforsaken place. And then his father died. Rafe has
stayed on the Lazy W the whole time since

then. Guess he's here for good. Unless something goes to hell overseas or Sam gets in trouble again and needs Rafe to pull his tail out of
a crack."

"Sam? In trouble? How? And what could
Rafe do about it?"

Bob laughed wryly. "Sis, Rafe would—"

"Bring Sam a toothbrush," said Rafe from
the stairway.

Alana looked up. Rafe was leaning against
the wall, his hands in his pockets, his shirt
tightly across bunched shoulder muscles. For
all his casual pose, she sensed that Rafe was
angry about something.

Bob breathed a curse and an apology.

"I warned you, Rafe," Bob said. "I'm no
damn good at—"

"Burdette." Rafe's voice cracked with au-
thority. "Shut up. If you can't do that, talk
about the weather."

There was a charged silence for a moment.
Alana looked from Bob to Rafe and back
again. Although her brother had five inches
and fifty pounds on Rafe, Rafe didn't seem the
least bit intimidated by the prospect of a
brawl.

"Storm coming on," said Bob finally.
"Should be thunder in the high country by
midnight, rain down here before dawn. It's
supposed to clear up at sunrise, though. Part
of a cold front that's moving across the Rockies. Now, if you ask me, I think we should
roust those sleeping dudes upstairs and leave

for your lodge at dawn or as soon afterward as it stops raining."

"That," said Rafe distinctly, "is one hell of an idea. Do you suppose you can keep your feet out of your mouth long enough to sit a horse all the way to Five Lakes Lodge?"

"Didn't you know I'm a trick rider?" said Bob, his smile wide and forgiving.

"Who had chicken pox," retorted Rafe, but he was smiling, too.

"Now you got it," said Bob approvingly. "Keep that good thought until morning. And I'll practice biting my damned tongue. But only for a while."

"I'll hold you to it."

"Yeah. It goes both ways, Winter. Don't forget. I sure as hell won't. Goodnight."

Beneath the humor in Bob's voice there was something much harder.

Alana heard it, and she wondered if Rafe heard it, too.

And then she wondered why Bob, who was normally easygoing to a fault, was leaning on Rafael Winter.

5

RAFE SHOOK HIS HEAD AND said something harsh under his breath as Bob vanished. But Rafe was smiling when he turned to Alana.

"How did you hold your own?" he asked. "Sam and Bob together. My God. And Dave, too. Boggles the mind."

"What did Bob mean about your 'spotted past'?" asked Alana.

"Terrible work record," Rafe said laconically. "Moved around a lot. Remember?"

"And about Sam being in trouble?"

"He's not in trouble now."

"But he was?" persisted Alana.

"Everyone gets in trouble now and again."

Alana made an exasperated sound. "Am I permitted to ask about the dudes?"

Rafe's glance narrowed.

"Sure," he said. "Ask away."

"But will I get any answers?"

"Now I remember how you held your own with your brothers," Rafe said, smiling. "Stubborn."

"I prefer to think of it as determined."

"Good thing, determination."

Alana looked at Rafe's carefully bland expression, at the intelligence and humor that gave depth to his whiskey eyes, at the clean line of his lips beneath his mustache.

What she saw made her forget her unanswered questions. Rafe had taken off his hat, revealing the rich depths of color and texture in his hair. It was a very dark brown, with surprising gleams of gold, clean and thick and lustrous. No shadow of beard lay beneath his skin, which meant that he must have shaved before he picked her up at the airport.

The open collar of Rafe's shirt revealed hair darker than his mustache, more curly. Her glance went back to his forehead, where the rich brown hair had been combed back by his fingers.

Is it a memory or a dream, Alana asked herself silently, or did Rafe's hair once feel like winter mink between my fingers?

"What are you thinking?" he asked.

Rafe's voice was casual, as though he were asking the time.

Reflexively Alana responded to the offhand

tone, answering before she realized what he had asked or what her answer would reveal.

"Your hair," she said, "like winter mink . . . ?"

"Want to find out?"

"What?"

"If my hair feels like mink."

Rafe spoke as though it were a perfectly normal thing for Alana to do.

"Don't worry," he added softly. "I won't touch you at all. I know you don't want to be touched."

Rafe's voice was low, murmurous, as soothing as it had been in the Jeep when nightmare had overtaken Alana without warning.

"Go ahead and touch me," he said. "I promise I won't do anything but stand here. You're safe with me, Alana. Always. I'm the man who came to take you home."

Alana looked at the amber eyes and gentle smile while Rafe's voice surrounded her, caressing her. His hands were still in his pockets, his body was still relaxed. His posture told Alana that he understood and accepted her fear of being touched, held. Restrained.

"How did you know?" Alana asked, her voice trembling.

"That you didn't want to be touched?"

"Yes."

"Every time I touch you, you freeze. That's as good as words for me. Better."

Alana was caught by the emotion she sensed coiling beneath Rafe's surface calm.

He sent back my letter unopened, Alana

thought tensely. But did he dream of me, too? Is my coldness cutting him, making him bleed as I bled when my letter came back unopened?

Remembered grief ripped through Alana, shaking her.

That's in the past, she told herself harshly. I'm living in the present. Today, Rafe has shown me only kindness. And now I'm hurting him.

Alana wanted to hold on to Rafe, comforting both of them, but the thought of being held in return made her body tense to fight or flee.

"It isn't anything personal," she said in a strained voice.

"Are you sure it isn't something I've done?"

Alana looked at Rafe. His eyes were as clear as a high-country stream. Glints of gold and topaz mixed with the predominant amber color, radiating outward from the black pupil. He was watching her with strange intensity.

"I'm sure," she said, sighing, relaxing. "Very sure."

"Then what is it?" Rafe asked gently.

"I—I don't know. Since Jack died, I just don't like people touching me."

"Do you like touching people?"

"I—"

Alana stopped, a puzzled expression bringing her black brows together.

"I hadn't thought about it that way," she admitted.

Rafe waited, watching her.

And Alana watched Rafe, absorbing his silence and his restraint, the pulse beating slowly in his neck, the slide and coil of muscles across his chest as he breathed in the even rhythms of relaxation, waiting for her.

Slowly Alana's hand came up. He bent down to make it easier for her to touch him. Her fingers brushed over his hair lightly, hesitated, then quickly retreated.

"Well?" Rafe asked as he straightened, smiling. "Is someone going to skin me for a fancy coat?"

Alana laughed a little breathlessly.

"I'm not sure," she admitted. "It was so quick."

"Try again," he offered casually.

Alana climbed the stairs until she was on the same step as Rafe. This time her hand lingered as she allowed his hair to sift over the sensitive skin between her fingers. With a smile that was both shy and remembering, she lifted her hand.

"Better," Rafe said. "But you should take lessons from a professional furrier."

She made a questioning sound.

"Professionals rub the pelt with their palms and fingertips," said Rafe.

His glance moved from Alana's mouth to her glossy black hair.

"And they tease the fur with their breath," he said, "hold its softness to their lips, smell it, taste it, then gently slide the fur over their most sensitive skin."

Alana's breath caught. A shiver of pleasure spread through her at the thought of being touched so gently . . . by Rafael Winter.

"Do they really?" she asked.

"I don't know," Rafe admitted, his voice a teasing kind of velvet as he smiled down at her. "But that's what I'd do to you if you were a fur and I were a furrier."

Though Rafe hadn't moved any closer, Alana felt surrounded by him, by sensual possibilities that sent warmth showering through her.

Suddenly, vividly, memories from the times they had made love went through Alana's body like liquid lightning. She had spent so long trying to forget, yet the memories were as hot and fresh as though newly made.

Or perhaps her memories of Rafe's exquisite touch were merely hunger and dream entangled so thoroughly that truth was lost. Another kind of amnesia, more gentle, but just as filled with pitfalls in the present.

Yet Alana had just touched Rafe, and he had felt better than in her memories.

Rafe smiled as though he knew exactly what Alana was feeling. Before she could retreat, he pushed away from the wall and passed her on the narrow stairway without touching her. When he spoke his voice was no longer teasing, husky, intimate.

"Get some sleep," Rafe advised. "Bob and I weren't kidding about leaving at dawn. If you need anything, I'm in the room next to yours. Don't worry about making noise. The dudes are still on Virginia time. Sleeping like babes all in a row."

She stared at Rafe as he walked toward the living room.

"And Alana..."

Rafe turned back toward her, his face half in light, half in shadow, his eyes the radiant gold of sunset rain.

"Yes?" she asked.

"Don't be afraid. Whatever happens, I'm here."

Rafe vanished into the living room before Alana could answer.

Slowly she walked upstairs to her room, hoping at every moment to hear Rafe's footsteps behind her.

Only silence followed Alana to her bedroom.

The exhaustion of sleepless nights combined with the familiar background sounds of the ranch to send Alana into a deep sleep. She slept undisturbed until clouds gathered and thickened, stitched together by lightning and torn apart by thunder.

Then she began to sleep restlessly, her head moving from side to side, her limbs shifting unpredictably, her throat clenching over unspoken words.

Riding next to Jack, arguing.

He's angry and the clouds are angry and the mountains loom over me like thunder.

Spruce and fir and aspens bent double by the cruel wind. Wind tearing off leaves, spinning them like bright coins into the black void, and the horses are gone.

Screaming but no one can hear, I'm a single bright leaf spinning endlessly down and down and—

Cold, sweating, Alana woke up, her heart hammering against her ribs, her breath ragged. She looked at the bedside clock. Three-forty. Too soon to get up, even if they were leaving at dawn.

Lightning bleached the room, leaving intense darkness behind, trailing an avalanche of thunder.

Suddenly Alana felt trapped.

She leaped out of bed, yanked open the door, and ran into the hallway. She raced down the stairs and out onto the front porch. Incandescent lightning skidded over the land, separated by split seconds of darkness that were almost dizzying.

Frightened, disoriented, a broken scream tearing at her throat, Alana turned back to the front door.

A man came out, walking toward her.

At first Alana thought it was Rafe; then she realized that the man was too tall. But it wasn't Bob. The walk was different.

Lightning came again, outlining the man, revealing his pale hair, long sideburns, blunt nose, narrow mouth, and eyes so blue they were almost black.

Jack.

Past and present, nightmare and reality fused into a seamless horror. Helpless, terrified, shaken by thunder and her own screaming, Alana scrambled backward, hands flailing frantically,

*running, scrambling, falling, and everywhere ice and
lightning, thunder and darkness and screaming.*
  Falling.
  I'm falling . . . !

This time Alana could hear the screams tearing apart her throat. But it wasn't Jack's name
she screamed as she spun toward the void.
  It was Rafe's.
  The front door burst open and slammed back
against the wall. Abruptly Jack disappeared between one stroke of lightning and the next.
  Shaking, holding on to herself, Alana told
herself that Jack was a product of her imagination, a waking nightmare from which she
would soon be freed.
  Then she saw Jack laid out on the porch,
Rafe astride him, Rafe's forearm like an iron
bar across Jack's throat.
  Panic exploded inside Alana, shards of ice
slashing through her, paralyzing her. Jack was
so much bigger than Rafe, as big as Bob, bigger, and Jack could be so cruel in his strength.
  Then her paralysis melted, sliding away into
darkness and lightning as Alana realized that
Rafe was in control. It was Jack who was
down and was going to stay that way until
Rafe decided to let him up again.
  Bob ran out onto the front porch, flashlight
in one hand and shotgun in the other. He saw
Rafe and the man beneath him.
  "What in the hell—?" began Bob.
  Then he saw Alana backed up against the
porch railing, terror in every line of her face,
her hands clenched around her throat.

"Sis? Oh, God!"

Bob started for her, holding out his arms.

Alana screamed.

Rafe came to his feet in a single powerful lunge. He stood between brother and sister.

"Don't touch her," Rafe said flatly.

"But—" began Bob.

Lightning flared again. Bob saw Rafe's face, hard and utterly savage. Without another word, Bob backed up.

Rafe turned with the same fluid power that he had used to come up off the porch floor. As he looked at Alana, his eyes burned with rage and regret. He ached to gather her in his arms, to hold her, to feel her melt and flow along his body as she accepted his embrace.

And he knew that was a dream, and she lived in nightmare. Broken Mountain was destroying their future as surely as his "death" once had.

"It's all right, wildflower," Rafe said quietly. "I won't let anyone touch you. Not even me."

Numbly Alana nodded, hearing the word *wildflower* echo and reecho in her mind, a name from the deep past, before Rafe had died and been reborn, killing her without knowing it.

Wildflower.

A name out of dreams.

A name out of nightmares.

"Bob," Rafe said without turning around, "pick up Stan and get the hell out of Alana's sight. *Now*."

Bob had no desire to argue with the whiplike voice, the poised fighting stance, the muscles visibly coiled across Rafe's naked back, ready to unleash violence. Silently Bob bent over, levered the man called Stan to his feet, and dragged him into the living room.

The screen door banged shut behind them like a small crack of thunder.

Distant lightning came, revealing Rafe's face, harshness and yearning combined.

Alana blinked, half expecting Rafe to vanish.

He stayed before her, outlined by forked lightning, a man both lean and powerful, wearing only jeans, and regret was a dark veil across his features.

Instinctively Alana swayed toward him, needing the very comfort that her mind wouldn't let her take.

Rafe stood without moving, looking at her slender body shaken by shudders of cold and fear, his own private nightmare come true. He would have put his arms around her, but he knew that she would only scream again, tearing both of them apart.

In the end, Rafe could not help holding out his hand to Alana. It was a gesture that asked nothing, offered everything.

"Hold on to me, wildflower," he said softly. "If you want to."

With a small sound, Alana took Rafe's hand between her own. She held on to him with bruising intensity. He didn't object. Nor did he so much as curl his fingers around hers. She took a shuddering breath, then another, fighting to control herself.

"I thought—" Alana's voice broke.

She bent over, pressing her forehead to the back of Rafe's hand. He was as warm as life itself, flowing into her, giving her peace. She swallowed and spoke without lifting her head.

"I thought he was J-Jack."

Rafe's left hand hovered over Alana's bent head, as though he would stroke her hair. Then his hand dropped to his side and remained there, clenched in a fist.

He was afraid to touch her, to frighten her and rend the fragile fabric of trust being woven between them.

"Stan is one of the dudes," Rafe said quietly, but emotions turned just beneath the smooth surface of his voice, testing his control. "Stan is big, like Jack was. And blond."

Alana shuddered and said nothing.

"If I had known that the first time you saw Stan it would be in the lightning and darkness, a storm, like Broken Mountain—" Rafe didn't finish. "I'm sorry, wildflower. For so many things."

But the last words were said so softly that Alana wasn't sure she had heard them at all. For a moment longer she clung to Rafe's hand, drawing strength and warmth from him, the nightmare draining away, fading like thunder into the distance.

Slowly Alana's head came up. She drew more deep breaths, sending oxygen through a body that had been starved for it, paralyzed by fear to the point that she had forgotten to breathe. Gradually the shuddering left her body, only to return as shivers of cold rather than fear.

For the first time she realized that she was wearing only a thin silk nightshirt, which the icy rain had plastered across her body. The vivid orange cloth was nearly black where water had touched it, as dark as her eyes looking up at Rafe.

Alana shivered again, and for an instant Rafe held his warm hand against her cheek. A single fingertip traced the black wing of her eyebrow with such exquisite gentleness that she forgot to be afraid. Tears stood in her eyes, magnifying them. Tears flowed down silently, tears as warm as Rafe's hand.

With dreamlike slowness, Alana turned her face until her lips rested against his palm. When she spoke, her breath was another caress flowing over his skin.

"Thank you for understanding," Alana whispered.

Rafe's body tensed visibly as he fought his impulse to hold Alana, to turn her lips up to his own, to taste again the warmth of her, to feel her respond. He knew that if he reached for her she would retreat, terrified.

And that knowledge was a knife turning inside him.

Slowly Alana released Rafe's hand. For a moment he held his palm against her cheek, then he withdrew.

"I feel like such a fool," said Alana, closing her eyes. "What must that poor man think of me?"

"Stan thinks he was a real horse's ass to come barging outside after you in a storm, scaring you half to death," said Rafe, his voice like a whip once more. "He's lucky I didn't take him apart."

Alana made a sound of protest.

"It was my fault, not his," she said. "I'll have to apologize."

"Like hell. Stan will apologize to you, in good light, when you can see him clearly. *And then he will stay away from you.*"

Rafe's words were clear and hard, like glacier ice. Alana realized that he was furious, but not with her. He was enraged with Stan, because Stan had frightened her.

Then she realized that Rafe was also furious with himself, because he hadn't prevented her from being frightened.

"It wasn't your fault," whispered Alana.

"The hell it wasn't."

Then, before she could respond, Rafe was talking again.

"You're shivering. Are you ready to go back inside?"

Alana hesitated. The thought of seeing the man who looked so much like Jack disturbed her deeply. But she had no choice. She refused to spend the rest of her life at the mercy of her own fears.

She clenched her hands at her sides, took a deep breath, and lifted her chin.

"Yes, I'm ready," Alana said.

"You don't have to." Rafe's voice was gentle despite his tightly leashed anger. "I'll go in and tell Bob you'd rather not meet Stan right now."

"No. I've got to stop being so damned . . . fragile."

"You've been through too much, too recently. You've been through more than anyone should have to bear. Don't be so hard on yourself. Ease up. Give yourself a chance to heal."

Alana shook her head.

She wasn't healing. The nightmare was getting worse, taking over more and more of her waking hours.

"Life goes on, Rafe. The biggest cliché, and the one with the most truth. I have to go on, too. I have to leave those six days behind me. *I have to.*"

For an instant Rafe closed his eyes, unable to bear either Alana's pain or her courage.

"Just like a wildflower," he whispered. "Delicate and tough, growing in the most difficult places."

He opened his eyes and held his hand out to her.

"Will you let me help you?" Rafe asked.

After a moment's hesitation, Alana put her hand in Rafe's. The warmth of his skin was like fire, telling her how cold her own body was.

"Thank you," Rafe said simply.

Then he opened the door and led Alana back into the living room, where her nightmare waited.

6

BOB AND STAN WERE SITTING in the living room, talking about storms and high-country trout. Both men looked up, then away, clearly not wanting to intrude if Alana needed privacy.

Rafe plucked a flannel shirt off a coatrack standing near the door, draped the colorful plaid folds over Alana, and turned toward the two men.

Instantly Stan stood up.

Alana took a quick breath and stepped backward until she came up hard against Rafe's chest. Over Alana's head, Rafe smiled coldly at the blond, muscular giant who was every bit as tall as Bob.

"Alana Reeves, meet Stan Wilson," said Rafe. "Stan, you'll understand if Alana doesn't want to shake hands. You have an unnerving resemblance to her recently deceased husband."

For a long moment, Rafe and Stan measured each other.

Stan nodded, a brief incline of his head that was almost an apology. Then his head moved slightly as he looked toward Alana.

At the sight of Stan's cobalt-blue eyes, Alana made a small sound. Like Jack. Just like Jack. Only the solid warmth of Rafe at her back kept her from falling into nightmare again.

"I'm sorry, Mrs. Reeves," Stan said. "I sure didn't mean to frighten you like that."

Relief uncurled deep inside Alana. The voice was different, entirely different, deeper, permeated by the subtle rhythms of the Southwest.

"Please call me Alana," she said. "And I'm sorry for—"

"You have nothing to apologize for," said Rafe, cutting across Alana's words. "Now that Stan is aware of the situation, I'm sure he won't take you by surprise again."

Rafe's voice was smooth and polished, steel hard, having no soft surfaces that might admit argument. His eyes were narrowed, watching Stan with the intensity of a cougar stalking deer.

Again, Stan hesitated before responding. Again, Stan nodded slightly, though his expression was as hard as Rafe's.

Alana looked from one man to the other and then to Bob, whom she feared would be worried about the fate of his dreams for a dude ranch. If Stan Wilson had an awful vacation at the Broken Mountain Dude Ranch, he would hardly recommend the place to his wealthy clients.

Yet Bob didn't look upset. He looked more like a man making bets with himself, and winning.

When Bob realized that Alana was watching him, he smiled at her.

"Some homecoming, sis," Bob said, shaking his head.

"Yes," she whispered. "Some homecoming."

Yawning, Bob looked at the wristwatch he always wore.

"Well, there's not much point in me going back to sleep," Bob said, stretching. "I'll start working on the pack string. Stan, you said you wanted to watch a real cowboy at work. Still game?"

The faint challenge in Bob's voice brought a smile to Stan's face.

Quickly Alana looked away. The smile was like an echo of Jack, charming and boyish. Stan was a very handsome man . . . and Alana's skin crawled every time she looked at him.

It wasn't rational or fair to Stan, but it wasn't something she could control, either.

"I'll be glad to help you," drawled Stan, "seeing as how you're such a puny thing."

Bob looked startled, then laughed out loud. He clapped Stan on the shoulder and led him toward the kitchen. Bob's voice drifted back as the two huge men left the room.

"Merry left some coffee warming. We'll need it. And I've got a jacket that I think will fit you, seeing as how you're such a puny thing, too."

Listening, Alana realized that her brother liked Stan. That was different from before, from Jack. Bob hadn't liked Jack at all. None of the Burdettes had.

Alana heard Stan's laughter trailing back into the living room, laughter as charming as his smile. Yet, unlike the smile, Stan's laughter didn't remind Alana of Jack. Jack had rarely laughed, and never at himself.

Even so, she was glad that Stan was out of sight. It was unnerving to catch a glimpse of him out of the corner of her eye, blond shades of Jack stalking behind her. She let out a long sigh as the kitchen door slammed, telling her that the two men were on the way to the barn.

"Okay?" asked Rafe, feeling the deep breath Alana had taken and let out, for her back was still pressed against his chest.

Alana nodded. "He—he's nice, isn't he?"

Rafe grunted, a sound that told her nothing.

"Bob likes him," said Alana.

"They're a lot alike," Rafe said dryly. "Muscle and impulse in equal amounts and places."

"Between their ears?" suggested Alana.

"Sometimes." Rafe sighed. "Just sometimes."

Alana shifted her weight slightly. The movement reminded her that she was standing very close to Rafe, all but leaning on him. The contact didn't bother her. He wasn't touching her. She was touching him.

The difference was both subtle and infinitely reassuring. The warmth of Rafe's bare chest radiated through the flannel shirt and her damp silk nightshirt, a warmth as natural as the embers glowing in the living room hearth.

For an instant Alana wanted to turn and wrap herself in his warmth, chasing away the chill that had come the day they'd told her that Rafe was dead.

She shivered again, but not from cold.

"You should try to sleep a little more," Rafe said. "You're still on West Coast time."

He was so close to Alana that she felt the vibration of his chest as he spoke, the subtle movement of his muscles as he bent slightly toward her, and the brush of his breath over her ear. She closed her eyes, savoring a tactile intimacy that demanded nothing from her.

"I feel safer here with you," she said simply.

Alana felt Rafe's quick, subdued breath and realized what she had said. She tensed, knowing that if Rafe accepted her unintended invitation and put his arms around her, she had only herself to blame.

The worst of it was that part of her very much wanted his arms around her.

And part of her panicked at the thought of being held.

Suddenly Alana wondered if Jack had been

holding her when they fell, if that was why she froze at a man's touch.

Does my mind equate the act of being embraced with falling and terror and death? Alana asked herself silently.

She stiffened, listening intently, hoping to hear an inner voice say *yes* or *no*, hoping to tear the veil of amnesia and look upon just a few minutes of those six missing days.

The only answer, if answer it was, came in the sudden coldness of her skin, nausea turning in her stomach, her heart beating quickly, erratically.

"What's wrong?" asked Rafe, sensing the change in Alana. Then, sadly, "Does being close to me frighten you?"

"No, it's not that. I was thinking of Jack."

Behind Alana, Rafe's expression changed, tightening in anger and defeat. But his voice was neutral when he spoke.

"Did you love him?"

Alana closed her eyes.

"No," she said flatly. "I didn't love him."

"Then why did you marry him so fast? Not even two months after—"

Abruptly Rafe stopped speaking.

"They told me you were dead," Alana said, her voice ragged. "Music was all that was left to me. And that meant Jack, a voice to make angels weep."

"I'm sorry," said Rafe, stepping backward. "I had no right to ask."

Rafe's voice was neutral, distant, and Alana's back felt cold without his warmth. She spun around, suddenly angry, remembering the letter that had come back, Rafe's own handwriting telling her that he didn't want to say anything to her, not even good-bye.

"That's correct," Alana said tightly. "You have no right. You didn't even open my letter."

"You were another man's woman."

Rafe's voice was as opaque as his eyes, his mouth a thin line of remembered anger beneath his dark mustache.

"I never belonged to Jack. Not like that."

"You were his wife. Didn't that mean anything to you?"

"Yes," Alana said harshly. *"It meant you were dead!"*

Tears spilled suddenly down her cheeks. She spun away, wanting only to be alone, not to be torn between a past she couldn't change and a present that was trying to destroy her.

"Alana, please don't turn away."

Rafe's voice was gentle, coaxing, making subtle music out of her name. She knew without turning around that he was holding his hand out to her, asking her for something she could not give.

Trust. Caring. Warmth. Passion. Love. All the things she needed but no longer believed in. Not really.

Those things had been taken away from her once too often. She had survived her mother's death. She had survived her lover's death. She had survived her husband's death.

Now Alana was trying to survive a different

kind of death, a shattering loss of belief in her own strength, her own mind, her music. Now she was trying not to ask herself if it was worth it, any of it, if there was no end to fear and loss and death.

"I'm sorry, wildflower. I shouldn't have brought up the past. It's too soon. You're too close to what happened on Broken Mountain."

Rafe walked to Alana, not stopping until he felt the cool, rough flannel he had draped around her shoulders rubbing against his chest. She sensed his arm moving and held her breath, anticipating his touch, not knowing whether she would run or scream or stand quietly.

It was agony not to know, not to be able to trust anything, most of all herself.

"No," Alana said hoarsely, stepping away. "I can't take any more. Leave me alone, Rafe."

"Is it the letter? Is that what you can't forgive me for?" Rafe asked sadly.

"No. It's worse than the letter, although that was bad enough, losing you a second time . . ."

Alana's voice died.

"If not the letter, what?" Rafe said softly, urgently. "What have I done? *What are your memories?*"

At first Alana thought she wasn't going to tell him. Then words rushed out of her in a bittersweet torrent.

"After you, I couldn't bear another man's touch. God, how Jack hated you! You ruined me for any other man."

Rafe's face changed, all anger and urgency gone, only hunger remaining. He reached for Alana and could not help protesting when she flinched away.

"Alana. Don't. Please."

She turned and looked at Rafe with eyes that were wild and dark, shadows as deep as despair.

"Jack got even with me, though," Alana whispered. "Somehow he ruined me for any man at all. Even you!"

Alana turned and fled up the stairs, not stopping even when Rafe called out her name in a voice hoarse with emotion, a cry out of her dreams and nightmares.

She locked the bedroom door behind her and stared out the window until dawn came, bringing color and life to the black land. She watched the world change, born anew out of the empty night.

Just as the last star faded, she heard Bob's voice.

"Sis? You awake?"

Alana realized she was shivering, her skin icy, roughened by gooseflesh. Every muscle ached with the tension that hadn't left her since Broken Mountain. Now she faced another day like all the other days.

But not quite. This day would bring the exquisite torture of being close to the only man she had ever loved. So close and yet so very, very far away.

Dream and nightmare and nothing in between, no safety, no port in the unending, violent storm.

"Alana?"

"Yes," she said tiredly. "I'm awake."

"Don't sound so happy about it," teased Bob.

Alana tugged the flannel shirt more firmly around her, opened the door, and pulled her mouth into the semblance of a smile.

"Morning, little brother," she said, grateful that her voice sounded better than she felt. "Is it time for me to cook breakfast?"

"Nope. Merry's doing the honors this morning. I just came up to get your gear."

Alana gestured toward the small duffel bag on the bed.

"Have at it," she said.

"That's all?"

"This is a pack trip, right? I don't think the trees will care how I'm dressed," Alana said, shrugging.

"Er, right."

Bob gave his sister a sidelong glance, then asked softly, "Are you sure you're up to this?"

"What does that have to do with it?" asked Alana sardonically. "Ready or not, here life comes."

She smiled to take the sting out of her words, but she could tell from Bob's look that she hadn't been very convincing.

"It's okay, Bob. Not to worry. I'm doing fine. Just fine."

He hesitated, then nodded. "Like Dr. Gene says, Burdettes are survivors. And you're the

toughest Burdette of all, sis. You taught the
rest of us how to survive after Mom died."

Alana blinked back sudden tears.

"Would you mind very much if I hugged
you?" she asked.

Bob looked startled, then pleased. Remembering Rafe's blunt instructions, Bob kept his
arms at his sides while Alana gave him a hard
hug.

"You're stronger than you feel," said Bob,
patting her slender shoulder.

Alana laughed strangely and shook her
head.

"I hope so, baby brother. I hope so."

"Are you—are you remembering anything
now that you're home?" asked Bob in a rush.
Then, "Damn, there I go! Rafe will nail my
dumb hide to the barn if he finds out."

Alana stiffened at Rafe's name.

"What happens between me and my brother
is none of Rafe's business."

Bob laughed. "Don't you believe it, sis. That
is one determined man. Makes a pack mule
look positively wishy-washy."

She looked narrowly at her brother.

"You don't resent Rafe, though, do you?"
Alana asked.

Surprised, Bob stared down at Alana. His
dark eyes, so like her own, narrowed as he
measured the emotion on her face.

"Rafe is quite a man. I don't resent learning
from him. Granted," said Bob with a smile,
"he's a jealous son of a bitch. I thought he was

going to fieldstrip Stan and feed him to the coyotes."

Alana blinked, seeing the previous night through Bob's eyes, a totally different view.

"Jealous?" she asked.

Bob snapped his fingers and waved his hands in front of her face.

"Wake up, sis. Stan wouldn't have minded, er, soothing you. And Rafe has made it pretty plain that . . ."

Shrugging, Bob shut up, his caution for once getting the better of his tongue.

"Rafe cares about you," Bob said, "and Stan is bigger, stronger, and better looking than Rafe. No surprise that Rafe's jealous."

"Stan's bigger," agreed Alana, "but it was Stan who ended up flat on his back. And there's more to looks than blond hair, bulging muscles, and a big smile. A lot more."

Bob grinned. "Does that mean you've forgiven Rafe for not opening your letter?"

Alana's face changed, darkness and grief clear on her features. Bob swore.

"Goddamnit, sis. I'm sorry. I'll never learn when to keep my big mouth shut."

"Sure you will," said Rafe from the doorway, "even if I have to pound the lessons into your thick skull one by one with a twenty-pound sledgehammer."

Alana spun around and saw Rafe lounging against the door frame, his rich brown hair alive with sunlight, his mouth hard and yet oddly sensual, his face expressionless except for the whiskey eyes burning with suppressed emotion.

Distantly she wondered how Bob could think that Stan was better looking than the utterly male Rafe.

And then Alana wondered how much of the conversation Rafe had overheard.

"Morning, Rafe," said Bob with a cheerful grin.

He turned and grabbed Alana's duffel off the bed, ignoring both of them.

Rafe simply looked at Alana. The flannel shirt she still wore was in shades of russet and orange and chocolate brown. The long tails came nearly to her knees, and the sleeve cuffs lapped over her fingertips, making her look very small, very fragile. Only in her face and in her movements did her strength show, a woman's strength made of grace and endurance.

A wildflower with pale cheeks and haunted eyes, watching him.

The sound of Bob unzipping Alana's duffel bag seemed very loud in the silence. He rummaged for a few seconds, muttered under his breath, and went to the closet where she had left her clothes after the last disastrous visit.

Bob ran a critical eye over the contents of the closet, then began pulling bright blouses and slacks off hangers. He hesitated between a scarlet dress and a floor-length indigo wraparound that was shot through with metallic gold threads.

"Which one of these travels best?" asked

Bob, looking over his shoulder at Alana.

With a start, Alana pulled her attention away from Rafe. She saw Bob in front of her closet, his arms overflowing with color and silk. In his large hands, the clothes looked exquisitely feminine, as intimate as French lingerie.

"What are you doing?" asked Alana.

"Packing for my big sister," Bob said patiently. "As cute as you look in Rafe's flannel shirt, that wasn't what I had in mind when I told the dudes we dressed for dinner. This is a classy operation, remember?"

Alana looked down at the big flannel shirt folded around her like a warm blanket.

Rafe's shirt.

The thought disturbed Alana. She had assumed that the shirt belonged to Bob.

"Sis? Anybody home?"

"Oh. Um, the dark blue one packs best."

Bob began folding the wraparound with more determination than expertise.

Alana started to object, then shrugged. Whatever Bob did to the silk could be steamed out at the other end. But when he went back to the closet for more clothes, and then more, she finally protested.

"How long are we staying on Broken Mountain?" she asked.

"As long as it takes," Bob said laconically, folding bright clothes.

"As long as what takes?"

"Finding out what—"

Abruptly Rafe's voice cut across Bob's.

"As long as it takes to convince the dudes that Broken Mountain is a good place to send clients. Right, Burdette?"

Bob gritted his teeth.

"Right," he said, folding clothes industriously. "I'm counting on your cooking to win them over, sis."

"But—" began Alana.

"But nothing," Bob said suddenly.

His dark eyes looked at Alana with a combination of affection and maturity that was new to him.

"You signed on for the duration, sis. Get used to the idea. No running out this time, no matter what happens. We'll come after you if you do. Right, Rafe?"

"Right," said Rafe, looking narrowly at Bob. "You're learning, Burdette."

"And not a sledgehammer in sight," pointed out Bob, smiling widely.

Rafe glanced at Alana and saw her baffled look.

"Better get dressed," Rafe said as he went back into the hallway. "Breakfast is getting cold."

Bob zipped up Alana's bag and left her standing in the room with a bemused look on her face.

"Hurry up, sis. Like Dad always used to say, 'You can't keep the mountain waiting.' "

The phrase from her childhood gave Alana a dizzying sense of déjà vu. She remembered her first pack trip up Broken Mountain. She had been only nine and wild with pride that her fa-

ther was taking her on a fishing expedition, just
the two of them together. It had been a wonderful time, full of campfires and long conversa-
tions while stars moved in slow motion
overhead like a silent, glittering symphony.

It hadn't been like that the last time, when
she and Jack had gone up the mountain.

Six days gone.

Six blank days poisoning past memories,
poisoning each day, poisoning her; Broken
Mountain looming over her with inhuman patience, waiting, waiting.

For what? Alana asked silently. For me to
die, too?

You can't keep the mountain waiting.

With a shudder Alana turned away from
her thoughts, dressed quickly, and went
downstairs. The thought of food didn't appeal
to her. She avoided the dining room, where
she heard laughter and strange voices, Stan's
and the woman whom Alana hadn't officially
met. She didn't feel up to meeting Janice Simp-
son right now, either.

Quietly Alana let herself out the front door,
then circled around to the barn where the pack
mules waited patiently.

There were five horses lined up at the hitch-
ing posts. One horse was a magnificent Appaloosa stallion. Two were good-looking bays,
their brown hides glossy in the sun. Of the two
remaining horses, one was as black as midnight and one was a big, dapple-gray gelding.

Alana went to the black mare and stood for
a moment, letting the velvet muzzle *whuff* over

her, drinking her scent. When the mare returned to a relaxed posture, accepting Alana's presence, she ran her hand down the animal's muscular legs and picked up each hoof, checking for stones or loose nails in the shoes.

"Well, Sid," Alana said as she straightened up from the last hoof, "are you ready for that long climb and that rotten talus slope at the end?"

Sid snorted.

Alana checked the cinch and stirrup length, talking softly all the while, not hearing Rafe approach behind her.

"Good-looking mare," said Rafe, his voice neutral.

Alana checked the bridle, then stepped back to admire the horse.

"Sid's a beauty, all right, but the best thing about her is the way she moves," Alana said. "She just flattens out those mountain trails."

"Sid?" Rafe asked, his voice tight.

"Short for Obsidian," explained Alana, returning to the bridle. "You know, that shiny black volcanic glass."

"Yes, I know," he said softly. "You say she has a good trail gait?"

"Yes," Alana said absently, her attention more on loosening the strap beneath the bit than on the conversation. "Riding her is like riding a smooth black wind. A real joy. Not a mean hair on her shiny hide."

"She didn't mind the talus?" continued Rafe in a voice that was restrained, tight with emotion.

"No. The gray didn't like it much, though," said Alana, rearranging the mare's forelock so it wouldn't be pulled by the leather straps.

"The gray?" Rafe asked.

"Jack's horse," she said casually, gesturing toward the big dapple-gray gelding. "It—"

Alana blinked. Suddenly her hands began to shake. She spun and faced Rafe.

"It balked," she said urgently. "The gray balked. And then Jack—Jack—"

She closed her eyes, willing the memories to come. All that came was the thunder of her own heartbeat. She made an anguished sound.

"It's gone!" Alana cried. "I can't remember anything!"

"You remembered something," said Rafe, his whiskey eyes intent. "That's a start."

"Jack's horse balked. Six seconds out of six days." Alana's hands clenched until her fingernails dug deeply into her palms. "Six lousy seconds!"

"That's not all you remembered."

"What do you mean?"

"Sid. You walked out here today and picked her out of a row of horses without any hesitation at all."

"Of course. I've always ridden—" Alana stopped, a startled look on her face. "I can't remember the first time I rode Sid."

"Bob bought her two months ago. He hadn't named her by the time you and Jack came up. You named her, Alana.

"And then you rode her up Broken Mountain."

7

THE FIRST HALF OF THE eight-hour ride to the fishing cabins on the Winter ranch wasn't strenuous. The trail wound through evergreens and along a small, boulder-strewn river that drained a series of lakes higher up the mountain. The air was vibrant with light and fragrance.

The horses' hooves made a soothing, subtly syncopated beat that permeated Alana's subconscious, setting up tiny earthquakes of remembrance beneath amnesia's opaque mantle.

Little things.

Simple things.

Sunlight fanning through a pine branch, stilettos of gold and quivering green needles.

The ring of a horse's steel-shod hoof against stone. The liquid crystal of a brook sliding through shadows. The creak of a saddle beneath a man's shifting weight.

The pale flash of blond hair just off her shoulder when Jack's gray horse crowded against Sid's side.

No, not Jack's horse, Alana corrected instantly. Stan's horse. Jack is dead and the sky over Broken Mountain is clear. No clouds, no thunder, no ice storm poised to flay my unprotected skin and make walking a treacherous joke.

There was sunlight now, hot and pouring, blazing over her, warming her all the way to her bones. She was hot, not cold. Her hands were flexible, not numb and useless. Her throat wasn't a raw sore from too many screams.

It was just rigid with the effort of not screaming now.

Deliberately Alana swallowed and unclenched her hands from the reins. She wiped her forehead, beaded with cold sweat despite the heat of the day.

She didn't notice Bob's concerned looks or the grim line of Rafe's mouth. When Rafe called for an early lunch, she thought nothing of it, other than that she would have a few minutes of relief, a few minutes longer before she had to face Broken Mountain's savage heights.

Alana dismounted and automatically loosened the cinch. She was a little stiff from the ride, but it wasn't anything that a bit of walking wouldn't cure.

Janice, however, wasn't as resilient. She groaned loudly and leaned against her patient horse. Rafe came up and offered his arm. Janice took it and walked a few painful steps. Alana watched the woman's chestnut hair gleam in the sun and heard Janice's feminine, rueful laughter joined by the deep, male sound of Rafe's own amusement.

Slowly the two of them walked back down the line of horses on the opposite side of the trail, coming closer to Alana, who was all but invisible as she leaned on Sid.

Envy turned in Alana as she watched Janice with Rafe. To be able to accept touch so casually. To laugh. To feel Rafe's strength and warmth so close and not be afraid. To remember everything.

Did Janice know how lucky she was? And did she have to cling so closely to Rafe that her breasts pressed against his arm?

Alana closed her eyes and choked off her uncharitable thoughts. Obviously Janice wasn't at all accustomed to riding. Her legs must feel like cooked spaghetti. Yet she hadn't complained once in the four hours since they had left the ranch.

Bob had demanded a brisk pace, wanting to reach Five Lakes Lodge on Broken Mountain before the late-afternoon thundershowers materialized. The hard ride hadn't been easy on the two dudes, who weren't accustomed either to riding or to the increasingly thin air as the trail climbed toward timberline.

But no one had objected to the pace. Not even Stan, who had good reason to be feeling irritable.

Stan, who had been first screamed at and then attacked with no warning, laid out flat, choking beneath Rafe's hard arm.

Blood rose in Alana's cheeks as she remembered last night's fiasco. She put her face against the smooth leather of the saddle, cooling her hot skin.

Stan came up on the other side of Janice and took her arm, supporting her. She smiled up at him in rueful thanks. The smile was vivid, inviting, a perfect foil for Janice's clear blue eyes. Stan smiled back with obvious male appreciation.

"I'll leave you in Stan's capable hands," said Rafe, withdrawing. "But don't go too far. We have to be back on the trail within half an hour."

The big blond man looked at the meadow just beyond the trees, where several trails snaked off in various directions.

"Which trail?" asked Stan.

"That one."

Rafe pointed toward the rugged shoulder of Broken Mountain, looming at the end of the meadow.

Janice groaned and rolled her eyes.

"Only for you, Rafe Winter," she muttered, "would I get on that damned horse again and ride up that god-awful trail."

Alana lifted her head and looked over Sid's back with sudden, intense curiosity. Janice's words, her ease with Rafe, everything about the two of them together added up to people who had known each other longer than a few hours. Stan, too, seemed familiar with Rafe, more like an old friend than a new client for Broken Mountain Dude Ranch.

As Janice and Stan hobbled off down the trail, Rafe smiled after them with a combination of affection and amusement. Alana watched both the smile and the man, and she wondered how well Rafe knew Stan and Janice.

Especially Janice.

As though Rafe sensed Alana's scrutiny, he looked up and saw the black of her hair blending perfectly with Sid's shiny hide. Other than her eyes and hair, Alana was hidden behind the horse's bulk.

"You know them," Alana said when she saw the whiskey eyes watching her. Her voice sounded accusing.

Rafe waited for a long moment, then shrugged.

"I used to travel a lot. The two of them were my favorite agents." He smiled swiftly, amused by a private joke. "We've done a lot of business together, one way or another."

"She's very attractive."

There was a question mark in Alana's eyes, if not in her voice.

Rafe glanced in the direction of Janice, now well down the trail, leaning on Stan.

"Yes, I suppose she is," said Rafe, his voice indifferent. Then he turned suddenly, pinning Alana with amber eyes. "So is Stan."

"Not to me."

"Because he reminds you of Jack?"

Alana thought of lying, then decided it was too much trouble. It was hard enough to keep dream separate from nightmare. If she started lying to herself and to Rafe, it would become impossible to separate the threads of reality from the snarl of amnesia and unreality.

"Stan isn't attractive to me because he isn't you."

Rafe's nostrils flared with the sudden intake of his breath. Before he could speak, Alana did, her voice both haunted and unflinching.

"But it doesn't matter that you're attractive to me and other men aren't," she said, her voice low, "because it's too late."

"No."

Rafe said nothing more. He didn't have to. Every line of his strong body rejected what she said.

Slowly Alana shook her head, making sunlight slide and burn in her black hair.

"I can't handle any more, Rafe," she said, a thread of desperation in her voice. "I can't handle you and the past and today, what was and what wasn't, what is and what isn't. Just getting through the days is hard enough, and the nights . . ."

Alana took a sharp breath, fighting to control herself. It was harder each hour, each minute, for her mind was screaming at her that with every moment, every foot up the trail to Broken Mountain, she came closer to death.

Her death.

It was irrational. She knew it. But knowing didn't stop the fear.

"Seeing you and then remembering the days before and knowing that it will never again . . ." said Alana in a rush.

Her breath came out raggedly, almost a sob. She closed her dark eyes, not wanting to reveal the hunger and fear and helplessness seething inside her.

"I just can't!" Alana said.

"No," countered Rafe, his voice both soft and certain. "I lost you once. I won't lose you again. Unless you don't want me?"

Alana made a sound that was halfway between a laugh and a sob.

"I've never wanted anyone else, for all the good that does either one of us," she said. "It wasn't enough in the past, was it? And it isn't enough now. *Even you can't touch me.*"

"It's been hardly a month," Rafe said reasonably. "Give yourself time to heal."

"I'm starting to hate myself," she said.

Alana's voice was husky with the effort it took to speak rationally about the panic that was turning her strength to water and then draining even that away.

"I'm a coward," she whispered. "Hiding behind amnesia."

"That's not true!"

Alana looked longingly at Rafe, an unattainable dream.

"Yes, it is," she said. "I shouldn't have come back. I'm getting worse, not better."

Rafe's face showed an instant of pain that made Alana catch her breath.

"Was it better for you in Portland?" he asked, his voice quiet, almost without inflection.

Slowly Alana shook her head.

"No. When I slept the nightmares came, more each time, and worse. I'd wake up and fight myself. Hate myself. That's why I'm here. I thought . . ."

Rafe waited, but when Alana didn't say any more, he asked, "What did you think?"

She took a deep, shuddering breath, then another.

"I thought there was something here for me, something that would help me to be strong again. Something that would . . ."

Alana's voice broke but she went on, forcing herself to tell Rafe what she had told no one else.

"Something that would let me sing again," she whispered.

Rafe wondered if he had heard correctly. Her voice was so soft, so frayed.

"What do you mean?" asked Rafe.

"I haven't sung since Broken Mountain. I can't. Every time I try, my throat just closes."

Alana looked at Rafe desperately, wondering if he knew how much singing meant to her.

"Singing was all I had left after you died," she said. "And now I can't sing. Not one note.

Nothing. You're alive now, and I can't bear to be touched. *And I can't sing.*"

Rafe's eyes closed. He remembered the sliding, supple beauty of Alana's voice soaring with his harmonica's swirling notes, Alana's face radiant with music and love as she sang to him.

He wanted to reassure her, protect her, love her, give her back song and laughter, all that the past had taken from her and from him. Yet everything he did brought Alana more pain, more fear.

She could not sing.

He could not hold her.

Rafe swore softly, viciously. When his eyes opened they were clear and hard, and pain was a darkness pooling in their depths.

"I'll take you back down the mountain, Alana. And then I'll leave you alone if that's what you want. I can't bear hurting you like this."

"Rafe," she said, catching her breath, touching his cheek with fingers that trembled. "None of this is your fault."

"All of it is," he said harshly. "I leaned on Bob to get you back here. Now you're here and everything I do hurts you."

"That isn't true," said Alana.

She couldn't bear knowing that she had hurt Rafe. She had never wanted that, even in the worst times after her letter had come back unopened.

"Isn't it?" Rafe asked.

He looked at her with narrow amber eyes.

His anger at himself showed in his lips, sensual curves flattened into a hard line.

"No, it isn't true," she whispered.

But words weren't enough to convince Rafe. Alana could see his disbelief in his grim expression. If she could have sung her emotions to him, he would have believed her, but she couldn't sing.

Hesitantly she lifted her hand to Rafe's face, the face that had smiled and laughed and loved her in her memories, in her dreams. He had always been a song inside her, even in the worst of times.

Especially then, when nightmare and ice avalanched around her, smothering her. He had given her so much, reality and dream and hope. Surely she could give something of that back to him now, when his eyes were dark with pain and anger at himself.

Alana's fingertips pushed beneath the brim of Rafe's Stetson until it tipped back on his head and slid unnoticed to the ground. Fingers spread wide, she eased into the rich warmth of his hair.

"You do feel like winter mink, Rafael," she murmured, giving his name its liquid Spanish pronunciation, making a love song out of the three syllables. "Rafael . . . Rafael. You feel better than in my dreams of you. And my dreams of you are good. They are what kept me sane since Broken Mountain."

Alana felt the fine trembling that went through Rafe, the outrush of his breath that was her name. For an instant she was afraid he would touch her, breaking the spell.

Instead, he moved his head slowly, rubbing against her hand like a big cat. He closed his eyes and concentrated on the feel of her fingers sliding deeply through his hair.

His sensual intensity sent a new kind of weakness through Alana, fire licking down her fingers and radiating through her body, fire deep inside her, burning.

Rafe's dense brown lashes shifted as he looked at Alana, holding her focused in the hungry amber depths of his eyes.

"I've dreamed of you," he said. "Of this."

Alana said nothing, for she could not. Her fingers tightened in his hair, searching deeply, as though she would find something in his thick male pelt that she had lost and all but given up hope of ever finding again.

Even when the sound of Janice and Stan walking back up the row of horses reminded Alana that she and Rafe weren't alone, even then she couldn't bring herself to withdraw from the rich sensation of his hair sliding between her fingers.

Bob's voice cut through Alana's trance.

"Twenty minutes to trail time, everyone," he called from the front of the line of pack mules. "If you haven't eaten lunch, you'll regret it."

Slowly, reluctantly, Alana released the silk and warmth of Rafe's hair. Just before her hand dropped to her side again, her fingertips paused to smooth the crisp hairs of his mustache, a caress as light as sunshine.

He moved his head slowly, sliding his lips over the sensitive pads of her fingers. When her hand no longer touched him, he bent swiftly, retrieved his hat, and settled it into place with an easy tug.

"Bob's right about food," Rafe said, his voice husky and warm. "You didn't have breakfast."

Alana shook her head, though it hadn't been a question.

"I forgot to pack lunch," she admitted.

"Merry packed enough for twenty in my saddlebag." Then, smiling, Rafe added in a coaxing voice, "Share it with me, Alana. Even wildflowers have to eat something."

Beneath his teasing was real concern. Alana was thinner than he had ever seen her. Too thin, too finely drawn, like an animal that had been hunted too long.

"Roast beef, apples, homemade bread, chocolate chip cookies . . ." he murmured.

Alana's mouth watered. She licked her lips with unconscious hunger.

"Sold," she said breathlessly.

She and Rafe ate in the shifting shade of a windblown pine. They sat side by side, almost touching, sharing his canteen. The mint-flavored tea Merry had made for Rafe tasted extraordinary in the clean mountain air.

Alana ate hungrily, enjoying food for the first time in weeks. Rafe watched her, smiling. This, too, had been part of his dreams. Alana and the mountains and him.

When everything else in his life had reeked

of death and betrayal, he had dreamed of her.

"Saddle up," called Bob.

Alana stopped, her hand halfway into the paper bag of cookies. Rafe scooped up the bag and handed it to her.

"Take them," he said, smiling.

"Are you sure? I don't want you to be hungry just because I was too stupid to remember my own lunch."

"There's another bag of cookies in there," Rafe assured her, gesturing to the saddlebags draped across his leg. "Apples, too."

He dug into the supple leather pouch and pulled out two apples.

"Here," he said. "One for you and one for Sid."

Rafe stood and pulled Alana to her feet with one hand, releasing her before she had time to be afraid.

"I'd better help Janice," he said. "She's going to be sore."

Alana winced slightly, flexing her legs.

"She's not the only one," Alana muttered. "Although, considering that it's been more than a year since I rode this hard, I'm not very sore at all."

Then Alana heard the echo of her own words. Her face changed, tension coming back to her in a rush.

"That's not true, is it?" she said, her voice raw. "It hasn't been a year. It's been less than a month. Why can't I remember?"

"Alana," said Rafe urgently.

He bent over her, so close that he could see

the pulse beating in her throat, smell the minty sweetness of her breath. Close but not touching her, afraid to hold her and bring back nightmares in place of dreams.

"Alana, don't. Clawing at yourself won't help you heal."

She drew several long, ragged breaths. Her eyes opened again, very dark but not as wild. She nodded almost curtly, then turned and went back to her horse, clutching a bag of cookies in one hand and two forgotten apples in the other.

The rest of the ride became a waking nightmare for Alana. It began with the first of the five Paternoster lakes, so named because they were strung out like beads on a rosary, shining circles of blue water joined by silver cascades.

The first, lowest lake was at six thousand feet and the highest was just above eight thousand. Pines grew down to the shores of the lower lakes, making dark green exclamation points against the silver-gray boulders that embraced the transparent water. The first lake was beautiful, reflecting the sky in endless shades of blue, serene and quiet.

And after one look, Alana felt fear rise and begin to prowl the corridors of her mind. She heard thunder belling from a cloudless sky, saw violent lightning in every golden shaft of sunshine, heard Jack's voice where nothing but ravens spoke from high overhead.

Gradually, without realizing it, Alana's hands tightened on the reins until Sid fretted, tossing her sleek black head. After a time, Alana's nervousness was reflected in Sid's actions. A line of foam grew around the steel bit. The horse's long, easy stride became a mincing walk. Streaks of sweat radiated from Sid's flanks despite the coolness of the air.

The pressure of Alana's hands on the bit increased by subtle increments until finally Sid stopped. But even then the pressure didn't decrease.

Sid shook her head repeatedly, seeking freedom from the bit.

"Alana."

Rafe's voice was soft and undemanding, despite the harshness of his expression as he watched Alana's blank, unfocused eyes. He leaned over and pulled forward slowly on the reins, easing them out of her rigid fingers. Gradually the thin leather strips slid free, ending the relentless pressure of the bit.

"It's all right, wildflower," murmured Rafe. "I've come to take you home."

Alana blinked and looked around with eyes that were still caught between nightmare and reality.

"Rafael . . . ?"

"I'm here."

Alana sighed and flexed hands that were cramped from the tension of hanging onto reins as though they were a rope pulling her up out of a nightmare. She started to speak, couldn't, and swallowed. The second time she tried, her throat no longer closed around her dead husband's name.

"Jack and I rode this way."

Beneath the shadow of the hat brim, Rafe's narrowed eyes looked like brilliant lines of topaz. He knew that the trail they were on was only one of three trails that led to Five Lakes Lodge. If Alana recognized this particular trail, she must be remembering at least parts of the six lost days.

"You're sure," said Rafe, no question in his voice.

She nodded stiffly. "The first storm began here."

"The first?"

"There were several, I think. Or was it just one long storm?"

She frowned intently, reaching for memories that vanished even as she touched them.

"I don't remember!" Then, more calmly, Alana said, "I don't remember."

She closed her eyes, hiding the shadows that haunted her.

When Alana finally opened her eyes again, she was living only in the present. Rafe and the two horses were waiting patiently. No one else was in sight.

"Where is everyone?" she asked.

"Over the next ridge. I told them we'd catch up later, if you felt well enough."

Distantly Alana wondered what the two dudes thought of her. A woman with strange moods. Hysterical.

Crazy.

The word kept ringing in Alana's mind, an interior thunder drowning out the rational words she kept trying to think of, to cling to.

"Am I crazy?" Alana wondered aloud, not realizing she had spoken. "Or does it matter? If sanity is terror, is there peace in madness? Or is there only greater terror?"

Abruptly Alana shuddered.

"You aren't crazy," Rafe said, his voice gentle and angry and sad. "Do you hear me, Alana? You aren't crazy. You've been beaten and terrified. You've seen your husband killed and you damn near died yourself. And then you were out of your head with shock and exposure. You've hardly eaten at all and slept even less since Broken Mountain."

Wide-eyed, Alana watched Rafe, feeling his words sink into her like sunlight.

"You aren't crazy," he said. "You're just at the end of your physical resources, driven right up to the edge of hallucination in order to keep reality at bay until you decide there's no choice but to face it."

Alana listened, heard the certainty of Rafe's voice, heard the state of her mind and body described so precisely in his deep tones.

"How did you know?" she asked achingly.

"It happens to people when they're pushed too hard, too long."

Slowly Alana shook her head. "Not to strong people. Like you. I used to think I was strong."

Rafe laughed. It was a harsh sound, almost cruel.

"Anyone can be broken, Alana. Anyone. I know. I saw it happen in Central America time and time again."

"Rafe," she whispered.

"They said that I died. For a long time I believed them. It was like dying, only worse. There was no end to it. And then it happened again here."

Alana searched Rafe's eyes and found emotions she had never seen in him before. Violence and hatred and a rage so deep it went all the way to his soul.

"What . . . what happened in Central America?" asked Alana.

Rafe's expression changed, becoming remote, shutting down, shutting her out. The muscles in his jaw flexed and he spoke slowly, with a reluctance that told Alana more than his words.

"I've never told anyone. But I'll tell you. On Broken Mountain, I'll tell you. Unless . . ." Rafe looked at her swiftly, concerned again. "Unless you want to turn back. I'll take you back, Alana. If that's what you want. Is that what you want?"

"I want to trust myself again, to trust my mind and my memory and my emotions," she said in a rush. "I want to be *me* again. And I want . . ."

Rafe waited, an expression of restraint and longing drawing his face into taut planes and angular shadows.

"What do you want?" he asked softly.

"You," Alana said simply. "I was never more myself than when I was with you."

But even as she spoke, she was shaking her

head, not believing that what she wanted was possible.

Rafe held out his hand, palm up, not touching Alana but asking that she touch him. She put her palm lightly on his.

"I'm yours, wildflower," said Rafe. "I have been since I saw you on that exposed trail with a lame horse and lightning all around. You were brave then. You're even more brave now."

"I don't feel brave."

"You came back to Broken Mountain. You're honest with yourself, and with me. If that isn't courage, I don't know what is."

Rafe's voice was deep and sure, conviction reflected in every syllable and in the amber clarity of his eyes as he watched her, approving of her.

With fingers that shook slightly, Alana brushed away the tears that starred her eyelashes. Teardrops gleamed on her fingertips as she almost smiled at him.

"Thank you," she said.

"For telling the truth?" Rafe smiled sadly. "I have a lot more truths for you. But not now."

"What do you mean?"

"My truths wouldn't help you now. And that's what I want. To help you, and me. We'll heal each other and then the past will stay where it belongs. In the past. Memories, not nightmares."

Rafe held out his other hand, palm up.

Alana put her hand in his, felt the strong

pulse in his wrist beneath her touch, saw the glitter of tears transferred from her fingertips to his smooth, tanned skin. Unerringly, he found the pulse point of her wrists and rested lightly against it, savoring the strong flow of her life beneath his fingertips.

"Are you ready for the mountain?" asked Rafe softly.

Slowly Alana withdrew her palms, letting his touch caress her from wrists to fingertips.

"I'm ready," she whispered.

8

F OR THE REST OF THE TRIP, Rafe and Alana rode side by side when the trail permitted. When it didn't, Alana rode first. When pieces of the nightmare condensed around her, she looked over her shoulder to reassure herself that it was Rafe rather than Jack who followed her.

The fragments of nightmare and memory came unexpectedly, out of sequence, tormenting Alana because she couldn't be sure whether it was true memory or false nightmare that stalked her. When she heard Jack's voice raised in anger, she didn't know if it came from the far past or the recent past, or if the words were a creation of her own mind trying to fill in the six missing days.

Sometimes there was no doubt. The sound of wind through the aspens, the shiver of yellow leaves, the song sticking in her throat . . .

Those were real. Those she had heard before, seen before, felt before, and remembered only now. She and Jack had rested by the second lake, there, down by the glacier-polished boulder. They had drunk coffee from their individual canteens and watched trout fingerlings rise in the turquoise shallows.

Then the wind had come again, moving like a melancholy hand over the lake, stirring reflections into chaos, bringing the scent of the heights and storms boiling down.

Jack had watched the clouds seething around the lonely ridges. He had smiled. And he had said . . .

What had he said? Alana asked herself. Something about the land. Something. . . . Yes, that was it: *I always knew this country was good for something. I just never knew what.*

And then he had laughed.

Shivering, Alana drew an imaginary jacket around her shoulders. Sid stumbled slightly, jarring her into the present.

Alana loosened the reins, giving the horse more freedom. She looked over her shoulder. Rafe was there, riding the big Appaloosa stallion, his hat pulled low against the restless wind. She sensed his quick regard, his concern for her. She waved slightly, reassuring him that she was all right.

Other fragments of memory returned, hoofbeats following, wind twisting and booming between ridges, ice-tipped rain. An argument . . .

She and Jack had argued over something. The storm. And the fishing camp. She had wanted to stay at the Five Lakes Lodge until the storm passed. Jack had refused, even though the fishing camp's five buildings were deserted and looked as though they had been empty for years.

In the end Jack had won, but only because Alana couldn't bear to see the site of her greatest happiness standing blank-eyed and empty, cabin doors ajar and porches heaped with dead needles and random debris.

Everywhere she turned, she had seen shadows of Rafe. Every breath she drew had reminded her of the first time Rafe had made love to her, in the loft of the main cabin with a storm coming down, surrounding them. But she hadn't been afraid then. She had been an aspen shivering, and Rafe the mountain wind caressing her.

Sid snorted and shied as she came around the shoulder of an old landslide. Again, Alana was jarred out of the past. Bob was waiting there, riding the big bay mare that was his favorite.

"Everything okay?" asked Bob.

His dark glance roamed his sister's face, looking for and finding signs of strain.

"Yes," Alana said tightly.

"You don't look it," he said, blunt as only a brother can be.

"I'm remembering a few things. Little things."

"That's great!"

"Is it?" she countered quickly. Then, "Sorry. Of course it is."

"Have you told Rafe about remembering?"

Before Alana could answer, Bob was talking again, words rushing out in excitement and triumph.

"He was right!" Bob said, delight in every word. "He said you'd remember once you were here and knew it was safe. And neither doctor would let him go to Portland because—"

"*Burdette.*"

Rafe's whiplash voice stopped Bob's tumbling words.

Bob looked startled, then stricken. "Oh, God, I really stepped in it this time. Damn my big mouth anyway."

Rafe gave Bob a narrow glance that spoke volumes on the subject of loose lips and secrets.

Alana looked from Rafe to Bob, questions in her eyes, questions Rafe knew he would have to answer, questions whose answers she wasn't ready to hear. So he chose his truths and half-truths carefully.

"I told you I leaned on a few people to get you here," said Rafe.

Uncertainly, Alana nodded.

"When Merry couldn't be chief cook and tour guide, I thought of you," Rafe said. "It would be a perfect opportunity to get you back home, where you belonged."

Then Rafe looked toward Bob and spoke in a soft, cold voice. "Isn't that how you remember it, Burdette?"

"Rafe leaned like hell," Bob agreed, looking relieved. "Sis, you aren't mad, are you? I mean, about coming home? We just want what's right for you."

Alana sighed, caught as always by her affection for the brother who rarely had an unspoken thought.

"No, baby brother, I'm not mad. Maybe," she added, smiling crookedly, "I'm not even crazy."

Bob drew in his breath sharply. "Alana, what in hell gave you the idea that you were crazy?"

"What would you call it when someone runs scared from six missing days?"

"I'd call it shock," Rafe cut in smoothly. "Survival reflex. In a word, sanity."

He looked from Alana to Bob.

"Let's get to the camp," Rafe said. "That storm won't hold off forever."

There was an urgency in his voice that allowed no argument. He didn't want Alana to be caught in the open in a storm. Not now. She was off balance, easily startled, too tired. Too fragile.

She needed rest now, not a resurgence of nightmare and violence. It was enough that she had begun to remember. More than enough. He didn't want the past to rise up and rend the delicate fabric of trust binding her to him.

He didn't want her to remember too much, too soon. If she did, then he would lose her again. Only this time there would be no hope. She would be lost to him irrevocably, forever.

Don't remember all of it, wildflower, Rafe prayed silently. Not yet. Give us time to love again.

"Move it, Burdette," Rafe said aloud. "The storm won't wait much longer."

At Rafe's curt signal, Bob set a fast pace to the cabins. Rafe hoped that riding hard would keep Alana's mind in the present rather than in the nightmare he saw too often in her eyes.

Even after they reached the cabins, Rafe watched Alana without seeming to while she prepared supper. He saw no signs that the storm building outside the cabin was bothering her.

After dinner, Bob and Stan went to Janice's cabin for a round of poker and conversation. Alana didn't go. She spent as little time as possible near Stan.

Rafe, too, turned down the offer of cards. His excuse was the flies that needed to be tied for tomorrow's fishing. But he doubted Bob was fooled. He was certain Stan wasn't fooled. The cynical gleam in the big man's eyes said he knew Rafe wanted to be alone with Alana.

As Alana finished setting the table for tomorrow's breakfast, Rafe came back from turning off the generator for the night. He shrugged out of a yellow slicker that sparkled with rain. So far, the evening storm consisted mainly of fat drops randomly sprayed and distant mutters of thunder stalking elusive lightning.

Alana adjusted the wick on the kitchen light until it burned with a clear, steady glow. Rafe hung his slicker on a hook by the back door.

"Hope the dudes don't mind kerosene lamps," said Alana.

"So long as they can see the cards, they'll do just fine. Besides, it will nudge them into bed at a decent hour. Trout rise early. If you want to catch them, you'd better rise early, too."

Eyes the color of whiskey measured the signs of fatigue on Alana's face.

"You should think about going to bed," Rafe said.

"It's hardly even dark," she protested, despite the tiredness welling up in her.

She didn't want to be alone. Not yet. Not with lightning and thunder loose among the peaks.

"It won't be completely dark until nearly ten," Rafe said reasonably. "That's too late for you, if you're going to get up at five to cook breakfast. Tell you what, I'll do breakfast tomorrow. You sleep in."

"No," said Alana quickly. "You look like you haven't been sleeping too well, either. Besides, I came here to cook and that's what I'm going to do. If I get too tired, I'll take a nap tomorrow afternoon."

Rafe looked as though he was going to protest. Then he let out a long breath.

"Will the light bother you if I work down here for a while?" he asked.

Alana looked at the loft bedroom that was simply a partial second story. One "wall" of the room was a polished railing that prevented anyone from wandering out of bed and taking a fall to the living room floor. Curtains could be drawn across the opening of the loft, but that cut off the welcome currents of warmth rising from the hearth. Even though it was only the first week of September, the nights at sixty-three hundred feet crackled with the promise of winter.

"You won't bother me," said Alana. "I always sleep with the light on now."

Again, Rafe paused. Again, he said nothing, merely looked at Alana with eyes that saw everything, accepted everything, even her fear. Knowing that he didn't withdraw from or judge her gave Alana a small measure of acceptance of her own irrational feelings.

"Go to sleep, Alana. If you need anything, I'll be in the downstairs bedroom. So will Bob, unless he plays cards all night like a young fool." As Rafe turned toward the dining room, he added, "There's plenty of hot water for a bath."

The thought of a tub full of steaming water made Alana close her eyes and all but groan with pleasure.

"A hot bath. Damn. That's my idea of roughing it," she said emphatically.

Smiling, Rafe turned back to Alana. He leaned against the door between the living room and dining room.

"From what Dad told me, Mother and Grandmother felt the same way," Rafe said.

"How about you?"

"I'm not all that upset at having hot water," Rafe drawled. "Only thing that bothers me is that damn noisy generator. As for the rest, this is home for me. It took me a lot of years and pain to realize it, but it was worth it."

Slowly Rafe looked around the lodge, enjoying the vivid Indian blankets and brass camp lamps, the suede furniture and a fireplace big enough to stand in. Luxury and simplicity combined. The generator provided electricity for the refrigerator, the water pump, and the lights. The kitchen stove, which also heated water for the cabin, burned wood.

All that was lacking was telephone service. His father had taken care of that by adding a shortwave radio and a repeater on the nearby ridge. By tradition, though, the radio was reserved for emergencies.

Alana watched Rafe quietly, sensing his pleasure in his surroundings, a pleasure she shared. She had loved the Lazy W's lodge and cabins from the first time she saw them, when she and Rafe had raced a storm and lost. They had been drenched and laughing when they arrived.

They would have been cold, too, but the bright currents of passion that raced through them made a mockery of cold. He had started a fire in the hearth to dry their clothes. Then he had led her up to the loft and taught her about other kinds of fire, and the beauty that a man and a woman in love can bring to each other.

Alana blinked, coming back to the present, bringing with her part of the past's shimmering warmth. She saw Rafe watching her with hungry whiskey eyes, as though he knew what she had been thinking.

Or perhaps it was simply that Rafe, too, was remembering a storm and a loft and the woman he loved burning in his arms.

"I laid out your things in the bathroom," Rafe said.

"Thank you," Alana said, her voice almost husky.

Rafe nodded and turned away, leaving her alone.

The bath relaxed Alana, taking the soreness from her body and the tightness from her mind. When she pulled on the long, soft cotton nightgown and went up to the loft bedroom, Rafe was nowhere in sight.

The hearth fire was blazing hotly, ensuring that she wouldn't be chilled by the trip from the bathroom to bed. The bed itself had also been warmed. The metal warmer was still hot to the touch, the coals from the fireplace still glowing when she opened the lid. The covers had been turned down, inviting her to slide in and sleep deeply.

"Rafael," Alana said softly, though she

knew he couldn't hear. "Oh, Rafe, why does it have to be too late for us?"

There was no answer, unless the bed itself was an answer, a bridge between past and present, a promise of warmth and safety.

With a sigh, Alana discarded her robe and slid underneath the covers, pulling them up to her chin as she snuggled into the haven Rafe had so carefully prepared for her. Sleep came quickly.

So did dreams.

As the storm outside the cabin strengthened, dreams twisted into nightmares called by thunder and wind screaming from the ridge lines. A lake condensed around Alana . . . *a landscape subtly blurred, like water pushed by the wind. A glacier-polished boulder stood crookedly, laughing.*

Jack was laughing and the sound was colder than the wind.

Rain swirled, laughing, showing clear ice teeth, stirring water and rocks and trees until another lake condensed. Small, perfect, utterly real but for the shadows of terror flowing out of the trees.

Jack's arms reaching for her, his words telling her of desire and his eyes telling her of death. Jack holding her despite her struggles and then pain came, pain and terror and her screams tearing apart her world.

Alana woke with her heart pounding and her skin clammy. She was breathing in short, shallow bursts. She had recognized the third lake in her nightmare, but not the other lake, the beautiful lake surrounded by horror.

Jack, too, was new, unrecognizable, desire and death inextricably mixed. A raw nightmare, a horrible compound of today's memories and . . . what?

Truth? Imagination? Both? Neither? Alana asked herself frantically. Jack wanted me, yes, but only as the other half of Jack 'n' Jilly. He didn't want me as a woman.

And if he had, it wouldn't have mattered. I didn't want him. I never wanted any man but the one I loved and couldn't have. Rafael Winter. Jack didn't like it, but he finally accepted it—after I told him I would leave him if he ever touched me again.

Is that what we argued about on Broken Mountain?

Shivering, Alana wrapped her arms around her body and let reality condense around her once more. It was so long ago, all of it, on the far side of a six-day gap in her mind that might as well be eternity.

So far away and so futile. Jack was dead and she was not, not quite. She couldn't sing, she couldn't be touched, she couldn't love. But she was alive.

And so was Rafael Winter.

Lightning burst silently into the room, bleaching everything into shades of gray and a white so pure her eyes winced from it. Thunder came, but only slowly, telling of a storm retreating down the mountainside.

Taking a deep breath, Alana lay back once

more, trying to sleep. Even as her head touched the pillow, she knew that it would be futile. Her body was too loaded with adrenaline and the aftermath of nightmare to go back to sleep right away.

She got up, barely feeling the chill. Her deep green nightgown settled around her ankles. The soft T-shirt material clung and flared as she walked to the edge of the loft. The tiny silver buttons that went from her collarbones to her thighs sparkled like raindrops in the muted light from the living room.

Below Alana, engrossed in the multicolored materials spread before him on a table, Rafe worked quietly. His back was to her, so she couldn't see precisely what he was doing.

Alana hesitated long enough to be startled by another burst of lightning. Then she went quickly down the stairs. The battery-powered clock over the mantel told her it was just after eleven.

Though Alana would have sworn that she'd made no noise, Rafe knew she was there.

"Take the chair that's closest to the fire," Rafe said without looking up from the small vise in front of him.

Alana pulled out a chair and sat, careful not to come between Rafe and the light radiating from the kerosene lantern. He was focused on a tiny hook held in a small vise. Silently, delicately, he tied an iridescent bit of feather to the hook's shank using gossamer thread.

In the warm light Rafe's eyes were almost gold, his lashes and hair nearly black. Horn-rimmed half glasses sat partway down his nose, magnifying the work in front of him. Deft, tapered fingers handled special tweezers and dots of glue no bigger than the tip of a needle. He wound the thread once more around the shank of the hook, made a half hitch, tugged gently, and cut the thread.

"There are two schools of thought about fly-fishing," said Rafe as he picked up a delicate shaft of iridescent black feather. "One school is that you attract a trout by presenting it with something it's never seen before, something flashy but not frightening. Like this."

Rafe opened a small metal box. Inside were neat rows of flies, their sharp hooks buried in the wool fleece that lined the box. The fly that Rafe selected was nearly as long as his thumb. The colors were bright, a whimsical combination of blue, yellow, and rose that culminated in graceful silver streamers reminiscent of lacy wings.

"Now, Bob swears by this Lively Lady," Rafe said, neatly replacing the fly in its box. "And I admit to using it a time or two when the fishing was so bad I'd tried everything but a DuPont spinner."

"What's a DuPont spinner?"

"Dynamite," Rafe said dryly. "The Lively Lady is outrageous, but it's more sporting than shock waves."

"Does it work?" asked Alana, watching the play of light over the hair on the back of Rafe's hand.

"Only for Bob." Rafe smiled crookedly.

"The times I used it, you could hear the fish snickering all up and down the canyon."

Alana smiled and almost forgot to jump when lightning flicked again, washing the room with shards of white light. Rafe's deep, calm voice smoothed off the jagged edges of the night for her.

"What's the other kind of fly-fishing?" she asked.

"The kind that imitates natural conditions so exactly that the trout can't tell the difference," said Rafe.

His voice was casual yet reassuring, as though he sensed the fear that had driven Alana out of bed and downstairs to the table where he worked. He set aside the fly he had just tied and picked up a hook that already had been wound with mink-brown thread.

"Usually at this time of year, all you have left are larger, darker flying insects," Rafe said. "Most of the smaller bugs have all been killed off in the same frost that turned the aspens pure gold. I'm a little short on autumn flies, so I decided to do a few tonight."

As Rafe talked, his fingers searched delicately among the boxes. There were feathers and tiny, shimmering drifts of fur, as well as nylon and tinsel and Mylar threads of various thicknesses. It was as though he searched with his touch as well as his eyes, savoring the subtle differences in texture with skilled, sensitive fingertips.

There was no sense of hurry or frustration in Rafe's actions. If the thread he chose was stubborn or slippery, refusing to wrap neatly around the hook's shank, he didn't show any impatience. He simply smoothed everything into place and began again, his fingers sure, his expression calm, his mouth relaxed.

With eyes darker than the night, Alana watched Rafe's every movement. He had rolled up the sleeves of his navy-blue flannel shirt past his elbows. Dark hair shimmered and burned with gold highlights as his arms moved. Muscles tightened and relaxed, making light slide over his skin with each supple movement of his body. Beneath the skin, veins showed like dark velvet, inviting her fingers to trace the branching network of life.

"It's important to match environments precisely if you hope to lure a trout out of the depths of a lake or a river," said Rafe, tying a tiny bit of deep red feather to the body of the hook.

"Why?" Alana asked softly.

"It's so quiet down where they hide, safe and deepest blue. But being safe isn't enough for living things. They need more. They need to touch the sun. At least," Rafe added, smiling, "the special ones do."

Alana watched Rafe's face, her eyes wide and intent, feeling his words slide past the fear in her, sinking down into her core, promising her something for which she had no words, only a song that couldn't be sung.

"So my job is to tempt a special trout out of those safe, sterile depths," said Rafe. "To do that, I have to know what's happening around the fish. If dun-colored mayflies are flying, then a black gnat will be ignored by my special trout, no matter how beautifully the fly is tied or presented."

Deftly he added a radiant filament of black to the shank of the hook.

"You see," Rafe added softly, "my special trout is neither stupid nor foolish. It's unique and strong and wary. Yet it's hungry for the sun."

Tiny shafts of color shimmered as Rafe worked, feathers as fragile as they were beautiful. He handled them so gently that not a single filament was crushed or broken.

When he had taken whatever tiny contribution he needed for the fly he was making, his fingers smoothed the remaining feather, making each iridescent shaft into a graceful arch once more. Tufts of color curled and clung to his fingertips as though thanking him for understanding their delicacy and beauty.

Alana closed her eyes and let memories rise, welcoming them the way a flower welcomes sunlight. Rafe had touched her like that the first time, his strength balanced with his understanding of her innocence.

And she had responded, sighing and curling around him, clinging to his fingertips while his lips feathered across her breasts until she sang a love song that was his name. He had called to her in return, the exquisite beauty of his hands caressing her until she knew nothing but him, felt nothing but ecstasy shivering through her as she sang his name.

Then he had come to her like gentle lightning, moving deeply until she learned what it
was to die and be reborn in the arms of the
man she loved.

To be touched like that again, exquisitely . . .

Alana shivered deep inside herself, a tiny
ripple that was reflected in the subtle color
high in her cheeks.

Glancing up, Rafe saw the faint flush and
rapid pulse beating just above the soft emerald
neckline of Alana's nightgown. For an instant
his fingers tightened and the color of his eyes
became a smoky amber fire.

Then he forced himself to concentrate again
on his work, knowing it wasn't time yet. He
must be patient or he would frighten her back
into the bleak safety of withdrawal from memory, from life.

From him.

Alana's brief, ragged breath sounded like
fire flickering inside the glass cage of the kerosene lamp. She opened her eyes and watched
Rafe, wanting to touch him, to savor the textures of his hair and skin as delicately as he
was savoring the materials with which he tied
flies.

Yet if she did, he would touch her in return
and she would be afraid. Then she would de-
spise herself for her fears.

"Dad never used flies," said Alana, her
voice husky as she searched for a safe topic.
"Worms or metal lures only. Spinning rods.
That's what I was raised with."

"A lot of people prefer them," Rafe said.

His voice was calm, neutral, demanding nothing of her.

"But you don't?"

Rafe smiled slightly as he tied another tiny piece of feather onto the mink-brown body of the fly.

"I prefer the special fish, the shy and elusive one hiding deep in the secret places known only to trout," he said. "To tempt that trout out of the depths and into the sunlight will require all my skill and patience and respect."

He turned a feather, letting light wash over it from various angles, admiring the play of color.

"But wouldn't it be easier to fish down deep rather than to try and lure the trout to the surface?" asked Alana, watching Rafe intently.

"Easier, yes. But easy things have so little value."

Rafe looked up at Alana over the dark rims of his glasses. His eyes were gold, as hot as the flame burning in the lantern.

"The trout should want the fisherman," he said. "Otherwise it's a simple exercise in meat hunting. I want to create a lure so perfect that only a very special trout will rise to it."

"And die," Alana said, her voice almost harsh.

"No," Rafe said very softly. "My hooks have no barbs."

Alana's eyes widened. She looked at the hooks set out on the table, flies finished and half finished and barely begun. Each hook was

a clean, uncluttered curve, not a single barb
to tear at the flesh. She looked back up into
Rafe's amber eyes and felt the breath stop in
her throat.

"Would you like to learn how to fly-fish?"
he asked.

While he waited for an answer, he turned a
golden pheasant feather in the lamplight, making color run in iridescent waves over the
shaft.

"I'd be all thumbs," said Alana.

Rafe laughed softly and shook his head.
"Not you."

She held out her hands as though to convince him of her awkwardness. Slowly he ran
the feather from her wrists to her palms to her
fingertips, stroking her with the delicacy of a
sigh, seeing her response in the slight tremor
of her fingertips.

"Your hands are just right," Rafe said.
"Graceful and long and very, very sensitive."

Alana's breath came in raggedly as she saw
Rafe's expression. She knew that he was remembering being touched by her, the sensual
contrast of her hands against the male contours of his body, the heat and pleasure she
had brought to him.

"You'll enjoy it," continued Rafe softly. "I
promise you."

"I—yes," Alana said quickly, before she
could change her mind and be afraid again.
"After breakfast?"

"After breakfast."

Rafe turned his attention to the hook in his

vise. He released the hook and carefully buried the sharp tip in the fleece-lined box.

"Can you sleep now," he asked, "or would you like me to sit next to your bed for a while?"

Then he looked up, catching and holding Alana's glance with his own.

"I wouldn't touch you unless you asked me to," Rafe said. "And I don't expect you to ask."

"I know," Alana said, her voice low.

And she did. She trusted him.

The realization sent a quiver of light through the dark pool that fear and amnesia had made in the depths of her mind.

"Would you mind staying with me?" she whispered. "For just a few minutes? I know it's childish—"

"Then we're both children," said Rafe easily, cutting across her words, "because I'd rather sit with you than be alone."

Alana brushed his mustache with her fingertips.

"Thank you," she breathed.

The touch was so light, it was almost more imagined than real. Yet she felt it all the way to her knees.

And so did he. His eyes were tawny, reflecting the dance of flame from the lamp.

"My pleasure," Rafe said.

Then he looked away from Alana, not wanting her to see his hunger.

"Go upstairs before you get cold," Rafe said. "I'll clean up here."

"Can I help?"

"No. It will just take a minute."

Alana hesitated, then turned away as Rafe began deftly sorting materials and stacking small boxes onto a tray.

But as soon as she no longer watched him, Rafe looked up, ignoring the brilliant materials at his fingertips. Motionless, entirely focused on Alana, he watched as she climbed up the narrow stairs to the loft.

The glossy black of her hair caught and held the lamplight like stars reflected in a wind-ruffled midnight lake. The green of her nightgown clung and shifted, revealing and then concealing the womanly curves beneath. Her bare feet looked small, graceful, oddly vulnerable beneath the swirling folds of cloth.

Silently, savagely, Rafe cursed Jack Reeves.

9

ALANA OPENED THE CAST-
iron stove door, using a pot holder that had
been crocheted by Rafe's grandmother. Inside
the belly of the stove, a neat pattern of wood
burned brightly, sending vivid orange flames
licking at the thick iron griddle above.

"So far, so good," Alana muttered.

She closed the door, adjusted the vent,
dipped her fingers into a saucer of water, and
flicked drops on the griddle. Water hissed and
danced whitely across the griddle's searing
black surface.

"Perfect."

The kitchen was washed in the golden
warmth of a kerosene lamp, for it was at least

147

half an hour until dawn. The smell of bacon and coffee permeated the lodge and spread through the crisp air to the other cabins, prodding everyone out of bed.

From just outside the kitchen door came the clean, sharp sound of Rafe splitting wood for the stove. It was a strangely peaceful sound, a promise of warmth and a reminder that Rafe wasn't far away.

The rhythm of a song began to sift through Alana's mind, working its way down to her throat. She hummed almost silently, not knowing what she did. It was only the barest thread of sound, more a hope of song than song itself.

Alana picked up the pitcher of pancake batter and poured creamy circles onto the griddle. When the bubbles burst and batter didn't run in to fill the hollows, she flipped each pancake neatly. Soon she had several stacks warming at the back of the stove next to the thick slices of bacon she had already cooked and set aside.

As she poured more batter onto the griddle, she sensed someone walking up behind her.

"I don't need any more wood yet, Rafe," Alana said, setting aside the pitcher as she turned around. "Not until I—*oh!*"

It was Stan, not Rafe, who had come up behind Alana. Reflexively she took a step backward, forgetting about the hot stove.

"Watch out!" said Stan, reaching toward her automatically, trying to prevent her from being burned.

Alana flinched away, bringing the back of her hand into contact with the cast-iron stove. She made a sound of pain and twisted aside, evading Stan's touch at the cost of burning herself again. Again, he reached for her, trying to help.

"Don't touch her."

Rafe's voice was so cold, so savage, that Alana almost didn't recognize it.

Stan did, though. He stepped back instantly. When his blue eyes assessed the fear on Alana's face, he stepped back even more, giving her all the room she needed.

"What in hell do you think you're doing?" demanded Rafe.

His voice was flat and low, promising violence. The stove wood he had carried inside fell into the wood box with a crash that was startling in the charged silence.

Though Rafe hadn't made a move toward Stan, the blond man backed up all the way to the door between the dining room and the kitchen before he spoke.

"Sorry," muttered Stan. "Bob and I thought Alana might need help with . . . whatever."

"Bob and you? Christ," snarled Rafe. "That's an idiots' duet if ever there was one."

Stan flushed. "Now look here, Winter."

"Go tell Bob that if Alana needs the kind of *help* that you had in mind, I'll be the first one to suggest it. Got that?"

Stan's mouth flattened, but he nodded his head curtly, accepting Rafe's command.

"That was your free one," Rafe said grimly. "Do you read me?"

Again, Stan nodded curtly.

Rafe turned his back on Stan and went to Alana. He held out his hand.

"Let me see your burn," Rafe said softly.

The change in his voice was almost shocking. Warm, gentle, reassuring, it seemed impossible that the words came from the same man who had flayed Stan to the bone with a few razor phrases.

"It's all right, wildflower," murmured Rafe. "I won't hurt you."

With a long, shuddering release of breath, Alana held out her burned hand to Rafe.

He looked at the two red bars where her skin had touched the stove and felt rage like raw lightning scoring his gut. Turning on his heel, he went to the refrigerator and pulled out a handful of ice. He dampened a kitchen towel, wrapped the ice, and held it out to Alana.

"Put this over the burns," he said gently. "It will take away the pain."

Numbly Alana did as Rafe said. Within seconds the pain from the seared flesh was gone.

"Thank you," she said, sighing. Then, "It seems that I'm always thanking you."

He took the spatula from Alana and scraped off the pancakes that had begun to burn.

"Funny," Rafe muttered, "it seems that I'm always hurting you."

"It wasn't your fault. It wasn't Stan's, either. It was my own foolishness," said Alana.

"Bullshit," Rafe said in a clipped voice.

He scraped charred batter off the griddle with short, vicious strokes.

"You wouldn't be here if it wasn't for me," he said, "and neither would Stan."

Alana was too surprised to say anything.

With a disgusted sound, Rafe threw the spatula onto the counter and turned to Alana. His eyes were nearly black with the violence of his emotions.

"Forgive me?" he asked simply.

"There's nothing to forgive."

"I wish to Christ that was true."

Abruptly Rafe turned back to the stove and began greasing the griddle.

"I'll finish cooking breakfast," he said.

"But—"

"Sit down and keep those burns covered. They aren't bad, but they'll hurt unless you leave the ice on for a while."

Alana sat on the kitchen stool and watched Rafe covertly. He cooked as he did everything, with clean motions, nothing wasted, everything smooth and sure. The stacks of pancakes grew.

By the time everyone was seated in the dining room, there were enough pancakes to feed twice as many people as were around the table. At least it seemed like that, until everyone began to eat. The altitude and crisp air combined to double everyone's appetite.

Even Alana ate enough to make her groan. At Rafe's pointed suggestion, Bob did the dishes. Stan insisted on helping, as did Janice.

Rafe set out fishing gear while Alana packed lunches.

There were still a few stars out when Rafe led the two dudes to a stretch of fishing water and gave advice on the most effective lures and techniques to use in the extraordinarily clear water.

When Bob turned to follow Rafe and Alana back up the trail, Rafe gave him a long look.

"I promised to teach Alana how to fly-fish," Rafe said. "For that, she definitely doesn't need an audience."

"I won't laugh," said Bob, his lips quirked around a smile. "Much."

"You won't laugh at all," Rafe said smoothly, "because you're not going to be around."

Bob looked quickly at Alana, but she shook her head. He shrugged and accepted the fact that he wasn't going fishing with his older sister.

"Oh, well," Bob said. "I promised Stan I'd show him how to use the Lively Lady. Bet we catch more than you do."

"You'd better," retorted Alana. "Rafe uses barbless hooks. If we're going to eat trout, it's up to you, baby brother."

"Barbless?" asked Bob, giving Rafe a swift look. "Since when?"

"Since I was old enough to shave."

"Hell of a way to fish," Bob said, turning away. "A man could starve."

"Fishing is more than a way to feed your rumbling gut," pointed out Rafe.

"Depends on how hungry you are, doesn't it?" retorted Bob over his shoulder as he walked down the trail.

"Or what you're hungry for," added Rafe softly.

He turned to Alana.

"Ready?" he asked.

"Um . . ."

"I've got a spot picked out by the lake. Lots of room and nothing to tangle your line on the back stroke."

"You're assuming that I'll get enough line out to tangle," Alana said, smiling wryly.

Rafe's soft laughter mixed perfectly with the sound of the stream flowing along the trail.

Though the sun hadn't yet cleared the ridges, predawn light sent a cool radiance over the land, illuminating the path and making boulders look as though they had been wrapped in silver velvet. In the deep pools where water didn't seethe over rocks, trout rose, leaving behind expanding, luminous rings.

Silently, letting the serenity of the land and the moment seep into Alana, Rafe led her to a narrow finger of glacier-polished granite that almost divided the lake into two unequal parts. As she stepped out onto the rock shelf, Rafe touched Alana's shoulder and pointed across the lake.

A doe and two half-grown fawns moved gracefully to the water. While the fawns drank, the doe stood guard. Beyond them the granite face of Broken Mountain flushed pink beneath the gentle onslaught of dawn. The sky was utterly clear, a magic crystal bell ready to ring with exquisite music at the first touch of sunlight.

The doe and fawns retreated, breaking the spell. Alana let out her breath in a long sigh.

Rafe watched her for an instant longer, then began assembling his fishing rod.

"Have you ever used a fly rod before?" he asked.

"No."

Alana watched intently as the long, flexible rod took shape before her eyes.

"I've always wondered how a fly rod works," she admitted. "With spinning rods, the weight of the lure is used to pull line off the reel. But there's no weight worth mentioning in a fly."

"With fly rods, the weight of the line itself is what counts," Rafe said. "The leader and the lure barely weigh anything. They can't. Otherwise they land with a plop and a splash and scare away any fish worth catching."

Using a smooth, complicated knot, he tied a nearly weightless fly onto the thin, transparent leader. Then he pulled a length of thick fly line off the reel, showing her the line's weight.

"Handled correctly, the fly line will carry the fly and set it down on the water as lightly as if the fly really had wings," Rafe said. "The point is to mimic reality as perfectly as possible. The leader is transparent and long enough that the fish doesn't associate the heavy fly line lying on the surface with the tasty insect floating fifteen feet away."

Alana looked at the opaque, thick fly line.

"If you say so," she said dubiously.

"See that fish rising at about two o'clock?" asked Rafe.

She looked beyond Rafe's hand to an expanding ring. It was at least fifty feet out in the lake.

"Yes, I see it."

"Watch."

With his right hand, Rafe held the butt of the fly rod near the point where the reel was clamped on. With his left hand, he stripped line off the reel. As he did so, his right hand began to move the rod forward and back in a smooth, powerful arc.

Kinetic energy traveled up the rod's supple length, bending it with easy, whiplike motions, pulling line from the reel up through the guides. With each coordinated movement of Rafe's arm, line leaped out from the tip of the rod, more line and then more, until it described fluid curves across the luminous sky.

Silently, smoothly, powerfully, Rafe balanced the forces of line and rod, strength and timing, gravity and flight, until an impossibly long curve of line hung suspended between sky and water. Then he allowed the curve to uncurl in front of him, becoming a straight line with the fly at its tip.

Gently, gently, the fly settled onto the water precisely in the center of the expanding ring left by the feeding trout. Not so much as a ripple disturbed the surface from the fly's descent. It was as though the fly had condensed out of air to float on the dawn-tinted mirror of the lake.

And then there was a silver swirl and water boiling as the trout rose to the fly.

The rod tip lashed down at the same instant that Rafe began pulling line in through the guides with his left hand. The supple rod danced and shivered as the trout tail-walked across the dawn like a flashing silver exclamation point.

Line slid through Rafe's fingers, drawn by the trout's power. But slowly, gently, the line returned, drawn by his sensitive fingers, until finally the trout swam in short curves just off the granite shelf, tethered to Rafe by an invisibly fine length of leader.

Just as the first rays of sunlight poured over the lake, the trout leaped again. Colors ran down its sleek side, forming the iridescent rainbow that gave the fish its name.

In reverent silence, Rafe and Alana admired the beauty swimming at their feet. It would have been a simple matter for Rafe to unhook the net at his belt, guide the fish into the green mesh, and lift it from the water. Instead, Rafe gave an expert flick of his wrist that removed the hook from the cartilage lining the trout's mouth.

There was a moment of startled stillness, then water swirled as the trout flashed away.

"See how easy it is?" murmured Rafe, watching Alana with eyes as luminous as dawn. "It's your turn now."

* * *

For what seemed like the hundredth time, Alana stripped line from the fat reel, positioned her hand to feed line from reel to rod, lifted her right arm, and began the forward and backward motion that was supposed to send line shooting up through the guides on the rod.

As she stroked the rod forward and back, line inched up through the guides and started to form the lovely, fluid curve that was the signature of fly-fishing.

And then the curve collapsed into an ungainly pile of line on the rock shelf behind Alana.

"I waited too long on the forward stroke, didn't I?" Alana muttered. "All the energy that was supposed to hold up the line went *fffft*."

"But you got out nearly twice as much line," pointed out Rafe, his voice and smile encouraging her.

"And before that, I broke three hooks on the rock, hooked myself on the back stroke, hooked you on the back stroke, lashed the water to a froth on the forward stroke, tied ruinous knots in your beautiful leader, and in general did everything but strangle myself on the fly line."

Alana shook her head, torn between frustration and rueful laughter. Rafe had been incredibly patient. No matter how many times the line or the leader snarled hopelessly, he had neither laughed at her nor gotten angry. He had been gentle, reassuring, and encouraging. He had praised her and told funny stories about the monumental tangles he used to make when he was learning how to fly-fish.

"Alana," said Rafe softly, capturing her attention. "You're doing better than I did the first time I had eight feet of limber rod and fifty feet of fly line in my hands."

She grimaced. "I don't believe it. I feel so damn clumsy."

"You aren't. You're as graceful as that doe."

"Outrageous flattery," she said, smiling, "will get more knots tied in your line."

Alana positioned the rod again. "Here goes nothing."

Not quite nothing. A rather impressive snarl came next. Rafe untangled it with the same patience he had displayed for the last hour.

As he turned the rod over to Alana once more, he hesitated.

"If it wouldn't bother you," Rafe said quietly, "I could stand behind you, hold on to your wrist, and let you get the feeling of the timing. And that's all it is. Timing. There's no real strength involved. Fly-fishing is a matter of finesse, not biceps."

Alana nibbled on her lower lip as she eyed the deceptively simple appearance of fly rod and reel.

"All right," she said. "Let's give your way a try. Mine sure hasn't done much."

Rafe stepped into position behind Alana. Less than an inch separated them, for he had to be able to reach around her to guide the rod. He stood for several moments without touching her, letting her get used to his presence very close behind her.

"Okay so far?" he asked casually.

"Yes. . . . Just knowing that you understand how I feel makes it easier," Alana admitted in a low voice.

She took a deep breath. The mixed scents of high-country air and sunshine and Rafe swept over her. His warmth was a tingling sensation from her shoulders to her knees. She felt his breath stir against the nape of her neck, sensed the subtle movements of his chest as he breathed, the slight catch of his flannel shirt against hers.

"Ready?" asked Rafe.

Alana nodded, afraid to trust her voice. The breathlessness she felt had little to do with her fear of being touched.

"Take up the rod," he said.

She lifted the fly rod into position.

"I'm going to put my hand around your wrist and the rod at the same time," said Rafe. "Okay?"

She took a deep breath. "Okay."

He reached around Alana until his hand covered hers and wrapped around the rod.

The contrast of his tanned skin against her hand was arresting. It reminded Rafe of just how smooth Alana's skin was, how pale where the sun had never touched it, how incredibly soft when she had welcomed his most intimate caresses.

For an instant Rafe closed his eyes and thought of nothing at all.

"All right so far?" he asked.

His voice was too husky, but there was nothing he could do about that any more than he could wholly control the growing ache and swelling of his desire.

"Yes."

Alana's breath drew out the word until it was almost a sigh. The warmth and strength of Rafe's fingers curling around her hand fascinated her. She wanted to bend her head and brush her lips over his fingers. Just the thought of feeling his skin beneath her mouth made liquid fire twist through her.

Rafe took a quiet breath and hoped that Alana had no idea of how her closeness threatened his carefully imposed self-control.

"Now, remember," he said. "The rod is only supposed to move in the arc between ten and two on our imaginary clock. That's where the greatest power and balance are. You go above or below that and you'll get in trouble. Ready?"

Alana nodded.

Rafe guided her arm and the rod through the short arc between ten and two, counting softly as he did.

"*One*, two, three, four. Now *forward*, two, three, four. And *back*, two, three, four."

Smoothly, easily, the rhythm flowed from Rafe to Alana and then to the rod. She felt the energy curl up the length of the rod, pulling line through the guides, bending the rod tip at the end of the arc. Then came the soft hiss of line shooting up and back over her shoulder just before the rod came forward smoothly, en-

ergy pouring up its length on the forward
stroke, fly line shooting out magically, Rafe's
voice murmuring, counting, energy and line
pulsing along the rod.

Alana felt the rhythm take her until she
forgot everything but Rafe's voice and his
warmth and the line suspended in curving
beauty above the silver lake.

And still the rhythm continued, unvarying,
serene and yet exciting, line pulsing out like a
soundless song shimmering, lyrics sung in silence and written in liquid arcs curving across
the dawn.

"Now," murmured Rafe, bringing the rod
forward and stopping it precisely at ten
o'clock. "Let it go."

Line hissed out in a long, ecstatic surge.
Gracefully, delicately, the fly line, leader, and
fly became a part of the lake. Not so much as
a ripple marred the perfect surface of the water at the joining.

Alana let out a long breath, enthralled by
the beauty of the line uncurling, the sweeping
blend of energy and rhythm, the timeless con-
summation of line and lure and silver water.

"That was . . . incredible," she said softly.
"Thank you, Rafe."

"What for?"

"For your patience. For teaching and sharing this with me."

Rafe felt the shifting surface of Alana's body
against his as she sighed. He wanted to close
his arms around her, enfolding her. He

wanted to feel her flow along his body as she fitted herself against him.

At the very least, he wanted to be able to trace the velvet edge of her hairline with the tip of his tongue, inhaling the sunlight and womanly scent of her, testing the resilience of her flesh with gentle pressures of his teeth.

Ruthlessly Rafe suppressed the hunger that pulsed through him, tightening his body with each heartbeat, drawing it upon a rack of passion.

"You're a joy to teach," Rafe said in a quiet voice. "You should take it easy for a while, though. You're using muscles you didn't know you had. Why don't we just sit in the sun and be lazy? There's a patch of grass and wildflowers farther up the lake."

"Sounds wonderful," said Alana.

As she spoke, she stretched the muscles in her shoulders by twisting them from side to side. She didn't hear the subtle intake of Rafe's breath as she accidentally rubbed against him when she straightened again.

"But aren't you supposed to be helping the dudes, too?" Alana asked.

"They know one end of a fishing rod from the other."

Rafe took the fly rod from Alana, removed the hook, and wound in the line. He began breaking the rod into its component parts with quick movements of his hands, working with an economy and expertise born of long familiarity.

Alana watched Rafe's skilled fingers and the

flex of tendons beneath the rolled-up sleeves of his navy flannel shirt.

"The dudes aren't what I expected," she said.

Rafe looked up suddenly. His whiskey glance pinned her.

"What do you mean?" he asked quietly.

The intensity of his voice belied the softness of his tone.

"Stan's looks, for one thing," Alana said, shrugging. "I'm having a hard time getting used to seeing Jack's ghost. Poor Stan. He must think I'm more than a little unwrapped."

"He'll survive," said Rafe unsympathetically.

"I know. It's just a bit awkward." Alana sighed. "He and Janice have been such easy guests. They don't complain. They don't expect to be waited on. They're funny and smart and surprisingly fit."

Rafe made a neutral sound.

"Not many people could have ridden the trail to Broken Mountain one day and popped out of bed the next morning ready to slay dragons—or even trout," Alana said dryly.

Rafe shrugged.

"And no matter how strange I act," Alana said, "the two of them take it in stride. Even Stan, when I literally ran screaming from him, acted as though it was his fault, not mine."

Rafe said something savage under his breath.

Abruptly Alana laughed. "I guess the dudes are as unusual as the dude ranch."

"Luck of the draw," he said tersely.

With quick motions Rafe slipped the rod into its carrying case.

"The fact that these good sports are your friends has more to do with it than luck," retorted Alana.

Rafe's eyes narrowed into topaz lines. "What are you hinting at?"

"I know what you're doing, Rafe."

"And what is that?" he asked softly.

"You're helping Bob get started."

Rafe said nothing.

"You know how much he needs cash to buy out Sam and Dave," Alana persisted, "and you know Bob doesn't want to destroy the land to make a quick cash killing. So you beat the bushes for friends who could help Bob launch a dude ranch."

Rafe grunted.

"Don't worry," added Alana quickly, resting her hand for an instant on Rafe's arm, "I won't say anything to Bob. I just wanted you to know that I appreciate what you're doing for him. He's got four left feet and he keeps them in his mouth most of the time, but he's a good man and I love him."

With a long, soundless sigh, Rafe let out the breath he had been holding. He smiled ruefully at Alana as he packed away the last of the fishing gear.

But Rafe said nothing about Bob, neither confirming nor denying her conclusions.

In companionable silence, Alana and Rafe walked along the margin of the lake, skirting boulders and gnarled spruces. Spring and summer had come late to the high country this year. Wildflowers still bloomed in the sheltered places, making windows of color against the pale outcroppings of granite. Delicate, tenacious, radiant with life, drifts of wildflowers softened the harsh edges of rock and stark blue sky.

At the head of the third lake, a broad cascade seethed over slick rocks into the shallows. The cascade drained the second, higher lake in the chain. That lake was invisible behind the rocky shoulder of Broken Mountain.

The cascade itself was a pale, shining ribbon of white that descended the granite slope in a breathtaking series of leaps. The sun was more than halfway to noon, pouring transparent warmth and light over the bowl where the third lake lay.

Rafe stopped in a small hollow that was a hundred feet from the cascade. Evergreens so dark they were almost black formed a natural windbreak. Topaz aspens burned in the sunlight and quivered at the least movement of air, as though the trees were alive and breathing with tiny, swift breaths.

Rafe pulled a waterproof tarp from his pack. Silver on one side, deepest indigo on the other, the tarp could gather or scatter heat, whichever was required. He put the dark, heat-absorbent side up, knowing that the ground was cool despite the sun. Spread out, the tarp made an inviting surface for two people to eat or sleep on comfortably.

"Hungry?" asked Rafe, lifting Alana's pack off her shoulders.

Alana was about to say no when her stomach growled its own answer.

With an almost soundless chuckle, Rafe went to his backpack. Quickly he pulled out a snack of apples, hard-boiled eggs, and chocolate raisins.

Alana's stomach made insistent noises. She looked chagrined.

"It's the air," said Rafe reassuringly, concealing a smile.

"If I do everything my stomach tells me to, I won't be able to fit into my clothes," she grumbled.

"Then buy new ones," he suggested, uncapping a canteen full of cold tea. "Ten more pounds would look good on you."

"You think so?" she asked dubiously.

"I know so."

"My costume designer is always telling me to lose more weight."

"Your costume designer is as full of crap as a Christmas goose."

Rafe divided the food between Alana and himself.

She smiled blissfully. "In that case, I'll have another handful of chocolate raisins."

"What about me?" asked Rafe, his voice plaintive and his eyes brilliant with amusement.

"You," she said with a sideways glance, "can have my hard-boiled egg."

Rafe laughed aloud and pushed his pile of

chocolate raisins over to Alana's side of the tarp. He left her egg in place. But when Alana reached for the new pile of sweets, he covered it swiftly.

"Nope," he said, smiling at her. "Not until you eat the egg and the apple."

"Slave driver."

"Count on it," said Rafe.

He bit into his own apple with a hearty crunching sound.

They ate slowly, enjoying flavors heightened by clean air and healthy appetites. When she had eaten the last chocolate raisin, Alana sighed and stretched luxuriously. The exuberant splash of the cascade formed a soothing layer of sound between her and the rest of the world. Nothing penetrated but Rafe's occasional low-voiced comments about fly-fishing and ranching, and the silky feel of high-country sunshine.

"Why don't you take a nap?" he suggested finally.

Alana caught herself in mid-yawn. "There's something sinful about taking a nap before noon."

"In that case, let's hear it for sin." Rafe smiled crookedly. "Go ahead, wildflower. You didn't get enough sleep last night, or a lot of nights before that."

He unbuttoned his flannel shirt, revealing a dark blue T-shirt beneath. With a few quick motions, he shaped the thick flannel shirt into a pillow.

"Here," Rafe said to Alana. "Use this. I don't need it."

Alana tried to object but couldn't get any words past the sudden dryness in her mouth.

Even in her dreams, Rafe had not looked so overwhelmingly male. The T-shirt defined rather than concealed the slide and coil of muscles. With every movement Rafe made, every breath he took, his tanned skin stretched over a body whose latent power both shocked and fascinated her.

Suddenly Alana wanted to touch Rafe, to trace every ridge and swell of flesh, to know again the compelling male textures of his body.

She closed her eyes but still she saw Rafe, sunlight sliding over his skin, sunlight caressing him, sunlight burning in his eyes and her blood.

"Alana?" Rafe's voice was sharp with concern.

"You're right," Alana said in a shaky voice. "I haven't been getting enough sleep."

Rafe watched as she stretched out on the tarp, her cheek against the shirt he had rolled up for her. He would rather she had used his lap as a pillow, but was afraid if he suggested it, the relaxed line of her lips would tighten with tension and fear.

Yet for a moment, when Alana had looked at him as though she had never seen him before, Rafe had hoped . . .

"Better?" he asked, watching Alana's body relax into deep, even breathing.

"Yes."

"Then sleep, wildflower. I'm here."

Alana sighed and felt herself spiraling down into a sleep where no nightmares waited.

10

WHEN ALANA WOKE UP, the sun was on the other side of noon. She rolled over sleepily and realized that she was alone.

"Rafe?"

No one answered.

She sat up and looked around. Through the screen of evergreens and aspens she saw Rafe outlined against blue water. He had found another rock shelf leading out into the lake. He was standing at the end of the granite finger. The fly rod was in his hands. Line was curling exquisitely across the sky.

For a few moments Alana watched, captured by the grace of the man and the moment when line drifted soundlessly down to lie upon still water.

Except Alana couldn't actually see the line touch the surface of the lake, because trees blocked her view.

She stood up and started toward the shoreline, then realized that once Rafe saw her, he would probably stop fishing and start teaching her once again. She wasn't ready for that. She felt too relaxed, too at peace—and too lazy—to attempt anything that required concentration.

What she really wanted to do was to sit quietly, watching Rafe and the lyric sweep of line against the high-country sky.

Alana looked back down the lakeshore to where she and Rafe had been earlier. She saw no place to sit and watch him that wouldn't immediately bring her into Rafe's view.

She looked left to the cascade dancing whitely down rocks turned black by water. Rafe was facing away from the cascade, looking down the lake toward the cabins. The position gave him a hundred feet in front of the fly rod and an equal amount in back without anything to obstruct the motion of the line.

And he was using every bit of that two hundred feet.

On tiptoe, Alana peered through the wind-twisted branches of a fir, holding her breath as the curve of the fly line grew and grew, expanding silently, magically. Rafe's left arm worked in perfect counterpoint to his right as he stripped line off the reel, almost throwing fly line up through the guides as his right arm pumped smoothly, sending energy coursing through the rod.

"How are you doing that?" muttered Alana, knowing Rafe couldn't hear her. "You aren't a magician, are you?"

She stepped farther to her left, but she still couldn't see exactly what Rafe was doing to make the line lengthen so effortlessly. With a small, exasperated sound, she worked her way along the increasingly rugged shoreline, trying to find a spot that would allow her to watch Rafe without being seen.

Alana leaped from stone to stone, avoiding the small boggy spots where coarse grass and tiny flowers grew, until she found herself confronted by the barrier of the cascade. She turned around and looked back at Rafe, who was about sixty yards away from her by now.

Unfortunately, she still couldn't see what he was doing with his hands. Nor could she go any farther forward without coming up against the cascade. She could either go back, or she could go up the boulder-tumbled slope.

With a muttered word, Alana looked at the jumble of stone rising on either side of the frothing water. She wouldn't have to go very far up the cascade to get the view she wanted. Just far enough to allow her to look over Rafe's shoulder, as it were. If she didn't get too close to the water, the climb wouldn't be too hard. Besides, she had been raised hiking and scrambling along mountain rivers and up steep slopes.

Alana turned and began climbing over the lichen-studded boulders. Twenty feet away, the cascade churned and boiled, making both mist and a cool rushing thunder. She avoided the slippery rocks, seeking the dry ones.

Within a few minutes she was breathless, gaining two feet in height for every foot forward. She persisted anyway, scrambling and balancing precariously, until she stood on a ledge of granite that was barely eighteen inches deep.

She stopped because there was no other choice. In front of her rose a slick outcropping of rock six feet high, and not a handhold in sight.

"Well, this had better be far enough."

When Alana turned to look, it felt like the earth was dropping away beneath her feet. Unexpected, overwhelming, a fear of heights froze her in place.

Twenty feet away, the cascade frothed down the steep mountainside, water seething and racing, white and thunder, and wind whipping drops of water across her face like icy rain. Thunder and ice and the world falling away, leaving her *helpless, spinning, darkness reaching up for her*.

Alana clung to the rough face of the granite and closed her eyes, struggling to separate nightmare and memory and reality.

The feeling of falling didn't stop. The boom of water over rock became remembered thunder. Drifting spray became ice-tipped winds and her screams were lightning as memory and nightmare and reality became one.

Cold.

God, it was cold, cold all the way to the center of the earth. Jack with anger twisting his face. Jack cursing her, grabbing her, hitting her, and the storm breaking, trees bending and snapping like glass beneath the wind.

Like her. She wasn't strong enough. She would break and the pieces would be scattered over the cold rocks.

Running.

Scrambling.

Breath like a knife in her side. Throat on fire with screams and the storm chasing her, catching her, yanking her backward while rocks like fists hit her, bruising her, and she screamed, clawing and fighting.

But she was swept up, lifted high, helpless, nothing beneath her feet, and she was falling

screaming

and Rafe was calling her name.

You're safe, wildflower. I've come to take you home.

Distantly Alana realized that she had heard the words before, over and over, Rafe's voice reaching out to her, peeling away layers of nightmare until only reality remained.

"You're safe, wildflower. I've come to take you home."

Shaking like an aspen in a storm, Alana clung to the rock face. She sensed Rafe behind her, heard his voice, felt the warmth of his body along her back, Rafe standing between her and the drop-off at the end of the rocky ledge.

"R-Rafe," Alana said shakily.

It was the only word she could say.

"I'm here, wildflower. You're safe," he murmured, his words and the tone of his voice soothing her. "You're safe."

Alana let out a breath that was more a sob.

"Rafe? I'm so s-scared."

She couldn't see the darkness of his eyes or his savage expression so at odds with the reassurance of his voice.

"I know," Rafe said. "You had a bad time up along the lakes, even if you don't remember it. Or," softly, "did you remember?"

Alana shook her head.

"Then why are you frightened?" he coaxed. "Is it because I'm close to you? Are you afraid of me?"

She shook her head again. "No."

Though weak, her voice was positive. It wasn't Rafe she feared.

For an instant, Rafe closed his eyes. A strange mixture of emotions crossed his face. Then his eyes opened. Relief eased the tightness of his mouth and brought light to his eyes again.

"What is it, then?" he asked. "Can you tell me?"

"Height," said Alana in a trembling voice. "I'm afraid of heights now and I never was before, not until Jack fell and I guess I fell, too."

The words tumbled over each other like water in the cascade. She made a ragged sound.

"Rafe, I felt so good when I woke up a few minutes ago. All morning I hadn't thought about Jack or Broken Mountain or the missing days. I hadn't thought about anything since breakfast but fly-fishing and sunshine and you being so patient and gentle with me."

"I'm glad you enjoyed the morning," Rafe said, his voice low and husky. "I know that I haven't enjoyed anything so much in years."

"Do you mean that? Even though I ruined your line and scared every fish away?"

Rafe's lips brushed against Alana's shoulder in a caress so light she didn't feel it.

"I'll buy a hundred miles of leader," he said, "and let you tie knots in every inch of it."

Alana let out her breath in a rush, then took another breath. She almost felt brave enough to open her eyes.

Almost.

"Don't make any rash promises," she said shakily, trying to make a joke even though her voice wouldn't cooperate. "I'll hold you to every one of them."

"Wildflower," whispered Rafe, brushing his cheek against her glossy hair, "brave and beautiful. I'd carry away Broken Mountain stone by stone if that would let you come to me again with a smile on your lips."

The words were a warmth unfolding in the center of Alana's icy fear. As fear melted away, some of her strength returned.

She opened her eyes. The rough granite textures of rock were only inches from her face. On either side of her shoulders, close but not touching her, were Rafe's arms. His hands were flattened on the rock as he stood behind her, his legs braced, his feet wide apart on the narrow ledge, his body between her and any danger of falling.

Slowly Alana put one of her hands over his. The warmth of him was almost shocking.

"But I'm not brave," she said, her voice tight with anger at herself.

Rafe's laughter was as harsh as it was unexpected.

"Bravery isn't a square jaw and a thick head," he said. "Bravery is standing toe-to-toe with fear every minute of every hour, never knowing if you're going to get through this second, and afraid the next second might be one too many."

Alana's breath stopped. It was as though Rafe were in her mind, reading her thoughts, putting into words what she had only sensed without understanding.

"And the worst of it is that you're strong," Rafe said, "so you survive when others would have broken and gone free, crazy free, but you survive day after day no matter how bad it gets. And it gets very bad, doesn't it?"

Alana nodded, unable to speak.

So Rafe spoke for her, and for himself.

"Some of those days are endless," he said,

"and the nights . . . the nights are . . . unspeakable."

Alana's grip on Rafe's hand was so tight that her nails left marks on his skin.

"How did you know?" she whispered.

"I've been there, Alana. Like you, I've served my time in hell."

She whispered Rafe's name as tears slid from her eyelashes down her cheeks, crying for him and for herself.

His lips brushed her neck very lightly. She wouldn't have felt it if she hadn't been so sensitized to him, his emotions, his physical presence, Rafe like a fire burning between her and the freezing blackness that came to her in nightmares.

Alana bent her head until her lips touched the back of Rafe's hand. She kissed him gently, not withdrawing even when his hand turned over and cradled her cheek in his palm.

Slowly Rafe leaned down, unable to resist the lure of Alana's tears. He murmured her name as his lips touched her eyelashes, catching the silver drops. He expected her to stiffen at the caress, at the knowledge that she was trapped between his strength and the granite face of the mountain.

She turned her cheek to his lips, leaning lightly against him, her eyes luminous with emotion. He kissed the corner of her mouth, delicately stealing the tears that gathered there, until finally there were no more tears.

"Are you ready to climb down now?" Rafe asked softly.

Alana took a ragged breath, then looked beneath Rafe's arm to the rocks tumbling away to the lake.

Everything spun for an instant. She closed her eyes and hung on to him, hard.

Rafe saw the color leave Alana's face even before he felt her nails digging into his arms and the shaking of her legs against his. Quickly he leaned inward, bracing Alana against the rock with his body so that she wouldn't fall if her legs gave way.

"Don't be afraid," said Rafe softly, urgently. "I'm not going to hold you or hurt you in any way."

There was an instant of stiffness before Alana sighed and nodded her head, unable to speak.

When Alana accepted his presence, his reassurance, relief came in a wave that for an instant left Rafe almost as weak as she was.

And with relief came hunger for Alana, the hunger that had haunted Rafe ever since he had come back to find the woman he loved married to another man . . . desire and rage burning Rafe like acid every time he saw a picture of Alana with Jack, Country's Perfect Couple, happiness condensed into two smiling faces on millions of album covers.

Ruthlessly Rafe suppressed both desire and the corrosive memories of rage. He ignored the sweet warmth of Alana's body pressed along his as he braced her against the cold granite.

"I'll support you until you aren't dizzy," he

said, his voice even, calm. "Tell me when you can stand again."

Eyes closed, Alana savored the sound of Rafe's deep voice, his warmth and reassurance, and his patience. If he didn't condemn her for being foolish, for being afraid, she wouldn't condemn herself, either.

"Alana?" asked Rafe, unable to see her face. Concern made his voice almost harsh.

"It's all right," Alana said.

And as she spoke, she realized that it really was all right. When she stopped being disgusted with herself, when she stopped being afraid of fear, she was able to react more rationally.

Rafe's strength and closeness made Alana feel as she should, protected rather than threatened. She sighed and felt the shaking in her legs diminish.

"You didn't frighten me, Rafael. I looked down the mountain, that's all."

He let out his breath with an explosive sigh.

"That wasn't a very bright thing to do, sweetheart."

Alana's mouth formed a smile that was gone as swiftly as it had come.

"I figured that out real fast," she said. "Now maybe you can figure out how I'm going to climb off this damned ledge with my eyes closed."

"Gracefully, smoothly, and quickly," murmured Rafe, brushing Alana's neck with his lips, not caring if she felt the caress, "like you do everything else."

"Including tie knots in your leader," retorted Alana.

Her voice was almost steady, but her eyes were still tightly closed.

"Most especially tying knots in my leader," he answered, laughing softly against her hair. "Ready?"

"To tie knots? I was born ready for that, obviously. No practice needed. Perfect tangle on the first try."

Then Alana took a deep breath.

"Rafe," she said softly, "I really don't want to open my eyes."

"How else can you admire the gorgeous tangles you make?"

"Braille," she said succinctly.

"Okay. Braille it is." Rafe hesitated. "For that to work, I'll have to be very close to you, Alana. Sometimes I'll have to take your foot and place it, or hold you, or even lift you."

"*No.*"

Then she spoke quickly, desperately, wanting to be sure Rafe understood how important it was.

"Don't lift me, Rafe. *Please.* That's my worst nightmare, my body being lifted high and then falling and falling and Jack— Oh, God," she said, horrified. "Jack. He fell. He fell into the darkness and rocks, and the water was like thunder everywhere and he died and—"

Alana's throat closed around screams and her eyes opened dark and wild, dilated with terror and memories that faded in and out like a nightmare.

Rafe ached to hold her, but he was nearly certain it would trigger the terror he sensed seething beneath her words, waiting to claim her.

"Hush, wildflower," Rafe murmured. "I won't lift you. You're safe with me."

Slowly Alana's eyes focused on the strong hands braced on either side of her. She made a despairing sound.

"Rafe, each time I come closer to remembering but never close enough. And each time I'm so afraid. Does it ever end?"

"It will end," Rafe said, his voice a curious mixture of reassurance and shared pain. "It will end. And you'll survive. Like the wildflowers survive ice and darkness, sure of the summer to come."

His lips brushed her nape.

"You're strong, Alana. So strong. I know you don't believe that now, but you are. If you didn't go under before, you won't go under now. Believe me. I know. I've been there, too. Remember?"

Alana put her forehead against Rafe's hand and fought to control her breathing. After a few minutes, she succeeded.

Only then did Rafe say quietly, "We're going to climb down, now. You'll have to help me, Alana."

"H-How?"

"You'll have to trust me," he said simply. "If you don't, you'll panic and then I'll have to knock you out and carry you down. I don't want to do that, Alana, even though I could do it and never leave a bruise on your body. Your mind, though . . ."

Alana shuddered, not noticing how intently Rafe was watching her.

"Being knocked out and carried down the mountain would be your worst nightmare come true, wouldn't it?" Rafe asked softly.

The words went through Alana's mind like a shock wave. Was that her nightmare? Being knocked out and carried?

Slowly, hardly even realizing it, Alana shook her head.

"No, that's not my nightmare. My nightmare is being lifted and then thrown, something throwing me away and then I'm falling, falling forever, ice and darkness and death."

Rafe's voice was calm, but his eyes were burning with the rage that came to him every time he thought of Alana hurt, frightened, screaming his name.

But none of his emotions showed in his voice.

"Then you won't panic if I have to hold you?" he asked matter-of-factly.

"I don't know," said Alana starkly. "I guess we'll just have to find out the hard way, won't we?"

"Yes, I guess we will."

When Alana felt Rafe move away, felt the cool wind on her back where his warmth had been, she wanted to cry out in protest. For a moment she simply stood, eyes closed, hands pressed against cold stone.

"About one foot below and slightly to your left is a flat stone," Rafe said.

He watched while Alana crouched slightly and felt around with the toe of her walking shoe, trying to find the surface he had described.

"Another inch down," he said. "That's it. Good."

Legs braced, arms outstretched but not touching her, Rafe followed Alana's progress.

"Now your right foot," he said. "Straight down, more, just another few inches. There. Feel it?"

Alana's answer was a drawn-out sound of relief when she felt the rock take her weight. She thought of opening her eyes again, but she didn't trust herself not to freeze.

Rafe described the next step, then the next, his hands always hovering just above Alana without touching her. He talked constantly, encouraging her.

Slowly Alana backed down the steepest part of the slope.

"Now, use your left foot," Rafe said. "This is a tricky one. There are two rocks close together. You want the one on the left. No, not that one, the—*Alana*."

The rock turned beneath her foot, throwing her off balance. Rafe grabbed her and held her in a hard grip, but only for an instant. Carefully he put her back on her feet.

Other than a choked cry when the stone first slid out from beneath her foot, Alana had made no protest, even when Rafe's hands closed around her arms. Yet she was very pale, and her hands shook noticeably as she searched for support among the tall boulders. Shudders rippled through her body.

Rafe sensed that Alana had fallen into nightmare again. Gently he turned her until she was facing him. He kept his hands on her shoulders, more to give her contact with the world than to support her.

"Alana, open your eyes. Look at me, not at the lake or the rocks. Just at me."

Slowly Alana's black eyelashes parted.

Rafe was only inches from her, his amber eyes narrowed and intent. His mustache was a deep, rich brown shot through with metallic highlights of bronze and gold. The pulse in his neck beat strongly, hinting at the heat and life beneath his tanned skin.

"It's daylight, not night," Rafe said softly. "It's warm, not icy. Jack is dead. You're alive and safe with me."

Mutely Alana nodded. Then she sighed and leaned against him.

Rafe wanted very much to put his arms around her, to hold her against his body and rock her until both of them felt only the other, knew only the other, comfort replacing fear.

But, like Alana, Rafe was afraid if he held her, there would be only fear and no comfort at all.

"I'm sorry you were frightened," murmured Rafe, smoothing his cheek against her hair.

"I was—but I wasn't. Not really." Alana took another long breath. "I knew after I called your name that you wouldn't let me fall."

And Rafe knew that Alana hadn't called his name. Not *this* time.

If she thought she had, she was still caught between the past and the present, a hostage to fear. Yet she had trusted him not to let her fall.

That, at least, hadn't changed.

After a few moments, Alana straightened and stood on her own.

"Let's finish it," she said, her voice flat.

"Aren't you going to close your eyes?"

"I don't think so. It's not as steep here, is it?"

"No. If you're going to take a look, though, do it now, when I'm close enough to catch you if you get dizzy."

Alana's mouth relaxed into a tiny smile. "I can't see through you, Rafe."

He turned partially, just enough to give her a brief view of the tumbled slope behind him. As he turned, he watched her face, ready to grab her if vertigo struck again.

Other than a flattening of her mouth, Alana showed no reaction. Even so, Rafe stayed very close for the first few steps. She glanced at him and tried to smile.

"I'm all right now," she said.

Rafe nodded, but he remained within reach of her. Together they worked their way down the last of the slope. When there was only lake in front of them, they stopped.

With a sense of triumph, Alana turned and looked back. She shook her head as she realized that the slope, which had seemed so steep and deadly from above, didn't look like much at all from the bottom.

"Fear always looks like that from the other side," Rafe said quietly.

Alana looked from the mountainside to the man beside her. Rafe's understanding of what she had been through, and his acceptance of her fear, untied knots deep inside her as surely as he had untied the snarls of fly line she had created. She put her palm against his cheek, savoring his warmth and the masculine texture of his skin.

"Rafael," she murmured, making music of his name. "You make me believe that someday I may even sing again."

Rafe turned his head until he could kiss the slender palm that rested against his cheek. He whispered Alana's name against her hand and smiled as her fingers curled up to caress his lips. Slowly Alana's other hand crept up to Rafe's head, hungry for his warmth and the smooth thickness of his hair between her fingers.

Moving as slowly as Alana did, Rafe tilted his head down until his lips could slant across hers. The kiss was so gentle that it was impossible to tell the exact instant when it began.

Alana neither hesitated nor pulled back when she felt Rafe's mouth caress hers. Instead, she whispered his name again and again, lost in the sensations that came as his lips brushed slowly against hers. His mouth moved from side to side with gentle pressures that made her fingers tighten in his hair, pulling his head closer in silent demand.

The tip of Rafe's tongue slid lightly over

Alana's lower lip, then traced the curves of her mouth until she sighed and her fingers kneaded down his neck to his shoulders, seeking the long, powerful muscles of his back. Her mouth softened, fitting itself to his.

When Alana's tongue touched first his lips, then his teeth, Rafe made a sound deep in his chest. His hands clenched at his sides as he fought not to give in to his hunger to hold her, to feel her body soften and flow over his as surely as her mouth had.

Hesitantly Rafe touched the warmth and sweetness of her tongue with his own. Even then she didn't retreat. The kiss deepened until the sound of his own blood beating inside his veins drowned out the cascade's rushing thunder.

Rafe heard Alana call his name with hunger and need, a sound out of his dreams. As gently as a sigh, his fingers dared to touch her face, the smooth curve of her neck, the slenderness and feminine strength of her arms. When she showed no fear, he rubbed his palms lightly from her shoulders to her hands and back again.

She murmured and moved closer to him, letting his heat radiate through her. He shifted his stance, fitting her against him, touching her very gently with his hands while the sweet heaviness of desire swelled between them.

Alana forgot the past, forgot the nightmare, forgot everything but the taste of Rafe and the rough velvet of his tongue sliding over hers. Fire shimmered through her, called by his hunger and her own, fire melting her until she sagged against him, giving herself to his strength.

Rafe's arms circled Alana, holding her as she held him, molding her against the heat and hunger of his body. She responded with a movement that brought her even closer, standing on tiptoe, trying to become a part of him.

And then she moved sinuously, caressingly, stroking his body with her own.

With a ragged sound, Rafe let his arms close around Alana. As his arms tightened, they tilted Alana's hips against his thighs. The movement lifted her just enough that for an instant her toes lost contact with the ground.

In that instant, Alana went from passion to panic.

11

EVEN AS ALANA TRIED TO wrench free of his embrace, Rafe realized what had happened. Cursing himself, he released her completely.

"I'm sorry."

They both spoke quickly, as one, identical words and emotions.

"It's not your fault."

Again their words tangled, each hurrying to reassure the other.

When Alana would have spoken again, Rafe gently put his fingers across her mouth.

"No," he said in a husky voice. "It's not your fault. I should have known better than to hold you. I thought I could trust myself. But

I'd forgotten how sweet and wild you are. Even in my deepest dreams, I'd forgotten."

Alana's black lashes closed. She tilted her face down so that Rafe couldn't see her expression until she was more certain of her self-control. When she looked at him again, there was no fear in the dark clarity of her eyes, only apology and the luminous residue of passion.

"Did you really dream of me, Rafael?" Alana asked, music and emotion making her voice as beautiful as her eyes.

"Yes," he said quietly. "It was all that kept me sane in hell."

Alana's breath caught at the honesty and pain in Rafe's voice. Her eyes searched his expression.

"What happened?" she asked.

Rafe hesitated. "It's not a pretty story. I'm not sure it's something you want to know."

"If you can stand to tell me, I can stand to hear it."

When Rafe still hesitated, Alana took his hand and started back along the lakeshore, leading him with a gentle pressure of her fingers.

"Never mind," she said. "We'll eat lunch and then we'll lie in the sun and count aspen leaves. Remember?"

The darkness left Rafe's eyes. His lips curved into an off-center smile.

"I remember," he said. "The first one who blinks has to start all over again."

"After paying a forfeit."

"Of course," Rafe said in a husky voice. "I remember that part very well."

A sideways look into his brilliant whiskey eyes told Alana that Rafe indeed hadn't forgotten. Her fingers tightened in his as he brought her hand up to his lips. He rubbed his mustache teasingly over her sensitive fingertips. Then he nibbled on the soft pad of flesh at the base of her thumb.

"What's that for?" asked Alana breathlessly.

"I blinked," admitted Rafe. "Didn't you see me?"

"No. I must have blinked, too."

"That's one you owe me."

"But we haven't started counting aspen leaves yet," Alana pointed out.

"Well, if you're going to get all technical on me, I guess I won't start keeping score until after lunch."

Smiling, Alana led Rafe to the hollow where they had left their backpacks. While he retrieved the fishing gear he had abandoned when he heard her scream, Alana set out a lunch of sandwiches and fruit.

They ate slowly, letting the sun and silence dissolve away the last residue of fear and nightmare. When Rafe was finished, he stretched out on his back with his hands linked behind his head.

After a few moments he said lazily, "Twenty-three."

"What?"

"I counted twenty-three aspen leaves before I blinked."

"You can't even see any aspens from where you are."

"Sure I can," Rafe said, his voice deep. "Just off over your shoulder."

Alana turned and looked. Sure enough, a golden crown of aspen leaves rose above a thick screen of dark evergreen needles.

"You blinked," Rafe said. "How many?"

"Eleven."

"That's two you owe me."

Saying nothing more, Rafe resumed staring over her shoulder.

"Aren't you ever going to blink?" asked Alana finally.

"Nope." Then, "Damn. Got me. Thirty-seven."

Alana shifted until she could look at the aspen without twisting around. She counted swiftly, then groaned when she blinked.

"It's coming back to me now," she said. "I used to lose this game all the time."

Rafe smiled. "Yeah. I remember that best of all. That's three you owe me."

He settled into counting again.

After a long pause he said, "It's coming back to me now. The trick is not to stare too hard—and be sure the wind isn't in your face. Then—damn. Forty."

Alana got as far as thirty-five before she blinked. She groaned again.

"That's four," Rafe said.

"Aren't you worried about collecting?" Alana asked, for he had made no move to kiss her.

Rafe's glance shifted.

"Are you?" he countered in a soft voice, watching her.

Alana's breath shortened, then sighed out.

"I don't know," she admitted, remembering both the pleasure and the panic she had felt by the lakeshore.

"Then I'll wait until you know," he said simply.

Alana propped herself on her elbow and rolled over to face Rafe. He ignored her, counting quickly, aspen leaves reflected in his amber eyes.

She looked at the grace and strength of him as he lay at ease, legs crossed at the ankles, jeans snug over his muscular thighs and lean hips. The dark blue T-shirt had pulled free of his pants, revealing a narrow band of skin the color of dark honey. A line of hair so deeply brown that it was almost black showed above the low-riding jeans. Where the shirt still covered him, it fit like a shadow, smooth, sliding, moving when he did, a cotton so soft that it had felt better than velvet against her palms when she had touched him by the lake.

"Seven thousand six hundred and ninety-two," Rafe said.

"What?"

"Seven thousand six hundred and ninety-two."

"You can't have counted that many leaves without blinking," she protested.

Rafe smiled. For the last few minutes, he had been watching Alana rather than aspen leaves, but she hadn't noticed because she had been watching every part of him except his eyes.

And her smile told him that she very much approved of what she saw.

"Would you believe two thousand?" Rafe asked innocently.

Alana shook her head so hard that the motion sent her silky cap of hair flying.

"Two hundred?" asked Rafe.

"Nope."

"Fifty?"

"Well . . ."

"Sold," Rafe said smoothly. "That's five you owe me."

"But I haven't had my turn yet."

"Think it will do any good?"

Alana sighed and stared very hard at an aspen, but all she saw was the image of Rafe burned into her mind, into her very soul. She blinked to drive away his image, then groaned when she realized that single blink had cost her the contest.

"Fifteen," she said in disgust.

Rafe smiled and turned his attention back to aspen leaves quivering in the breeze. When Alana's fingers touched his cheek, his counting paused, then resumed. When her hand slid up the arm that was pillowing his head, his counting slowed. When her fingertip traced the supple veins showing beneath his skin, her touch sliding slowly up and down the sensitive inner side of his arm, Rafe stopped counting altogether.

"You're cheating, wildflower," he said in a husky voice.

"I finally remembered."

"What did you remember?"

"How I used to win this game."

"Funny," he said, "I remember us both winning. Every time."

"I wish—" Alana's voice broke. "I wish that it could be like that again. I wish you had never gone away that last time."

She took a ragged breath and then asked the question that she had asked herself a thousand times since she had learned that Rafe was alive.

"What happened, Rafe? What did I do to deserve your silence?"

He didn't answer for so long that Alana was afraid he would refuse to answer at all.

"Do you mean the letter I returned to you?" he asked finally.

"Yes, but even before that. Why did you let me believe you were dead? Other people knew you were alive, but not me. I didn't find out until a year ago."

"I thought you were happily married."

Alana searched Rafe's expression with eyes that were too dark, remembering too much of pain and not enough of happiness.

"How could you believe that?" she asked. "I loved you. I thought you loved me."

"I did."

"Then how could you believe I loved Jack?"

Rafe's lips flattened into a grim line. "It happens all the time to soldiers. The Dear John syndrome. One man goes off to war and another man stays to comfort the girl who was left behind."

"It wasn't like that," whispered Alana. "I married Jack because singing was all I had left after they told me you were dead. It was a business marriage."

"Alana—"

"He never touched me," she said, talking over Rafe. "I wouldn't let him. I couldn't bear to be touched by any man but you."

Rafe closed his eyes. When they opened again, they were hard, focused on the past, a past that had nearly destroyed him.

"I didn't know," he said. "All I knew was that six weeks after I 'died,' the woman who once said she loved me became half of Country's Perfect Couple. Everywhere I turned I saw Jack 'n' Jilly, America's favorite lovers, singing songs to each other, love songs that were beautiful enough to make Broken Mountain weep."

"Rafael . . ." Alana's voice frayed.

"Let me finish," Rafe said tightly. "I may never talk about it again. God knows I'd just as soon forget it, every second of it."

"The way I did?" she asked, her voice flat, all music gone. "That wouldn't make it better. Believe me, Rafe. Forgetting the way I did just makes it worse in the long run. I can't imagine anything more awful than my nightmares."

Rafe closed his eyes and let out a long, harsh breath.

"I know," he said. "I learned the hard way

that forgetting or ignoring doesn't make anything go away. So I'm going to tell you something that's buried in filing cabinets in the Pentagon and in the minds of the very few men who survived. Something that never happened at all, officially."

Alana said nothing, afraid to move, straining to hear Rafe's low voice.

"I told you I was in the army," he said. "Well, I was, but in a very special branch of it. I was trained in counterinsurgency, with special attention to rural areas." He smiled grimly. "Really rural. God, but I learned to hate jungles."

After the silence had stretched for several moments, Alana touched Rafe's arm with gentle fingers.

"What happened?" she asked, her voice soft.

"Four years ago, I'd just about decided that I'd rather fight lost causes with my thick-skulled father in Wyoming than fight lost causes in the jungles of Central America. I owed the army some more time, though."

Alana waited, remembering. When Rafe had asked her to marry him, he had also told her that they would be separated a lot of the time for two more years. Then he would quit the army and come back and marry her.

"Just before I left Wyoming the last time, some of our men were taken prisoner along with a native guerrilla leader," Rafe said. "There was no chance of getting our men back through regular diplomatic means, because the men weren't officially there in the first place. The records had them posted to Chile or West Germany or Indochina, anywhere but Central America."

Motionless, Alana listened.

"We couldn't just write off the men," Rafe said, "even though word was that nobody survived prison there for long. And we needed that guerrilla leader. My group was asked to volunteer for a rescue attempt."

Alana's eyes closed, knowing what was coming next.

"You volunteered," she said, her voice barely a thread of sound.

"I knew the men who had been caught. One of them was a very good friend. Besides," Rafe said matter-of-factly, "I was good at what I did. With me leading the raid, it had a better chance of succeeding."

She took a deep breath and nodded. For the first time, some of the agony she had gone through four years ago began to make sense.

"I understand," she said quietly.

"Do you?" Rafe asked.

He looked directly at Alana for the first time since he had begun to speak of the past.

"Do you really understand why I left you?" he asked. "Why I *volunteered* to leave you?"

"You couldn't have lived with yourself if you had stayed safe and the other men had died," Alana said simply, stroking the hard line of Rafe's jaw with a gentle fingertip. "That's the kind of man you are. You'd never buy your own comfort with another person's life."

Rafe kissed the finger that had moved to caress his mustache.

"Most women wouldn't understand."

"Most women never know a man like you."

"Don't kid yourself," Rafe said harshly. "I'm no hero. I scream just as loud as the next guy when the rubber-hose brigade goes to work."

Alana's eyes widened darkly as the meaning of Rafe's words sank in. She touched his face with gentle fingers, smoothing away the lines of rage that had come when he remembered the past.

"You're a man of honor, Rafael. That's all anyone can ask."

For long moments Rafe said nothing, responding to her with neither look nor words. Then he let out his breath.

"I'm glad you think so, Alana. There were times I didn't think much of myself. Men died. I was their leader. I was responsible for their lives."

"They were soldiers. Volunteers. Like you."

"And I led them right into hell."

Alana's fingers smoothed the grim lines bracketing Rafe's mouth.

"Was there another way you could have done it?" she asked softly.

"No." His voice was bitter. "That's how I knew I'd led them into hell. The road there is paved with the best intentions. The better the intentions, the deeper you go.

"And all the way down you know that there was nothing you could have done differently, that if you were put in the same position again you'd do the same thing again, the honorable thing . . . and you'd take the same good people down with you.

"And that," he said savagely, "is my definition of hell on earth."

Words crowded Alana's throat, all but choking her. She spoke none of them, sensing that the only words that could help Rafe right now were his own. She caressed him gently, her fingers smoothing his skin in undemanding touches that told him she was there, listening, sharing his pain as much as she could.

"I've thought about that mission a lot," Rafe said after a time. "But I've never said anything to anyone since I was debriefed."

"You couldn't."

"It wasn't so much the security regulations that kept me quiet. I just never found anyone who I thought would understand what it was like to be scared every second of every day, to be scared and fight not to show it, to face each dawn knowing that it probably wouldn't be better than yesterday and often it would be worse."

Alana touched Rafe's wrist, felt the life beating beneath his supple skin.

"Not many people know what it is like to serve an indeterminate sentence in hell," Rafe said. "Waiting and listening to the screams while the damned are tortured, waiting and

listening and knowing that soon you would be
screaming, too."

Alana made a stifled sound and turned very
pale. Yet after a brief hesitation, her hand
never stopped touching Rafe, giving him what
comfort she could while he relived a nightmare she could barely imagine, but could understand all too well.

The man she loved had been imprisoned
and tortured until he screamed.

Whatever memories I have hidden in my
nightmares, Alana told herself silently, Rafe's
must be worse, memory and nightmare alike.
Yet he survived. He is here, strong despite the
cruel violence of the past, patient with me despite my weakness, gentle with me despite the
brutality that he has known.

As Rafe continued talking, low-voiced and
intense, Alana took his hand and pressed it
against her cheek, as though simple touch
could take the agony and bitterness from his
past. And her own.

"I went into the jungle alone," he said,
"about three days ahead of the others. They
needed someone to get inside the prison for a
fast recon so we'd know how many of the men
were alive and able to walk on their own. It
was too dangerous a job to ask anyone to volunteer for."

Rafe stared past Alana, his eyes unfocused,
remembering. Yet even then his fingers moved
lightly against Alana's cheek, telling her that
her presence helped him as much as anything
could.

"I got into the prison without any problem," Rafe said. "Wire fences and a few perimeter guards. They were counting on the jungle and the prison's reputation as a hellhole to keep people away."

Rafe's fingers tensed on Alana's cheek.

"It was a hellhole, all right," he said. "What I saw there made me want to execute every guard, every government officer, everyone I could get my hands on. And then I wanted to burn that prison with a fire so hot it would melt through to the center of the earth."

Rafe closed his eyes, afraid that if they were open, Alana would see what he saw. Men chained and tortured, maimed and slowly murdered for no better reason than the entertainment of guards who were too brutal to be called men and too inventive in their savagery to be called animals. Grinning devils ruling over a green hell.

"I got the information and I got out," Rafe said. "The next day I led my men back in."

His eyes opened. They were clear and hard as topaz, the eyes of a stranger.

"As soon as we pulled out the men we came for, I went back to that prison. Three of my men came with me, against my orders. They were the three who had seen the wing where prisoners were tortured. The four of us freed every prisoner and then we blew that building straight back to the hell that had spawned it."

Alana held Rafe's hand against her lips, trying to comfort him and herself, rocking slowly.

"One of the men who came back with me

was injured. The other two carried him to the rendezvous while I stayed behind to cover the retreat.

"Some of the guards survived the blast. I held them off until my gun jammed. They caught me, shot me, and left me for dead in the clearing. The helicopter got away, though. I heard it lift off just after I was shot."

Alana made a low sound.

"I survived. I don't remember much about it. Some of the peasants hid me, did what they could for my wounds. Then the government soldiers came back. I was too weak to escape."

Alana bit her lips against the useless protests aching in her throat.

Rafe kept talking quietly, relentlessly, getting rid of the savage memories from the past.

"They took me to another prison just like the one I'd blown to hell. I knew there was no hope of rescue. My men had seen me shot. They would assume I was dead. Besides, you don't risk twenty men to save one, unless that one is damned important. I wasn't."

Wanting to speak, afraid to stop the flow of Rafe's words, Alana murmured softly against his palm and tried not to cry aloud. Her hands smoothed his arm and shoulder again and again, as though to convince herself that he really was alive and she was with him, touching him.

"I spent a long time in that prison," Rafe said. "I don't know why I didn't die. A lot of men did and were happy to."

Then Rafe turned and looked at Alana.

"That's not quite true," he said. "I know why I survived. I had something to live for. You. I dreamed of you, of playing the harmonica while you sang, of touching you, making love to you, hearing you laugh, feeling and seeing your love for me in every touch, every smile."

"Rafael," she whispered, and could say no more.

"The dreams kept me sane. Knowing that you were waiting for me, loving me as much as I loved you, gave me the strength to escape and to live like an animal in the jungle until I crossed into a country where I wouldn't be shot on sight."

Alana bent over to kiss Rafe, no longer caring if he saw her tears.

"And then," Rafe said, his voice flat, "I came home to find that the woman I'd loved enough to live for didn't love me enough to wait for me."

"That's not true!" Alana said, her voice a low cry of pain.

"I know. Now. I didn't know then. All I knew was what the papers told me. Jack 'n' Jilly. Perfect marriage. Perfect love. No one told me any different."

"No one knew," Alana said raggedly. "Not even my family. Jack and I worked very hard to keep the truth of our marriage a secret."

"You succeeded."

Rafe looked at Alana for a long moment, seeing his pain and unhappiness reflected in her dark eyes and pale face. He touched her lips with his fingertip, loosening the tight line of her mouth.

"I left the army as soon as my time was up," Rafe said. "My father was dead by then. I came back to the ranch as bitter a man as has ever watched the sun rise over Broken Mountain. Until a year ago, I ran the ranch through my lawyers and lived out of the Broken Mountain fishing camp. Alone."

Alana closed her eyes against the tears she couldn't control.

"If only I had known you were alive . . ." she whispered.

"But I wasn't sure that I was alive," Rafe said. "Not really. Most of my time was still spent in hell. No one on this side of the mountain even knew that I hadn't died. Except Sam, and he wouldn't tell anyone."

"Sam?" Alana asked, startled.

"He took some training in Panama. Different outfit. Civilian, not military. We worked together once, just before I left the army. He's a good man, if a bit hardheaded. And that's all I have to say on the subject of Sam Burdette."

Alana started to object, then realized that it would do no good. Rafe might share his own secrets with her, but her brother's secrets were not Rafe's to share. She looked at Rafe with eyes that understood, eyes as dark as midnight, as dark as her nightmares.

"When did you decide to tell people that you were alive?" she asked.

"I didn't. It just happened."

Rafe shook his head slowly, remembering his rage and bitterness at life and the woman who had married another man just six weeks after her fiancé had been declared dead.

"I ran into Bob one day in the high country," Rafe said. "He was fishing that crazy fly he favors. And he went straight down the mountain to you."

Without realizing it, Alana's fingers tightened on Rafe's arm as she remembered the moment that Bob had burst into the house talking about Rafe Winter, a man come back from the dead—and looking like it. Hard and bitter, eyes as cold as a February dawn.

Rafe. *Alive.*

And Alana was married to a man she didn't love.

"A day later," Rafe said, watching her, "Bob brought me a letter. I recognized your handwriting on the envelope. I looked at it for a long, long time."

"Why didn't you—" she began.

"I knew I couldn't open my own Dear John letter," Rafe interrupted savagely. "I couldn't force myself to read the words describing your perfect marriage, perfect career, perfect man, perfect lover. I couldn't read the death of my dream written in your own hand, the dream that had kept me alive when most of me hurt so much that death looked like heaven itself."

Alana shook her head. Tears fell from her tightly closed eyes. With a ragged sound, she put her head on Rafe's chest and held him until her arms ached. She couldn't bear the thought of Rafe being tortured, dreaming of her, surviving because he loved her.

And then coming home to find her married.

"What was in the letter?" Rafe asked.

His voice was so soft that it barely penetrated the sound of Alana's tears.

"The truth," Alana said hoarsely. "I was going to leave Jack. When I was free, I was going to write to you again, if you wanted me to."

"But you didn't leave Jack."

"No." She drew a ragged breath. "When I lost you a second time, I thought nothing mattered. I went back to Jack."

Rafe's eyelids flinched. It was the only sign he gave of the pain within him at the thought that he had sent her back to Jack Reeves.

"But when I knew you were alive," Alana said, "I couldn't stay with Jack. Not even to save our singing career. So we lived separately, but very discreetly."

Slowly she shook her head, remembering the past.

"Separation wasn't enough," she whispered. "You didn't want me, hadn't even cared for me enough to tell me you were alive, but I had to be free of the sham marriage. I had lived with lies for too long. When you were dead, the lies hadn't mattered to me. Nothing had mattered except singing.

"That's how I survived, Rafe. I sang to the memory of the man I loved, not to Jack. Never to him."

"And then," Rafe said bitterly, "I wrote

your death sentence on an envelope and sent it back to you."

"What?"

Rafe swore savagely.

Alana trembled, not knowing why he was so angry with himself.

"What did you mean?" asked Alana, her voice shaking as she looked at Rafe's narrowed eyes. "Why was that envelope my death sentence?"

"It sent you back to Jack Reeves."

"What—"

"The answer is in your nightmares," Rafe said, cutting off Alana's question.

Her eyes searched Rafe's, looking for answers but seeing only herself reflected in the clear amber.

"How do you know?" she asked.

"That, too, is in your nightmares."

Rafe's hands came up to frame Alana's face.

"There's something else in those lost days, wildflower," he murmured, kissing her lips gently. "There's the moment you saw me, knew me, turned to me."

He kissed her again, more deeply.

"Rafe—"

"No," he said softly. "I've told you more than the good doctor wanted me to. But I thought it might help you to know that something other than horror is buried with those six missing days."

12

FOR A LONG TIME THERE WAS only silence and the rushing sound of the distant cascade.

Rafe's expression told Alana that questioning him would be futile. He had the same closed look that he had worn when he talked about leading his men into hell.

But it angered her that Rafe knew something about her six lost days and wouldn't tell her.

"Why?" Alana asked finally, her voice harsh. "Why won't you help me?"

"You didn't know Jack was dead. People told you he was. How much help was that?"

Alana searched Rafe's topaz eyes.

"But—" she began.

"But nothing," he interrupted in a flat voice. "Did knowing Jack was dead help you remember anything?"

Alana clenched her hands.

"No," she said.

"Did waking up in that hospital beaten and bloody tell you how you got hurt?"

Silence. Then, tightly, "No."

"Did reading about Jack's death in every newspaper help?"

"How did you know?" she whispered.

"In some ways you're a lot like me," Rafe said simply.

"But if you'd tell me what you know, it would help me sort out reality from nightmare."

"The doctors don't think so. They're afraid I might tell you something you don't want to know."

"What?"

"I might tell you that your nightmares are pieces of the truth."

Rock and ice and wind, something lifting her, throwing her out into the darkness
falling
she was falling and rocks waited below, waited to break her, hatred breaking her.

Alana made a small sound and went pale. She wrapped her arms around herself as she felt the cold of nightmares congeal inside her, fear and truth freezing her. She closed her eyes as though it would shut out the fragments of nightmare.

Then she wondered if it was memory that she was shutting out, reality chasing her through her nightmares, truth saying to her, *remember me.*

Rafe reached for Alana, wanting to gather her into his arms and comfort her.

When his hands touched her, she gasped and flinched away.

Rafe withdrew instantly, but the cost of controlling himself made muscles stand out rigidly along his jaw. He looked at Alana's pale skin and black lashes, her mouth shaped for smiling but drawn by fear into a thin line, the pulse beating too quickly in her throat.

With a soundless curse, Rafe closed his eyes. The doctors were right. Telling her wouldn't help.

Even worse, it could hurt her.

At first Rafe had been afraid that Alana would remember too soon, before he had a chance to win her love again. Now he was afraid that she wouldn't remember soon enough, that she would lose faith in herself and then tear herself apart.

Yet Rafe couldn't bring back Alana's memory for her, no matter how much he wanted to. The bitterness of that knowledge made the brackets around his mouth deeper, harder.

"If telling you everything I know about those six days would stop you from freezing when I touch you, I'd shout the truth from the top of Broken Mountain," Rafe said, his voice rough with suppressed emotion.

Alana said nothing.

"My God, don't you know that I'd do anything to have you in my arms again?" Rafe whispered. "I want you so badly. I want to hold you, comfort you, love you . . . *and I can't.* All I can do is hurt you again and again."

Rafe's hands became fists. With a quick movement, he rolled over until his back was turned toward Alana.

"It's like Central America all over again," he said harshly, "only it's worse because this time it's you I'm leading into hell, knowing with every step that there's no other way, knowing and hating myself just the same."

His laugh was a short, savage sound.

"Christ," Rafe said harshly, "I don't blame you for shrinking away every time I touch you."

The raw emotion in Rafe's voice called Alana out of the depths of the nightmare as nothing else could have. She knew what it was like to feel snarled and helpless, hating yourself, feeling as though everything you did made the tangle worse, not better.

The thought of Rafe feeling that way because of her made Alana ache with tears she couldn't shed. In just the past day, Rafe had given so much to her, laughter and protection, patience and companionship, subtle passion, and, above all, acceptance.

She might rail at herself for being weak, she

might be angry and disgusted with herself . . .
but Rafe was not.

When she was close to hating herself, he had
told her about strength and weakness and survival, torture and the breaking point every human being has. He had told her about his own
time in hell, and in doing so he had coaxed
her out of the depths of her own self-disgust.

Rafe had given her hope when all she had
was nightmare.

And for that she flinched when he touched
her.

"Rafael," murmured Alana, touching his
arm.

He made no response.

She shifted her position until she was on her
knees. She leaned over Rafe, stroking him
from the thick silk of his hair down to the
corded tension of his neck. She repeated his
name again and again, a slow litany that was
nearly a song.

Her hand moved down, trying to loosen the
rigid muscles of his shoulders and back. The
dark cotton of his T-shirt felt like warm velvet
to her. Her fingers kneaded the hard flesh beneath. He felt so good to her, heat and smooth-
ness and strength.

With a sigh, Alana bent over until she could
put her lips just below the dark brown of his
hairline. Rafe's neck was warm and firm,
tanned skin stretched tautly over tendons,
tempting her tongue to taste and trace each
subtle change in texture.

She kissed him lightly, lingeringly, before

she gave in to temptation and touched his skin with the tip of her tongue. He tasted of salt and heat and man, slightly rough where his beard began and amazingly smooth on the back of his neck.

Delicately Alana's teeth closed on Rafe's neck, testing the resilience of the muscle beneath. He moved his head and shoulders slowly, increasing the pressure of her teeth on his flesh, making her hand slide over the muscles of his back.

Rafe tasted good, felt good. Alana wanted to touch and savor more of him. Her fingers dug into the bunched muscles beneath her hand as her teeth tested the male power of his shoulders.

Rafe arched against her touch like a hungry cat.

The honesty of his response made an equal hunger sweep through Alana, a hunger that only Rafe had ever called from her. She wanted to lie down next to him, to fit her body along his, to feel his passion surround her as she surrounded him.

Yet even as fire licked through her, melting her, Alana knew that if Rafe's arms closed around her, she would freeze. And in freezing, she would hurt him cruelly. Then she would hate herself all over again.

"Oh, Rafe," she said, her voice breaking on his name, "what are we going to do?"

"What we're doing right now feels wonderful."

"But I'm afraid I'll freeze."

Alana's words trembled with fear and the beginning of anger at herself.

"Does touching me frighten you?" Rafe asked.

Alana made an odd sound that could have been laughter.

"Touching you is like singing, Rafael. Only better."

She heard his breath come in sharply and felt the fine tremor that went through his body.

"Then touch me as much as you want," he said simply.

"That isn't fair to you."

Rafe's back shifted beneath Alana's hand, urging her to explore him, telling her more clearly than words that he wanted to be touched by her.

"Remember when you were nineteen?" he asked.

Alana's hand hesitated, then slid up Rafe's back to his hair. Eagerly her fingers sought the warmth of him beneath the thick pelt.

"Yes," she whispered. "I remember."

"You didn't object then."

"I didn't know what I was doing to you. Not really. Virgins can be very cruel."

"Did I complain?" asked Rafe, laughter and memories curling just beneath his words.

"No," she said softly.

"Did I ask for more than you wanted to give?"

"No. Never, Rafael."

"I never will."

With a smooth motion, Rafe rolled onto his back and looked at her with eyes that were clear amber, brilliant with emotion and desire.

"Do you believe me?" he asked.

"Yes."

"Then touch me."

"Even though I can't . . ." Alana's voice faltered.

"Yes," said Rafe swiftly, almost fiercely. "However much or little you want. Everything. Anything. I've dreamed of you for so long. Touch me, wildflower."

Hesitantly Alana's hands came up to frame Rafe's face. Her lips brushed across his while her fingers again sought the silky brown depths of his hair. With a sigh, her breath mingled with his and she knew again the heat and textures of his mouth. She made a throaty sound of pleasure as his taste spread across her tongue.

Forgotten sensations stirred, awakening. The kiss deepened into a timeless sensual joining as they gave themselves to each other, knowing only one another.

Finally, Alana lifted her mouth and looked at Rafe with eyes that remembered passion.

"The first time you kissed me like that," whispered Alana, "I thought I would faint. I think I could faint now. You take the world out from under me."

"Are you frightened?" Rafe asked quietly, watching Alana with smoky amber eyes.

She smiled slowly and shook her head.

"With you, there's no danger of falling,"

Alana said. "With you, I'm as weightless as heat balanced on fire."

She bent her head and kissed Rafe again, savoring every instant, every changing pressure of tongue on tongue, the heat and pleasure of his mouth joined with hers.

Her hands slid from his hair, caressing him with each tiny movement of her fingers. One hand curved around his neck just beneath his ear, her palm fitting perfectly against the slide and play of muscle as he moved his mouth across hers. Her other hand slid down his arm, only to return as her fingers sought the warmth of his skin beneath the short sleeve of his T-shirt.

She stroked Rafe, murmuring her pleasure as she felt him flex against her touch. Her hand slid higher until her palm rubbed his shoulder under the soft T-shirt. Catlike, Rafe arched into her caress, telling her how much he liked having her hand on his bare skin.

When Alana's mouth left his and she began to nibble on his mustache and his neck and finally, delicately, his ear, Rafe made a deep sound in his throat. She responded by tracing the outline of his ear with her mouth, then caressing him with slow, probing touches of her tongue that made his breath quicken.

"I remember how I shivered the first time you did that to me," whispered Alana, her breath warm against Rafe. "Do you remember?"

"Yes," he said huskily. "You had goose bumps all the way up and down your arms."

"Like you, now."

"Like me, now."

Alana's tongue touched Rafe's neck just as her teeth closed on his skin. Rafe moved his head, urging her to touch more deeply, to bite harder. Her teeth pressed into his flesh and she felt the male power in the tendon sliding beneath her mouth.

He had caressed her like that when the storm had chased them to the Broken Mountain cabin. His bite had been just short of pain and had brought a pleasure that had left her weak.

With a small sound, Alana caressed Rafe's neck down to his shoulder until her teeth closed on the T-shirt. Her hands kneaded down his chest to the warm band of skin where his shirt had pulled free of his jeans.

When her fingers touched his naked skin, Rafe's breath came in sharply. His weight shifted as his arms moved.

Alana waited, frozen, anticipating his embrace.

"It's all right," Rafe said softly. "See? No hands."

And it was true. Rafe had moved, but only to put his hands behind his head, fingers tightly laced against the nearly overwhelming temptation to touch Alana as she was touching him.

Alana smiled and relaxed against Rafe's side.

"Does that mean I can still touch you?" she asked.

He smiled just enough to show the tip of his tongue between the serrations of his teeth.

"What do you think?" he asked in a deep voice.

Alana's approving glance went from the rich pelt of Rafe's hair down the hard, masculine length of him.

"I think," said Alana, "that it's a miracle I kept my hands off you until I was twenty."

"And here I thought I was the one who deserved a medal."

"That's probably true," Alana admitted, her eyes brilliant with memories of a storm and a cabin loft. "I didn't know what I was missing. You did."

"Not really," Rafe said softly. "You were unique, sweet and wild, as generous as summer. You gave yourself to me so completely that you made me realize that I'd never made love to a woman until you. Not completely. And I've never made love since. Not completely."

"Rafael," Alana said softly, pleasure and pain and regret in a single word.

"I'm not asking you for anything," he said. "I know you're not ready to give yourself again. That doesn't mean I've forgotten how it was between us once—and how it will be again.

"But not now, this instant," Rafe added, regret and certainty evenly balanced in his deep voice. "I don't expect that now. It's enough that you're touching me, that you're here with me, that you're alive."

Alana felt the heat of Rafe's skin beneath her fingers, the tempting, silky line of hair curling down below his navel, and the sharp, involuntary movement of his body as her fingers slid beneath the soft T-shirt. She traced the long muscles of his torso from his waist to his ribs.

Eyes closed, smiling, Alana let her hands savor Rafe's strength and stillness and the changing, compelling textures of his body beneath her palm. Her fingers searched among the crisp hairs on his chest, alive to the feel of him, the silk and the hardness and the heat of him.

And Rafe watched her, wanting her.

Without stopping to think, Alana tugged at his T-shirt, impatient with even the soft cotton restricting the freedom of her touch. She had the T-shirt bunched up beneath his arms before she realized what she was doing.

"I'm sorry," Alana said raggedly, her eyes still closed. "I wasn't thinking."

"I was."

Rafe's voice was deep, caressing.

"What were you thinking?" she whispered. "That I'm a tease?"

"Open your eyes and I'll tell you."

His voice was gentle, coaxing, an intangible caress that made Alana shiver.

Her eyes opened slowly. She saw her hands against Rafe's chest, his nearly black hair curling up over her slender fingers. Her hands flexed sensuously, pressing her nails against his skin.

"What are you thinking?" she asked, watching his eyes as her nails bit gently into his flesh with tiny, sensual rhythms.

"I was thinking of the first time we made love. When I unbuttoned my shirt, you looked at me as though you'd never seen a man before, but I knew damn well that you lived with three brothers. And now," added Rafe softly, "you're looking at me like that again."

"Am I?" asked Alana, her voice barely a breath of sound.

"Do you want to take off my shirt?" Rafe asked, his eyes watching her with hungry intensity.

"Yes."

Alana bent to brush her lips across Rafe's mouth, loving the feel of him, firm and sweet, answering his heat with her own. She felt his lips smile beneath her caress; then his tongue moved teasingly over her mouth until she smiled in return.

"Then what are you waiting for?" asked Rafe. "Take off my shirt."

As he spoke, he unlocked his hands and stretched his arms above his head.

Alana's hands moved up Rafe's body, pushing the soft folds of T-shirt over his chest, his head, his arms, until the shirt fell aside, forgotten. Her breath came in, then went out in a long sigh as she ran her hands freely from Rafe's fingertips to his waist. His breath sounded more like a groan as he laced his hands behind his head once more.

For an instant, Alana hesitated. Then Rafe's

body twisted sinuously beneath her hands, asking to be touched. She whispered his name as she bent down and kissed him, hungry for the feel of his tongue against hers. Her palms rubbed slowly over his chest, stroking him, enjoying him. When her nails scraped gently over his nipples, she felt him shiver. Her fingertips circled him caressingly, then tugged at the small, hard nubs. His tongue moved sensually in her mouth, stealing her breath until she was dizzy.

With a ragged sound, Alana shifted her position and sought the powerful contours of Rafe's shoulders, tasting and biting and kissing him until her mouth slid down and found the hard male nipples her fingers had teased. Her teeth closed lightly over him. She felt the tension in him, felt his body flexing, felt the powerful muscles of his arms harden beneath her palms.

Memories raced through her, burning her.

"Funny," Alana murmured, rubbing her cheek over Rafe's chest, "I never thought of you as really strong, until the storm and the cabin loft."

Rafe smiled, though his fingers were so tightly laced around each other that his hands ached.

"Thought I was a weakling, did you?" he said, his voice soft but almost rough, hungry and laughing at the same time.

"Weakling?"

Alana laughed against Rafe's ribs before she turned her head and began caressing the long muscles of his torso with slow movements of her cheek and hand.

"No," she said. "But Dad was six foot five, and my brothers were all over six feet tall when they were twelve. Bob was six foot six and weighed two hundred and twenty pounds when he was fourteen."

"Whatever attracted you to a shrimp like me?" asked Rafe.

The question ended in a groan when the hard tip of Alana's tongue teased his navel.

"First it was your eyes," she said, her voice blurred as she caressed the taut skin of Rafe's stomach. "Like a cougar, clear amber and more than a little untamed."

"And that made you want to tame me?"

"No. It made me want to be wild with you."

Rafe's hands clenched until the fingers went numb. He tried to speak, but Alana's fingers had gone from his waist down to the hard muscles of his thighs. He could think of nothing except her touch and the fierce ache of hunger swelling so close to her hand.

"But I didn't know it then," continued Alana, kneading the long muscles that flexed and shifted beneath her fingers, "not in so many words. I just knew I got a funny, quivering feeling deep inside whenever you looked at me in a certain way."

"What way?"

Rafe fought to keep his voice even despite the waves of hunger that hammered through his blood. His fingers twisted against each other until bone ground over bone.

"The way you looked at me when you took off my wet blouse and hung it by the fire," Alana said.

Her breath was a warm flow across the naked skin above Rafe's waist.

"The way you looked at me when you peeled off that soaking, lacy bra," she whispered. "And then you touched me until I couldn't stand by myself. Do you remember?"

"God, yes." Rafe closed his eyes, remembering. "You were barefoot. Your jeans were black with rain and outlined you perfectly, those beautiful legs and hips. . . . Did you know that my hands were shaking when I took off your blouse?"

"Yes," she whispered, her fingers clenching for an instant on Rafe's leg. "I was trembling, too."

"You were cold."

"Was I?" she asked.

Her voice was almost breathless as she caressed Rafe's navel again, biting him gently.

"I burned when you touched me," Alana whispered. "Your hands were so warm on my skin."

"I didn't mean to undress you, not at first. But once I started, I couldn't stop. You were so beautiful, wearing only firelight. I couldn't stop looking at you, touching you."

"I didn't want you to stop. I felt like the most exquisite woman ever born when you looked at me, when you kissed me, touched me. And your body fascinated me."

Alana traced the line of skin just above

Rafe's jeans with her tongue. Her hand smoothed his thigh, enjoying the feel of his strength, remembering.

"When I finally touched you," she said, "every bit of you tightened until each muscle on your body stood out. You felt like warm steel. You feel like that now."

"*Alana.*"

The word was involuntary, a response torn from his control when he felt her hand settling over him.

"I found out how strong you were then," Alana whispered. "You lifted me high, then let me slide slowly, slowly down your body. So strong, yet so gentle. The eyes of a mountain cat and the hands of a poet."

Alana's mouth caressed Rafe's skin as her fingers unfastened his jeans, seeking him beneath layers of cloth, finding him. Her breath came out raggedly.

"And the rest of you so very male," Alana said huskily.

She rubbed her cheek across Rafe's stomach, then she turned her mouth to his skin and kissed him quickly, fiercely.

"Alana," Rafe said, his voice hoarse as he moved reflexively, sensually against her hand. "I can't take much more of this."

"Then don't," she said simply.

She traced the rigid muscles of his arm with one hand, feeling the mist of passion and restraint that covered his body.

"You've given me so much," she said. "Let me give you something in return. It's not as much as either of us wants, but it's all I have right now."

Rafe closed his eyes for a moment, knowing if he looked at Alana, he wouldn't be able to keep his fingers locked behind his head.

Her hand moved again in a devastating, sensual glide of flesh over flesh. Fire thickened in Rafe's veins, fire pooling heavily beneath Alana's hand until he could only twist against the sweet agony of her touch. He groaned aloud, his breath hissing between clenched teeth.

"Oh, God . . . don't," he said hoarsely.

"Rafael," said Alana. "I can't give myself to you now, but you can give yourself to me. Please, give yourself to me. Let me know that I've been able to bring you some pleasure. I need to know that."

Her voice was husky and urgent as she rubbed her cheek against his hot chest.

Rafe's eyes opened, an amber hot enough to burn.

"Look at me," he said.

Alana lifted her head. He saw the silent plea in her dark eyes, saw the fire and fierce pleasure when he moved against her hand, and he knew that she had been utterly honest with him.

Slowly he unlocked his fingers, but he moved only one hand, and then only to hold it out to her. When her lips pressed against his palm, his hand shifted, gently bringing her mouth up to his. What began as a simple brush of lips deepened with each heartbeat until it became a kiss of shattering hunger and sensuality.

And then he gave himself to her as freely and generously as she had given herself to him four years ago, in a cabin warmed by firelight and love.

13

ALANA PULLED THE BUB-
bling, spicy apple pie out of the oven, using
oversize pot holders that felt as soft to her
touch as Rafe's T-shirt had. She smiled to herself as she set the second pie on the wooden
counter to cool, feeling more at peace than she
had in a long time. Notes of music kept gliding through her mind, chased by lyrics that
hadn't yet condensed into songs.

"What is that marvelous smell?" asked Janice from the doorway.

"Pie," said Alana, turning and smiling over
her shoulder at the tall, slender woman.

"A miracle," Janice said.

Alana smiled. "Actually, it's just dried apples, sugar, and spices."

"In this wilderness, on that stove, those pies are a miracle," said Janice firmly. She looked at Alana with blue eyes that missed nothing. "Anything I can do to help?"

"I've got everything under control, but thanks anyway."

Janice smiled. "Must be a wonderful feeling."

"What?"

"Having everything under control."

Alana looked startled for an instant. Then she nodded slowly.

It was true. Since she had awakened in the hospital, she had felt as though her life was out of her control, as though she was a victim instead of a person. Fear had eroded her self-respect and confidence.

But today she had been able to talk and laugh with Rafe. Today she had taken the first steps toward overcoming her fear of heights. Today she had realized that Rafe respected and cared for her despite her amnesia and irrational fears.

Rafe had accepted her as she was, imperfect, and then he had given himself to her instead of demanding that she give herself to him.

"Yes," Alana said quietly. "It's an incredibly good feeling."

Janice's eyes narrowed in an instant of intelligent scrutiny that Alana didn't notice.

"I'm glad," said Janice, unmistakable satisfaction in her voice.

Alana looked up quickly, seeing for the first time the compassion in the other woman.

"Rafe told you about my husband, didn't he?" Alana asked.

Janice hesitated while her shrewd blue eyes measured the emotions apparent on Alana's face.

"Don't be angry with him," Janice said finally. "Rafe just wanted to be sure that Stan and I wouldn't accidentally hurt you."

Frowning, Alana wiped her hands on the enormous white apron that she wore.

"It's not fair to ask you to walk on eggs so I won't be upset," Alana said. "This trip is for your pleasure, not mine."

Janice smiled. "Don't worry. We're having a ball."

Alana looked at her with skeptical dark eyes.

"Uh-huh," Alana muttered. "Sure you are— when I'm not screaming at Stan or stealing your fishing guide."

"Stan's a big boy," said Janice dryly. "And as for Rafe, he showed us the water and we caught our limit. Besides, he cleans the trout for us and you whip up hot apple pies. What more could we ask?"

Laughing and shaking her head, Alana gave in.

"You two are very special dudes," Alana said. "If other clients are half as easy to be around, Bob will think he's died and gone to heaven. Most dudes can't find their way downhill without directions and a hard push."

From the next room came the sound of cupboard doors being opened and closed briskly.

"Hey. sis," called Bob from the dining room, "where did I put the dishes last night after I washed them?"

Janice and Alana exchanged a look and burst out laughing. Bob stuck his head in the kitchen.

"What's so funny?" he asked.

"You wouldn't understand," said Alana. "But that's all right. I love you anyway."

She stood on tiptoe and kissed Bob's cheek quickly.

He looked surprised, then very pleased. He started to hug Alana in return, then stopped, remembering. He patted her shoulder with unexpected gentleness and put his blunt index finger on the tip of her nose.

"You look better, sis. Rafe was right. You needed to be home."

Then Bob shook his head and smiled, giving Alana a somewhat baffled look. He still wasn't used to seeing his sister as a contemporary rather than as a substitute mother.

"What?" Alana asked.

"How did you get to be so small, anyway?" Bob said in a rueful voice.

"You grew up."

He smiled. "Yeah, guess so. Why don't you go get dressed? I'll whip up the potatoes and get everything on the table."

Alana blinked, startled by the offer. Then she blinked again, several times, fighting back sudden tears. Bob was being as protective of her as he was of Merry.

"Thanks," Alana said, her voice husky. "I'd like that."

She showered quickly, then climbed into the loft wrapped in Bob's oversize terry cloth robe, which she had found hanging from a peg in the downstairs bathroom. She stood in front of the closet and tried to choose from the array of clothes that Bob had packed for her.

After an unusual amount of time, she decided on a pair of heavy silk slacks that were a rich chocolate color. The blouse she chose was long sleeved and the color of fire, its sensuous texture and folds in stark contrast to its businesslike cut.

Automatically Alana began to button up the blouse so the chain she always wore was concealed. Then she stopped, realizing that she no longer had to hide Rafe's engagement gift. It no longer mattered if people asked her about the unusual design of the necklace.

Jack was dead.

She no longer had to conceal the fact that half of Country's Perfect Couple wore another man's gift in the vulnerable hollow of her throat.

Alana smoothed the collar open. The elegant symbol of infinity shifted and gleamed with each movement of her head. She touched the symbol with her fingertip and felt another tiny bit of peace settling inside her, another step on the way to rebuilding her strength.

For the first time since she had awakened in

the hospital, she began to believe that she not only would survive, but would be able to love again.

Even if her nightmares were true.

"Alana?" Rafe's voice came from the bottom of the steep stairway. "Are you ready?"

"Almost," she whispered, too softly for Rafe to hear. "Almost."

She hurried downstairs, truly hungry for food for the first time since the six missing days. High-country air had a magical effect on her appetite.

It was the same for everyone else. Even after a dinner of trout, potatoes, green beans, and biscuits, everyone found room for a piece of pie.

Rafe sliced and served the warm apple pie to the accompaniment of good-natured complaints as to which person was or wasn't getting the biggest piece. Bob and Stan swapped pieces with each other several times before Rafe gave in and put the last piece of pie between them.

Smiling, Rafe watched Alana as she ate the last bite of the generous slice of pie he had cut for her. When she threw back her head and sighed that she was too full to move, he saw the gleam of gold in the hollow of her throat.

With a callused fingertip, he traced the length of the chain and its elegant symbol.

"You still wear this," he said softly.

"I've never taken it off since you gave it to me."

Rafe's eyes were tawny in the late-afternoon

light that was streaming through the window, tawny and very intent.

"Not even after I sent back your letter?" he asked, searching her eyes.

"Never. It was all I had left of you."

The back of Rafe's finger caressed Alana's throat.

"I wish we were alone," he whispered. "I would like very much to kiss you. Many times. Many places. Would you like that, wild-flower?"

A suggestion of color bloomed beneath Alana's skin. She smiled and smoothed her cheek against Rafe's finger.

"Yes," she murmured. "I'd like that."

Then Alana looked across the table and saw Stan watching her closely, his eyes so blue they were almost black, his fair hair shimmering in a shaft of sunlight that came through the cabin window and fell across his thick shoulders. Quickly she looked away, still unable to accept Stan's unnerving physical resemblance to Jack Reeves.

When Stan asked Rafe about a particular kind of dry fly, Alana turned to Janice and asked the first question that came to mind.

"Somehow you aren't what I'd expect a travel agent to be. How did you choose that career?"

There was a sudden silence, then a determined resumption of the casual conversation taking place around the women.

Alana looked at Rafe suddenly, wondering if she had done something wrong.

Rafe ignored her, apparently caught up in his talk with Stan.

"I'm sorry," Alana said to Janice. "Did I ask the wrong question?"

Janice's smile had a wry twist as she glanced sideways at Rafe.

"I'd say you asked just the right one," Janice said.

Rafe looked up sharply but said nothing.

"I used to be a psychiatrist," Janice explained. "After ten years, I burned out. So many problems. So few solutions."

Her voice was light but her eyes were narrowed against memories that still had the power to hurt her.

Alana thought of what had happened to Rafe, to her, to Jack. *So many problems. So few solutions.*

"So I became a special kind of travel agent," Janice said. "I match people with the kind of vacation that will do the most for them."

"Solutions," said Alana.

"Yes."

Alana wanted to ask more. Suddenly she was very curious about Janice's past, about the pressures that had driven her to change careers.

And about Rafe, who had known Janice before.

"Would you like to hear about what happened?" asked Janice.

"If you don't mind," Alana said.

Janice and Rafe exchanged a quick look. He

raised his dark eyebrows slightly, then shrugged.

Janice turned back to Alana.

"I used to work for the government, like Rafe," said Janice.

Though she spoke quietly, at her first words Stan and Rafe's conversation died.

Stan gave Janice a hard look, then looked questioningly at Rafe. Rafe ignored him. Stan seemed about to speak when a gesture from Rafe cut him off.

"Men and women who work under impossible conditions," Janice said calmly, "often have trouble living with themselves. If something goes wrong and people die, or if nothing goes wrong and people die anyway, the person in charge has to live with it."

Alana looked at Rafe. His eyes were hooded, unreadable.

"The key words are *in charge*," Janice said. "These are intelligent people who care about the world. They are the actors, not the audience. They are in control of themselves and of life."

Janice smiled wryly and took a sip of her coffee.

"At least," she added softly, "they *think* they're in control. Then it all goes from sugar to shit and they're left wondering what hit them. My job was to explain that it was reality that ran over them and left them flat."

Stan made a sound halfway between protest and laughter. When Janice looked at him, he winked. The smile she gave him was both gentle and sensual.

Alana sensed the nearly intangible currents of affection and respect that flowed between the two people.

"People come in all kinds," Janice said, turning back to Alana, "but the ones I dealt with usually fell into three categories. The first was people who couldn't cope with an unpredictable, unforgiving reality and simply fell apart."

Alana looked down at the bit of pie left on her plate and wondered if she was one of the ones who couldn't cope.

"In the second category were the people who survived by stuffing down their feelings of inadequacy, bewilderment, and fear. These people did exactly what they had been trained to do and they did it magnificently."

Alana looked at Rafe. He was watching her. For an instant he put his fingertip on the golden symbol she wore around her neck.

"The third category," Janice said, "was made up of people who had so little imagination or such great faith in 'going by the book' that they had the same untouchable serenity that religion gives to some people."

"It must be nice," Alana said.

"I wouldn't know," Rafe answered.

Janice picked up her coffee cup, sighed, and put it down again without tasting the dark brew.

"People in the first category, the ones who couldn't cope, didn't last long as operatives,"

Janice said bluntly. "The third type, the ones who went by the book, did very poorly in the fluid world of fieldwork. We tended to put them in office positions as soon as they were discovered."

"And the second category?" Alana asked Janice, but it was Rafe whom she watched.

"Those in the second category did most of the work," Janice said. "They were the survivors, the people who got the job done no matter what it cost them."

The brackets around Rafe's mouth deepened.

"Unfortunately," Janice said, glancing quickly at Rafe, "sooner or later the survivors paid a high psychic price when they were confronted by the randomness of reality and the fact that Superman exists only in cartoons."

Alana touched the corner of Rafe's mouth as lightly as he had touched her necklace. He turned and brushed a kiss over her fingertip.

"Real men bleed and make mistakes," Janice said softly. "If, once the crisis is past, the survivors can't deal with their feelings of weakness, can't accept that all any person can do is his or her best . . . well, then they begin to hate themselves. If they can't accept the fact that they can be afraid, be hurt, even be broken and *still* be damned fine, brave, effective human beings, then they tear themselves apart."

Alana's hand trembled. Rafe caught it between his own, kissed her palm, and released her.

"My job was to help the survivors accept their own limitations, their humanity. I was supposed to help them accept themselves." Janice stared out over the table, seeing something from the past. "Because if they couldn't accept their humanity, I lost them. I—lost—them."

Janice's hand clenched into a fist, softly pounding the table with each word.

Impulsively Alana put her hand over the other woman's.

"It wasn't your fault," Alana said quickly. "You couldn't open up their hearts and make them believe in their own worth. All you could do was care, and you did."

Janice looked at Alana for a long moment. Then Janice's lips shaped a sad smile.

"But when you love them, and you lose them," Janice said, "it hurts like hell. After awhile there was one too many, and I quit."

Alana looked quickly at Rafe, wondering if he had been the "one too many" for Janice.

"You did all anyone could," Rafe said quietly, "and that was a lot more than most."

"So did you." Janice's blue eyes measured Rafe. "Did you think that was enough?"

"No," he said, meeting her eyes without flinching, "but I'm learning to live with it. Finally."

Janice looked at Rafe for a long moment, then smiled gently.

"Good for you, Rafe Winter," she said. "Very good. It was a near thing, wasn't it?"

Janice turned and looked at Alana.

"The strongest ones," Janice said quietly, "have the hardest time. They go the longest before they come up against human limitations. And then they blame themselves. They reach a state where they are, in effect, at war with themselves. Some survive even that. A lot don't."

Alana looked at Rafe with dark, haunted eyes. The thought of how close she had come to losing him forever was like a knife turning in her soul.

"For the strong ones," Janice said, "it's a case of the sooner they accept their own limitations, the better. There are very few ways to win a war with yourself, and a whole lot of ugly ways to lose."

There was silence. Then Janice set down her coffee cup and said briskly, "Enough of my past. Who's going to catch the biggest fish tonight?"

"I am," Bob and Stan said at the same moment.

The two big men looked at each other, grinned, and began placing bets on the outcome.

Rafe and Janice exchanged knowing glances and shook their heads.

After Bob and the guests left, Alana stood and began to clear the table. Rafe immediately took the plates out of her hands.

"You look too elegant to handle dirty dishes," he said. "Come sit in the kitchen and talk to me."

Alana looked at Rafe in disbelief. He was

wearing black wool slacks and a tailored black
shirt made of a wool so fine it felt like silk.
The supple fabric fit him like a shadow, outlining the power of his arms and shoulders.

"You look too elegant, too," Alana said.

She touched the black fabric where it pulled
lightly across Rafe's chest. The warmth of him
radiated through the shirt to her hand, making
her want to rub her palm against him, to curl
up next to him like a cat by a fire. And then
she wanted simply to hold him, to comfort
him, to take away whatever hurt she could
from his past.

Alana had no doubt that Rafe was one of
the very strong ones whom Janice had talked
about, the ones who had the hardest time accepting their own limitations.

"What are you thinking?" Rafe asked, his
voice deep, velvety.

"That you're one of the strong ones."

"So are you."

The thought startled Alana. She didn't feel
strong. She felt weak, useless, foolish, hiding
from herself and reality behind a wall of amnesia and irrational fears.

Before she could protest, Rafe spoke, his
voice quick and sure.

"You are strong, Alana. You were only a
child, yet you held your family together after
your mother died. When you thought I was
dead, you saw your best chance of emotional
survival in a singing career, and you took it.

"And when another crisis came, you fought

for life. You fought as bravely and fiercely as anyone ever has."

"Then why am I afraid?" whispered Alana.

"Because it wasn't enough," Rafe said grimly. "You came flat up against the fact that Wonder Woman, like Superman, doesn't exist in the real world."

"I didn't think that I was Wonder Woman."

"Didn't you? Who was the strongest Burdette, the one everyone came to when dreams and favorite puppies died? Your dad? No way. It was years before he was worth a damn after your mother's death. As for Jack—"

Alana's mouth turned down in a sad, bitter smile.

"Jack was a user," Rafe said, his voice clipped. "If it hadn't been for your discipline, your intelligence, your sheer ability to take apart a song and put it back together in a new, vivid way, Jack would have been just another beer hall tenor."

"He had a fine voice."

"Only with you, Alana. He knew it better than you did. He used you to make the world more comfortable for himself. And he acted as though using you was his God-given right."

Alana closed her eyes, hearing her own unwanted thoughts coming from Rafe's lips.

"I used him, too," she whispered. "I used him to survive after they told me you were dead."

"Were you the one who demanded marriage?"

Alana shook her head. "I just wanted to sing."

"That's what Bob said. He remembered Jack hounding you and then finally telling you that if you wouldn't marry him, he wouldn't sing with you."

"Yes," Alana whispered, her voice shaking.

"Jack knew exactly what he wanted, and he knew how to get it. When it came to his own comforts, he was as selfish as any man I've ever known."

"But he didn't want me, not as a wife, not as a woman."

Rafe laughed harshly.

"Wrong, Alana. You didn't want *him*. He could have your singing talent, but he couldn't have you. Easy street was more important to Jack than sex, so he accepted your conditions."

"I didn't want him to want me," Alana said.

Her voice was strained, her eyes tightly closed, memories and nightmares turning. She shivered despite the warmth of the cabin, for she was feeling again the cold afternoon before the storm, hearing fragments of words, *Jack cursing, reaching for her.*

"I think—" Alana's voice broke, then came back so harshly that it sounded like a stranger's. "I think Jack wanted me on Broken Mountain. I think we fought about it."

From the front porch came the sound of Stan's laughter as he and Bob shouldered each other to see who would be first through the door.

Alana swayed alarmingly. Her eyes opened, black with memories and nightmare combined.

"No," she whispered. "Oh, God, *no*."

14

ALANA DIDN'T HEAR THE
clatter of plates as Rafe put them on the table
and stood close to her, not touching her, prepared to catch her if she fainted.

Rafe was afraid she was going to do just
that. Her skin was as pale and translucent as
fine china. Her pupils were dilated to the point
that only a small rim of brown remained.

"Jack was laughing," Alana whispered.

Rafe's eyelids flinched. He bit back the
words he wanted to say, the futile cry that she
shouldn't remember. Not yet. Reality was brutal.

And Alana looked so fragile.

"The lake was ice cold and Jack was laughing at me," she said. "All my clothes, my sleeping bag, me—soaked and so cold. He said I could sleep in his sleeping bag. For a price. He said he'd be glad to warm me up."

Rafe's breath came in swiftly.

Alana didn't notice. She heard nothing but the past that haunted her.

"At first, I didn't believe him," she said numbly. "Then I tried to ride out. He grabbed my braids and yanked me out of the saddle and kicked Sid until she bolted down the trail. He—he hit me. I couldn't get away. He wrapped my braids around his hand, holding me, and he hit me again and again."

Rafe's expression changed, pulled by hatred into savage lines of rage, the face of a man who had once gone through a jungle hell like an avenging angel.

Alana didn't see. Her wide eyes were blinded by the past that she had hidden from herself, but not well enough.

Not quite.

"Then Stan tied me and dumped me on a rock ledge by the lake," Alana said. "He said we wouldn't go down the mountain until I changed my mind. 'When we come down off this damned mountain, you're going to heel for me like a bird dog.' And then he laughed and laughed."

Rafe reached for Alana with hands that trembled, rage and love and helplessness combined.

He couldn't touch her.

"But Jack didn't want me," Alana said in a

raw voice. "He just wanted to—to break me. I think he must have hated me."

Alana's eyes closed slowly. She made an odd sound and covered her mouth with her hand.

"It was so cold. The lake and the rock and the night. Cold."

The words were muffled, but Rafe heard them, felt them like blows.

Helpless.

In the silence of his mind, Rafe cursed the fact that Jack Reeves had died quickly, painlessly, a hundred feet of darkness and then the deadly impact of granite.

Alana drew a deep, shuddering breath. When her eyes opened, they were focused on the present. She ran shaking fingers through her hair. Short hair. Hair that couldn't be used as a weapon against her, chaining her.

"That's why I cut off my braids," Alana said, relief and pain mixed in her voice. "I'm not crazy after all."

"No." Rafe's voice was soft and yet harsh with the effort of holding his emotions in check. "You're not crazy."

"Are you sure?" she asked, trying to smile. "Because I have a really crazy thing to ask you."

"Anything. Anything at all."

"Run your fingers through my hair. Take away the feel of Jack's hands."

Rafe brought his hands up to Alana's head, ready to retreat at the first sign of returning fear. Gently he eased his fingers through her soft, short hair.

Slowly closing her eyes, Alana concentrated on the sensation of Rafe's strong fingers moving through her hair. She tilted her head against his palms, increasing the pressure of his caresses.

Chills of pleasure chased through her.

"More," she murmured.

Rafe's fingers slid deeper into the midnight silk of Alana's hair, rubbing lightly over her scalp, caressing her.

"Yes," she sighed.

Alana moved against his hands, increasing the contact, deepening the intimacy, until the heat of Rafe's hands surrounded her, taking away memories, warming her.

When Alana opened her eyes, Rafe's face was very close. His concentration on the intimate moment was as great as hers. So was his pleasure. By quarter inches he lowered his mouth to hers, waiting for the least sign of the fear that might come when she realized she was caught between his hands and his lips.

Alana's answer was a smile and a sigh as her lips parted, welcoming Rafe. He kissed her very gently, not wanting to frighten her. Her arms stole around his waist, held him.

"You feel so good," Alana whispered against Rafe's lips. "So warm, so alive. And you want me. Not to break, but to cherish."

She kissed him slowly, savoring the heat of him, shaping herself to him, absorbing him like a flower absorbing sunlight.

"So warm," she murmured.

Rafe felt Alana's breasts press against him as her arms tightened around him. Hunger swept through him, a fierce surge of fire.

"Very warm," he agreed, smiling, nibbling on the corner of her mouth.

One of Rafe's hands slid from Alana's hair to her shoulder, then to her ribs. Instead of retreating, she moved closer. Her scent and sweetness made the breath stop in Rafe's throat.

Slowly he moved his hand away from the soft temptation of Alana's breast. With light touches he ran his right hand over her back, enjoying the resilience of her body. His left hand rubbed through her hair, then stroked her neck.

Finally, slowly, he moved his left hand to her back until he held her loosely in his arms.

"I'm not frightening you, am I?" Rafe asked huskily.

Alana shook her head and burrowed closer to him.

"I love your warmth, Rafael. When I'm close to you like this, I can't even imagine ever being cold again."

The front door slammed open.

"Hey, sis, where did I put the—oops, sorry!"

Rafe glanced up over Alana's black cap of hair.

Stan, who had followed Bob inside, gave Rafe a long, enigmatic look.

"Lose something?" asked Rafe mildly, keeping his arms around Alana.

"My net," admitted Bob. "I had it when I came in for dinner, but I can't find it."

"Last time I saw your net," Rafe said, "it was leaning against the back door of the lodge."

"Thanks."

Bob walked quickly around the dining room table and out the back door. When he realized Stan wasn't following, Bob called back over his shoulder to the other man.

"Come on, Stan. Don't you know a losing cause when you see one?"

The instant Alana realized that Bob wasn't alone, she stiffened and turned to face the living room.

Stan was walking toward her.

Quickly Alana spun around, holding on to Rafe's arms as though he were all that stood between her and a long, deadly fall.

"Stan," Rafe said.

Rafe's voice was quiet, yet commanding.

Stan paused, waiting.

"The trout are rising," Rafe said. "Why don't you try that dark moth I tied for you? *The one we both agreed on.*"

"You sure it will get the job done?" Stan asked sardonically. "You have to be real careful with trout. If they get away, they're even harder to lure the next time."

"What I've made matches the environment almost perfectly," Rafe said, choosing each

word with care. "That, and patience, will get
the job done. Ask Janice."

Stan paused, then nodded.

"I'll do that, Winter. I'll do just that."

Without another word, Stan brushed past
Rafe and Alana. In a few seconds, the back
door banged shut.

"Two bulls in a china shop," Rafe muttered,
resting his cheek against Alana's hair.

Alana shifted in Rafe's embrace. Immediately he loosened his arms. She moved closer,
kissed him, and stepped back.

"I'm going to change clothes and then do
the dishes," she said. "You should get into
fishing clothes and help Stan win his bet with
Bob."

"I'd rather stay here. With you."

"I'm all right, Rafe. Really. Stan startled me.
He looks so damn much like Jack."

"Are you afraid that Stan is going to pick
you up and throw you in the lake?" asked
Rafe, his voice easy, casual.

Alana stood very still for an instant before
she slowly shook her head.

"No. I don't think . . ."

Her voice died and her eyes were very dark.
She said nothing more.

"What is it?" asked Rafe softly, coaxingly.

"I don't think that was the worst of it," she
said starkly.

"Alana," he whispered.

She stepped away from Rafe.

"I need to think," Alana said, "but when
you're near, all I can think about is how good

you feel, how patient you are with me, how much I want to reach back four years and touch love again. Touch *you*."

She took a breath and let it out slowly. "I'll catch up with you at sunset, when it's too dark to fish."

"That's two hours from now," protested Rafe. "You won't even know where Stan and I will be."

"Sound carries in this country. And Stan has the kind of voice that carries, period. I'll find you."

"We'll be fishing just below the cascade," Rafe said. "If you don't show up before sunset, I'm going to stuff Stan into his own net and come looking for you." Then, softly, he said, "I wanted to fish with you tonight."

"Oh, no," Alana said, shaking her head. "I can hear your fly line whimpering for mercy right now."

Rafe's smile flashed, softening the hard lines of his face.

"But," Alana added, running her fingertips across his mustache, "I'd love to watch you fish. You please me, Rafael Winter. You please me all the way to my soul."

Then Alana turned and slipped from Rafe's arms. Hungrily he watched her walk across the living room to the loft stairs. His skin tingled where she had touched him, her scent was still sweet in his nostrils, and he wanted her so much that he hurt.

Abruptly Rafe turned away and went to the downstairs bedroom. With quick motions he changed into his fishing clothes. Then he let himself out of the cabin quietly, knowing if he saw Alana again, he wouldn't leave her.

Alana changed into jeans and a sweater and had the kitchen cleaned long before sunset. Her mind was working as swiftly as her hands. She reviewed what she remembered about the six missing days, and what she didn't.

She remembered parts of the ride up the trail with Jack. Then the first night . . .

Was it the first night when Jack and I fought? Alana asked herself silently.

Frowning, she stacked wood in the stove for the morning fire.

Three days in the hospital, of which she remembered only one. That left three days unaccounted for.

No, two.

We must have spent one day traveling to Wyoming and one night at the ranch house, Alana thought. So it must have been the first night on Broken Mountain, up by the lake, when Jack threw me and my clothes and my sleeping bag into the lake.

Alana's body tightened as she remembered what had followed. Jack had slapped her all but senseless when she had tried to run from him. That was the night she had spent curled over herself on a piece of granite, shivering.

That's why I'm so cold in my nightmares, Alana realized. Memory and nightmare combined.

She let out a long breath, feeling better

about herself. Not all of her fears were irrational.

But then, why does the sound of a storm terrify me? Alana asked herself.

The wind hadn't been blowing that night. It hadn't been storming. No lightning. No ground-shaking thunder. Alana was certain of it. If that night had been the ice-tipped storm of her nightmare, she would have died of exposure before morning.

Yet wind and thunder and ice were a vivid, terrifying part of Alana's nightmares.

"The storm must have come the second night on Broken Mountain," Alana whispered, needing more than the cabin's silence to comfort her. "The night I fell."

The night Jack died.

"Why did Jack untie me? Did I give in, go to him?"

The sound of her own questions made Alana shudder. She wasn't certain she wanted to know if she had traded her self-respect for a dry sleeping bag and cold sex with Jack. Prostitution, in a word.

Alana waited, listening to her own silences, sensing her body's response to her thoughts.

Nothing changed. No nightmare closing around. No fear. No sense of connection with hidden reality.

"All right," Alana said tightly. "It's probably not that. Did Jack get too drunk to be patient? Did he untie me, rape me, beat me?"

Once more, Alana waited, forgetting to breathe, anticipating the return of nightmare as her waking thoughts closed in on the truth.

Once more, nothing came.

When Alana remembered Jack hitting her, her stomach turned over and her breath came shallowly.

When she thought of submitting to him, there was . . . nothing. When she thought of being raped, there was . . . nothing. No fear, no desire to scream, no sickness rising in her throat, no chill, no hammering heart or cold sweat. None of the physiological signals that had warned her in the past when she was approaching the truth.

If the truth could even be approached.

Abruptly Alana pulled off her apron and went to find Rafe, unable to bear any more questions, any more answers, any more fear and silence.

The path to the lake was overgrown, clearly showing the bruised grass that marked the passage of at least two people. Alana walked quickly, barely noticing the crimson cloud streamers stretched across the sky. Nor did she see the deep amethyst mountain slopes crowned by luminous ramparts of stone, nor the fragrant shadows flowing out of the forest around her.

The path approached the lake at an angle in order to avoid an area that was a bog in the early summer and an uneven, rough meadow in the fall. Winding through the trees, yielding only occasional glimpses of the water, the path kept to the forest until the last possible moment.

Alana heard Rafe and Stan before she could
see them. At least, she heard Stan, his voice
pitched to carry above the exuberant thunder
of the cascade. She could only assume he was
talking to Rafe.

Then Stan's voice came clearly and Alana
was certain. He was talking to Rafe.

"No, you listen to me for a change, Captain
Winter, *sir*," Stan said sardonically. "I've got
a nasty mind for situations like this. I was
trained to have a nasty mind."

There was a pause, but whatever Rafe re-
plied was lost in the sound of the cascade.
Alana hesitated, then continued toward the
lake, screened by spruce and aspen.

"Try this scenario on for size," Stan said.
"There's a woman you've wanted for years.
Another man's woman. It grinds on you real
hard. So the woman you want and the man
you hate come up here for a little camping
trip."

Alana froze in place, suddenly cold.

She didn't want to hear any more, but she
couldn't move.

"You wait around, see your chance, and
chuck good old Jack over the nearest cliff,"
continued Stan. "Then you go to collect the
spoils."

". . . half-assed pop psychol . . ." Rafe's
voice wove in and out of the cascade's throaty
rumble.

Stan's voice was as clear as thunder.

"But she's not used to that kind of violence," Stan said. "She runs away. She spends

a night in the open, cold and exposed. And then she just shuts it all out, forgets."

". . . leave the thinking to people with . . ."

"Her amnesia leaves you with a real problem," Stan said, ignoring the interruption. "If she remembers, it doesn't matter whose friend the sheriff is. Your ass is in a sling."

Alana took a ragged breath and continued down the trail. She stumbled like a sleepwalker, using her hands to push herself away from the rough trunks of the trees that seemed to grow perversely in front of her feet, as though to hold her back.

". . . crock of . . ." Rafe's voice faded in and out of the cascade's thunder.

"I'm not finished," cut in Stan, his voice very clear, carrying like a brass bell across the evening. "You can save yourself by marrying her. She won't go telling tales on her own husband."

"Jesus, you've been reading too many tabloids."

"Maybe. From what Bob tells me, good old Jack wasn't much of a loss to this world, so it's not like Alana is going to spend a year mourning the son of a bitch. Besides, it's plain enough that she likes you."

"You noticed," Rafe said sarcastically.

"You've got a little problem, though. If she remembers before you marry her, you're up shit creek without a paddle."

"Then why am I helping . . ."

Alana leaned forward, straining to hear all of Rafe's words. She couldn't. Unlike Stan,

Rafe's voice became softer, not louder with anger.

Rafe was furious.

"Are you really helping her to remember?" retorted Stan. "Then why in hell won't you let me off the leash?"

". . . Janice."

"Janice would do a marine crawl through hot coals for you, Winter, and you damn well know it!"

"I'd . . . same for . . ."

Alana left the trees behind and began walking over the rocks and logs that were between her and the lake. Each step brought her closer to the men.

Closer to their words.

"And I'm supposed to just shut up and go along with the program," shot back Stan.

"Hell of an idea, hotshot!"

"Maybe, and maybe not. That's a damned good woman you're hunting, Winter. I'm not real sure she wants to be caught. I think she should remember first. That's the only way her choice will have any meaning. That's the best chance she has of surviving."

"Is that what Janice thinks?" Rafe asked.

Alana was less than fifty feet away, close enough to hear Rafe clearly. He and Stan were facing one another. If the men noticed her slow progress toward them, they made no sign.

"I'm not sure Janice is able to think straight where you're involved," said Stan.

Alana stopped, held by the stark pain in Stan's voice.

"There's nothing between me and Janice," Rafe said. "There never was."

Stan hesitated, then made an odd gesture, turning his hands palms up as though to accept or hold something.

"I'd like to believe that. I really would."

"Believe it," Rafe said.

"Hell, it doesn't matter right now. It wouldn't matter at all, except that I don't want Alana trapped because Janice allowed emotion to louse up her judgment."

"She hasn't."

"If it all goes to hell," Stan said, "I don't want Janice blaming herself. She's been through enough of that on your account. But that doesn't matter, either. Not up here. It's just like the bad old days. All that matters is the mission."

"Then quit screwing it up."

"You've got two more days," Stan said flatly. "If your way doesn't work by then, I'll try mine."

When Rafe spoke, the suppressed violence in his voice curled and cracked like a whip, making Stan flinch.

"If you do anything that hurts Alana," Rafe said, "you'll go back down Broken Mountain the same way Jack Reeves did—in a green plastic bag. Do you read me, corporal?"

"I'm not a corporal anymore. And you're not a captain."

Stan turned slightly.

For a moment Alana thought he had spotted her, for she was directly in his line of sight.

Suddenly Stan made a swift feint toward Rafe. At the first hint of movement, Rafe swiftly assumed a fighting stance. Legs slightly bent, hands held slightly apart at chest level, he waited for Stan to move again.

"You're as fast as ever," Stan said, something close to admiration in his voice.

Stan moved again very quickly, his big hands reaching for the other man. Rafe stepped into the attack, pivoted smoothly, and let Stan slide by, not touching him except for the hand that closed around Stan's wrist.

With fluid grace, Rafe twisted Stan's arm and brought it up behind his back, applying pressure until Stan was on his knees. Stan's blond hair shimmered palely in the twilight as Rafe bent down, his face a mask of cold rage.

"*No!*"

Rafe's head snapped around at Alana's scream. When he saw the frightened, hunted look on her face, he released Stan and started toward her.

"Alana!" Rafe said.

Alana spun away from him and ran back into the forest.

Rafe started after her, then realized that chasing her would only increase her fear. With a soundless snarl, he turned on Stan, who had made no move to get to his feet.

"You knew she was there, didn't you?" Rafe demanded.

Stan nodded and smiled grimly.

"I saw her out of the corner of my eye," he agreed. "That's why I jumped you. Think it reminded her of something, old buddy?"

"Get up."

Rafe's voice was soft and deadly.

"So you can take me apart?" Stan asked, smiling oddly. "No way, Winter. I've seen what you can do when you're mad. I think I'll just sit out this dance."

"And I think," Rafe said, spacing each word carefully, showing how much his control cost, "that if you don't get out of my sight, I'll take you apart anyway."

15

WIND FLEXED AND FLOWED
around the lodge, bringing with it the sound
of laughter. After the laughter came words
without meaning, wind, more laughter.

Alana rolled over in bed, tangling in the
covers for the tenth time and wishing that everyone would enjoy the poker game with a little less enthusiasm.

She wondered if Rafe was with the happy
card players. Then she remembered his fury at
Stan. She doubted that Rafe was in the last
cabin, laughing and drawing cards.

Stan's accusations turned and prowled inside Alana's mind like the wind. She wanted
to reject them out of hand, completely, yet

they kept finding weaknesses in her resolve, cracks in her wall of refusal, little doubts clinging like tentacles.

From the moment Alana saw Rafe at the airport, she had been certain that he still loved her. It wasn't a thoughtful conclusion; it was instinct, pure and simple and very, very deep. Yet assuming that Rafe loved her was groundless, even ridiculous.

He had believed she was happily married six weeks after his "death" had been reported. A year ago he had returned her letter unopened. Before yesterday, nothing had happened to make him believe any differently.

Before yesterday, Rafe must have hated her.

Then why did he pressure Bob to get me home? Alana asked silently. Why has Rafe been so very gentle, so understanding, from the moment he met me at the airport?

No answer came but that of the wind blowing over mountains and forest and cabin alike.

Did something happen on Broken Mountain? Alana wondered. Something that I can't remember, something that made Rafe believe my marriage to Jack was a desperate sham from the beginning?

The wind curled and shook the cabin like a powerful, transparent cat.

A chill condensed in Alana. She pulled the covers closer and rolled over again, seeking the comfort that had never come to her since Broken Mountain.

Yet no matter where she turned, she kept

hearing Stan's voice, Stan's accusations.

They horrified her.

Is the truth that brutal? Alana cried silently. Did Rafe pursue me to save himself?

Was Jack's death less than accidental?

Is that why Rafe refused to tell me what happened on Broken Mountain?

Waves of coldness swept over Alana, roughening her skin. She lay very still, curled around herself, shivering despite the blankets heaped on top of her.

Alana knew that Rafe was capable of deadly violence. He had been trained for it, was skilled in it, had lived with it for most of his adult life. But she couldn't believe that he was capable of such sly deception, that he would coolly plan to murder Jack and then seduce and marry her in order to ensure her silence.

That didn't sound like the Rafe she had known, the Rafe she had loved.

The Rafe she still loved.

If Stan had accused Jack of such vicious lies, Alana would have been sickened—*but she would have believed.*

Jack had been a totally selfish man. Jack had been capable of smiling lies and chilling cruelties, whatever it took to bend the world to his comfort.

Jack had been capable of cold-blooded murder.

Alana's stomach moved uneasily. Cold sweat broke out over her body. Suddenly she couldn't bear the clammy sheets and slack, heavy blankets any longer. She needed the lively warmth and flickering companionship of a fire.

She sat up in bed and groped for her housecoat. All she found was the thick robe she had borrowed from the downstairs bathroom. Impatiently she pulled on the indigo robe, letting the sleeves trail down over her knuckles. The hem was long enough to brush the tops of her toes.

Groping along the wall, Alana worked her way down the inky darkness of the stairway. The living room was empty, without light. The fireplace ashes were as cold and pale as the moon.

Rafe hadn't been in the lodge at all tonight. He hadn't seen or spoken to Alana since she had run from him through the forest. After her irrational panic had passed, she had waited for Rafe by the trail.

He hadn't come.

Finally, when the moon had risen in pale brilliance over Broken Mountain, Alana had given up and gone inside, shivering with cold and loneliness.

She struck a wooden match on the fireplace stone. Using its flickering light, she peered into the wood box. There was a handful of kindling and a few small chunks of stove wood. Not enough to warm the hearth, much less her.

With a dispirited curse, Alana let the top of the wood box fall back into place. She turned to go back to bed, then froze.

A subtle sound drifted through the cabin, a

distant keening that floated on the shifting mountain wind.

The strange, bittersweet music held Alana motionless, aching to hear more. She held her breath, listening with an intensity that made her tremble.

Music curled around her lightly, tantalizing her at a threshold just below memory, music curving across the night like a fly line, lengthening in grace and beauty with each surge of energy, each magic, rhythmic pulse.

Blindly Alana felt her way through the lodge to the front door, lured by the elusive music. She opened the door, shut it silently behind her, and held her breath, listening and looking.

There was laughter tumbled by wind, bright squares of light glowing from the cabin at the end of the row. Silhouettes dark against one curtained window, wordless movements of hands and arms, more laughter.

But no music.

It wasn't somebody's transistor radio or tape player that had slid through Alana's defenses, calling to her in a language older and more potent than words.

Yet there was nowhere else the music could be coming from. Of the three cabins that stretched out east of the lodge, only one was glowing with light, only one was brimming with laughter when people won or lost small bets. The two other cabins were empty, as black as night itself. Blacker, for the cabins had neither moon nor stars to light their interior darkness.

The wind stirred, blowing across the back of Alana's neck, teasing her ears with half-remembered, half-imagined music. Slowly she turned, facing west.

The fourth cabin was several hundred feet away, wrapped in forest and darkness, not really part of the fishing camp. No light gleamed from the cabin in welcome, no laughter swirled, no sense of brimming life came to her.

And then the music called to Alana, an irresistible lure drawing her closer with each note.

She stood and listened for a moment more, her heart beating hard, her blood rushing so quickly that it overwhelmed the mixed murmur of music and wind.

Without stopping to think, she stepped off the porch onto the overgrown path to the fourth cabin. Pine needles and sharp stones smarted against her bare feet, but she noticed them only at a distance. The small hurts meant nothing, for she had recognized the source of the music.

Rafe.

Rafe and his harmonica, mournful chords lamenting love and loss.

It was Alana's own song curling toward her across the night, drifting down on the seamless black surface of her despair, music shimmering with emotion. Once she had sung this song with Rafe. Once they had looked into each other's eyes and shared sad songs of death and broken dreams.

And they had smiled, certain of the power and endurance of their own love.

> *I heard a lark this morning*
> *Singing in the field.*
> *I heard a lark this morning*
> *Singing wild.*
>
> *I didn't know*
> *You had gone away.*
> *I didn't know*
> *Love had gone to yesterday.*
>
> *I heard a lark this morning*
> *Singing wild.*
> *I heard a lark this morning*
> *Singing free.*
>
> *Maybe tomorrow I'll know.*
> *Maybe tomorrow you'll tell me*
> *Why the lark sang.*
> *And maybe yesterday*
> *Never came.*
>
> *I heard a lark this morning*
> *Singing in the field.*
> *I heard a lark this morning*
> *Singing free.*
> *It did not sing for me.*

The music Alana had once picked out on her guitar now came back to her in haunting chords sung by Rafe's harmonica. The words she had written ached in her throat and burned behind her eyes.

Thick terry cloth folds wrapped around her legs, slowing her. She picked up the hem of the robe and began to run toward the cabin, not feeling the rough path or the tears running down her face, drawn by her music.

By Rafe.

The cabin stood alone in a small clearing. There was no flicker of candlelight, no yellow shine of kerosene lamps, nothing but moonlight pouring through the cabin windows in a soundless fall of silver radiance. Sad harmonies shivered through the clearing, shadows of despair braiding through the pale brilliance of moonlight.

Slowly, like a sigh, the song changed into silence. The last transparent notes of music were carried away on a cold swirl of wind.

Alana stood at the edge of the clearing, transfixed by music, aching with silence. Only her face was visible, a ghostly oval above the textured darkness of her robe and the sliding black shadows of evergreens flexing beneath the wind.

She hesitated, feeling the wind and tears cold on her cheeks. Then the mournful chords began all over, sorrow coming back again, unchanged.

I heard a lark this morning . . .

Alana couldn't bear to stand alone in the haunted, wind-filled forest and listen to her yearning song played by the only man she had ever loved.

Slowly she walked across the clearing, seeing only tears and moonlight, hearing only song and sorrow. She went up the cabin steps like a ghost, soundless, wrapped in darkness. The front door stood open, for there was neither warmth nor light to keep inside.

The cabin had only one room. Rafe was stretched out on the bed that doubled as a couch during the day. Only his face and hands were visible, lighter shades of darkness against the overwhelming night inside the cabin.

Silently, without hesitation, Alana crossed the room. She didn't know if Rafe sensed her presence. He made no move toward her, neither gesture nor words nor silence. He simply poured himself into the harmonica, music twisting through her, chords of desolation shaking her.

Alana knelt by the bed, trying to see Rafe's face, his eyes. She could see only the pale shimmer of moonlight, for the sad strains of music had blinded her with tears.

> *I heard a lark this morning*
> *Singing wild.*

With each familiar chord, each aching harmony of note with note, Alana felt the past sliding away, nightmare draining into song until she knew only music and no fear at all.

Swaying slightly, her body lost to the music,

Alana's mind slowly succumbed to emotions that were as wary and elusive as trout shimmering deep within a river pool. She didn't know how many times the song ended and began, notes curling and curving across her inner darkness, music drifting down, floating, calling her, luring her up from the dark depths of her own mind.

Alana knew only that at some point she began to sing. At first her song was wordless, a supple blending of her voice with the harmonica's smooth chords, clear harmonies woven between instrument and singer. The melody line passed between them, changed by one and then the other, renewed and renewing each other by turns.

And then, like a wild lark, Alana's voice flew free.

It soared and turned on invisible currents, swept up emotions and transmuted them into pouring song, a beauty so transparent, so flawless, that a shiver of awe rippled through Rafe. For an instant the harmonica hesitated. Then he gave himself to the music as completely as Alana had, pursuing the brilliant clarity of her voice, soaring with it, sharing her ecstatic flight out of darkness, touching the sun.

Finally there was nothing left of the song but the last note shimmering in the darkness, sliding into moonlight and the soft whisper of the wind.

Alana put her head in her hands and wept soundlessly. Rafe stroked her hair slowly, gently, until her lips turned into his palm and he felt her tears slide between his fingers. With careful hands, he eased Alana onto the bed beside him, murmuring her name, feeling her shiver as she came close to him. Her hands were cool when she touched his face, and she shivered again.

Rafe shifted until he could free the sleeping bag he had been lying on. He unzipped it and spread smooth folds of warmth over her. When he started to get out of bed, she made a sound of protest and sat up. He kissed her cold hands.

"Lie still," he said. "I'll start a fire."

But first Rafe closed the cabin door, shutting out the wind. He moved swiftly in the darkness, not bothered by the lack of light.

There was a muted rustle of paper and kindling, then the muffled thump of cured wood being stacked in the fireplace. A match flared in the darkness.

Alana blinked and held her breath, shivering again. Rafe's face looked like a primitive mask cast in pure gold, and his eyes were incandescent topaz beneath the dense midnight of his hair. For long moments he and the fire watched one another, two entities made of heat and potent light.

With the silence and grace of a flame, Rafe turned toward Alana, sensing her eyes watching him. He stood and came toward her, his expression concealed by shadow.

The bed shifted beneath his weight as he sat and looked at her face illuminated by the gliding dance of flames. Her eyes were both dark and brilliant, her skin was flushed, and her lips were curved around a smile. Reflected fire turned and ran through her hair in liquid ribbons of light.

"You are even more beautiful than your song," whispered Rafe.

His fingertip traced Alana's mouth and then the slender hand that rested on top of the sleeping bag. He took her hand and rubbed it gently between his palms.

"You're cold," Rafe said. "How long were you outside?"

Alana tried to remember how long she had stood in the clearing, but all that seemed real to her now was Rafe's heat flowing into her as he touched her.

"I don't know," she said.

Silently Rafe rubbed Alana's hand until it no longer felt cool to his touch. When his fingers went up her arm, he encountered the heavy cloth of the robe she wore. He made a startled sound, then laughed softly.

"So that's where it went," said Rafe.

"What?"

"My bathrobe."

"Yours?" asked Alana, surprised. "I thought it was Bob's. The sleeves come down over my knuckles and the hem drags on my toes and—"

"—I'm such a shrimp," finished Rafe, smiling.

"Rafael Winter," Alana said, exasperation and laughter competing in her voice, "you're more than six feet tall and must weigh at least a hundred and seventy pounds."

"Closer to one-ninety."

In startled reappraisal, Alana looked at the width of Rafe's shoulders, outlined by firelight.

"Those are hardly the dimensions of a shrimp," she pointed out.

"I know. You're the one who keeps thinking that my clothes belong to Bob."

Rafe's weight shifted, sending a quiver through the bed. Alana's breath caught as she sensed him coming closer.

"You're such a tiny thing," he said. "I'll bet you got the hem all muddy. Unless you're wearing high-heeled slippers?"

"No. Twice."

Rafe looked at Alana. A smile made firelight glide and gleam over his mustache.

"Twice?" he asked.

"I'm five feet five. Not a tiny thing at all. And I'm barefoot."

"Barefoot?"

All amusement was gone from Rafe's voice. He moved to the end of the bed and pulled aside the sleeping bag until he could see Alana's feet.

"There's glass on the path from here to the main cabin," Rafe said. "Not to mention sharp rocks and roots."

He hissed a curse as he saw thin, dark lines of blood on Alana's feet.

"You cut yourself," he said flatly.

Alana wiggled her toes. She tucked her feet

up beneath the warm sleeping bag.

"Little scratches, that's all," she said.

Rafe got up, went to the stove, and tested the water in the kettle. He had intended to make coffee, but when he found the harmonica on the kitchen shelf, he had forgotten about everything else.

Although the fire in the stove had long since died, the water was still warm. He poured some into a basin, took a bar of soap from the sink, and searched for a clean cloth. When he found one, he returned to Alana.

"Give me your feet," he said.

"They're fine."

Rafe flipped back a corner of the sleeping bag, captured one of her feet, and began washing the abrasions with warm water. He sat sideways on the end of the bed, resting her ankle on his thigh.

"Rafe," Alana protested, squirming slightly.

"Rafe what? Am I hurting you?"

"No," she said softly.

"Tickling you?"

Alana shook her head, watching Rafe as he washed her feet and rinsed them carefully. Then he examined the cuts with very gentle touches, making sure that all the dirt was out.

"Hurt?" he asked.

"No."

"I don't have any antiseptic in this cabin."

"I don't need it."

"Yes, you do," countered Rafe in a firm voice. "Dr. Gene made a big point about how run-down you were, fair game for any bug that came along."

"Dr. Gene is wrong."

Rafe grunted, then smiled crookedly.

"I take it back," he said. "I do have some antiseptic here, after a fashion."

Alana watched while Rafe took rag, soap, and basin back to the tiny corner kitchen. He opened a cupboard and pulled out a fifth of Scotch. He knelt by the end of the bed, one of her feet in his hand.

"I'll bet it stings," she said.

"Bet you're right. Bet that next time you go walking you'll remember to wear shoes, tenderfoot."

Using the tip of his finger, Rafe applied whiskey to the first cut. Alana's breath came in sharply. He blew across the cut, taking away some of the sting. Then he went to work on the next scrape, applying Scotch, blowing quickly, his eyes and the whiskey glowing gold in the firelight.

When Alana's breath hissed out over the last cut, Rafe's fingers tightened on her foot.

"Why am I always hurting you?" he asked.

Pain turned in his voice, tightening it into a groan. He bent his head until he could kiss the delicate arch of Alana's foot. His lips lingered on her skin in silent apology for having caused her pain, no matter how necessary it might have been.

One hand cradled the arch of her foot, warming her, while the other hand stroked from the smooth skin at the top of her foot to the graceful curve of her ankle. He caressed her warmly, hands and mouth moving over her, savoring the heady mixture of Scotch and her sweet skin.

"Rafael," cried Alana softly.

Her toes flexed and curled against his palm with an involuntary sensual response.

Rafe's whole body tightened as he fought a short, savage battle with himself for control. With an invisible shiver of rebellion, his hands obeyed the commands of his mind.

Swiftly he put Alana's feet under the sleeping bag and tucked it around her.

"Rafe . . . ?"

Without answering, he stood and went to the fire. Using swift, abrupt motions, he added wood to the fireplace until the flames rushed upward into the night with a sound like wind. Only then did he turn from the savage leap of flames to face Alana.

"Warm enough?" he asked neutrally.

"No."

She shivered slightly, watching Rafe with dark eyes, wondering why he looked so hard, so angry.

He crossed the room in three strides, grabbed the daybed, and pulled it closer to the fire with an ease that shocked Alana. Because he was so gentle with her, she kept on forgetting how powerful he really was.

Rafe turned away from Alana and watched the fire with eyes that also burned.

"How's that?" he asked. "Better?"

"Not as warm as your hands felt," Alana

said softly. "Not nearly so warm as your mouth."

Rafe spun toward her as though she had struck him.

"Don't," he said, his voice harsh.

Alana's eyes widened. Then her eyelashes swept down, concealing her confusion and pain. But nothing concealed the change in her mouth from smiling softness to thin line, happiness flattened by a single word.

Rafe saw and knew that he had hurt Alana once again. He swore silently with a savagery that would have shaken her if she had been able to hear him.

"I'm sorry," Alana whispered. "I thought—"

Her voice broke. She made a helpless gesture, then slid out from beneath the sleeping bag and stood up, pulling the robe tightly around her. His robe.

"I thought you wanted me," she said.

"That's the problem. I want you so much I get hard just looking at you. I want you so much that I don't trust myself to be petted and then to let you go. I want you—*too much*."

The gesture Rafe made was as curt as his voice.

"A thousand times I've dreamed of having you in my arms," he said, "of loving you, touching you, tasting you, and then burying myself in your softness, feeling you loving me deep inside your body until nothing is real but the two of us and then there is only one reality. *Us*."

Alana made a breathless sound that could have been Rafe's name. His words had washed over her in a torrent of desire so consuming that she could barely breathe.

Rafe looked away from her to the fire raging in the hearth.

"I've dreamed too often, too much," he said bluntly. "You'd better go, wildflower. Go now."

Instead, Alana sank back onto the bed, for her legs felt too weak to support her. She thought of Rafe holding her, her body helpless beneath his strength as he became a part of her, and then she waited for the fear to come, freezing her.

Fire came instead, freeing her.

Slowly Alana stood. She walked soundlessly across the short distance separating her from Rafe. He stood with his back to her, his neck corded with tension.

When her arms slid around his waist, his whole body stiffened.

"I'm yours, Rafael," she said softly.

16

ALANA FELT THE TREMOR that went through Rafe at her words. Then she felt the slide and flex of powerful muscles as he turned in her arms and looked down into her eyes. Watching her, waiting for the least sign of withdrawal, of fear, he closed his arms gently around her.

Rafe's arms tightened slowly, inevitably, drawing her against his body. He gathered her close and held her with the power and hunger that he had fought so long to conceal from her.

Alana tilted back her head and watched Rafe through half-closed eyes. Her lips parted, hungry for his kiss.

With a muffled groan, Rafe bent his head

and took what she offered, searching the softness of her mouth with hard, hungry movements of his tongue. The force of his kiss bent
her back over his arm, but she didn't protest.

Instead, she clung to him with fierce joy,
giving herself to his strength. She sensed that
he was testing her, trying to discover if she
would freeze, trying to find out while he could
still stop himself and let her go.

Rafe shifted Alana in his embrace, holding
her head in the crook of one arm and bringing
her hips against him with the other. She answered with a soft moan and a supple movement of her body that sent whips of fire
flicking over him.

Despite the passion and power of Rafe's embrace, he was careful not to lift Alana off her
feet. He didn't want to test either of them to
that extent, for he suddenly knew that he
couldn't let her go.

He had dreamed of Alana too long, and this
was too much like his dreams, cabin and firelight and her sweet, passionate abandon in his
arms.

"You aren't afraid," Rafe murmured against
Alana's lips, pleading and urging and asking
at the same time.

"I'm not afraid of you."

Slowly Alana turned her head from side to
side, rubbing her moist lips over Rafe's, savoring the heat and life of him.

"You were never the one I feared," she
whispered.

Alana felt one of Rafe's strong hands slide

up to her neck, felt gentle fingers trace the gold chain he had given to her, felt the slight roughness of his fingertip resting on the rapid pulse beating beneath her soft skin. She sighed and softened against him even more.

His head moved and his lips slid down Alana's neck until his tongue touched her pulse so delicately that he could count her rapid heartbeats. Then his hand shifted, sliding inside her robe until the firm curve of her breast fit into his hand and her heartbeat accelerated wildly.

"Yes," Rafe said hoarsely. "This is my dream. Your response, your hunger, the way your nipple rises against my palm, wanting my touch."

Alana's body curved against Rafe, enjoying the hard muscles of his thighs, the heat of him as he moved against her, the texture of his flannel shirt beneath her palms. With a small sound, she slid her hands up to his head and buried her fingers in his hair.

"Winter mink," she said, sighing. "Thick and soft and silky."

She flexed her fingers sensually, shivering as Rafe arched against the caress, his whole body tightening against her, stroking her.

"I'd like to feel you all over me," Alana said. "All of you. All of me."

"You're going to," Rafe promised.

He bit her neck in a caress that was neither wholly gentle nor wholly wild.

"Every bit of you," he said deeply. "Every bit of me."

Yet even as Rafe spoke, his embrace gentled. The certainty that Alana wasn't going to run away brought a greater measure of control back to him. He no longer felt driven to steal what he could before she became afraid.

Alana wasn't retreating from his strength. She was coming closer to him with every breath, every heartbeat, every touch.

Rafe untied the heavy robe with slow motions. Then he took it from Alana with hands that cherished the pleasure of the moment and the woman who turned to him, smiling.

When Rafe dropped the robe onto the bed, the indigo cloth shimmered invitingly in the firelight. He didn't notice. He saw only Alana and the soft, floor-length nightgown that was the color of a forest at dusk.

Tiny, flat, silver buttons flickered, reflecting the dance of flames. The silver flashes tempted Rafe's finger to trace the shining circles from Alana's throat to her thighs. His hand lingered on the buttons, gently kneading the slight, resilient curve of her stomach before continuing down.

When he stroked the soft mound at the apex of her thighs, her breath rushed out. He stroked more deeply, shaping the thin gown to Alana's hidden curves, cupping her in his palm. She moaned and her fingernails dug into his shoulders.

Rafe laughed softly, triumph and hunger combined. And then he groaned as Alana's satin heat reached out to him, spilling over him like sunrise.

"You tempt me without mercy," he said, his voice deep.

"Look who's talking," Alana said shakily.

Slowly Rafe retreated, tracing once again the line of tiny buttons until it stopped just below the hollow of Alana's throat. His fingers moved over the first button, trying to open it.

But the button was very small, very stubborn, and his hand was less than steady, for every breath he took was infused with the elemental perfume of Alana's desire.

"This nightgown would try the patience of a saint," Rafe muttered, amusement and passion mixed equally in his voice.

Alana bent her head to brush her lips across Rafe's fingers. Her teeth closed delicately on his knuckle. Her tongue slid between his fingers, caressing the sensitive skin.

"You're not helping," he said.

"The neckline is wide enough that I don't bother with the buttons."

"But I've dreamed so many times of undressing you slowly, so slowly . . ."

When Alana looked up, Rafe was smiling and very serious. The heat of his eyes made her feel deliciously weak.

"I'm going to enjoy each button, Alana. Each new bit of you revealed. And when I'm done, I'm going to look at you wearing nothing but firelight."

The shimmering promise in Rafe's eyes sent an answering fire through Alana.

"I won't even touch you at first," he said, brushing the back of his fingers lightly across

Alana's soft lips. "I'll just look at you and remember all the times I could see you only in my dreams. I've dreamed of that, too, a dream within a dream."

Alana trembled, caressed as much by Rafe's words as she was by his hands.

Rafe saw her shiver, felt the warm rush of her breath against his fingers. He moved both hands to the line of buttons, but he became distracted when Alana's breasts brushed against the sensitive skin of his inner wrist.

It felt so good that Rafe couldn't resist moving his wrists lightly against her soft, firm curves. Alana's breasts changed as he stroked her, until her nipples stood boldly against the tantalizing softness of her nightgown.

Rafe bent his head and caressed the tip of one breast with his teeth. The response that shivered through Alana made him want to groan with pleasure and raw need combined. He wanted to part her soft thighs and feel the silky heat of her welcome washing over him. He wanted that until he was shaking with his hunger.

But he wanted the dream, too. He wanted that even more.

Reluctantly Rafe's hands returned to the tiny buttons. One by one he unfastened them until Alana's skin glowed between dark green folds of cloth. She watched with eyes that also glowed, and her breath made soft, tearing sounds in the hushed darkness.

Rafe kissed the satin warmth of Alana's skin, following the yielding line of buttons with his mouth. Slowly, sensuously, his tongue slid down her body, following the buttons that melted away, unveiling her for his caresses. In a silence that shivered with possibilities, he tasted the heat and sweetness of his dream.

He paused to cherish one breast, then the other, caressing her with teeth and tongue until Alana moaned and her fingers tangled helplessly in his hair. Only then did he continue down, his hands less steady, his breathing quicker, the taste and feel of her consuming him while passion pooled heavily, urgently, between his thighs.

With a swift, supple motion Rafe knelt in front of Alana, his fingers moving over the remaining buttons until they were all undone. Gently he tugged at the cloth. Soft folds clung to each feminine curve for breathtaking moments. Finally, reluctantly, the gown slid to the floor, yielding the secrets of Alana's body.

For the space of several breaths, Rafe simply looked at Alana. Her skin was flushed by firelight and passion. Her breasts rose smoothly and their tips glistened from the caresses of his mouth. The rich contrast of her dark nipples against her glowing skin held his eyes for a long moment, and then he looked at the tempting midnight gleam of hair below her narrow waist.

When the tip of Rafe's tongue teased Alana's navel and his hands found the taut swell of her hips, she swayed even closer to him, calling his name. He closed his eyes, letting the sound and scent and feel of Alana sink into him, healing and inflaming him at the same instant.

He had dreamed of this so many times, of touching her until she was too weak to stand and then carrying her to the bed, caressing her softness intimately until she cried aloud her need for him.

But now Rafe was afraid to lift Alana, to carry her. He was afraid he would shatter both dream and reality with a single incautious act.

Rafe brushed his mouth across Alana's stomach, savored again the sweetness of her breasts, taut and flushed with heat, beneath his hands. Dream and reality fused into a passion that raged at the restraint he imposed on himself.

Quickly he came to his feet, ignoring the hammer blows of desire in his blood, the talons of need raking him until he could count his heartbeat in the hardened flesh between his legs. With impatient hands he pulled off his own clothing and threw it aside.

At the sound of Alana's swiftly drawn breath, Rafe turned toward her, suddenly afraid that she would flinch from the blunt, heavy reality of his desire.

And then Rafe stood motionless but for the tremors of hunger ripping through him, a hunger that increased with each instant. Alana was looking at him the same way he had looked at her, raw yearning and hunger and tenderness combined. Her eyes reflected fire as she touched him with hands that shook, want-

ing him with a force that made her whole
body tremble like an aspen in the wind.

Alana's fingers went from Rafe's shoulders
to his thighs in a single, shivering caress that
almost destroyed his control. For an instant he
let her fingertips trace the hard outline of his
desire and count the heavy beats of his blood.
Then he caught her hands between his own.

"No," said Rafe hoarsely.

"But—"

"If you touch me again, I'll lose control. This
time, let me touch you. Next time you can
tease me until I go crazy, but not this time.
This time is too much like my dreams. This
time it's all I can do not to pull you down and
take you right here on the cabin floor."

Alana closed her eyes, knowing if she
looked at Rafe right now she would have to
touch him. With a graceful motion she turned
away and stretched out on the daybed. Only
then did she open her eyes and look at the
man standing beside the bed, Rafe with firelight licking over his powerful body, molten
gold pooling in his eyes, the most beautiful
thing she had ever seen. When she spoke, her
voice was a soft, husky song.

"Then come dream with me, Rafael."

He came down onto the bed and gathered
Alana into his arms in one continuous movement. He held her as though he expected
something to wrench her from his embrace,
ending the dream, leaving him to awaken
hungry and despairing, the past repeating it-

self endlessly, dream sliding into waking nightmare.

Alana felt Rafe's mouth demand hers, felt his arms close powerfully around her, felt the bruising male strength of his body, the hardness and the hunger of him; and she returned the embrace, holding on to him with every bit of her strength.

After a long time, Rafe drew a deep, shuddering breath and released her.

"I'm sorry. I didn't mean to hurt you," he said, kissing Alana gently, repeatedly, tasting her with each word, unable to stay away from her for more than a second at a time.

"You didn't hurt me."

Rafe touched Alana gently. His hand trembled as it moved from her temple to her lips. Eyes closed, she twisted blindly beneath him, seeking to hold him again, to feel the heat and power of his body against hers, sliding within her, moving with her.

With a throttled groan, Rafe trapped Alana's restless hands. He kissed her palms, bit her fingertips and the flesh at the base of her thumb, sucked lightly on her wrist and the inside of her arm. She moved against his loving restraint, wanting more than his inciting, teasing caresses.

Rafe laughed softly and watched Alana with smoky golden eyes. He stroked her body almost soothingly, and when he spoke his voice was deep, husky with memory and desire.

"At first," he said, "after they tortured me, I dreamed only of revenge. Blood and death and the devil's laughter. But later . . ."

Rafe's head bent until he could touch the tip of Alana's breast with his tongue.

"Later, hatred wasn't enough to keep me alive," he said. "It was for some men, but not for me. That's when I began to dream of you, deep dreams, dreaming all the way to the bottom of my mind, dreaming with everything in me."

Rafe's teeth closed lightly, tugged, then he took Alana's nipple into his mouth and cherished her with changing pressures of his tongue until she cried his name and her love again and again.

"Yes," he whispered, smoothing his mustache across her taut nipple until she shivered, "I heard you calling for me when I wanted to die, calling for me and crying . . . and so I lived, and I dreamed."

The words came to Alana like another kind of caress sinking into her soul, Rafe's voice dreaming of her while his hands and mouth moved slowly over her, memorizing her as she burned beneath his touch.

Strong fingers stroked down her stomach, her thighs, sensitizing her skin until her breath came in raggedly. When his cheek slid up from her thigh and ruffled the blackness of her hair, she moaned his name. His hands smoothed the curve of her legs, pressing gently, asking silently. Her legs shifted beneath his touch, giving him another measure of his dream.

When Rafe felt the waiting heat and need of

Alana, his hand shook. She was even softer than his dreams, hotter, more welcoming. His fingers slid over her, cherishing and parting her in the same loving caress.

Alana tried to say Rafe's name, but she could only moan while he caressed her deeply, telling her of his dream and her beauty as she moved sinuously, helplessly, clinging to his touch.

When his mouth brushed over her, tasting and teasing her, she gave up trying to speak, to think. She cried for him with each ragged breath, each melting instant, fire spreading in rhythmic waves through her body.

Rafe moved over Alana slowly, covering her body with his own, sliding into her, filling her, and she came apart beneath him. Motionless, rigid, he listened to the song of her ecstasy, better than his dreams, wilder, hotter, sweeter.

And then Rafe could hold back no longer. He moved within Alana's melting heat, sliding slowly, fiercely, then more quickly. She called his name huskily, tightened around him, holding him with all her strength.

They moved together, wound tightly around one another, sharing each heartbeat, each rhythmic melting of pleasure, until neither one could bear any more. Rafe cried out and gave himself to Alana even as she gave herself to him and to the incandescent ecstasy they had created.

Finally they knew the shimmering silence and peace that followed such a complete sharing.

It was a long time before Alana stirred languidly and looked up at Rafe. He was watching her with smoky amber eyes that remembered every touch, every cry, every moment, everything.

She smiled and smoothed his mustache with fingers that still trembled.

"I love you, Rafael Winter."

Rafe gathered Alana against his body a little fiercely, like a man hardly able to believe that he wasn't dreaming.

"And I love you, Alana. You're a part of me, all the way to my soul."

He kissed her eyelids and her cheeks and the corners of her smiling lips, and he felt the kisses returned as quickly as they were given.

"As soon as we get off the mountain," Rafe said, "we'll be married. On second thought, the hell with waiting. I'll get on the radio and have Mitch fly in a justice of the peace."

Rafe felt the change in Alana, tension replacing the relaxed pressure of her body against his. He lifted his head and looked into her dark, troubled eyes.

"What is it, wildflower? Your singing career? You can live with me and write songs, can't you? And if you want to do concert tours, we'll do concert tours."

Alana opened her mouth. Words didn't come. But tears did, closing her throat.

"I'd like to have kids, though," Rafe added, smiling. "Boys as clumsy as me and girls as graceful as you. But there's no rush. You can do whatever you want, so long as you marry me. I can't let you go again."

"Rafael, my love." Alana's voice broke and tears spilled over her long eyelashes. "I can't marry you yet."

"Why?"

Rafe looked at Alana's dark eyes. Where passion had recently burned, there were only shadows now.

"Because Jack has been dead only a month?" Rafe asked bluntly. "The marriage was a mistake. A pretend mourning period would be a farce."

"Jack has nothing to do with it."

"Then——"

Alana touched Rafe's lips with gentle fingertips, silencing him.

"I want to be the woman who gives you children," she said softly. "I want to live with you and love you all the way to death and beyond, because I can't imagine ever being without you again."

Rafe took Alana's hand and kissed her palm with lips that clung and lingered over her skin. He began to gather her gently into his arms, then stopped.

She was still speaking softly, relentlessly.

"But I can't marry you until I can trust myself not to shatter into a thousand pieces with every thunderstorm," Alana said. "I can't marry you until the sight of a big, blond stranger doesn't send me into a panic. I can't marry you until I can come to you whole, confident of myself, of my sanity."

Alana felt Rafe's retreat in the withdrawal of his hand, saw it in the narrowing of his eyes and the expressionless mask that replaced a face that had been alive with love for her.

"Until you remember what happened on Broken Mountain?" asked Rafe, his voice neutral.

"Yes. Before I marry you, I have to be able to trust myself," she said, pleading with him to understand.

"Trust yourself—or me?" retorted Rafe.

The amber eyes that measured Alana were remote, as cool as his voice, showing nothing of the pain that his words cost him.

"I trust you more than I trust myself," Alana said.

Her voice was urgent, almost ragged, and her eyes searched Rafe's face anxiously.

"Then trust me to know what's best for us," he said. "Marry me."

Alana shook her head helplessly, wondering how she could make Rafe understand.

"So much for trust," said Rafe, his voice clipped.

"I trust you!"

"Yeah. Sure." He said something savage beneath his breath. "Well, at least I know how long you were standing by the cascade today. Long enough to hear Stan. Long enough to believe him. Long enough to kill a dream."

"No!" Alana said quickly. "I don't believe Stan. You aren't like that. You couldn't kill Jack like that!"

Rafe's laugh was a harsh, nearly brutal

sound that tore at Alana almost as much as it tore at him. With a vicious curse, he rolled off the bed and began pulling on his clothes.

When Rafe snatched up his shirt, the harmonica fell out of the pocket onto the floor. Firelight ran over the instrument's polished silver surface, making it shine.

He scooped up the harmonica, looked at it for a long moment, then tossed it casually onto the bed.

"Rafe?"

"Take it. Souvenir of a dream," Rafe said roughly, kicking into his boots. "I won't need it anymore. Any of it."

Alana picked up the harmonica, not understanding, not knowing what to say, afraid to say anything at all.

But when Rafe pulled open the cabin door and started to walk into the night, Alana came off the bed in a rush and threw her arms around him, preventing him from leaving.

"Rafe, *I love you*," she said against the coiled muscles of his back, holding on to him with all her strength.

"Maybe you do. Maybe that's why you forgot."

Rafe started to move away, but Alana's arms tightened, refusing to let him go.

The pain that had come with her refusal to marry him raged against Rafe's control, demanding release. He jerked free of Alana's arms and spun around to face her, his pain naked in his expression—and his anger. Yet when he spoke, his voice was so controlled, it lacked all inflection.

"I tried to be what you wanted, wildflower. I tried everything I could think of to lure you out of your isolation. I reassured you in every way I could. And it wasn't enough."

Rafe's voice roughened with each word, sliding out from his control. To see Alana in front of him right now, so lovely, so unattainable, to lose her all over again . . .

Rafe made a harsh sound and closed his eyes so that he wouldn't touch her, hold her, stir desperately among the ashes of impossible dreams.

"No matter how carefully I constructed my lures, you didn't want them enough to trust me," he said. "Finally, I even tried music. I hadn't played the harmonica since the day I found out you were married. I had played it too often for you, loving you with music the way I never could with words. After you married Jack, even the thought of touching that harmonica made me blind with rage."

"Rafael," Alana began, but he talked over her.

"Music had always been irresistible to you. So I picked up that beautiful, cruel harmonica and I called to you with it."

Tears trembled in Alana's eyelashes. "Yes."

"And you came to me."

"Yes."

"You sang with me."

"It was the first—"

But Rafe was still talking, and his eyes were as haunted by pain as his voice.

"You made love with me more incredibly than in my dreams," he said. "But it wasn't enough to make you trust me. Nothing will be enough for you."

"That's not true!"

"What's true is that you may never remember what happened on Broken Mountain. And even if you do—"

Rafe shrugged and said nothing more.

Tears and firelight washed gold down Alana's cheeks. Her hands reached for him.

"No," Rafe said gently.

He stepped away, out of reach of her slender hands.

"I once said my hooks were barbless, Alana. I meant it. I can't bear hurting you anymore. You're free."

Frozen in disbelief, Alana watched as Rafe turned and walked away from her, Rafe passing from silver moonlight into dense ebony shadows, Rafe moving as powerfully as the wind, leaving her alone with the echoes of her pain.

And his.

"*Rafael . . . !*"

Nothing answered, not even an echo riding on the wind.

17

FOR A LONG TIME ALANA stood in the cabin doorway, staring into moonlight and darkness, unaware of the cold wind blowing over her naked skin. Finally, the convulsive shivering of her body brought Alana out of her daze.

She closed the door and stumbled back into the cabin. With shaking hands she pulled on her nightgown, but her fingers were too numb to cope with all the tiny, mocking buttons. She kept remembering Rafe's long fingers unfastening the buttons one by one as his mouth caressed her body with fire and love.

With a choked sound, Alana grabbed Rafe's heavy robe. The harmonica tumbled free of the indigo folds and fell gleaming to the floor. She hesitated, looking at the firelight caressing the harmonica's chased silver surface.

Then she bent and picked up the instrument and put it deep in the robe's soft pocket. She pulled the robe tightly around her and sat at the edge of the broad granite hearth, staring into the hypnotic dance of flames.

But all her eyes saw was the darkness that came after fire was lost.

Eventually dawn came. Alana realized she was cold. The rock hearth she sat on was cold. She ached from the chill of unforgiving stone.

Cold.

Stone.

Darkness.

Heart hammering, Alana tried to move but could not. She was chained by stiffness and memories summoned by the icy touch of granite.

"Rafe—"

Alana's voice was hoarse, as though she had spent the night calling futilely for help that never came.

But not last night.

She had called all through the darkness nearly four weeks ago, when she had spent the night on the rock ledge by the lake. She hadn't called to Jack that night. She remembered now.

She had called to Rafe, crying his name again and again, cries that had come from deep inside her, from the love for him that was as much a part of her as her own soul.

Jack had laughed.

Cold. Helpless. A prisoner tied to stone.

It was devastating to be so helpless, to know that beyond the tiny, icy circle constricting her, there was a world of heat and sunlight and laughter and love.

And none of those things could reach her.

Cold.

Ice raining down. Darkness and wind lifting her, tearing her from . . .

"No!" said Alana fiercely, denying her nightmare. "There's no ice here. I'm in a cabin. I'm not tied by that lake. I'm not waiting helplessly for Jack to come and either free me or maul me. I'm not a tiny, shivering aspen leaf at the mercy of cold winds. I'm Alana. I'm a human being."

Her body shivered convulsively, repeatedly.

"Get up," Alana whispered hoarsely to herself. *"Get up!"*

Slowly, stiffly, she pulled herself to her feet. She moved awkwardly toward the cabin door. When she finally managed to open it, she saw that a new day was pouring down the stone ramparts in a thick tide of crimson light.

Alana stared up at Broken Mountain's ruined peak, rocks shattered and tumbled, cliffs and miniature cirques sculpted by winters without end.

She climbed down the cabin's steps to the clearing. Her feet were too cold to feel the impact of sharp stones. She hurried to the main lodge, wanting only to get dressed before Bob got up and saw her and asked questions that she had no way to answer and no desire to hear.

Stumbling in her haste, Alana went up the lodge's steps. For an instant she was paralyzed by the thought that Rafe might be inside, that she would run to him and he would turn away from her again, leaving her freezing and alone.

A nightmare.

No, worse than that, for in Alana's nightmares Rafe didn't turn away from her, he came to her and—

Alana froze in the act of opening the door.

Rafe. In her nightmares. Like Jack.

Shaking, suddenly clammy, dizzy, Alana leaned against the closed door, wondering if it was memory or nightmare or a terrible combination of both that was breaking over her, drenching her in cold sweat.

Rafe had been on Broken Mountain.

He had told her as much. He had told her that with the horror she had buried beneath a black pool of amnesia, there was an instant of beauty when she had turned to him.

Did Rafe tell me that only to help me remember? Alana asked silently. Did he use the promise of beauty like a single, perfect lure drifting down onto the blank surface of my amnesia, luring me beyond its dark, safe depths?

Alana waited for memory or nightmare to come and answer her questions, freeing her.

Nothing came but the too-fast beating of her heart, blood rushing in her ears like a waterfall . . .

Ice and darkness and falling, she was falling to the death that waited below!

With a hoarse cry, Alana wrenched herself out of nightmare. She opened the lodge door and hurried up the loft's narrow stairway. She pulled on clothes at random, caring only for warmth.

The fiery orange of Alana's sweater heightened the translucent pallor of her face and the darkness below her eyes. She rubbed her cheeks fiercely, trying to bring color to her face.

It didn't help. Her eyes were still too dark, too wide, almost feverish in their intensity. She looked brittle and more than a little wild, as though she would fly apart at a word or a touch.

Abruptly Alana decided that she would find Rafe. She would find him and then she would demand that he tell her what he knew.

"To hell with what Dr. Gene said about what would or would not help me remember," Alana whispered savagely. "To hell with what everyone else thinks is good for me. *I have to know.*"

No matter how horrible the truth, it could be no worse than what Alana was enduring now . . . Rafe turning away from her, sliding into night, nothing answering her cry, not even an echo.

Alana heard someone in the kitchen. She went down the stairs quickly, determination in every line of her body. She would confront Rafe now. She was through running, hiding, feeling screams and memories clawing at her throat.

But Rafe wasn't in the kitchen.

"Morning, sis," Bob said as she walked in.

His back was to her as he finished filling the coffeepot with water, but he had recognized her step.

"You're late, but so are the rest of us," Bob said. "Poker game didn't break up until after three."

Still talking, he turned toward her as he set the coffeepot on the hot stove.

"Janice is the luckiest—my God, Alana! What's wrong?"

"Nothing that coffee won't cure," she said, controlling her voice carefully.

Bob crossed the room in two long strides. He reached for Alana before he remembered Rafe's very explicit instructions about touching her.

"I'm going to see if you're running a fever," said Bob, slowly raising his hand to her forehead.

"I'm not."

Alana didn't step away from her brother's touch. Nor did she flinch. Finally she could see him clearly, no nightmare to cloud her eyes.

Bob's big palm pressed against Alana's forehead with surprising gentleness.

"You're cold," he said, startled by the coolness of her skin.

"Right. Not a bit of fever." Alana's voice was as clipped as the smile she gave her brother. "Have you seen Rafe?"

Bob's dark eyes narrowed. "He left."

"Left?"

"He told me he'd gotten a holler on the radio from the ranch. Something needed his attention right away. Said he'd radio us as soon as he got home."

"How long?"

"It's a long ride to his ranch house, even on that spotted mountain horse of his. Tonight, probably."

"When did he leave?"

"About an hour ago. Why?"

"No reason," Alana said, her voice as dry and tight as her throat. "Just curious."

"Did something happen between you two? Rafe looked as rocky as you do."

Alana laughed strangely.

"Did you know that Rafe was on the mountain four weeks ago?" she asked.

Bob gave her an odd look.

"Rafe was on Broken Mountain when Jack died," Alana said fiercely.

"Of course he was. How did you think you got off the mountain after you were hurt?"

"What?" whispered Alana.

"C'mon, sis." Bob smiled despite his worry. "Even you can't walk down three miles of icy mountain switchbacks on a badly wrenched ankle. The storm spooked all the horses, so Rafe carried you out on his back. If he hadn't, you'd have died up there, same as Jack did."

"I don't remember," Alana said.

"Of course not. You were out of your head with shock. Hell, I'll bet you don't even remember Sheriff Mitchell landing on the lake and flying you out of here in the middle of a storm. Mitch told me it was the fanciest piece of flying he'd ever done, too."

"I don't remember!"

Bob smiled and patted Alana's shoulder gently.

"Don't fret about it, sis. Nobody expects you to remember anything about the rescue. When I got to the hospital, you didn't even recognize me."

"I—don't—"

"Remember," Bob finished dryly. "Hypothermia does that to you. Turns your brain to suet every time. Remember when we went after that crazy rock climber way up on the mountain? By the time we found him, he had less sense than a chicken. He did fine after we thawed him out, though."

Alana looked at Bob's very dark eyes, eyes like the night, only brighter, warmer.

Eyes like her own before she had forgotten.

But Bob remembered and she didn't. Even when he told her, she could hardly believe what she was hearing. It was like reading about something in the newspaper. Distant. Not quite real.

Rafe had carried her down Broken Mountain.

She didn't remember.

No wonder Rafe hadn't told her what had happened. Telling her would do no good. Being told wasn't the same as remembering, as *knowing*.

Rafe had saved Alana's life, and she didn't even know it. He had carried her down a treacherous trail, ice and darkness all around, risked his own life for her.

And to her it was as though it had never happened.

"Rafe waited for you to remember after you ran out of the hospital," Bob said.

"I didn't. Remember."

She hadn't remembered, hadn't called Rafe, hadn't even known that he was waiting back on Broken Mountain.

Waiting for her.

"Yeah," Bob said. "Rafe figured that out for himself. So he gnawed on me to get you back here."

Numbly Alana nodded. She had come home, and Rafe had treated her with gentleness and understanding, asking nothing of her, giving everything. When being in the mountains frightened her, he apologized as though he were responsible.

Rafe had shared her pain to a degree that she hardly believed even now. He had given her all the reassurance he could. And never once had he shown how much she was hurting him.

He had loved her, cherished her, done everything possible for her, except remember. No one could remember for her.

That she must do for herself.

"Sis?" asked Bob, his voice worried. "You better sit down. You look like death warmed over."

"Thanks a lot, baby brother."

Alana's voice was as thin as the smile she gave Bob. She forced her throat to relax, using the discipline she had learned as a singer.

It was important that Bob not worry about her.

It was important that he not hover or watch over her, preventing her from doing what must be done.

It was important that she act as though there was nothing wrong with her that breakfast and a day lazing around the lake wouldn't cure.

Nothing wrong.

Absolutely normal.

"Check the wood box in the kitchen, okay? I don't want to run out of fire halfway through the eggs."

Alana's voice sounded calm, if a little flat. The smile she gave Bob echoed her voice precisely.

"Why don't you let me do breakfast?" asked Bob, a worried frown creasing his forehead. "You go sit and—"

"I'll sit later," she interrupted, "while you and the dudes are out fishing. I have a place all picked out. Grass and sunshine and a perfect view of aspen leaves."

Alana's throat constricted as she remembered counting aspen leaves with Rafe while he lay quietly with his hands locked behind his head, smiling and aching as she touched him.

Rafe.

She closed her eyes and forced herself to take a breath.

"Get cracking on the wood box, baby brother. I don't want to spend all day in the kitchen."

Bob hesitated, then went out the back door of the cabin. A few minutes later the clear, sharp sound of a ten-pound maul splitting cured wood rang through the dawn.

Carefully thinking of nothing at all, Alana moved through the kitchen, letting the routine of cooking and setting the table focus her mind. Whenever her thoughts veered to Rafe, she dragged them back ruthlessly.

First she had to get through breakfast. When everyone was safely caught up in fishing, when she was alone with only her erratic memory, then she would think of Rafe.

Thinking of him would give her the courage to do what had to be done.

A moment of panic rippled through Alana. A piece of silverware slipped from her hands and landed with a clatter on the table. With fingers that trembled, she retrieved the fork and put it in its proper place. She finished setting the table just as Janice came in.

"Good morning," Janice said cheerfully.

"Morning. Coffee's ready."

"Sounds like heaven. Is Rafe up yet?"

"Yes. I'll get you some coffee."

Quickly Alana turned away, avoiding the scrutiny of the other woman's eyes. The former psychiatrist was entirely too perceptive for Alana's comfort right now.

"Is that Rafe chopping wood?" asked Janice, falling into step beside Alana.

In an instant of memory that almost destroyed her control, Alana's mind gave her a picture of Rafe working by the woodpile four years ago. His long legs had been braced, his shirt off, the powerful muscles of his back coiling and relaxing rhythmically as he worked with the ax beneath the July sun, chopping stove wood. She could see him so clearly, the heat and life of him so vivid, she could almost touch him.

Yearning went through Alana like lightning, hunger and love and loss turning in her, cutting her until she could feel her life bleeding away.

"No," whispered Alana.

Desperately she pushed away the memory. If she thought of Rafe right now, she would go crazy.

Or crazier.

Before Janice could ask any more, Alana said, "Bob drew the short straw this morning."

Despite Alana's efforts to keep her voice normal, Janice looked at her sharply.

"You look a bit feverish," Janice said. "Are you feeling all right?"

"Fine. Just fine."

Alana poured coffee. Her hand shook, but not enough to spill the coffee.

"Tired, that's all," Alana said. "Altitude, you know. I'm not used to it. That and the cold nights. God, but the nights are cold on Broken Mountain."

And I'm babbling, added Alana silently, reining in her thoughts. And her tongue.

She handed Janice her coffee.

"Breakfast will be ready in about twenty minutes," Alana said.

Janice took the cup and sipped thoughtfully, watching Alana's too-quick, almost erratic movements around the kitchen.

"I thought I heard a horse ride by earlier this morning," Janice said. "Before dawn."

"That must have been Rafe," said Alana very casually.

She concentrated on laying thick strips of bacon across the old stove's huge griddle. Fat hissed as it met the searing iron surface.

"Rafe left?" asked Janice, startled.

"He has to check on something at the ranch. He'll be back later."

And pigs will fly, thought Alana, remembering Rafe's pain and anger. He won't come back until I'm gone. I've used up my chances with him. Rafael, I never meant to hurt you. Never . . .

Alana's hand shook, brushing against the griddle. She took a steadying breath and thought only about getting through breakfast.

One thing at a time. Now, this moment, that meant frying bacon without blistering herself through sheer stupidity.

Later she would think about Rafe leaving her, about his pain, about what she must do, about remembering.

Later. Not now.

"I hope everyone likes scrambled eggs," Alana said.

She went to the refrigerator and opened the door. No light came on. Rafe had forgotten to start up the generator. She pulled out a bowl of fresh eggs, then went to the back door and called to Bob.

"Do you know how to start up the generator?"

"Sure thing." Bob gestured toward a pile of split wood with the maul he was holding. "How much do you need?"

Alana remembered the night before, when she had found the living room wood box all but empty.

"Enough for the fireplace, too," she said. "You'll want a nice fire tonight."

"What about you?" asked Bob dryly, looking over his shoulder at Alana. "Don't you want a nice fire tonight, too?"

I won't be here tonight.

But the words were silent, existing only in Alana's mind.

"Does that mean I have to chop it myself?" she retorted, her voice sounding rough.

"Just teasing, sis," answered Bob. "You

never could split wood worth a damn."

He swung the maul again, burying its edge deep in the wood, splitting it easily into two smaller pieces.

Alana turned back to the stove. She was relieved to see that Janice had gone. The woman's eyes were just too intent, too knowing.

Breakfast was an ordeal Alana hoped never to have to repeat. The toast was impossible to chew, much less swallow. She forced herself to eat anyway. If she didn't, Bob would stick to her like a mother hen for the rest of the day, worrying over her.

Alana couldn't allow that to happen. So she ate grimly, washing down eggs and bacon with coffee, eating as little as she thought she could get away with.

As soon as Bob finished, he looked at Alana, then at Stan and Janice.

"I'm going to stay behind and help Alana with the dishes," Bob said. "Rafe thought you should try the water on the north side of the lake, where that little creek comes in. Some real big trout hang around there, feeding on whatever washes down."

"Sounds good to me," Stan said.

"Rafe suggested using dark flies," Bob added, "or the grasshopper imitation he tied for each of you. Me, I'm going to use the Lively Lady."

Alana got up, her plate and silverware in her hands.

"I'll take care of the dishes," she said, grateful that her voice sounded casual rather than desperate, the way she felt. "If you're doing dishes while Stan is fishing, he'll get the prize for the biggest fish."

"What prize?" asked Bob.

"Apple pie," Alana said succinctly. "Winner takes all."

A friendly argument began over big fish and winner taking all of the pie. In the end, everyone stayed and helped Alana with the dishes. When the last lunch had been packed and the last dish was draining on the counter, she turned and smiled rather fiercely at everyone.

"Thank you and good-bye," she said. "The trout are rising. The best fishing time of the day is slipping away. Have fun. I'll see you for dinner."

Stan and Janice exchanged glances, then left the kitchen. Alana looked expectantly at Bob.

"I'll leave in a while," Bob said, smiling genially and reaching for an apron. "Stan needs a handicap in the trout sweepstakes. I'll help you with the pie."

Alana looked at Bob in disbelief. Determination showed in every line of his face. He didn't know what was wrong, but he plainly wasn't going to leave until he did.

"You'll have a long wait," she said finally. "I'm going to take a bath. A very long, very hot bath. And no, baby brother, I don't need you to scrub my back."

Bob had the grace to laugh. But the laugh faded quickly into concern.

"You sure?" he asked softly.

"I've never been more sure of anything in my life." Alana's eyes held her brother's. "It's all right, Bob. Go fishing. Please."

Bob expelled a harsh breath and ran his hand through his black hair.

"I'm worried," he said bluntly. "Rafe looked like hell. You look worse. I feel like the guy who grabbed for the brass ring and came up with a handful of garbage. I want to help you, but I'm damned if I know what to do."

"Go fishing," Alana said.

Her voice was soft and very certain.

"Hell," Bob muttered. Then, "I'll be at the north side of the lake if you need me. Why don't you come over for lunch?"

"I'll probably be asleep."

"Most sensible thing you've said today," retorted Bob.

He looked pointedly at the dark circles beneath his sister's eyes. Then he threw up his hands and walked out of the kitchen.

"We'll be back for dinner about five," he called over his shoulder.

"Good luck," said Alana.

A grunt was Bob's only reply.

She held her breath until she heard the front door of the cabin close. Then she ran to the window and looked out. Bob had picked up his rod, net, and fishing vest. He was stalking over the lake trail with long, powerful strides.

"Take care," whispered Alana. "Don't be too mad at me. You did everything you could. Like Rafe. It's not your fault that it wasn't enough. It's mine."

Alana pulled off her apron with shaking hands and hung it on a nail by the back door. Then she raced upstairs and began stuffing warm clothes into the backpack she had found in her closet.

Broken Mountain could be cold, brutally cold. She of all people knew that.

Alana went back down the stairs, listening to her racing heart and the harsh thump of her hiking boots on the wooden stairs. She ran to the kitchen and began throwing food into the backpack. Cheese, raisins, granola, chocolate. She closed the flap and secured it tightly.

For a moment Alana stood and looked around the kitchen, wondering what she had forgotten.

"A note," she said. "I have to leave a note."

Alana scrambled through kitchen drawers, looking for paper and a pencil. But when she found them, she couldn't think of anything to say.

"How can I explain in words something that I barely understand myself?" Alana asked, staring helplessly at the paper.

Yet she had to write something.

She owed Bob that much. If he came back early and found her gone, he would be frantic.

Alana bent over and wrote quickly:

If Rafe calls, tell him I've gone to find the lark.
This time it will sing for me.

18

ALANA WALKED ALONG THE trail, grateful for the trees screening her from the lake. Through the breaks in the forest, she could see three people spaced out along the north side of the water. Bob looked no bigger than her palm. Bits of sound floated across the lake to her, fragments without meaning.

When she came to a fork in the trail, she hesitated for a moment. The right-hand path wound back to the lake, coming out just in front of the cascade where she had overheard Stan and Rafe arguing. The left-hand path skirted the worst of the rock jumble that caused the cascade.

Alana adjusted the backpack and turned

onto the left fork of the trail. Once past the fork, the trail began the long climb to the top of Broken Mountain.

The first part of the climb consisted of long switchbacks looping through the forest. Before Alana had gone half a mile, she wished she had Sid to do the work for her. But taking the horse would have been too great a risk. Sid would have spent the first mile neighing to the horses hobbled in the meadow behind the main cabin. Short of a siren, nothing carried better in the high mountains than the neigh of a lonely horse.

Sunlight quivered among aspen leaves and fell silently through evergreen boughs. The air was crisp, fragrant with resin, motionless but for the occasional stirring of wind off the lake. The cascade's distant mutter filtered through the forest, telling Alana that she was approaching one of the open, rocky sections of the trail. She would have to be careful not to be spotted by the fishermen below.

The forest dwindled, then vanished as the trail crawled over a steep talus slope. Broken stone of all sizes littered the ridge. The thunder of the cascade came clearly across the rocks. To the right of the trail the land fell away abruptly, ending in the sapphire depths of the lake.

Alana took one look, then did not look again. Fixing her eyes on the rugged ground just in front of her feet, she picked her way across the talus. For the first hundred yards her breath came shallowly, erratically. Then she regained control of her breathing. Slowly her fear of heights diminished, giving strength back to her legs.

Just before Alana dropped out of sight over a fold of Broken Mountain, she turned and looked down at the lake. Wisps of brilliant white cloud trailed iridescent shadows over the water, emphasizing the clarity and depth of both lake and air.

Alana's heart beat faster and her palms felt clammy, but she forced herself to look at the north shore. There were three specks, dark against the gray granite of the shoreline.

Three fishermen.

No one had spotted Alana and run after her to bring her back. With luck, no one would even notice that she was gone until dinnertime. And then it would be too late to come after her.

No one rode or walked high mountain trails at night unless a life was at risk.

Besides, even when Bob discovered that Alana wasn't at the lodge, he wouldn't know where she was. The last place he would expect to find her was farther up Broken Mountain, all the way up to the first and highest lake, up to the lip of the cliff where water leaped into darkness, standing in the exact spot where Jack had died and she had lost her mind.

Surely there, if anywhere, I'll remember, Alana told herself. Surely there, where conditions most exactly match the environment of my nightmare. . . .

There she would rise from the bleak, safe

pool of amnesia into the transparent light of reality. There, if anywhere on earth.

If Alana didn't remember right away, she would simply stay until she did, sleeping on a rock by the lake if she had to. She would do whatever she must to remember. Then she would accept whatever came.

In truth, now there was little at stake. That was why she finally had come to Broken Mountain.

She had nothing left to lose.

Alana climbed steadily through the morning. Though the second lake was less than two miles from the cabins, it took Alana three hours to make the climb. Part of the problem was the altitude. Another part was the roughness of the trail.

The hardest part was her own fear. Every step closer to the first lake was like a pebble added to her backpack, weighing her down.

By the time she scrambled up the saddle of land that concealed the second lake, Alana was sweating freely and felt almost dizzy. She stood and looked down on the tiny, marshy stretch of water. More pond than true lake, during the driest years the second lake existed only on maps. This year, though, the winter had been thick with snow and the summer ripe with storms. The water was a rich wealth of silver against the dense green of meadow and marsh plants.

The lake had been full the last time Alana was there. Clouds seething and wind bending the aspens, wind shaking the elegant spruce trees, storm winds moaning down the slopes.

It hadn't rained, though. Not then. Just clouds and a few huge water drops hurled from the heights by the wind.

Thunder had been distant, erratic. The peak next to Broken Mountain had been mantled in blue-black mist and lightning. But not Broken Mountain. Not then. Thunder hadn't come to Broken Mountain until the next night.

Seeing nothing but the past, Alana stared blindly at the ribbon of water nestled in a green hollow between folds of granite.

Remembering.

They had rested the horses there. She had gone to the edge of the small meadow and leaned against a tree, listening to the distant song of water over rock.

Jack had come up behind her, and she had wanted to put her hands over her ears, shutting him out. But she hadn't been able to then.

She was remembering now, Jack and the argument and the mountain rising cold and hard . . .

"Jilly, don't be stupid about this. We won't be famous forever. A few more years, that's all I ask."

She wanted to scream with frustration. Jack simply wouldn't accept that she couldn't go on with the farce of Country's Perfect Couple.

She had to be free.

"Jilly, you better listen."

"I'm listening," she said flatly. "I'm just not agreeing."

"Then you don't understand," he said confidently. "As soon as you understand, you'll agree."

"You're the one who doesn't understand. You're not getting your way this time, Jack. You shouldn't have demanded that I marry you in the first place. I shouldn't have given in."

Not looking at Jack, she ran her hand down the long black braids that fell between her breasts.

"It was a mistake," she said finally. "A very bad mistake. It's time we faced it."

"You're wrong. Think about it, Jilly. You're wrong."

"I've thought of nothing else for several years. I've made up my mind."

"Then you'll just have to change it."

She had turned suddenly, catching the black look he gave her. Then Jack had shrugged and smiled charmingly.

"Aw, c'mon, Jilly. Let's stop arguing and enjoy ourselves for a change. That's why we're here, remember?"

Yes, Alana was remembering.

Too late. Rafe was gone. She was remembering.

And she was afraid.

Alana shuddered and shifted the weight of her backpack, letting echoes and memories of the past gather around her as she climbed.

At first she remembered small things, a little bit at a time, minutes slowly building into whole memories. The closer she came, the higher she climbed on Broken Mountain, the thinner the veil of amnesia became—and the greater her mind's rebellion at what she was demanding of herself.

Alana no longer told herself that her rapid heartbeat and dragging breaths came from altitude or exertion. She was struggling against fear just as she had struggled against Jack's stubborn refusal to face the reality of her decision to leave him.

Suddenly Alana realized that she had stopped walking. She was braced against a rock, shaking, her eyes fixed on the last, steep ascent to the highest lake.

Broken Mountain rose behind the lake, granite thrusting into the sky. It waited for her, the cliff and the talus where wind howled and water fell into blackness and exploded far below on unyielding stone.

It waited for her, and she was terrified.

"Pull up your socks and get going, Alana Jillian," she said between gritted teeth. "Like Dad always said, you can't keep the mountain waiting. Besides, what do you have to lose that you haven't already lost?"

Nothing.

Not one damned thing.

Alana fastened her eyes on the trail just in front of her feet and began walking. She didn't look up, didn't stop, didn't think.

One by one, memories came, wisps of cloud gathering over the blank pool of amnesia, clouds and memories condensing into columns of white seething over the mountaintops, over her.

She stood at the edge of the tiny, hanging

valley where the first lake lay beneath the sullen sky. Thunder rumbled distantly, forerunner of the storm to come.

But not yet. The clouds hadn't met and wrapped around each other and the peaks. Only then would the storm begin, bringing darkness in the midst of day, black rain and white ice and thunder like mountains torn apart.

But not yet. She had a breathing space in the shelter of the stunted trees that grew in the lee of the mountain looming raggedly against the sky.

Broken Mountain.

At the base of the shattered gray peak lay the lake, mercury-colored water lapping at the very lip of the valley. Alana looked away from the white water leaping over the valley's edge, water falling and bouncing from rock to boulder, water exploding like thunder.

Jack flying out, turning and falling, white water and screams.

Alana slipped out of her backpack and went like a sleepwalker to the end of the trail.

Was it here Jack fell? she asked herself.

She looked over the edge, suffered a wave of dizziness and forced herself to look again.

No, it hadn't happened here.

Where, then? she asked herself impatiently.

The trail turned to the right, keeping to the trees. To the left was the end of the lake and the beginning of the waterfall, lake and rock and land falling away from the lip of the hanging valley.

Nausea turned in Alana, and a fear so great that it hammered her to her knees.

The lake. The lake lapping at the edge of space, water churning, thunder bounding and rebounding, darkness and screams. She was screaming.

No, it was the wind that screamed. The wind had come up at dawn and she shivered until Jack came to her. . . .

"Change your mind yet, Jilly?"

She closed her eyes and said nothing, did nothing, helpless, tied to stone.

"That's okay, babe. We've got all the time in the world."

"Untie m-me." Her voice came at a distance, a stranger's voice, harsh as stone scraping over stone.

"You going to listen to me if I do?"

"Y-Yes."

"You going to stop crying for that bastard Winter?"

Silence.

"I heard you, Jilly. Last night. Lots of nights. I'm going to break you of loving Winter, babe. I'm going to break you, period. When we get down off this mountain, you'll come to heel and stay there."

Alana listened, all tears gone.

She listened, and knew that Jack was crazy.

She listened, and knew that she would die on Broken Mountain unless she stopped crying and started using her head.

Her mind worked with eerie speed and clarity, time slowing down as she sorted through probabil-

ities and possibilities, certainties and hopes.

And then came understanding, a single brilliant fact: She must get Jack to untie her. Then the second fact: Jack's only weakness was his career; he needed her.

"If you l-leave me on this rock any longer, I'll be too s-sick to sing."

Jack put his hand on Alana's arm. It was cold enough to shock him. He frowned and fiddled with the zipper on his jacket.

"Are you going to listen to me?" he demanded.

"Y-Yes."

Jack untied her, but Alana was too stiff, too weak to move. He hauled her off the rock and set her on her feet.

She fell and stayed down, helpless, tied by a kind of pain that made her dizzy and nauseated. Finally feeling began to come back to her strained joints and limbs. Then she cried out hoarsely, never having known such agony.

Jack half dragged, half carried Alana to the camp, jerking her along, her braids wound around his hand. He dropped her casually by the fire. She lay there without moving, her mind spinning with pain. Eventually the worst of it passed and she could think.

She concealed the fact of her returning strength, afraid that Jack would tie her up again. When he spoke to her, she tried pretending that she was too dazed to answer. He hit her with the back of his hand, knocking her away from the fire. She lay motionless, cold and aching and afraid.

"You listen to me, Jilly. I need you, but there are other ways, other women who can sing. I've

been sleeping with one of them. You can sing circles around her, but she comes to heel a hell of a
lot better than you do. Don't be more trouble than
you're worth."

Alana shuddered and said nothing.

It seemed hours before the moment came that she
had been waiting for. Jack went to get more wood.
She came up off the ground in a stumbling rush,
running in the opposite direction, seeking the cover
of the forest and the mountainside.

That was the beginning of a deadly game of hide-
and-seek. Jack called to her, threats and endear-
ments, both equally obscene to Alana's ears as she
dodged from tree to thicket to boulder, her heart as
loud as thunder.

Storm clouds opened, drenching the land with
icy water mixed with sleet. Weakened by cold, her
mind fading in and out of touch with reality,
Alana knew she was running out of time and possibilities.

Her only chance was to flee down the mountain.
She had begun working toward that from the first
moment, leading Jack around the lake until he was
no longer between her and escape.

Now only the margin of the lake itself lay between her and the trail down Broken Mountain,
the lake where water lapped over boulders and then
fell down, down, to the rocks below. There was no
shelter there. No place to hide from Jack.

Lightning and thunder shattered the world into
black and white shards. Ice sleeted down, freezing
her.

And then a rock rattled behind her, Jack coming,
reaching for her.

Water rushing down, cold, and darkness waiting, lined with rocks, ice and darkness closing around, clouds seething overhead, lightning lancing down, soundless thunder.

Fear.

It was too cold, no warmth anywhere, only fear hammering on her, leaving her weak.

She tried to run, but her feet weighed as much as the mountains and were as deeply rooted in the earth. Each step took an eternity. Try harder, move faster, or get caught.

She must run!

But she could not.

Something had caught her braids, jerking her backward with stunning force.

Jack loomed above her, anger twisting his face, her braids wrapped around his fist. Jack cursing her, grabbing her, hitting her, and the storm breaking, trees bending and snapping like glass beneath the wind.

Like her. She wasn't strong enough. She would break and the pieces would be scattered over the cold rocks.

Jack slipped on the rocks where white pebbles of sleet gathered and turned beneath his boots. He let go of Alana's braids, breaking his fall with his hands.

Running. Scrambling.

Breath like a knife in her side.

Throat on fire with screams and the storm chasing her, catching her, yanking her backward while rocks like fists hit her. She was broken and bleeding, screaming down the night, running.

Caught. Her braids caught again in Jack's fist,

ice sliding beneath her feet, wind tearing at her, Jack lifting her as she screamed, lifting her high and when he let go she would fall as the water fell, down and down over the lip of the valley, exploding whitely on rocks far below.

Clawing and fighting. But she was swept up, lifted high, helpless, nothing beneath her feet, earth falling away and her body twisting, weightless, she was falling, falling, black rushing up to meet her and when it did she would be torn from life like an aspen leaf from its stem, spinning away helplessly over the void.

She called to Rafe then.

Knowing that she was dead, she cried Rafe's name and her undying love for him into the teeth of the waiting mountain.

And Rafe answered.

He came out of the storm and darkness like an avenging angel, his hands tearing her from Jack's deadly grasp.

At the last instant Rafe spun aside from the drop-off, balanced on the brink of falling. With certain death in front of him and Alana at his feet, Rafe whirled and launched himself in a low tackle that carried Jack away from Alana, helpless at the edge of the cliff.

The two men grappled in the darkness, pale sleet rolling beneath their feet, their struggles bringing them closer to the brink with each second.

Rafe kicked away, freeing himself and coming to his feet in a poised, muscular rush. Jack staggered upright, his hair shining palely with each flash of lightning, his face dark with hatred. He leaped blindly for Rafe.

But Rafe wasn't there. He slipped the attack with a supple, disciplined movement of his body, leaving nothing but night between Jack and the lip of the cliff.

Jack had an instant of surprise, a scream of fury and disbelief, and then he was falling, turning over slowly, screaming and falling into night.

Silence came, and then the sound of Alana's tearing screams.

"It's all right, wildflower. I've come to take you home."

Alana shuddered, giving her mind and her body to the cold and blackness. . . .

Alana stirred and slowly surfaced from memories. She was surprised to find that it was day rather than evening, fair rather than stormy, and she was huddled on her knees rather than unconscious in Rafe's arms.

She shook her head, hardly able to believe that she wasn't still dreaming. Rafe's words had sounded so real, so close.

She opened her eyes and saw that she had walked to the treacherous margin of rock and water and cliff. With a shudder, she turned away from the edge—and then she saw a man silhouetted against the sun.

She froze, fear squeezing her heart.

Rafe's face tightened into a mask of pain when he saw Alana's fear.

She had remembered and he had lost her.

"Stan was right," Rafe said, pain roughening his voice. "You were running from me, too. You didn't want to believe that the man you loved was a killer."

"No!"

Alana's voice shook, making a ragged cry out of the single word.

"Yes," said Rafe flatly. "I killed Jack Reeves. And you remembered it."

"It wasn't like that," Alana said quickly. "Stan was wrong. You didn't come up the mountain planning to kill Jack and seduce me and—"

"But Jack's dead," Rafe interrupted. "I killed him."

"You were saving my life!" Alana said, trying to understand why Rafe's face was so closed, so remote.

Rafe shrugged.

"So it's manslaughter, not murder one," he said curtly. "Jack's dead just the same."

"It was an accident!" she cried fiercely. "I saw it, Rafe! I know!"

"Technically, yes, it was an accident," Rafe said, his voice as controlled as his expression. "When I ducked, I didn't know that Jack would go over the cliff."

Alana let out a ragged breath.

"But there's something about the fight that you still haven't faced, Alana." Rafe spoke slowly, clearly, leaving no room for evasion or misunderstanding. "When I saw Jack trying to kill you—after that instant, Jack Reeves was a dead man walking. There was no way I'd let him leave the mountain alive."

Alana's eyes closed, but it wasn't in horror

at what Rafe was saying. It was the pain in him that made her flinch.

"You knew that," Rafe said. "Yet you couldn't stand knowing that the man you loved was a murderer. So you forgot. But not well enough. Somewhere, deep inside you, you knew. You didn't trust me enough to marry me."

"That's not true!" said Alana desperately. "You saved my life! You—"

"It's all right, wildflower," Rafe said, cutting across Alana's urgent words. "You don't owe me anything. You gave it all back to me that night."

"But—"

"When you were certain you were going to die, you screamed, but not for mercy or revenge. You called to me, telling me that you loved me. *And you didn't even know I was there.* In those few seconds you wiped out all the bitterness that had been destroying me since I found out you were married."

"Rafael," she whispered.

"You don't owe me anything at all. Certainly not trust."

Alana looked at Rafe wildly.

"But I do trust you!" she cried.

Rafe's mouth turned down in a sad travesty of a smile.

"I don't believe you, wildflower."

Before Alana could say anything more, Rafe turned toward the trail where his big spotted stallion stood patiently.

"We'd better go," Rafe said. "Bob has prob-

ably found your note by now, and mine. He'll
be beside himself with worry."

Rafe began walking toward his horse. After
a few steps, he realized that Alana wasn't following. He turned back and saw that she was
still sitting on a rock very near the edge of the
cliff.

"Alana?"

She sat motionless, watching Rafe, her eyes
dark.

"I'll need your help," she said distinctly.

With a few swift strides Rafe was at Alana's
side. He knelt in front of her and began running his hands from her knees to her feet.

"Did you wrench your ankle again?" he
asked. "Where does it hurt?"

"Everywhere," Alana said softly. "You'll
have to carry me."

Rafe's head snapped up.

He searched Alana's eyes and her expression, afraid to breathe, to hope. Even when she
had given herself to him in the moonlit cabin,
he had not dared to lift her, to hold her helpless above the ground.

And now she was at the edge of the same
cliff Jack had held her over, held her high
above his head, getting set to throw her out
into darkness and death.

Silently Alana held her arms out to Rafe.

He stood and looked down at her for a long
moment. Then he bent and caught her beneath
her arms.

Slowly Rafe lifted Alana to her feet, waiting
for the first sign of fear to tighten her body.

He held her almost level with him, her toes just off the ground.

She smiled and put her hands on his shoulders.

"Higher, Rafael. Lift me higher. Lift me over your head."

"Alana—"

"Lift me," she whispered against his lips. "I know you won't let me fall. I'm safe with you, Rafael. You aren't like Jack. You won't throw my life away. *Lift me.*"

Rafe lifted Alana as high as he could, held her, watched her smile, felt her trust in the complete relaxation of her body suspended between his hands.

Then he let her slide slowly down his body until their lips met in a kiss that left both of them shaken, clinging to each other.

They rode the same way down the mountain, clinging to each other, whispering words of love and need. Rafe's arms were wrapped around Alana and her hands were over his as he guided the big stallion along the trail.

Rafe was the first one to spot the plane bobbing quietly on the third lake.

"Sheriff Mitchell," Rafe said. "Bob must have hit the panic button."

Alana shrank against Rafe and went very still.

For the rest of the ride she was silent, her hands clinging to Rafe's wrists, her mind racing as she tried to figure out ways to protect the man she loved.

No matter what Rafe says, he isn't at fault for Jack's death, Alana thought. Jack brought it on himself. Rafe doesn't deserve to be punished for Jack's selfishness, his murderous rage.

Yet Alana was afraid that was exactly what would happen.

Sheriff Mitchell was sitting on the porch of the lodge, his feet propped against the rail. When he heard the big stallion's hoof strike a rock, Mitch looked up.

"I see you found her," Mitch said, satisfaction in his voice. "Just like I told Bob you would."

Alana spoke before Rafe could.

"My memory is back. Jack's death was an accident, just like Rafe said. It was icy and Jack fell and I passed out from shock and cold."

Mitch looked at Alana oddly. His homely face creased into a frown.

"That's not what Rafe told me," the sheriff muttered. "He said that Jack tried to kill you, they fought, and Jack ended up dead. Is that how you remember it?"

Alana made a helpless sound and looked over her shoulder at Rafe. He kissed her lips.

"I told Mitch everything when we rode back in to bring out Jack's body," Rafe said. "When we came off the mountain, you were gone."

"But—but that's not how the newspapers explained Jack's death," said Alana.

Mitch shrugged.

"Well," the sheriff said, "I didn't figure that justice would be any better served if we went to the hassle of arraigning and then acquitting

Rafe on a clear-cut case of justifiable homicide."

Alana's breath caught. She turned and looked at the sheriff with hope in her eyes.

"And then there would have been reporters hounding you for all the bloody details," the sheriff drawled, "what with Jack being such a famous son of a bitch and all. You didn't need that. You were having a hard enough time staying afloat as it was."

Alana let out a long sigh of relief.

"So I told the reporters the only truth that mattered," the sheriff concluded. "In my opinion, Jack's death was legally an accident."

Mitch paused and looked at Alana, his gray eyes intent. "Unless you remember it some other way and want to change the record?"

"No," Alana said quickly. "Not at all. I just didn't want Rafe to be punished for saving my life."

Mitch nodded. "That's how I had it figured."

He pulled out a pipe from his jacket pocket, struck a match, and held it to the bowl. He sucked hard a few times, then looked at the lake.

"Well, now," Mitch said, changing the subject with finality, "what's the fishing been like?"

Rafe tilted his head and kissed the nape of Alana's neck.

"You're too late, Mitch. I just caught the most beautiful trout on the mountain."

Mitch grinned around a cloud of pungent smoke.

"Keeper size?" he asked dryly.

Rafe laughed and slid off the big stallion. When he was on the ground, he held his arms out to Alana.

She smiled and let him lift her out of the saddle. For a few moments he held her off the ground, enjoying the sensation of her body pressed against the length of his own.

"Definitely keeper size," Rafe said.

Mitch laughed.

"Unless," Rafe whispered too softly for Mitch to hear, "the trout doesn't want the fisherman?"

Alana kissed Rafe gently, brushing her lips across his mouth as her fingers slid deeply into his thick hair, dislodging his Stetson.

The front door of the cabin slammed open.

"Mitch, when in hell are you going to— Alana! Are you okay?"

Mitch laughed. "Bob, are you blind? She's never been better."

Reluctantly Rafe released Alana so that she could reassure her brother.

"I've remembered," she said, turning to face Bob. "And I'm fine. I'm sorry I worried you."

"Hell, sis, it was worth it!" Bob turned to yell over his shoulder. "Stan! Janice! Alana's got her memory back!"

There was a triumphant whoop from the cabin. Janice and Stan ran out onto the porch. Stan looked at Alana, wrapped securely in

Rafe's arms, relaxed and smiling, obviously not afraid.

Then Stan turned and gave Janice a thorough, hungry kiss.

Bob looked startled.

Rafe simply smiled.

"I think I'd better make a complete introduction this time," Rafe said. "Bob, meet Mr. and Mrs. Stan Wilson."

When Stan finally let go of Janice, she smiled.

"Now we can wash out the blond highlights and get rid of the blue contacts," she said to Stan. "If I open my eyes, I feel like I'm kissing a stranger."

Alana watched, speechless, as Stan removed his dark blue contacts, revealing eyes that were light green.

"Blond highlights?" asked Alana weakly.

"Yep," said Janice, tugging on a lock of Stan's fair hair. "I'm used to my man being a sun-streaked brown, not a California blond."

"I don't understand," Alana said.

"I'm afraid you've been caught in a conspiracy," said Janice gently. "But it was a conspiracy of love. When Rafe told me what had happened to you, I told him to give you a few weeks to remember on your own. Then he called again and told me you weren't sleeping, weren't eating, were having nightmares—"

"How did you know?" asked Alana, turning to Rafe.

"I told you, wildflower. You're a lot like me."

"In short," summarized Janice, "you were tearing yourself apart. Rafe thought that if you came back here, you would see him and know that you were safe, that it was all right to remember what had happened. I agreed, so long as you came willingly. If you came back it would mean that you wanted to remember. That you wanted to be whole again."

"Some travel agent," Alana said dryly. Then, "Oh. You're still a practicing psychiatrist, aren't you?"

"One of the best," said Rafe, his arms tightening around Alana. "Damn near every word we said in front of you was vetted by Janice first."

"Not every word," Janice said crisply, looking sideways at Stan. "I nearly choked my husband when I found out about the fight by the lake."

Stan almost smiled. "Yeah, I know. I don't take orders worth a damn. We've argued about Rafe a lot," said Stan, flashing Alana a pale green glance. "I thought she was too gentle on Rafe after he got back from Central America. And then, when she couldn't put him back together, it took two years for me to coax her into marriage."

Janice looked surprised. "Two years! You only asked me out two months before we were married!"

"Yeah. So much for being subtle. I wasted twenty-two months tiptoeing around, thinking that you held it against me that I was the one who'd been wounded. If it wasn't for me, Rafe would have flown out of the jungle with the rest of us."

Rafe started to say something, but Stan cut him off.

"No way, buddy. I'm not finished. I thought you were being too gentle with Alana to get any results. Hell, I didn't even know you had that much gentle in you! I'm still having a hard time believing that you're the same man I worked with in Central America."

Stan shook his head. "Anyway, I wanted to stir up Alana, to make her think. I didn't believe you'd snuffed good old Jack to get Alana. If you'd wanted to do that, you wouldn't have waited almost four years, and you sure as hell wouldn't have been caught after you'd done it. You're too smart for that."

"Thanks . . . I think," said Rafe dryly.

Alana looked from Stan to Janice to Rafe. Finally she gave her brother Bob a long, considering look. He flushed slightly.

"You aren't mad, are you, sis?"

"Mad?" Alana shook her head. "I'm . . . stunned. I can't believe that you knew about the whole conspiracy and kept it a secret. Old in-the-ear-and-out-the-mouth Bob. I'm impressed, baby brother."

"It wasn't easy. I thought I'd blown it more than once," admitted Bob.

"We didn't tell him everything," Rafe said dryly. "Oh, he knew that he wasn't trying to start a dude ranch, but that's about it. He didn't know that I'd worked with Stan and Janice before. He didn't know that Stan was camouflaged as carefully as any lure I'd ever made. And he didn't know that Janice was a practicing psychiatrist."

"Well," Mitch said, "I'd better get down the mountain before the light goes."

"Can you fly back tomorrow?" asked Rafe.

"Sure. Need something in particular?"

"Champagne. A justice of the peace."

Mitch smiled. "Somebody getting married?"

Rafe looked at Alana, a question in his amber eyes.

"Damned right," she said, putting her arms tightly around Rafe. "This time, the trout is landing the fisherman."

19

ALANA STOOD BY THE hearth in the small cabin, wearing only Rafe's warm robe. She let the song fade from her lips, watching Rafe as he played soft notes on the silver harmonica.

He was stretched out on the bed, eyes closed, sensitive fingers wrapped around the harmonica as his lips coaxed beautiful music from it. He wore nothing but firelight, which clung and shifted with each breath he took. His hair gleamed like winter mink, alive with the reflected dance of flames.

Rafe looked up, sensing her watching him.

"Happy, Mrs. Winter?" he asked, holding out his hand.

"Very happy."

Alana took Rafe's hand and curled up beside him, enjoying the hard warmth of his flesh beneath her cheek.

"Even though you haven't remembered everything?" he asked quietly.

She looked at Rafe's eyes, gold in the firelight, and wanted nothing more than to be loved by him.

"I don't care anymore," Alana said, "because I'm not afraid anymore."

Rafe let out a long breath. Tenderly he traced the satin darkness of Alana's eyebrow with his fingertip.

"Good," he said softly. "I don't think you'll ever remember coming down the mountain. You were bruised, bloody, out of your mind with cold and shock."

His eyes closed, as though he was afraid she would see too much looking into them.

"Frankly," Rafe said in a low voice, "I'd forget it if I could. I loved you so much and I thought you were dying, that I'd come too late."

" 'Come too late,' " Alana repeated. "You say that as though you knew I needed you."

"I did."

"How?" whispered Alana. "Why did you come to the highest lake when I was there with Jack?"

"I can't explain it. I just . . . knew."

Rafe looked at the harmonica for a moment before he carefully set it aside.

"The night before I rode up Broken Mountain," he said, "I kept thinking I heard you calling me again and again. But that was impossible. I was alone at the ranch. Nothing but the wind. Yet by morning, I was wild, half crazy, certain that *you needed me*."

Rafe blew out a long breath. "I had no choice but to ride up the mountain and find you, Alana. It was irrational, crazy, but I had to do it."

"You weren't crazy," said Alana, trembling. "When Jack tied me and left me by the lake, I called for you all night long. I couldn't help myself."

Rafe's breath came in sharply. He rolled over and faced Alana, touching her as though she were a dream and he was afraid of awakening.

"If only I hadn't fought against it so hard," he said in a low voice. "I should have come to you sooner."

"It's a miracle that you came at all. You hated me."

"No," he said, kissing Alana's eyebrow, her eyelid, the corner of her mouth. "I never hated you. I wanted to, but I couldn't. We were tied too deeply to each other, no matter how far apart we were."

"Yes," she whispered, returning the tender kisses.

"That's why I couldn't ride away from you after we made love," Rafe said, "even though I thought you didn't trust me. Every time the wind blew down the canyon, I heard you calling me. I had to come back to you."

Rafe's fingertip traced Alana's lips. "I love you more than you know, more than I have words to say."

With slow, caressing movements, Rafe unwrapped the robe until Alana wore only firelight and the fine gold chain he had given to her. The elegant symbol of infinity gleamed in the hollow of her throat, speaking silently of love that knew no boundaries.

He gathered Alana close to his body, kissing her gently at first, then with a passion that was both restrained and deeply wild. She gave herself to the kiss, to him, melting in his hands, wanting him, loving him. He listened to the soft sounds that came from her, and he smiled.

"Yes," Rafe whispered, "sing of your love for me, a lifetime of love. And after that . . ."

His lips touched the golden symbol at Alana's throat, and he knew there would always be a song of love that knew no bounds.

Beautiful Dreamer

For Heather,
daughter, friend, fan

Prologue

❦

THE BLUE PICKUP truck was dirty, scratched by brush, and looked too battered to pull the faded single-horse trailer behind it. The truck's tires showed the scars of passage through four-wheel-drive country.

Like the man at the wheel, there was a lot more underneath than the rough outer surface revealed. Beneath the dust and marks of hard use, the tread on the tires was thick. The pickup's engine was powerful and well tuned. The mare riding patiently inside the trailer was hot-blooded and superbly trained. A single one of her colts would have been worth more than a new truck and trailer combined.

The truck went past a sun-faded road sign that said WELCOME TO RIVERDALE: POPULATION 47.

There was neither river nor dale to greet the visitor, but there was no law against dreams.

He parked the truck in front of a country store, got out, and stretched to his full height, casting a long, wide-shouldered shadow over the afternoon land. The

1

store was closed. A hand-lettered placard told anyone who cared that the door opened when and if the proprietor felt like it, and if it was an emergency, you should try around at the back. Cards stuck on the outside of the dirt-streaked front window asked for workers or work, tried to buy or sell ranch equipment, and generally served as an informal newspaper.

One of the cards said simply: *Rio, if you read this, head for Nevada. A woman on a ranch called Valley of the Sun needs you.*

He pulled off the card and tossed it into the glove compartment of his pickup. There were other papers in there, sheets and cards and scraps he had gathered all over the West in the past month. The notes said essentially the same thing.

Go to the Valley of the Sun.

He shut the compartment with a snap and went around to the horse trailer. "What do you think, Dusk? You game for a few more miles?"

The elegant mare snuffled through the trailer window and lipped lazily at his open collar. He rubbed her soft muzzle, stretched again, and waited.

When the wind breathed over the high plains, he listened for the sound of his name. It came as it always did, a long sigh that called, *Brother-to-the-wind.*

And he answered as he always had. *I'm here.*

The wind turned and swirled around him, pressing at his back, pushing him south.

"You sure, brother?"

The wind pressed harder.

He got back into the truck and headed south.

One

EVEN IN LATE OCTOBER, drought ruled the Nevada ranch known as the Valley of the Sun. Thirst was a dusty shadow clinging to all life. The wind was always restless, always whispering of distance and the secrets of an empty land.

To the east of the ranch, a range of mountains known as the Sierras Perdidas rose dark and silent above the dry landscape. The mountains themselves were lush with the gifts of water—valleys thick with grass, high slopes rippling with forests, and a few sheltered snow-fields glittering like diamonds far above the sunbaked afternoon.

Hope Gardener was too far away to see the snow-fields or the water-rich valleys or the forests, but she knew they were there. They were always there, a dream to tantalize the ranchers who lived with the dry reality of the high desert that lapped around the mountains like a sagebrush sea around green islands. Even so, Hope wouldn't have traded a single one of the tawny, thirsty, harsh sections of her ranch for all the Sierras Perdidas' easy beauty.

But she wouldn't have minded some of the Perdidas' tumbling wealth of water.

She wasn't greedy. She wasn't asking for a deep river that ran year-round, or even a stream that ran upside down, concealing its water a few feet beneath a dry riverbed. She wasn't asking for a lake shivering with wind and trout.

A pond, though . . .

Yes, just a pond. Sweet water that could ease her cattle's endless thirst. Water to soothe and nourish the tender roots of alfalfa and oat hay. Just one source of water that would stay wet no matter how dry and hard the rest of the Valley of the Sun became.

"Why not ask for hot and cold running money while you're at it?" she asked herself sardonically. "If you're going to dream, dream big."

Her generous mouth turned down in a smile at her own expense. She came from a family of dreamers. Not one of them had managed to be lucky or good enough to make the dreams real.

She had vowed to be different. She was going to be the Gardener who would make the Valley of the Sun profitable again. Or at least possible to live on without going bankrupt.

"Then I'd better get to work, hadn't I?" she asked her reflection in the dusty, cracked, sunstruck windshield.

Nothing answered her but the rumble of the diesel

engine and the wind keening through the open window of the ancient truck. She had stopped on top of a rise in the rough, one-lane dirt road to give the engine—and herself—a breather. The water truck dated from a time before power steering, automatic shift, and power brakes. Despite the strength of her deceptively elegant body, the truck gave her as much of a workout as she gave it. First gear was so cranky that she often parked on a slope and rolled downhill until she could coax the engine into second gear.

"C'mon, Behemoth. It's just you and me and my beautiful, thirsty cattle. Don't let me down."

As soon as she slipped the hand brake, the empty truck began to roll. She gathered speed in neutral until she had no choice but to engage the clutch or risk losing control of the truck on the steep slope. She double-clutched, shifted, muttered unhappily, and double-clutched again. This time the ancient water truck's gears grumbled and gnawed into place.

She patted the dusty instrument panel and settled in to wrestle the truck to the water tank. Road noises echoed around inside the truck's sun-faded cab. The steering wheel bucked hard in her hands. Instantly she braced her body and muscled the rented army-surplus truck back out of the ruts that drew tires like a magnet drawing iron dust. Muscles in her arms and her shoulders knotted in protest. She ignored the burning aches just as she ignored the exhaustion that had made her lose attention long enough to get trapped in the ruts.

"Just one more load," she promised herself. "Then you can kick back and watch Beauty and Baby drink."

At least, just one more load of water for today. To-morrow was another day, another time of Nevada's seamless sunshine baking the dry land, another string of hours when only dust devils moved over the empty land. *And this battered truck,* she reminded herself silently. *Don't forget poor Behemoth, lurching over this lousy road like a dinosaur on the way to extinction.*

Like the Valley of the Sun itself, dying.

Hope set her teeth and forced herself to pay attention to the potholed road rather than to her thoughts circling like vultures around the certainty of the death of her ranch and her dreams. She reminded herself that tomorrow could bring many things. Just one of them would be enough to keep her dream alive.

One of the old wells could begin producing water again, enough water to see a core of her breeding stock through this endless drought.

The price of beef could rise, allowing her to sell the cattle she couldn't water at break-even prices.

The bank could decide that the last hydrologist's report on Silver Rock Basin indicated a good probability of water and lend her enough money to go after it.

A hydrologist who wasn't a con artist might answer her ad and find the artesian river she believed flowed deep beneath her ranch.

It could even rain.

Hope leaned forward to peer out the dusty windshield at the Perdidas. A few wisps of water vapor clung to their rocky, rakish peaks. Not enough clouds. Not nearly enough. Rain might fall in the mountain high country in a day or two or three, but not in the high desert of her ranch, where the land cracked and bled sand and the cattle gathered around dry wells to bawl their thirst.

For an instant her reflection stared grimly back at her from the dirty glass. The western hat concealed everything about her face but the lines of worry and weariness thinning her otherwise full mouth. Her hazel eyes were just a flash of light within the dark shadow of the hat brim. Her loosely curling, bittersweet-chocolate hair was swept up and hidden from the sun beneath the battered crown of her hat. A few tendrils had escaped to lie along her neck, held there by the moisture that heat and the effort of controlling Behemoth had drawn from her fine-grained skin.

"Oh, boy, if your agent could only see you now," Hope muttered.

She made a face at the reflection of herself that faded even as her eyes focused on it, like a mirage shimmering above the empty desert.

"It's a good thing your fortune was in your legs, not in a pretty little-girl face. Because you aren't a little girl anymore. What will it be next birthday—twenty-six? And what do you want for your birthday, big girl? A well, you say? A nice, deep, clean, sweet, endless well?"

Hope's laughter was musical and humorous and sad. Almost twenty-six years ago her father had brought in a well that was nice and deep and clean and sweet. He had named it, and his just-born daughter, Hope. But the well hadn't been deep enough. Unless a miracle occurred, it would run dry by her twenty-sixth birthday.

The empty water truck rattled and shook down the steep grade to the Turner ranch boundary. More than miles separated the two ranches. One ranch had water. The other did not.

It was as simple and final as that.

No fences separated the two ranches. It wasn't necessary. No Turner cattle would wander miles away from water onto dry Gardener land. As for Gardener cattle, there had never been enough to wander anywhere. There had been plans, though, and dreams. Her grandfather's. Her father's. Her own.

And there had been the land, a land Hope loved as she had never loved anything else. Other girls had dreamed of boyfriends and babies, honeymoons and happily-ever-afters. Hope hadn't.

Any desire she might have had to share her girlfriends' dreams had died on her eighteenth birthday. What little trust in men and love she'd had after that night had been ground to nothing as she saw her own mother and Julie, her beautiful older sister, go through hell in the name of love.

Watching them had taught Hope to pour her faith and dreams and hungers into the land. Its tawny power called out to her senses as no man ever had.

The land endured and love did not.

Deep inside herself, she had always known that she was a woman born for enduring things. Unlike her mother, Hope knew she wouldn't be able to walk away from a man she loved. Unlike her sister, Hope couldn't go from man to man, leaving behind pieces of herself until nothing remained but a hollow smile.

A jerk from the steering wheel yanked Hope out of the unhappy past into the demanding present. She wrenched the steering wheel hard, holding the lumbering Behemoth to the rutted road.

The truck rounded a shoulder of the rugged hills and dropped down into a long, narrow valley. At the lower end of the valley, one of Turner's windmills rose thinly above the land. There was a startling flash of green around the machinery, sagebrush and willows and grass gone wild, a silent shout of vegetation signaling the presence of water.

The patch of lush green was just under ten acres. In the center of the ragged emerald saucer sat a circular metal tank that was filled to overflowing by the windmill's tireless turning. The windmill's metal straw went more than six hundred feet into the earth, sipping up water that was clean and cold and pure.

Cattle lay in the lacy shade of huge clumps of sagebrush and desert shrubs, chewing quietly, waiting for the sun to descend. The Herefords' russet hides made a rich contrast to the green oasis.

Despite Hope's weariness, she shouldered open the stubborn cab door and jumped lithely to the ground. A quick look beneath Behemoth's ungainly barrel assured her that the lower valve was closed tight. After a brief struggle with balky canvas coils, she connected the intake hose. There was another struggle to connect the hose to her patchwork pump.

The portable generator that ran the pump was so old that it had to be started with a hand crank. She had discovered the pump rusting in the barn almost three months ago. That was when she had the idea of hauling Turner water to Gardener cattle in the hope of surviving until the rainy season began.

At first it had been a trip every three or four days through the searing August sun to supplement her ranch's overworked wells. But by October the rains still hadn't come, not even to the high country of the Sierras Perdidas. She'd made the trip to Turner's well every two days, then every day. Twice a day. Four times a day. Dawn to dusk and then even longer as the drought continued and the water table fell more and more, slowly going beyond the reach of her ranch wells.

When the wind alone couldn't draw enough water from the depths of the land, she had connected portable generators to three of her windmills. Now, on the last day of October, her generators worked around-the-clock to bring up less and less water. And Hope— Hope worked until she couldn't lift her arms to drag Behemoth around one more bumpy curve. Only then did she sleep, a sleep haunted by the bawling of thirsty cattle.

She pulled off her leather work gloves, stuck them into the hip pocket of her jeans, and picked up the battered tin bucket that leaned against the pump. Like her cattle, Behemoth's radiator had a bottomless thirst.

A gust of unseasonably hot wind swelled through the narrow valley, making the windmill's arms turn with lazy grace.

As Hope reached to dip the pail into the huge circular trough, she hesitated, caught by the beauty of water welling over the lip of the metal pond. The fluid silver veil fell musically to the ground, creating a rich, dark ribbon of earth that cattle had churned into ankle-deep mud.

The mud didn't bother her. It made her envious. She would have moved heaven and earth to see mud like that around her own wells. Her stock tanks didn't overflow slowly, turning baked ground into a wealth of earth oozing with promise. Her own wells couldn't even keep up with the searching, dusty muzzles of her cattle.

Balancing on the plank walkway that she had made over the slick mud, she braced herself against the tank. Overflowing water was a cool shock against her thighs and a dark stain spread down her jeans. She set down the dry bucket, put her hat inside, and thrust her arms elbow-deep into the sweet water. She brought her cupped hands to her face in a silver shower of moisture and laughter that was as musical as the sound of water overflowing.

Deep within one of the nearby thickets, a horse moved restively at the sudden sound of laughter. The rider bent his dark head next to the horse's and murmured softly. The mare quieted, returning to her three-legged doze.

With the silence of a shadow, the man flowed out of the saddle. He had heard the truck's labored approach and had watched Hope's efforts to set up the makeshift hose that would fill the empty truck. He had lifted the reins to guide his horse out of the concealing brush to offer help, but something about her had stopped him.

Though obviously tired, she moved with the grace

of a wild thing as she filled the big truck's steaming radiator and coped with the ancient equipment. Slender, determined, she used an instinctive knowledge of leverage when her own strength wasn't enough to handle the awkward machinery. A hip braced here, a shoulder thrust there, a quick twist of her hands, and she coaxed the ragged canvas hose into place.

And then her laughter came, as bright and unexpected as water in a desert.

Now her faded jeans and shirt clung wetly to her, revealing a body as surprisingly lush as the dark tumble of her hair burning beneath the sun. She was long-legged, elegantly curved, and her breasts were completely outlined by the wet blouse.

He couldn't help responding to the picture she made as she stood arched against the sky, totally lost in her sensual response to the sparkling water pouring from her outstretched hands. He wondered if she would come to a man like that, nothing held back, nothing calculated, a quicksilver woman laughing and shimmering in his arms.

A slight smile softened the otherwise unyielding lines of his face. No wonder John Turner had kept trying to lure Hope into his bed by proposing marriage. If rumor was true, she kept turning him down, had been turning the rancher down since she came back to the ranch two years ago.

That had made him curious enough to ride his mare out to the well on a day that was hot enough to cure leather. He'd wanted to see a woman who cared more for a doomed ranch than she did for any man, even a rich white-eyes.

Any other woman would have given in to the inevitability of sinking water tables and drought-ridden land. Any other woman would have shaken off the Valley of the Sun's brutal demands like a dog coming out of water and would have been happy to curl up at Turner's big feet.

But not this woman. She was out here alone, a battered tin bucket in one hand and her dreams in the other.

Hope put on her hat, filled the bucket, primed the pump, pulled on her gloves with a few practiced motions, and began wrestling with the crank that was supposed to start the generator. The iron handle was long and had been in the direct sunlight. Even through leather gloves, the rough iron felt warm.

Like Behemoth, the machine was stubborn. Hope had to use both hands and a lot of determination just to make the crank turn. To make it turn fast enough to start the generator took every bit of strength she had.

With a grimace she forced her tired arms to drag the crank around quickly. The generator sputtered and almost caught. Encouraged, she worked harder, thinking of her beautiful black breeding cattle waiting by their hot, dry trough. Far too hot for October, nearly November. Far too dry.

If it wasn't for this wretched generator, she would have been forced to sell off the last of her range cattle and the first of her Angus. The thought gave strength to her aching arms. The generator coughed and shivered, but refused to catch.

"Let me help."

The quiet male voice startled Hope. She let go of the crank and whirled around.

Only the man's quickness saved her from getting a painful rap as the crank's long iron handle leaped upward, completing the circuit she had begun. He lifted her out of danger with one arm and with the other hand snagged the crank handle.

Automatically Hope balanced herself by putting her hands on his shoulders. Even as she wondered who he was, her senses registered the bunched strength of his arms and the long, resilient muscles of his torso and legs.

The man moved and she found herself safely on her feet again as suddenly as she had been snatched off them.

"I—thanks," she managed.

He nodded but didn't look away from the generator.

Hope watched while he worked the ancient machine with a power and coordination that fascinated her. He was well over six feet tall, long-limbed, wide-shouldered. The hair that showed beneath his battered Stetson was thick and straight, as blue-black as a raven flying through the desert sky. His clothes were dusty from riding, but otherwise clean. A shadow of satin-black hair showed in the open front of his faded blue work shirt. His skin was dark, almost mahogany. His boots were like his leather belt—supple, worn, of the highest quality. The buckle closing his belt was smooth silver with an intricate inlay of turquoise, coral, and mother-of-pearl.

She recognized the Zuni workmanship and the cryptic symbols telling of a shaman calling down rain upon the thirsty land. Gradually she realized that the buckle was not an ornament for this man. Like his hair and his skin, the symbols were part of his heritage.

The generator surged into life, sucking water from the circular trough. The hose leading to the truck began to swell. She watched as the man studied the generator, made an adjustment in the hose coupling, and listened with a cocked head to the engine's racket. In some ways he reminded her of her stallion, Storm Walker. There was a physical assurance about him that spoke of horizons explored, tests passed, and a primal awareness of his life in relation to the land around him.

The hose became as tight as a sausage. Water shot out in a fine spray from the coupling he had adjusted. There was less water wasted than usual, because he had tightened the coupling more securely than Hope ever had been able to.

"Sorry," she said, laughing and ducking as mist beaded her face. "I should have warned you about the connection."

He could have gotten away from the spray. Instead, he swept off his hat, unbuttoned his shirt, and let the cool water bathe him as he worked over the coupling.

She watched, fascinated in ways she didn't understand. Unlike most cowboys, the stranger didn't have a line of chalk-white skin beneath the band of his hat. Nor was his chest white beneath the open shirt. Despite the desert's harsh sun, it was obvious that he spent at least part of his time hatless and bare to the waist. It was also obvious that he was a man fully alive to all of his senses. His naked appreciation of the water struck a primitive chord within her.

His hands both coaxed and coerced the metal threads of the coupling into a tighter mating. As he worked, water drops beaded brightly over the tanned skin and smoothly coiling muscles of his arms and back. Slowly the spray diminished to little more than a sheen of moisture trickling from the corroded brass and sun-bleached canvas.

He shook back a thick wedge of hair from his forehead and replaced his hat. "Sometimes the best part of life is an accident that goes right." His voice was deep, calm, subtly gentled by a southwestern drawl.

With a brief touch he led her away from the noisy generator into the lacy shade of a clump of brush. Using quick glances, he checked the fat hose and the generator and the well.

"You can't be a cowboy," Hope said in a low voice, thinking aloud as she watched him.

He looked at her suddenly. She saw that his eyes were blue-black, clear, almost shocking in their intensity. They were also as aloof and private as a winter sky.

"Most cowboys have white foreheads and chests," she explained, feeling more than a little foolish.

His smile took her by surprise. At first glance she had simply thought of him as another range rider— taller than most, yes, and stronger, but still just one more cowhand. Then he had opened himself to the diamond spray of water and smiled, and his words had revealed the humor and intelligence beneath his tanned face.

She took off her work glove and held out her right hand. "Hope Gardener."

He held out his hand and said simply, "Rio."

Two

RIO'S BIG HAND enveloped Hope's. She had a distinct sensation of warmth and strength before his hand released hers. She watched him pull on his worn leather work glove again. Like his voice, his eyes, and his coordination, his hand was unexpected. Long fingers tapered to well-kept nails, hard strength that was careful of her softer flesh. It was the hand of a musician or a surgeon.

But there were scars across his knuckles, and a quickness that could either comfort or threaten.

The realization made uneasiness streak through her. She remembered another man with scarred knuckles. John Turner didn't have any comfort in him at all. Yet Rio did. She was certain of it. There was both gentleness and warmth in his smile.

More important at the moment, there was reassurance in his way of being close to her without crowding her sexually. Turner had been good at that kind of intimidation. He still was.

19

Sighing unconsciously, she relaxed with Rio as she had relaxed with few men since her eighteenth birthday.

"Rio," she murmured.

Her hazel eyes shifted focus, turning inward. She had heard that name before. Just Rio. No first or last or middle name. Spanish for "river." She tried to remember if it was Mason who had mentioned Rio.

"I keep thinking I've heard that name before," she said.

"Maps," he offered laconically, his smile lurking just on the point of release. "Rio Bravo. Rio Colorado. Rio—"

"Verde and Amarillo and Grande," she finished, her voice as dry as his. But unlike him, she smiled openly even though she sensed that he wasn't going to say any more about himself. "And a whole lot of other *rios* I've never even heard of, I'd bet."

"You'd win," he agreed. "The Indians were here first, but the Spanish knew how to write. And since white men couldn't wrap their tongues around Indian words . . ." Rio shrugged, not finishing his sentence. The maps spoke for themselves: Spanish rather than Indian names.

Without bothering to button his shirt, he swiftly tucked it into his jeans. "Hear you're looking for water."

She barely listened to his words. His quickness fascinated her, as did his grace. She decided that he was more like a mountain cat than a stallion. Or maybe he was some of both, a legend born out of its time, trapped in a century that had neither appreciation of nor use for myth. Nor, she admitted silently, for Indians themselves.

It must have been hell for a man of Rio's intelligence to suffer the casual abuse of bigots.

Then the meaning of Rio's near-question penetrated her wandering thoughts. "Er, yes. I ran several ads for a hydrologist."

" 'Willing to take risks,' " he quoted softly. "Like you. You're a gambler." His voice was dark and certain. "You're a dreamer, too. And I'm a man who finds water."

Hope's smile slipped. *Gambler. Dreamer.* Obviously he had read her ad and thought little of her chances of finding water. Grimly she waited for the rest of his act. She had heard it all before, from other con artists. The words varied, but the meaning didn't: she had a glowing, water-filled future if she would just trust him with her small savings.

Patiently, gathering her dream around her like armor, Hope braced herself for the disappointment of having this intriguing stranger turn into another con man who had come to the Valley of the Sun to see how many dollars he could wring from her hopes.

Even if he wasn't a con artist, she told herself bitterly, what made a drifting cowboy think that he could find water where certified hydrologists had failed? And what vast store of experience gave him the right to make fun of her and her attempts to save her ranch?

Because that was what he was doing. He was offering to work for her and at the same time he was saying that it was useless.

Gambler.

Dreamer.

"No." Hope's voice was as cool and impersonal as water flowing over the steel lip of the tank. "I'm neither a gambler nor a fool. I believe there is a fighting chance of finding artesian water beneath the Valley of the Sun. That's all I ask. A fighting chance."

Rio's dark eyes narrowed as he measured the change in her. Now he could believe that this slender, lonely young woman had refused John Turner and every other prowling male in the West's Basin and Range country. The Hope who was speaking now was someone who counted no unhatched chicks, asked no favors, and took no prisoners. She knew what she wanted.

And what she wanted was the land.

He understood that. The land was what he had always wanted, the only thing that he had taken from life: the West, all of it, rich and wild.

And he was the wind moving freely over the face of that land.

"Dreamer doesn't mean fool," he said quietly.

Though she said nothing, Hope's mouth flattened even more. She had watched her sister's dreams, and her mother's. Maybe all dreamers weren't fools, but the dreamers she knew had died too soon, too disillusioned, crying for men who never loved them in return.

Hope had learned that she couldn't control other people's dreams, but she could control her own. She could ask for only what was possible.

Artesian water, not a dream of love.

Water would give back to her the one enduring thing

in her life—the Valley of the Sun. The land had been here long before drought and men who didn't love enough. The land would be here long after all men were less than dust lifting on a dry wind.

"Ask Mason," Rio said. "Then decide."

He turned and walked back into the sagebrush clump. When he emerged a moment later, he was riding a mouse-gray mare that moved as though she had been born in the wild and only recently tamed. Yet the horse was no more an average slab-sided mustang than Rio was an average tongue-tied cowhand. The mare might have been raised wild, but Arab blood ran hot in her veins and intelligence glowed in her wide dark eyes.

"She's perfect," Hope said almost reverently, thinking of Storm Walker and the incredible foals that might come of such a mating. "If you ever want to breed her, bring her to—"

"Storm Walker," Rio interrupted. "I know."

He reined the mare around Hope, riding as he had walked, with economy and grace and power. A tiny motion of his left hand lifted the mare into a long lope. He merged his body with the animal's supple movements as though he was part of her.

"Yes. Storm Walker," Hope said finally.

She was talking to herself. Only a faint hint of dust in the air remained, proof that for a time she hadn't been alone. There was no sound but that of water falling into the rapidly filling barrel of the truck. The windmill turned slowly, bringing up more water. Despite that, the level in the tank kept dropping, liquid wealth transferred into Behemoth's steel belly, Turner water on its way to thirsty Gardener cattle.

The thought of using someone else's water didn't make Hope feel like a charity case. She would have done the same for any neighbor if she had been the one with abundant water and her neighbor's animals were bawling with thirst. John Turner had more than enough water for both ranches.

At one time her father had seen Turner's interest in her as the salvation of the Valley of the Sun. A marriage would mean money and water piped in from the Turner ranch. Her father had been wrong. Turner had wanted only Hope's body, not a woman to marry.

Then he had tried to take by force what she hadn't wanted to give.

From old habit her mind shied away from the terrifying night of her eighteenth birthday. Briskly she turned off the generator, uncoupled the hose, stuffed it into place on the truck's rack, fastened the stubborn clamps down, and swung into the cab. If she hurried, she might catch Mason before he had to drive out to the wells and refuel the generators. Mason would know about Rio. Mason knew about everyone who had ever left a mark in the West.

And despite her doubts about his honesty, Hope was certain that Rio had.

The thought of finding out more about him made her impatient with the road, the heavy truck, and her own feminine muscles. Skill, technique, and finesse could only accomplish so much. If she had Rio's easy strength, she would have gone twice as fast and not worried about losing control of the truck on the tight corners and deep ruts.

By the time Hope drove into the ranch yard and turned off the overworked engine, she was hot and tired all over again. Even in the late afternoon the sun hadn't lost any of its intensity. It was hot for the very end of October. Much too hot. Sweat had long since replaced cool well water on her skin.

She spotted Mason just as he climbed into the pickup truck that was the ranch's only other transportation.

"Mason!" she called.

As he turned and faced her, she leaped down out of the water truck's high cab. Even across the dusty yard she could see a smile send creases through his leathery face as he watched her. Beneath his worn Stetson, his collar-length, fine silvery hair stirred in the wind.

"You're back early," he said. "I left you some lemonade."

"How about ice?"

Even as she asked the question, she tried not to smile. She knew that the old man loved ice, and he hated refilling ice trays the way a cat hates mud. When she was gone all day, she usually returned to an empty freezer, a jumble of ice trays in the sink, and an embarrassed smile on Mason's lined face.

He tried to look offended and failed entirely. He chuckled. "You know me too good, gal."

"After all these years, I should hope so."

Slipping her arm through his, she led him into the relative coolness of the kitchen. Two years ago, when she had come back to the ranch to live full-time, she had taken some of the money she earned modeling hosiery and transformed the worn kitchen into a bright center of ranch life.

In January and February, when the long winds blew from the north, she and Mason played cribbage on the old oak table. As they played, she coaxed stories out of him, the lives of his father and uncles, grandfathers and great-uncles and great-grandfathers, the women they married, the children who died young and the ones who survived, the people who built and the people who destroyed.

The living history was shared with her in the gravelly, wry words of a man almost three times her age, a man whose ancestors had known the best and the worst the West could deliver. It was her own history, too, for Mason's family had worked alongside her mother's family in the Valley of the Sun for more than a hundred years.

Yet the ranch's beauty and history had never touched Hope's mother. She had hated the Valley of the Sun, had cursed its tawny heights and shadowed canyons with a depth of bitterness that had once terrified her younger daughter.

"Have you ever heard of a man called Rio?" Hope asked quickly. She didn't want to remember her mother, a woman who had loved and hated as deeply as anyone Hope had ever known.

"Big man, easy-moving, kind of an Indian look to him?"

"Ummm," she agreed. "With a smile that makes you believe in life everlasting."

Mason shot her a sideways glance. "Musta took a liking to you. Rio don't smile much."

"He was probably laughing at me," she said, remembering Rio's comments about dreamers and gamblers.

"Doubt it."

"He don't laugh much?" she suggested, imitating Mason's ungrammatical drawl.

"Good thing you got them pigtails cut, or I'd be pulling 'em sure as hell." Mason's smile faded as he reversed an old wooden kitchen chair and braced his arms across the back of it. "Rio don't laugh at nobody but fools. You may be stubborn as flint, but you ain't no fool."

She squeezed the old man's shoulder affectionately. Beneath her fingers he felt like a handful of rawhide braid. Age hadn't stooped him, or even slowed him very much. Except for the occasional arthritis in his hands, Mason was still nearly six feet of "hard times and bad water," as her father had once described his foreman, mentor, and best friend.

The refrigerator made a cool, companionable sound as she opened and shut it. She carried her glass of lemonade—no ice—to the table and sat down.

"What does Rio do?" she asked.

"Breaks horses."

Hope tried to match Mason's laconic description to the complex reality of the man called Rio. "Is that all?"

"If you're Rio, it's a good plenty. He's part horse hisself. Swear to it. Ride anything that grows hair. Gentle about it, too." Mason stretched his arms over his head with a force that made ligaments and joints shift and pop quietly. "Never knew him to bloody a horse, and he's rode more than one that had it coming."

Hope took a sip of the fresh, tart drink and sighed. "He said he was a man who found water. He said to ask you and then decide."

Though Hope wasn't looking, she sensed Mason's sudden and complete attention. Faded green eyes fastened on her with an intensity that somehow reminded her of Rio.

"He liked something about you," Mason said flatly. Then, seeing her tighten, he added, "Nope, not like that. Oh, you're plenty of woman and he's sure enough a hell of a man, but that won't saddle no broncs for Rio. If he said he'd look for water, it's because you did something he liked."

"He was at Turner's well. All I did was wrestle with that mulish generator."

Mason looked at Hope. The coltish girl of his memories had grown into a woman as beautiful as her mother had been. But unlike her mother, Hope didn't care about her own beauty. Nor did she hate the ranch. She was part of it, as deeply rooted in the land as the plants that tapped hidden water far below the desert floor.

Like her older sister, Hope had tousled dark hair and a generous smile that set men to dreaming. But Hope didn't see it, nor the men she drew. All she saw was the land, and she was willing to work for what she saw. Her sister hadn't been. Julie had been as pretty as a butterfly—and as useless when there was work to be done. As for Hope's mother, she simply hated the land too much to work it well.

"Rio liked your grit," Mason said, nodding to himself. "That's the only thing he respects. Grit."

"Well, I've plenty of that," she said, deliberately misunderstanding as she wiped her dusty face with the back of her equally dusty arm. "Can he do it?"

Mason's eyes narrowed and looked inward. "Honey, if there's water anywhere on the ranch, Rio will find it."

"How?"

The old man shrugged. "I heard it said he's a water witcher, a dowser, grandson of a Zuni shaman. I heard he was a soldier and a mapmaker. I heard he was raised in a Houston skyscraper and on an Indian reservation beyond the Perdidas. I heard he was educated east of the Rockies and knows the West better than any man alive."

"How much of that do you believe?" Hope asked curiously.

Mason lifted his battered, sweat-stained Stetson and settled it more firmly on his head. "All of it. And I'll tell you this," he added, pinning her with a shrewd green glance. "Rio's smart and quiet and faster than any rattler God ever made. He's part Indian and all man. He don't push worth a damn, and he's pure hell in a fight. I once saw him take apart three yahoos in less time than I could pour a cup of coffee."

"You make him sound—brutal."

Mason was eyeing Hope's lemonade when he sorted out what she hadn't quite said.

"Like Turner?" he asked bluntly.

She let out a breath. "Yes."

"Not a chance. Turner's bone-deep mean. He likes hurting people."

With difficulty Hope concealed a shudder. She knew that part of Turner's personality all too well.

"Rio's easygoing when easy gets it done, and no meaner than he has to be the rest of the time." Mason rubbed his aching knuckles and looked at her. "Honey, two of those three men Rio whipped had knives. There was a lot of loose talk about how they was going to skin out the breed that thought he was good enough to drink with white folks. Whatever those men got, they had coming, and then some."

She turned her head quickly, catching the hard look on Mason's face. "You really like Rio, don't you?"

"If God had seen fit to give Hazel and me kids," Mason said evenly, "I'd have died proud to sire a son like Rio."

For a minute Hope couldn't find any words to say. She had never heard Mason talk about anyone as he did Rio, not even the near-mythical figures out of his family's past.

"Where did you meet Rio?" she asked finally.

Mason hesitated. He lifted his hat again, settled it with a jerk, and said, "It's Hazel's story, really, but she wouldn't mind me telling you. Her sister's kids was in trouble, never mind what kind. Rio sorted it out."

Hope thought quickly, remembering what she knew about Mason's dead wife. Hazel's sister had married a half-Indian drifter. The man had vanished after a few years, leaving four children behind. Part-Indian children. It shouldn't have mattered—but there were still a lot of places where it did.

And Rio had "taken apart" three men who hated Indians.

"I see," Hope murmured. Then, quietly, "I hope those men learned a lesson."

"Doubt it. Can't teach a snake to ice-skate. But you can set your watch by this," he added with grim satisfaction. "Them three don't beat up on kids no more."

Hope decided that she knew all she needed to about the man called Rio: Mason respected him. Whether or not Rio could find water, at least he wasn't a vulture hoping to pick at the bones of her dreams.

"Thanks." She stood up suddenly and kissed his gray-stubbled cheek.

"You gonna do it?" he asked.

"Yes." She started for the phone, then stopped in dismay. "I don't know how to get hold of him."

"Don't worry." Mason smiled. "You turn around, he'll be there."

"But how will he know I want to hire him?"

"Same way the wind knows to blow."

Hope made an impatient sound.

Mason looked up, green eyes calm and certain. "He's Rio. He'll know."

Three

HOPE PUT HER hands on her hips and made an exasperated sound. " 'He's Rio. He'll know,' " she repeated mockingly. "Big help, Mason."

Mason just looked at her with wise green eyes.

"If you had pigtails," she muttered, "I'd pull them right off your stubborn head. I don't have time to wait for Rio to mysteriously *know* I want to hire him. I need water and I need it now!"

"You always were a headlong sort of gal," Mason agreed, smiling to himself. "I might be able to find Rio, for a price."

"What price?" Then she groaned, thinking of the list of chores that had to be done, chores that they both disliked doing.

"Ice cubes for a week," he said.

"Done." She smiled wickedly. "You're slipping, Mason. I always do the ice cubes."

"Yeah, but now I won't feel bad about it."

She laughed and shook her head, making light burn darkly through her loose curls. "How will you find Rio?"

"Easy. He's breaking horses for Turner."

"Oh."

Hope bit back a curse. She really didn't want to call the Turner ranch. Since she had come back to the Valley of the Sun to live, John Turner had pursued her relentlessly. The more often she refused him, the more determined he was to have her.

Grimly she nerved herself up for the call she had to make. Though she had outgrown her terror of him, she still despised him for his casual brutality. Just being polite to him was an effort that left her jaw aching. She hid her feelings because she knew that they would only make him more insistent. His arrogance had to be experienced to be believed.

"Has that son of— Has he been bothering you again?" Mason asked, his voice rough.

She shrugged. "Ever since his aunt's bank gave me a second mortgage on the Valley of the Sun, John seems to think he owns me."

"I may be near seventy, but so help me God, I'll pistol-whip that son of a bitch if he ever touches you again."

Hope put her hand on Mason's arm, both restraining and reassuring him. Even while her father was still alive, Mason had protected her as though she was his own daughter. In many ways he was an old-fashioned western man. He believed that if a woman said *no,* she meant it, and that was the end of the matter.

It was a belief John Turner didn't share. Like a spoiled child, he was obsessed by whatever he couldn't have. His father had prevented him from taking Hope eight years ago, but Big Jase Turner had died last winter, leaving no one to put a leash on his only son.

With a reflex that came from many years of practice, she buried the thought of the Turners and her father's futile dreams of a "good" marriage for his younger daughter. It had all happened a lifetime ago. Both fathers were dead, Hope's mother was dead, her sister was dead.

Hope was alive.

In surviving, she had learned the difference between a man's easy promises and the terrifying reality of his lust. But more important than yesterday and lies and a young girl's screams, today Hope was a woman whose ranch was dying beneath her feet. Next to that fact nothing mattered, certainly not the irretrievable past.

She picked up the receiver and dialed quickly. The housekeeper answered the phone on the second ring.

"Hi, Sally, this is Hope. I'd like to leave a message for one of your hands."

"I'll get John," Sally said quickly.

"No, there's no need to bother him."

It was useless. Sally was already gone. Hope closed her eyes and waited for the lord and master of the Turner empire to come to the phone.

Mason's eyes narrowed as he watched a mask settle over Hope's face. It had almost broken his heart when he had seen her dropped off by Jase Turner nearly eight years ago. Her face had been pale, bruised, and her expression far too old to belong to a laughing girl who had just turned eighteen.

Sighing, cursing under his breath, Mason rubbed his neck wearily. Thinking about the past always made him feel old and futile. The only good things about those years were Hazel and Hope's father, Wayne, and they were both dead now. And Hope, of course. She had come out of the past and she was alive. To hear her laughter on a winter morning made everything worth it. He would do whatever it took to make certain that she would never again forget how to laugh.

"Hello, John," Hope said neutrally. "I told Sally not to bother you."

"It's never a bother talking to you, baby doll."

"I'd like to leave a message for one of your hands. A man called Rio."

There was a fractional pause. When Turner spoke again, his voice wasn't nearly so warm. "What do you want with him?"

She waited for a long moment, letting the rude question echo, before she said crisply, "Sorry to disturb you. Good-bye."

"Wait! Don't be so stiff-necked. I'm just looking out for your interests. You can't trust every man, you know."

Hope thought of water and thirsty cattle and held her tongue. Turner's arrogance and rocklike insensitivity shouldn't surprise her anymore.

"This Rio is a drifter and a cocksman," Turner said baldly.

"I'm a big girl. I can take care of myself."

Now.

Neither of them said the word, but it was there between them. Hope hadn't been able to hold her own with a man when she was eighteen, but she could now. For that, she could thank John Turner. For that, she once had wished him and herself dead.

The thought almost made her smile now. It was hard to believe that she had ever been so young and naive.

"I thought you and Mason broke all your horses on your own," Turner said. "The ones you have left, that is. If you'd just give me the word, baby doll, I'd have you three deep in the best horses money can buy. And if it's Storm Walker that's giving you trouble, I'll be glad to put the spurs to him myself. He's too damn much horse for a woman."

With a grimace Hope schooled her voice to show nothing. When she spoke, she ignored his repeated proposal to become Mrs. John Turner. She also ignored his casual reminder that she had only five horses left, and one of them was a stallion that was a double handful of thunder to ride.

"If you see Rio, tell him I called," she said.

"He won't be in for several hours, maybe not for days. He's an independent bastard. You better tell me what you have in mind. He'll want to know what—"

"He already does," Hope cut in.

"Wait. Are you coming to the barbecue tomorrow?"

It was an effort to keep her voice civil, but she managed. She needed his water too badly to give way to her temper. "Sorry. There's just too much to do here."

"Baby doll, you're working that pretty ass to the

bone. You don't have to. I'll take care of you. I want to. You can keep your ranch. Hell, I'll even pipe water over for you. It'd be my wedding present to—"

"Thanks for passing on my message," Hope interrupted firmly, stopping the flow of unwanted words.

Turner laughed. "All right. But you're going to say yes one of these days."

Silently she hung up and turned to face Mason's knowing eyes.

"Still after you, huh?" the old man asked.

"It's just a game with him. If I said yes, he'd take off in the opposite direction like a chaparral cock."

Mason shook his head slowly. "Don't you believe it."

Her smile was small and tight. "I don't. But in a way, it's true all the same. If he had me, he wouldn't want me for more than a week or two. That's just the way he is. He's always been that way. He'll die like that."

"Yeah, and he'll die considerable before his time if he tries more than sweet-talking you."

Sudden tears burned behind Hope's eyes. She wrapped her arms around Mason. "I don't know what I'd have done without you," she whispered, hugging him hard. "I love you."

His large-knuckled hand smoothed her hair while he returned her hug. "You'd have been buried in ice cubes, that's what." Then, almost too softly for her to hear, he said, "I love you, honey." Then he turned her in his arms, swatted her paternally on her rear, and said, "Now, you git before them cows dry up and blow clean to the Perdidas."

"If Rio calls—"

"Gal, you ain't been listenin' to me," Mason interrupted impatiently. "Rio will find you. He don't need no help from me, and he sure don't need no swaggering, yellow-bellied son of a bitch like Turner to point the way."

Hope gave up. She gulped a fast swallow of lemonade and left Mason to enjoy the spoils of her hasty exit.

He took the glass, emptied it, and called after her from the porch, "Beans and beef at sundown."

"And salad," she yelled as she climbed into Behemoth's dusty cab. "There's lettuce, tomatoes, green onions, and mushrooms in the refrigerator."

"Rabbit food! You expect me to fix rab—"

The rest of his outraged words were lost in the roar of Behemoth's engine. It was no accident. Hope knew that while Mason might occasionally eat, and enjoy, "rabbit food," he felt it was beneath him actually to prepare it.

He would do it, though, cursing every crisp leaf. And he would enjoy it, both the crisp leaves and the cursing. The ride to town was long, which meant that fresh vegetables were rare at the ranch house.

Smiling, Hope drove past the home pasture where her breeding cattle clustered around the trough, their black coats dulled by dust. Alongside the dirt road there was a narrow pipeline pitted by sand and sun. The well that had once supplied the ranch house's needs had gone dry more than a quarter of a century ago. Her father had drilled the well deeper and then deeper still, until he struck dense bedrock where earthquakes had taken water-bearing layers of rock and shoved them beneath bone-dry slate. He had cursed and dug another well several miles away, on the far side of the buried fault.

The new well shared Hope's name. It was water from the Hope that had been piped down to the ranch house and its outbuildings.

Other, separate wells once had irrigated the nearby pastures and filled the cattle troughs to overflowing. No more, though. The fields were dead and the windmill-driven pumps that had once brought up water were disconnected, lifeless. The water that came out of the wells now wasn't enough to keep the prime on the pumps, much less supply the needs of the black Angus, the croplands, and the scattered troughs of the range cattle.

The well her father had named Hope wasn't dry. Not quite. But it couldn't produce enough water for cattle and the ranch house, too. So she had capped the pipe leading from the Hope to the ranch house, sold off some of the range cattle at a loss, and started hauling water to troughs both at the ranch and farther away.

When even that hadn't been enough, she had culled more range cattle, selling off pieces of her future in order to survive the endless dry months.

The croplands and ranch-house lawns were long dead, as were all but the oldest, most deeply rooted trees surrounding the buildings. She had been forced to let the vegetable gardens beyond the kitchen die, for she couldn't feed the plants' thirst and that of her cattle, too. She hauled water for the house from Turner's wells and fed it into the cistern buried beneath the ranch yard.

And still it wasn't enough.

Each day her ranch's single remaining well sent a little less water up to the thirsty surface of the ground. Each day the cattle needed a little bit more to drink. Each day dawned clear and bright in a barren sky.

It will rain soon, she vowed quietly.

Every drought, even the worst, had an end. All she had to do was survive until the rains came and the temporary water holes filled and the groundwater rose up again to fill the empty wells. Then grass would grow, cattle would breed and fatten and increase in number and size, and the Valley of the Sun would live again.

With the money she had saved from her modeling career, she could manage for another year. With luck, even longer. She could meet the balloon payment on the second mortgage that was due on January fifteenth. She could keep the ranch out of bankruptcy even longer if she took the money she had set aside for drilling a new well and used the funds to meet the ranch's monthly expenses.

But if she used up the well money, the ranch itself was doomed. The rains simply didn't come as they had a century ago, fifty years ago, even thirty years ago. Without a new well, a new source of year-round water, the Valley of the Sun would be virtually worthless for ranching.

With hungry eyes Hope looked at the tawny country flexed against the endless fall of sunlight. Big sage lifted its shaggy gray limbs overhead, making graceful, mysterious patterns against the blue bowl of the sky. Shadow creases of ravines outlined the muscular land as it rumpled up to meet the heights of the Perdidas to the east. Plants in subdued shades of green and bronze grew on the broad alluvial fans that swept out from the base of the mountains.

After a good storm, when runoff streams tumbled down into the low basins, there were temporary lakes where migratory birds flocked and wary desert animals left delicate, braided trails along the soft shorelines. In the winter the alluvial fans were green with grass and new growth, and bright with the streams that ran dry during the hot weeks of summer.

But now, too often, those same streams were dry longer each year, until ravines and pools that had once watered range cattle no longer even grew grass. That was when ranches drank deeply from their wells.

That was when wells failed.

The resinous, tangy smell of the high desert poured through the truck's open window. Hope breathed in deeply, letting the clean scent of the land revive her. The sun coming through the windshield was hot, though not nearly as hot as it had been three months ago.

But even then, even when the ranch baked beneath a brutal sun, Hope loved the land. The searing days only made the brief twilight more silky, and the nights were like drinking dark wine from an immense crystal chalice. There was no other place like the Valley of the Sun for her. Anywhere. She knew it as certainly as she knew her own name.

Hope turned off the ranch road onto a track that was little more than twin ruts. In the rainy season the ruts would soften, run like sticky wax, and then, for a short time, freeze in the cold northern winds. But by then it wouldn't matter if the road was impassable. In the season of winter rains and ice she wouldn't have to haul water to the widely scattered troughs.

Behemoth lurched and veered sideways like a hammerheaded horse determined to go back to the barn. Hope yanked the wheel and hung on until the truck was lined up with the road again. The ache in her shoulders told her that it was going to be all she could do to drag down the heavy canvas hose, connect it, and pull it to the dry steel trough through the milling, thrusting, thirsty cattle. Yet it had to be done at least once more today.

It should be done twice.

Hope didn't let herself think about it. Under her relentless grip the truck bounced over the top of a small rise and toward her namesake well.

Rio was there, waiting.

Four

꙰

HOPE BRAKED IN a turmoil of dust and crept toward the empty trough. Scenting Behemoth's cargo of water, cattle bawled and swarmed around the truck, making it impossible for her to get closer to the trough.

Without a word Rio swung into the saddle and went to work on the cattle, herding them aside. His mare worked neatly, precisely, gracefully, spinning on her haunches, turning cattle away from the truck with a well-trained cow pony's lack of fuss. Her rider was just as skillful. He rode the swiftly pivoting mare deftly, balancing his weight to ease the mare's work. The horse's motion swept through him, repeated in supple movements of his spine.

Thanks to Rio and his quick pony, Hope was able to park the truck right next to the empty circular tank. The trough was big, the size of a backyard swimming pool. Still inside the cab, she peered down into the tank.

45

It was empty.

She listened for the generator and heard only Behemoth's engine muttering. Her heart hesitated, then sank. The generator's cutoff switch must have tripped. That meant there wasn't enough water moving through the pump. The windmill itself was turning, but all it could bring up was a stream of water barely as wide as her little finger. As soon as the water fell from the cast-iron pipe into the trough, cattle sucked up every bit of moisture.

Hope watched a cow's big pink tongue lick at the damp metal. Ice settled in her stomach. The well her ranch depended on was all but dry.

The exhaustion she had been keeping at bay closed over her. She shut her eyes for a few seconds and fought against numbing fear. *She couldn't lose the ranch.*

Determination rose in her, pushing away fear and despair. The cab door rattled and slammed as she leaped down to the ground on the side away from the empty tank. She avoided the milling cattle easily. They wanted water, not her.

She glanced over the herd as she moved, automatically checking their condition with an experienced eye. The Herefords were lean and hard. Too lean. Too hard. They should have been sleek and placid, like Turner's cattle. But her range cattle had to search several miles beyond the well for their food and then walk back to the tank for water. Each day they had to go a bit farther to satisfy their hunger, and then a bit farther back to satisfy their thirst.

There was nothing she could do about the lack of natural feed except pray for rain. That, and make sure that her cattle had water to come back to. She knelt under Behemoth's metal belly and went to work, swearing silently as she fought to connect the slightly warped, definitely corroded coupling to the valve. Her arms shook and her shoulders cramped, warning her that she was close to the end of her strength.

There was a slight movement behind her, a brush of fabric along her thigh, and then Rio was beside her, lifting the hose from her straining hands. Gratefully she dropped her arms and watched him wrestle with the stubborn coupling.

"One of the threads is bent," she said as he tried to find a way to screw the hose on. "There's a trick to threading it. If you'll hold the hose up for me, I'll do the rest."

Before she finished talking, he moved the hose so that its brass coupling was just short of the valve's dark mouth. She reached through his arms to make the threads of valve and hose match. Without the weight of the wet hose dragging the end down, it was much easier. After a few false starts she succeeded in screwing the hose on enough so that she didn't have to hold the brass together with one hand and turn with the other.

Unconsciously she took a deep breath, bracing herself for the job of tightening the mulish coupling so that it wouldn't blow apart at the first pressure of water rushing through.

Rio felt Hope's deep breath in the stir of her breasts against his arm. When he glanced at her, he realized that she wasn't aware of the intimacy. She was focused on the stubborn coupling with the kind of intensity that came only from a combination of exhaustion and fear.

For the first time he noticed the marks that sweat had made on her face, the dusting of grit and the flush of heat, and her tempting, fine-grained skin. Strands of hair licked down from her hat and swayed across her face like dark flames. Her hazel eyes showed almost none of the green that had been visible in the pouring sun by Turner's well. Now her eyes were dark, too dark, just as her lips were too pale against her flushed cheeks.

Rio wondered how many times she had made the trip from Turner's well to her own dry land and thirsty livestock. She must be exhausted. Gently he covered her hands with his. Easing her fingers aside, he went to work tightening the coupling.

He was surprised at how difficult it was to keep the threads turning delicately and at the same time prevent the weight of the hose from jamming the two pieces of brass together at the wrong angle. The thought of Hope trying and failing and trying again and again to make the coupling work brought a hard line to Rio's mouth.

Where the hell is Mason? he asked himself silently. *This is no job for a woman's arms. How long has Hope been making these water runs by herself?*

"Thanks, that should do it," she said, pulling herself out from under the truck. "I'll get the wrench."

She came back very quickly. In her hand was a plumber's wrench as long as her arm and a lot heavier. Rio took the wrench from her, lifting it with an ease that she envied and that he took for granted. She watched his faded blue shirt strain rhythmically across his shoulders and biceps. He tightened the coupling with smooth, powerful motions of his arms. She waited, judging her moment, then began to tug at the hose, straightening it for the rush of water that would come soon.

"Stay put," he said. "I'll take care of it."

Her arms decided before her mind did. They dropped to her sides. She sighed and sat down, resting the back of her head against Behemoth's curved metal belly. Quietly she watched the desert-tanned man who was crouched so close to her that the faded jeans and shirts they both wore were almost impossible to tell apart. As he worked, she enjoyed the complex play of human muscle and tendon in the same way she had enjoyed watching his gray mare handle the impatient cows.

"Thanks," she said, rubbing her tired arms. "I owe you one."

Rio shook his head slowly. He was remembering Hope's beauty when she arched against the sky and her hands sprayed liquid diamonds over her beautifully curved body. It was an image he couldn't get out of his mind. She had been as vivid and unexpected as a rainbow in the desert.

And like a rainbow, she had given pleasure and asked nothing in return.

"No," he said quietly, "you don't owe me a thing."

She turned her head toward him, but he didn't look back at her. All his attention was for the stubborn coupling. When he finally finished, he slid out from beneath the truck and propped the wrench against a tire. Without a word he began dragging the heavy, stiff hose off its rack and into the trough.

Cattle bawled and shoved and crowded around the water tank. Though they kept trying, they couldn't quite wedge themselves between the truck and the trough. Rio and Hope wouldn't be trampled as long as they kept to Behemoth's bulky shelter.

He pitched his voice to carry over the noise of the cattle. "Ready."

When Hope didn't answer, and the hose remained slack, he glanced over his shoulder. She was propped against the dusty truck, eyes closed, soaking in every instant of rest like dry sand absorbing water. Contrasted with the truck's bulk, she looked very small, almost fragile.

"Hope?"

She opened her eyes and smiled up at him. With a grace that belied the exhausted shadows beneath her eyes, she picked up the heavy wrench, fastened it to the valve, and put her whole body into giving it a good solid turn.

Water swelled the hose and rushed over the lip of the tank, thundering hard and fast into the empty trough. Cattle bawled and crowded closer, jostling even the sturdy truck. When Rio was certain that the hose wouldn't leap up out of the trough and spray water everywhere, he slipped back under the ancient army vehicle and sat next to Hope.

"Eager little devils," he said, watching the forest of dusty legs milling beyond the truck's shelter.

"Beautiful little devils." Hope was smiling and her eyes were alight with pride in her cattle.

After a time the animals that had been first at the water tank allowed themselves to be pushed aside by their thirsty friends. The cattle that had shoved in for a drink earlier in the day, during Behemoth's first water run, waited on the fringes of the herd or grazed invisibly among the big sage and scattered piñon that grew over the gently folded land. The grazing cattle were the same ones that would be most eager tomorrow, up in the front of the crowd, shoving and bawling for their first taste of water in a day.

Hope didn't waste energy trying to talk over the noise of her cows. With a half-apologetic smile to Rio, she lay on her back in the dust, her head on her hat, her eyes closed. She felt light-headed with the pleasure of stretching muscles that were cramped from the day's demands.

This was one of the moments she waited for, when the hardest part of water hauling had been done and all that remained was uncoupling the hose, racking it, and driving Behemoth back to the ranch house. Sometimes before she left for home she would take off her clothes and slide over the lip of the huge tank. She would paddle quietly for a time before she rested her arms along the rim and floated, watching while glittering stars bloomed in the navy-blue depths of evening.

With an odd smile Rio watched Hope as she lay unself-consciously near him. He didn't know whether she was too tired for the usual flirtations or forthright advances of the women he had known in the past, or whether she simply didn't see him as a man because he wasn't all white.

Then he remembered the times he had turned and found her watching him, female approval clear in her expression. She was exhausted, not bigoted.

He was tempted to stretch out next to her, sharing the truck's bluntly curving shelter and resting his body at the same time. His day had begun well before dawn, when he had caught Dusk, saddled her, and rounded up some of Turner's skittish Thoroughbreds. The horses were as elegant as ballerinas, and about as much use for working cattle.

It was Turner's quarter horses that Rio truly enjoyed. They were muscular, cow-savvy, and quick, perfectly suited to use with cattle. By the time he was done, John Turner would have some of the best cow horses in Nevada.

Then Turner would ruin his quarter horses trying to win flashy buckles in rodeos. The man had no more sense of how to treat a horse than he did of how to treat hired hands, women, or the land itself. He took, but didn't give back. He didn't even suspect that he should.

Slouching farther down, Rio propped his head against a dusty tire and drew his feet out of the way of the eager cattle. He could have slept, but didn't. Instead he savored the peace of the moment, the cattle's thirst being slaked, the woman resting only inches from his thigh, the tactile memory of her breasts brushing against his arm.

With a silent curse he told himself what kind of fool he was even to look at Hope. *She's not a woman for bed today and good-bye tomorrow. So stop thinking about the way she looked outlined against the sky with her blouse shaping her the way I'd like to.*

Even if she came to me, asking for me, I'd only hurt her. Is that what I want? Do I want to give her a hand when she's down and needs me and then drag her off to bed like she's just one more Saturday night?

Hell, I outgrew that kind of screwing before I was old enough to drink.

Grimly Rio listened to his internal lecture. He approved each point with his intelligence and at the same time fought against them with every one of his fully alive senses. But despite his prowling masculine hunger, he made no move toward Hope.

Not a word. Not a gesture. Not even a hungry look.

Instinctively he knew beyond doubt or argument that she wouldn't give herself casually to any man. He also knew just as deeply that he didn't give himself at all to any woman, not really, not in any way that mattered. In the last thirty-three years he had learned many things about himself. One of them was that Brother-to-the-wind was more than his Indian name. It was his fate, and he had finally accepted it.

He had spent his life searching for something that was more powerful, more enduring, more beautiful, more compelling, than the endless sweep of the western lands. He had found no place, no person, capable of holding him when his brother the wind called to him, whispering of secret springs and shaded canyons where men never walked.

The other thing that Rio had learned about himself

on the way to growing up was that while he was born white, raised white until he was twelve, and educated white after sixteen, white women didn't want him. Not all of him. They didn't want his silences or his uncanny insights into life and the land.

Most of all, white women didn't want to have a child that was less white than they were.

He didn't really blame them. After what he had been through, he could write a book about being not white, not being Indian, not being anything to anyone but a pain in the butt.

Rio pulled his hat down over his eyes, shutting out the sight of Hope's vulnerable body within reach of his hungry hands. He subdued his desire with the same steel discipline that had kept his raging temper under control when he was growing up and blonde kids had baited him, calling him *breed* and *blankethead.* He had fought his tormentors with icy ferocity, but he hadn't killed any of them.

And he could have, even then.

When he was grown, most of the men who backed him into a corner depended on numbers or various weapons to make them strong. Rio had learned never to depend on anyone or anything but himself. It gave him an advantage in sheer ruthlessness that at first surprised and then overwhelmed his opponents.

It also made him very much a man alone. He had accepted that, too. *Brother-to-the-wind.*

Cattle milled and pushed, raising a dust that made the air a shimmering brass color. Water rushed out of Behemoth, thundering into the stock tank with a cool sound. The smells of cattle, water, and dust merged with those of sunlight, piñon, and sage.

The mixture of odors was soothing to Hope, familiar, reassuring. She sighed and relaxed even more. Exhaustion washed over her in waves, making her dizzy. She realized that she was on the edge of falling asleep miles from home while a big stranger half-lay nearby, so close to her that she could sense each stirring of his body as he breathed.

Yet she wasn't worried. Since her eighteenth birthday she had learned quite a bit about people in general and men in particular. Rio didn't give out the signals of a man who would leap on the first woman he found alone and unprotected. He had looked at her with veiled male appreciation, but he hadn't crowded her in any way.

Even if she hadn't been sure of her own instincts, she trusted those of Mason Graves. Any man he would be proud to claim for a son wouldn't be the kind of man to take advantage of people weaker than he was.

Hope's only regret about her present situation was that she didn't know Rio well enough to use his shoulder as a pillow rather than the dry, unforgiving ground. The thought of curling up against his living strength made her smile.

She was still smiling when she fell headlong into sleep.

Rio watched Hope for a long time, repeating to himself all the ways he was wrong for her and she was wrong for him. Then he lay down beside her and eased her head off the hard ground and onto his shoulder.

She stirred vaguely but didn't pull away. Instead she moved even closer, sighed, and relaxed against his body with a trust that made him want to shake her awake and tell her what fools they both were being.

Trying not to think at all, Rio lay utterly still, caught in the gentle, bittersweet pleasure of holding a woman in his arms who trusted him more than he trusted himself.

Five

🌿

THE SUN BALANCED in crimson glory on the black outline of a distant ridge. Long shadows reached under the
battered water truck, dark forerunners of night. The
stock tank was more than half-full. Its clean water reflected the last burning light of day.

No cattle milled around the tank. Having drunk their
fill, the Herefords were out grazing over the rumpled
land. The cattle looked like carved garnet statues set
among the nearly black flames of piñon trees.

The elegant gray mare dozed three-legged next to a
clump of sage that gleamed a ghostly silver in the rich
light. The single roping rein Rio preferred to use hung
loosely around her neck, allowing her freedom to wander as she pleased. She needed no physical tie, for she
was held by invisible bonds of training and her affection for the man who lay quietly beneath the old water
truck.

Rio looked from the thick, dark lashes lying along

Hope's cheek to the stunning transformations of sunset in a wild land. He had known many such times, days inevitably changed by condensing darkness, cool scented winds sweeping down from water-rich heights. Yet he had never known a sunset just like this one.

In the past he had been alone with the land, and now a woman lay in his arms as quietly as sunlight in a hollow.

It was a strange sensation to hold Hope, pleasure laced with uneasiness, as though he was a trespasser in an intriguing, forbidden land. He wondered if his Swedish grandmother had felt this way when she lay with her Indian lover, a Zuni shaman whose very existence was an affront to the Christianity that she had come to teach on the reservation.

The mare snorted and stamped her front foot, discouraging a persistent fly. It was the only sound Rio could hear. Even the wind was quiet.

Cool velvet shadows lapped over his feet. He knew it was past time for him to awaken the woman sleeping in his arms. He should have done it at least a half hour ago, when the hose had finished transferring the last of its water to the trough.

Reluctantly, gently, he shifted Hope's head back onto her hat. She made a protesting sound. He brushed his lips over her hair, breathed in the fragrance of land and woman and earth, and then leaned against the dusty tire once more, no longer touching her.

"Hope," he said softly.

She didn't stir.

He allowed his hand to rest on her shoulder, to

stroke it, to feel the woman-heat beneath the faded, dusty cotton. The temptation to slide his fingers into the shadowed opening of her collar swept over him, shaking him with its intensity. He wanted to touch the sweet curves of her breasts, to follow his hands with his mouth, to unwrap her, to take her right there, with the night blooming around them in a thousand luminous shades of darkness.

"Hope." The word was rough, almost painful, as though it had been dragged unwillingly from his throat.

She woke in a rush, disoriented.

He had been expecting it. He held her shoulder down so that she couldn't sit up before she was fully awake. His hand was all that saved her from cracking her head on Behemoth's metal belly in the first heedless instant of waking up.

Her eyes opened dark amber, a color as clear and pure as the evening itself. For a moment she was embarrassed; then she smiled crookedly, accepting the fact that she had fallen asleep on the most interesting man she had met in her life.

"Did my snoring keep you awake?" she asked wryly.

Rio had seen both the instant of unease and her humorous acceptance of reality. His smile transformed his face the way moonrise transforms night. Lines that had been harsh became gentle, and angles that had been forbidding became merely strong.

"Sorry to disappoint you," he said, "but you didn't snore even once."

"Must have been your lucky day," she said, stretching luxuriously. "God, I didn't know the ground could be such a soft mattress."

"It was," he said, referring to her first comment about luck. "It isn't," he added, referring to the softness of the ground.

She blinked and shook her head. Before she could ask for an explanation, Rio stood and went over to his horse. He led the mare to the tank and watched while she plunged her muzzle into the clean water.

After a few moments Hope stood, dusted off her jeans with her palms, and walked over to Rio. She would have given a lot for the freedom to peel off her clothes and float for just a few moments in the cool water. With a small sigh she turned away from the tempting liquid.

"The only water this tank will ever see is Turner water," Rio said, watching his mare drink. Then he turned quickly, catching the despair on Hope's face as his words sank in. "If you want me to drill here, forget it. It would be a waste of my time, your money, and your cows' lives."

Silently Hope counted the rings expanding through the water as the horse drank. It wasn't that Rio's words were untrue or even unexpected. But they were so very final.

It was the end of her dreams spoken in a stranger's calm, certain voice.

She wanted to protest, to ask Rio how he could be so sure, but she didn't. In the quiet, deep center of herself she didn't doubt him. She sensed that he knew the land in a way that couldn't be described or wholly understood. It had to be accepted on trust, the same way she trusted the sun to rise in the morning and stars to come in the evening.

Hope fought against the useless tears closing her throat. She felt defenseless, neither truly asleep nor yet awake, suspended between the end of one dream and the beginning of an unwelcome awakening.

She had enough money to drill her namesake well deeper. She didn't have the resources to find and drill an entirely new, probably much deeper well from scratch. She didn't realize how much she had secretly counted on being able to revive the Hope until now, when she finally and fully accepted the fact that her well was dead.

The despair was numbing.

"Hope—"

"It's all right," she said huskily, interrupting him. She knew that Rio hadn't meant to hurt her with his blunt assessment of her dream. "I understand."

He wondered if she truly did. Then he cursed himself for his unforgiving description of her well. Yet as long as she held on to an unrealistic dream, there would be no way to give her one that had at least a fighting chance of coming true.

And that was what she had asked him for. A fighting chance.

"I hoped that if I just drilled farther down, through the bedrock, I'd strike artesian water," she said in a low voice. Then, slipping through her defenses, came the dying cries of her dream. "Are you sure? How can you be so sure?"

"Yes. I'm sure."

Silently Rio watched her with eyes as deep and clear as the water she had hoped to find. He was sure. But he couldn't explain his certainty to Hope. It was a combination of instinct and education and long experience in dry lands.

"Well," she said, her voice steady despite its unusual huskiness, "thanks for being honest with me. You could have cleaned out my drilling account and then walked away."

"Is that what you heard about me?" Rio's tone was distant, hard.

She shook her head, making her hair shift and shimmer darkly in the dying light. "No. And even if I had," she added, meeting his eyes directly, "I wouldn't have believed it after being with you. You aren't a liar or a thief."

For a long moment they looked at each other, silently accepting what was being offered. She trusted him not to lie to her. He trusted her to believe him without any proof other than his word.

"If there's water on your land, I'll find it for you," Rio said. His voice was as soft and certain as when he had told her that the Hope well was dead.

She smiled sadly. "Unless the water you find is close to the surface, I can't afford to go after it."

"First let's find the water. Then we'll worry about drilling the well. I'll work nights and weekends here until I'm finished with Turner's horses. Then I'll work full-time."

"I can't afford to—"

"My pay will be room and board for me and my horse," he cut in, knowing what she was going to say.

"That's not enough."

"Do you have any old drilling equipment in your barn?" he asked.

"All the way back to the first well. Why?"

"We'll salvage what we can. I've got some equipment of my own that I'll have shipped in. Between us we'll put together a drilling rig that won't cost you much. Your biggest expense will be pipe, 'mud,' and fuel."

"And your fee," she said firmly. "It isn't fair that you work only for room and board."

His smile gleamed briefly in the dying light. His eyes were even darker now, as mysterious and radiant as the twilight expanding throughout the land. "It isn't fair that you have to do the work of three men just to hang on to your ranch."

She shrugged. There was no help for it, so there was no point in complaining about it.

"You're going to work until rain falls—or you do," he said dryly. "Right?"

His choice of words almost made her smile in spite of the grief of losing an old dream.

"I'm no different from anyone else," she said matter-of-factly. "I do what I can for as long as I can, and I hope to God that it will be enough."

Rio thought of the men and women he had met who had worked as little as they could for as short a time as possible, and bitched every step of the way about bad luck and bad people and the unfairness of a world that

didn't give them everything they had ever wanted.
Those were the people Rio avoided.

The other people—the ones like Hope who worked
their hearts out for a dream and didn't whine when the
going got rough—those were the people Rio was
drawn to as inevitably as rain was drawn to the thirsty
ground. Those were the people he helped, sharing their
dreams for a time, giving what he could, taking only
what they could afford in return.

When the dreams changed or came true, he moved
on like his brother the wind, speaking only in the wild
silences of the land, searching for something that neither he nor the wind could name.

"I'll help you," Rio said softly, "and hope to God
that it's enough."

"But I can't afford—" she began.

"I don't want money as payment. If I bring in a well,
I'll leave ten mares to be bred to Storm Walker. You'll
treat the mares and their foals as your own, no better
and no worse. From time to time I'll come to the Valley of the Sun, take the horses I want, and leave the
mares to be bred to your best stallion. For as long as
the water in my well flows."

When she started to speak, he put his finger on her
lips, surprising her into silence. There was sensuality
in the touch and something else, something indescribable that made her heart stop and then beat more
quickly, more deeply.

"Think carefully before you answer, Hope. Not one
of my wells has ever gone dry."

He lifted his hand, freeing her.

She closed her eyes, but still she saw Rio, his sundarkened skin, his eyes deep and clear as the night. Echoes of his velvet voice moved like a caress over her skin, touching her more deeply than anything ever had, even her dreams.

"Yes," she said, her voice as calm as his eyes. "Ten mares. Storm Walker." Then she looked directly at him. "And more, if you want. Horses, cattle, whatever. I have a lot of land and no water. Yet."

He watched Hope's expression, felt her truth, heard her trust in him, and knew both pleasure and uneasiness. He had taken one dream from her and given her another: water unending, sweet water reviving her dying ranch.

But he couldn't guarantee that the second dream would be any more possible than the first. He could only guarantee that if it *was* possible, he would give it to her.

"Sometimes there's no water to be found anywhere, by anyone." His voice was both quiet and rough.

She smiled wearily. "Yes, I know. If that happens, your mares will still be bred and the foals cared for until I no longer own the Valley of the Sun."

"No well, no payment."

"Your mares will be bred," she repeated, her voice firm. "Ship them in anytime." With a wry twist to her mouth she added, "Storm Walker will thank you for it. This last year I've had to use my four remaining mares for working cattle rather than for breeding."

Rio's smile gleamed in the gathering darkness. He held out his hand. She took it without hesitation, letting the warmth of him seep into her as the last of the sun's crimson light fled the sky. His touch was a warm, living reality that gave substance to all hopes, all possibilities, everything.

Eyes shining, heart beating rapidly, Hope allowed herself to dream again.

"For as long as the water flows," she said, pressing her hand against his, both clinging to and giving back his touch.

The echo of his own words went through Rio like a wild wind, shaking everything it touched. He wanted to tell Hope not to trust him so much, not to believe in him so deeply.

Yet that wasn't what he wanted to say, not really. She could trust him with her dream of water. Her heart was a different matter. And it was her heart that accelerated at his touch, making her pulse quicken visibly beneath the soft skin of her inner wrist.

And she wasn't even aware of it. He could see that as clearly as he had seen her courage and determination while she worked herself to exhaustion to save her cattle and her ranch from drought. She thought it was the new dream that was stirring her blood and her heart.

He knew that it wasn't, not entirely. The same sensual hunger burned in his own blood as the heat of her skin slid over his.

Rio couldn't draw back from Hope. Her dream was as deep and compelling as she was. That was why he wanted to—why he *must*—help her. He had stopped dreaming long ago. The emptiness that had come with the end of dreams was a void that even the wind couldn't fill.

"When can you start?" Hope asked. She felt oddly breathless, suspended between Rio's male warmth and the intimacy of desert twilight.

"I already have."

"You have? What did you do?"

"I looked at all your wells."

"Oh." Hope said no more.

Neither did Rio. There was nothing more to say. The Valley of the Sun's wells were dead.

She drew in a deep breath. "I see. Since you've already started working, it's past time for me to make good on my promise of room and board. Mason will have dinner waiting by the time we get back. Nothing fancy. Beef, beans, bread, and salad."

Rio's black eyebrows rose. "Salad?"

"Don't tell me," Hope said, groaning. "You're another one of those cowboys who can't stand rabbit food."

Gentle laughter curled around her like a caress, like his voice when he finally spoke. "No problem. I get real hungry for fresh vegetables."

"Good. We'll gang up on Mason and demand our rabbit rights."

Still smiling, Rio pulled the cold hose out of the stock tank and began wrapping the canvas coils around the rack bolted to the end of the truck. Hope helped as much as she could, feeding coils to him. By the time the hose was stowed away, they were both wet and more than a little muddy.

"Feel free to take a dip in the tank before you ride in for dinner," she said as she wiped her hands on her jeans. "I usually do. It's more fun than a basin bath at the ranch."

He smiled slightly. "Is that like a bucket bath?"

"Nope. Less luxurious. Buckets are bigger than our washbasin. Until I can take time out from watering cows to make another run to Turner's well, that's all there will be at home—a washrag and a basin of water. But," she added, smiling crookedly at him, "the washrag is of the highest quality."

Rio smiled in return, though he would rather have cursed. Obviously the water shortage at the ranch house was little short of desperate; Hope couldn't supply the house and the scattered range cattle at the same time. There simply weren't enough hours in the day or strength in her body to do what had to be done.

Again he wondered what had happened to Mason. It wasn't like him to let a woman work herself raw if he could help her out.

Without a word Rio turned toward his horse and whistled. The rising sound carried as cleanly as a hawk's cry through the silence.

The mare's head came up and she trotted over to Rio. He held the roping rein and looked at Hope.

"Give her a few seconds to get used to your lighter weight," he said. "She's the best night horse you'll ever ride."

"But—" she began.

"I'll take the truck," Rio continued without a pause. "Don't wait dinner for me. I'll be a while."

Automatically Hope's fingers closed over the rein he handed to her. She hesitated, then decided not to ask the obvious question about where he was going and what he was doing. She either trusted Rio or she didn't. In any case, she wasn't the kind of employer who needed to keep her men under her thumb at all times.

"Reverse gear is really dicey," she said. "Avoid it if you can. If you can't, I wish you luck. You'll need it. You'll have a hell of a time getting into another gear. I once backed ten miles to the ranch house so that Mason could work his magic on the gearbox."

Rio smiled at the picture.

"Keys are in the ignition," she continued. "Don't trust the fuel gauge. It always registers half-full. If you're going more than fifty miles, drop by the ranch house. Diesel is in the blue tank to the left of the barn. Gasoline is in the red tank."

Rio nodded, started toward the truck, then turned back with an odd expression on his face. "Are you always this trusting with strangers?"

"No," she said evenly. She looked, but couldn't see more than a hint of brighter darkness where Rio's eyes were. "I don't trust strangers at all." Then she smiled at her own expense. "And I don't sleep under trucks with them, either. What about you, Rio? Do you let strangers ride off with your horse?"

"Never."

The quiet word told Hope more than she had teasingly asked. No one but Rio had ever ridden the hot-blooded mare.

Before she could say anything more, he came to her, laced his hands together to make a stirrup, and lifted her onto Dusk. The mare minced restlessly for a moment before she arched her neck around and sniffed her unexpectedly small rider's muddy boot.

Hope murmured calm words and stroked the mare's warm, ghostly-gray neck. At a gentle pressure on the rein, the horse's ears came up and she stepped eagerly into the gathering darkness.

"See you at home," Hope said.

The words carried softly back to the man who stood motionless, watching her until she merged with the night.

Six

❧

By the time Hope rode into the ranch yard, she was wearing the jacket Rio had left tied behind his saddle. Despite being so tired that it was all she could do to stay awake, she almost hated to have the ride end.

Rio had been right about his mare. Dusk was the best night horse Hope had ever ridden. Most horses were balky or nervous to the point of wildness at being ridden alone into darkness. Not Dusk. She moved quietly, confidently, cleanly, like the man who had trained her. Even the sudden whistle of a startled dove's wings hadn't made her shy. As for the eerie harmonies of coyotes, Dusk had simply cocked her ears and walked on, unruffled.

Suddenly a rectangle of yellow light spilled out in the yard to meet Hope. Mason stood in the center of the light, silhouetted against the doorway.

"Nice pony," Mason said, satisfaction ringing in his voice. "Rio's?"

"Yep," Hope said, imitating Mason's laconic speech.

He waited, but she didn't say any more. "Truck break down?" he asked.

"Nope."

Mason waited.

Silence.

"You lookin' for trouble, gal?" he asked in exasperation.

Smiling, she reined the gray mare toward the barn. "Nope. Just dinner."

The old man mumbled something about serving her fried horse-apple pie and went back inside, banging the screen door behind him.

"Set an extra place," she called after him.

The door slammed open again.

"Rio's gonna do it?" Mason demanded. "He's gonna find water for you?"

"He's going to try."

Mason's whoop of triumph made the mare shy.

Hope was ready, because she had expected Mason's reaction. Even so, she had to grab the saddle horn or get dumped in the dust. The long-legged mare was very fast.

With a wary appreciation of her mount's speed, Hope dismounted. Her feet ached the instant they hit the ground. No matter how comfortable her battered cowboy boots might be, her feet were tired at the end of a day. So was she. She had been up since well before dawn. It would be the same tomorrow. And the day after that.

And every day until the rains came.

She led Dusk into a stall and rubbed her down thoroughly despite the fact that her arms cramped every time she lifted them above her shoulders.

"Are you hungry, girl?" she asked.

Dusk watched her with dark, liquid eyes.

"You're not as big as Storm Walker, but I'll bet you can eat as much as he can after carrying Rio around. That man is no lightweight."

The horse nudged her impatiently.

Hope laughed. "All right. You've more than earned it."

Humming quietly, she put several fat flakes of hay in the manger, poured grain in on one side, and hauled water for the stall trough from a spigot on the side of the house. She brushed the mare from forelock to heels, talking to her all the while. The flicking of black-tipped ears followed her words, but otherwise the mare was busy eating.

Only when Hope was certain that Dusk was content in her unfamiliar surroundings did she shut the stall door and walk slowly toward the ranch house. She was so tired that she felt like she was wading through mud. The thought of a long, hot, chin-deep bath made her want to moan.

"Then don't think about it," she muttered to herself. "There's enough water for drinking and for spit baths and not one drop more."

A basin of warm water waited for Hope in her bedroom. She peeled off her clothes, washed carefully, rinsed, and refused to let herself think about the bathtub across the hall. After a few swipes of the hairbrush through her dark, unquenchably curly hair, she went downstairs. Her stomach growled every inch of the way.

"Dinner?" she asked hopefully, hurrying into the kitchen.

"Light and set," Mason said, gesturing toward the table.

He hesitated as he reached for the gallon bottle of salad oil. It was heavy as well as slippery, and his hands hadn't been very cooperative for the past few days. He paused over the ingredients that were lined up on the counter, frowning as he tried to remember the ratio of vinegar to oil and salt to pepper for the salad dressing.

Hope could tell by the careful way Mason used his hands that the arthritis in his knuckles had flared up again. His pride, too, was in full flare. It was hard enough on his self-respect—and temper—when he couldn't handle the water truck and the hose for her. Not being able to handle kitchen work would be the final insult.

"I'll do it," she said easily. Then, as though she hadn't noticed Mason's difficulty with his fingers, she added with a wink, "You always use too much oil."

"Rabbit food," he said, his voice rich with disgust as he turned his back on the slick, treacherous bottle of oil. "When's Rio coming?"

"He said not to wait dinner."

"Then I'll just busy myself putting the *real* food on the table."

She snickered but didn't say a word.

He got out a heavy cast-iron frying pan and banged it onto an equally heavy iron burner.

"Price of beef went down half-cent a pound," he said.

Hope's smile slipped. She concentrated on making salad dressing.

Mason turned the burner up high. Blue and gold propane flames exploded around the black iron.

"Feed's up in cost," he said.

She hoped the icy fear in her stomach didn't show in her voice. "Ouch. Even if it's a mild winter, we'll be buying feed before spring."

"Nope."

She paused as she stirred the vinaigrette. "Why not?"

"Won't have no cows to eat it." Mason's faded green eyes looked squarely into hers. "Gonna have to sell some more range cows. You know it. I know it. Gotta be done."

Her face settled into stubborn lines. "Not yet. I can still water them for a while longer. Maybe it will rain soon."

"Maybe pigs will fly."

Head bowed, Hope beat the salad dressing until it was mostly froth.

Mason started to push the argument, then shrugged and let it go. As he had said more than once, she was stubborn but no fool.

"Don't kill yourself, honey." Butter sizzled in the frying pan. "Nothing's worth that." The solid weight of a steak smacked against hot iron. "We both know that the longer you wait to sell, the less them cows is gonna weigh. Natural feed's about gone and nothing's coming up to take its place. No rain."

Mason's matter-of-fact summary made Hope angry. Not because he was wrong, but because he was right.

"Then I'll haul feed," she said tightly.

He shook his head and didn't say a word. He knew that even if the two of them worked around-the-clock, they couldn't haul water and food to all the cattle.

Too many cattle.

Not enough hours in the day.

Not enough muscle between the two of them.

But Hope was young. She would have to discover her own limits. He had found his long ago, and the older he got the more those limits shrank in on him.

He stared at his swollen knuckles and cursed softly. He wasn't angry at life on his own account, but on hers. For her he would have endured the agonies of being young again, just to have the strength to help her build her dream. She was the daughter he had never had. He would have moved mountains for her if he could.

He couldn't. He could only love her.

Silently Mason lifted a corner of the steak, declared it cooked enough, and flipped it over.

After a time Hope quit beating the helpless dressing and put the beans and salad on the table. She heaped some of each on both plates. Then she opened the oven door and sniffed.

The tantalizing aroma of garlic curled up to her nostrils. At one time Mason had insisted that garlic bread was a foreign sacrilege that never should be allowed to mop up good American beef juices. Eventually he had become hooked on the pungent stuff.

"Eat it before the grease sets," he said, putting the sizzling beef in front of her.

She prodded the steak with her fork. "Did you hear that?"

"What?"

"It mooed at me."

Mason started to say something indignant before he saw the laughter lurking in her eyes. He smiled unwillingly, ruffled her just-brushed hair, and went back to the stove.

A low, sweetly rendered *mooooo* followed him.

He turned back quickly. An angelic-looking Hope was cutting into her bloody steak with every appearance of satisfaction.

"Mmmmmm," she said, chewing slowly. "Mason, nobody can almost cook a steak like you."

Smiling, singing off-key, a pleased Mason fried his own beef. It took even less time than hers had.

Soon the only sounds in the kitchen were those made by flatware against crockery plates, the occasional creak of old oak chairs when weight shifted forward or back on the seat, and the rapidly accelerating perk of the coffeepot as the liquid inside deepened in color and fragrance.

When Hope could eat no more, she took pity on the patient Mason and told him about the agreement she and Rio had made.

Mason listened quietly, nodded at the right moments, and smiled like a cat with feathers sticking out of its mouth. When Hope was finished talking, he wiped his mouth with a paper napkin and pushed back from the table.

"Well, better open the pipe to the water heater," he said.

She stared at him as though he had suggested frying one of the oak chairs for dessert. "What are you talking about?"

"Don't you want a bath, gal?"

"Well, of course, but—"

"Then don't keep me here jawing with you when bathwater could be heating up," he interrupted cheerfully.

"Mason." She spoke slowly, carefully, as though he was deaf or stupid or slightly crazy. "If I take a bath, there won't be any drinking water for tomorrow."

"Sure there will. Whole damn truckload."

Her mouth dropped open and stayed that way.

He snorted. "Look at you catching flies. What do you think Rio's doing out there on an empty belly, gal? Pushing that bastard truck around in the dark for the hell of it?"

Hope's mouth closed a lot more slowly than it had opened. "Do you really think . . ." she began wistfully, longing for a bath with every aching muscle in her body.

"Why don't you ask him yourself?"

The noise of the old water truck rattling into the ranch yard sounded loud in the sudden silence.

"Fast trip," Mason said. "Takes strength. Rio has it and then some."

Hope was too astonished for words. She hurried out into the front yard.

"Where do you want it?" Rio asked.

"I— You didn't have to do— Around back," she managed finally.

He looked past her into the night. *Around back* took in a lot of country, including the Perdidas cutting stars out of the clear night sky.

Laughing, she stepped onto the truck's running board and reached for the cab door. "I'll take care of it. You must be starved. Go in and eat."

Rio simply stared at her. He wasn't used to that kind of consideration from anyone, much less from a woman as tired as he knew Hope had to be. He smiled gently. "Thanks, but it won't take long for me to eat. You go on in and rest."

"After the water is put away."

He didn't argue. He knew how important every drop of water was to her. "Hang on."

She clung to the cab door as he eased the heavy truck around the house and up to a spot that had formerly been a lawn but now was little more than two tire tracks ground through a crust of dead grass. The pipe that had once brought water from the Hope had been cut and the stump threaded to allow the canvas hose to be coupled with it.

One look at the setup told Rio that it would be another wrestling match. He climbed down out of the cab, ready to do battle again with stubborn brass couplings and water-heavy hose.

Hope took a flashlight from the truck, bathing his hands in light while he coaxed the connection between the water truck and the buried cistern that served the ranch house. Soon water fattened the hose and fell into the nearly empty tank. Muted thunder rose from beneath their feet.

"How big is the tank?" he asked.

"It will hold half a truckload. Go in and eat. I'll watch over things out here."

He might have argued, but Mason stuck his head out of the back door and yelled, "Come and git it 'fore I feed it to the pigs."

"Do you have pigs?" Rio whispered to her.

"No, but I haven't had the heart to tell Mason."

"Too soft, huh?"

"For some people." Her smile was quick, but Rio caught its gleam. "Mason is one of them."

"Is Turner?" Rio asked, not knowing why.

Hope gave him a level glance. "I'm not around Turner long enough for it to matter either way."

"Sorry. None of my business."

She shrugged. "Everybody in a hundred miles has made it their business at one time or another. Why should you be different?"

He started to speak, then obviously thought better of it.

"Go ahead," she said with a sigh. "But please be original. Don't tell me Turner is an untrustworthy son of a bitch, because I already know it. Don't tell me that he's filthy rich, because I don't care."

"Is he crowding you?"

Something buried in Rio's voice, something dangerous, made Hope wish that it was light enough to see his expression clearly. "Nothing I can't handle."

"If that changes, let me know."

"You'll have to get in line after Mason," she said dryly.

"It would be a pleasure."

Hope didn't doubt that Rio meant every word. Obviously he and John Turner weren't very friendly. It wasn't surprising. Anyone with an ounce of self-respect had a hard time getting along with Turner.

And Rio, despite his easy manner, had plenty of pride.

"This here dinner of yours ain't getting any hotter, Rio," Mason called. "Gal, you git on back in here and set. That damn hose ain't going nowheres and you know it."

Hope hesitated, then played the light once more over the coupling. It was tight. Barely any drops escaped. She went to the truck and put the flashlight back in its place.

While Mason stood impatiently, Rio waited for her, then walked by her side toward the yellow light pouring out of the house. He said nothing to her, simply moved quietly, his long-sleeved shirt brushing against hers in a silent companionship that needed no words.

For an instant Hope forgot that she was exhausted and that tomorrow would be worse, not better. An absurd feeling of well-being swept through her, as unexpected as Rio's gentle smile. She wanted to laugh and hold her arms up to the brilliant stars and feel their billion bright possibilities cascading into her hands.

Instead, she simply watched Rio from beneath her long lashes. Rio, the man who had made her remember all those bright possibilities.

"Mason," Rio said, holding out his hand, "it's been a long time."

"Too long." He took the younger man's hand in his own gnarled grasp.

Only Hope noticed the instant of hesitation when

Rio saw Mason's swollen knuckles. Then Rio shook hands firmly but very gently, sparing the older man's arthritic hand.

The feeling of warmth that had stolen through Hope increased, melting the ice that had come to her stomach when she admitted that her best well was rapidly going dry. Knowing that Rio cared enough about Mason to spare his pride made her certain that she had been right to trust Rio.

"Judy sends her love," Rio said, "and the kids want to know if you'll be up for Thanksgiving. From the sound of it, they're having a three-ring circus for dinner."

Mason's glance slid to Hope, then away. "Maybe," he said, promising nothing.

Rio nodded, understanding that Mason wouldn't leave Hope alone on the family holiday.

She understood, too, and wanted to protest. Judy was Mason's sister-in-law, the last connection he had to the dead wife he had loved for forty-two years. But Hope didn't protest aloud. She and Mason had argued over the subject too many times. He wouldn't go on a trip without her, and the ranch couldn't be left untended overnight, much less for several weeks.

"Water's warm," Mason said, gesturing toward the basin and towel waiting just inside the service porch.

With the quick, efficient motions Hope had come to expect from Rio, he swept off his hat, rolled up his sleeves, and washed as much skin as he could reach. When he was finished he looked around at the yard.

Then he picked up the basin and flipped its contents on the ground where a wilted lilac bush struggled to survive in the lee of the porch.

More of the ice inside Hope melted. She caught Mason's eyes and smiled approvingly.

While Rio ate, Hope enjoyed the uncommon luxury of sitting and doing nothing more strenuous than drinking a cup of Mason's potent coffee. As she sipped, she let her mind drift, dreaming lazily of a time when the ground would be green rather than hard as stone, and her cattle wouldn't have to walk themselves thin just to get from food to water and back again.

Rio's deep voice and Mason's age-roughened tones wove in and out of her waking dreams. She didn't really listen until the men began discussing beef and water.

"How many head are you going to sell?" Rio asked as he forked a juicy chunk of steak into his mouth.

"Not a single cow," Mason said flatly.

Surprised, Rio looked up. In the artificial light his eyes were like midnight-blue crystal, startling against the tanned planes of his face and the rim of his jet-black lashes.

"Boss don't want to sell," Mason explained. He pointed toward Hope with the stem of the ghastly old pipe he loved and she refused to let him set fire to indoors.

Without another word, Rio went back to eating.

"Aren't you going to tell me that the price of beef will only get lower and the cattle thinner?" Hope asked him, her voice tight with the echoes of old arguments and refusals.

"Waste of time," Rio said. "You know your choices better than anyone in the room."

For a moment her new dream slid away from her, leaving her suspended in a cold present that had few choices, none of them pleasant.

"When you decide to cull the herd," Rio said matter-of-factly, "if I'm not here to help, use Dusk. She'll cut your work in half."

Hope nodded, unable to speak for the tears and the sudden fear squeezing her throat.

The more cattle she sold, the closer she came to the moment when she would have to auction off her beautiful Angus herd. They were the very soul of her dream of a new ranch, a new life, a future that held fat black cattle instead of the knife-lean Herefords of her nightmares.

In the water-rich future of her dream, the ranch house would ring with plans and laughter again. Maybe then she could dare to dream beyond the needs of the cattle to her own needs. Maybe then she could dream of a man who would love her, of having children who would grow up tall and straight on the land. . . .

Hope's empty coffee mug hit the table with a solid thump as she stood up, slamming the door on her treacherous thoughts. Not since she had turned eighteen had she allowed herself to dream of love and children. There was no point in dreaming about it now. She had other dreams, possible dreams, dreams that depended only on her own strength and determination rather than on the unknowable, undependable mind of a man.

In her lifetime she had found few men to respect. She had found none whose children she wanted to have.

Seven

✿

"THINK THE BATH water is hot yet?" Hope asked Mason.

"Not likely. But the buckets on the stove are near boiling. I'll haul 'em up for you."

"Don't bother," she said quickly. "Cook Rio another steak. He's doing the work of two men."

Before Mason could object, she went to the huge ranch stove. Two big buckets of water simmered over the hot flames. With them, plus some cool water from the faucet, she could have a lovely bath.

Hope picked some pot holders off a nail and reached for the wire handles that stood above the buckets. An instant later the pot holders vanished from her fingers and reappeared in Rio's big hands. With the easy strength that she envied, he lifted the full buckets off the flames and turned toward her.

"After you, ma'am," he drawled.

"Thank you," she whispered too softly for Mason to hear.

Rio nodded slightly, understanding and admiring her desire to protect the old man's pride.

While Rio followed her up the stairs, he admired something else. The womanly swing of her hips and the long, graceful line of her legs held his eye. The thought of sharing her bath teased his mind until he forced himself to think of something else.

Anything else.

Wanting a woman like Hope was at the top of his list of dumb things he could do. He was supposed to be smarter than to go looking for trouble.

He waited while she bent over and put the plug in the big, old-fashioned bathtub's drain. The feminine lines of her back and hips were even more alluring than her walk had been. Beneath the frosted glass globes of the bathroom lights, her hair had a rich satin shimmer that cried out to be stroked by a man's fingers.

She turned and looked over her shoulder at him with gold-flecked eyes and a generous mouth made for giving and receiving kisses.

"Ready?" she asked, wondering why Rio was watching her so intently.

Heat slammed out from the center of his body, hardening him in a rush of sensation that made his pulse beat heavily. He was more than ready. He was aching. His lips flattened into a line of disgust at his unexpected, unruly sexuality. He was acting like a kid with his first party girl—and God knew that he was no kid and Hope was no party girl.

Without a word he emptied buckets of scalding

water into the tub, turned, and left the steamy room and the woman who watched him with too many dreams in her eyes.

Drugged by heat and physical exhaustion, Hope dozed in the bath long after she was clean. Her dreams were a tantalizing mixture of water in all its forms—hot, cold, calm, racing, deep, shallow. And through all of it wove a midnight-blue river, deep and sweet, gentle and dangerous, longer than forever and more powerful than any drought. It called to her in Rio's voice, whispered to her the secrets of his midnight-blue eyes, caressed her flesh, and sank into her thirsty soul.

The sound of Behemoth rattling through the front yard startled her awake. The bathwater was still warm. She looked out the steamy window and saw the lights of the truck cutting through the night to the pasture where her Angus grazed in the darkness. The cattle bawled uneasily, then accepted the wheeled intruder. With only the moon's thin, cold smile for company, Rio began filling the stock trough.

Eager to talk with him even though she had nothing new to say, Hope washed and dried her hair. As she pulled on a clean shirt, the truck grumbled to life again. Hurriedly she yanked on her jeans and stuffed her bare feet into her boots.

Too late. Rio was already heading off into the night. She didn't have to ask or wonder where he was going. People and cattle alike needed more water in order to survive.

When she got downstairs, Mason had already gone to one of the ranch's two bunkhouses. He and his wife had converted the smaller bunkhouse into a home. But Hope didn't think Rio would be spending the night under Mason's roof. It wasn't that Mason was unfriendly. It was simply that the place was a cozy kind of mess.

Since Hazel's death, Mason's housekeeping had been of the lick-and-promise sort. He ignored Hope's offers of help. A lot of the bunkhouse hadn't been touched since the day Hazel had unexpectedly died. Mason had made it clear that he wanted it that way.

Hope hadn't argued. It was little enough comfort for the man who was the only family she had left.

But the state of Mason's bunkhouse meant that if Rio stayed at the Valley of the Sun, he would have to sleep in the other bunkhouse or in the house.

Hope rejected the possibility of the second bunkhouse as soon as she thought of it. It would take too long to clean out the pack rats, mice, spiders, and dust that had collected since the last of the ranch hands had left a year ago. Rio would have to use either the remaining upstairs bedroom in the ranch house or the daybed on the screened porch downstairs.

The thought of having him sleeping just down the hall from her upstairs room made a delicious sensation prickle over her body. Telling herself that she was being foolish, she made up the bed in the upstairs room and put out fresh towels. Then she made up the bed in the sunroom, shaking out the sheets and blankets with a brisk snap. To make the choice an even one, she set out towels on that bed, too.

Then she wrote a note and stuck it on the back door, telling Rio to take his pick of beds.

The note didn't say that she wanted him upstairs, that she wanted to fall asleep in his arms and wake up the same way. It certainly didn't hint of her hungry curiosity about his taste, the resilience of his body, the feel of him in passion.

"Don't be stupid," Hope said under her breath as she slid into her own bed. "He's here to find water, not to hammer me into a mattress."

She shivered at the sound of her own words. After Turner's bruising attack, she hadn't wanted any man to touch her.

Yet she couldn't think of Rio without wanting just that. To be touched by him.

The sound of the truck driving into the yard awakened Hope later in the night. The back door squeaked open. She held her breath and listened for the sound of a man's footsteps climbing the stairway.

The downstairs shower sputtered to life, shaking and hammering as water shoved air out of the pipes. Rio was as fast and efficient at showering as he was at everything else, because the water ran for only a few minutes.

She held her breath again.

A door creaked. It was the door that opened from the kitchen to the screened-in porch that ran along the back of the house.

Hope told herself that she wasn't disappointed. She

was still telling herself when she fell asleep. She didn't hear anything until her alarm went off in the small hours after midnight. Since she had worn her clean clothes to bed, it didn't take long for her to dress. She pulled on boots, jacket, gloves, and hat, and headed out into the darkness.

The predawn chill bit into unprotected flesh. Despite the lack of rain, it was still November. Hope's breath was a pale gust of steam that was absorbed instantly by the dry air, as though even the sky itself was thirsty for any bit of moisture.

The stars had a brittle brilliance that came only when there was almost no humidity in the air. A breeze stirred fitfully, bringing with it a cold promise. Winter was waiting to sweep down out of the north, riding on the back of the long, icy wind.

Hope rubbed her stinging nose, pulled her denim jacket closer around her body, and hurried into the barn. A rooster crowed like a rusty engine, then with greater force, although only an optimist would have said that dawn was near. Hens clucked and muttered as though resenting the rooster's loud summons to another day of pecking the dust and each other.

After she scattered food for the chickens, she checked the nests for eggs while the hens were busying their sharp little beaks on grain. The drought hadn't upset the chickens in the least. Fifteen eggs waited within straw nests like huge pearls within shapeless golden shells. She pulled a paper bag out of her jacket pocket, carefully put the eggs inside, and left the chickens to what they did best—eating and complaining.

When Hope went to check on Dusk, she saw that Rio had been up and in the barn. All the chores she usually did were already done. Fresh hay filled the mangers. All the horses were groomed, the stalls had been raked out. New straw gleamed on the floor of every stall.

Unexpectedly, her throat closed around tears or a protest or perhaps both. "Damn it, Rio. Didn't you get any sleep at all?" she asked huskily.

Dusk rubbed her head against Hope's chest. Automatically she petted the mare.

"Maybe he sleeps on his feet, like a horse."

Dusk rubbed harder, nearly knocking Hope off her feet.

She checked the side yard, wondering if maybe Rio had taken care of everything before he went to bed instead of after he got up. The dusty pickup truck that she and Mason used was gone. Mason was up and about already, and off on some errands of his own, leaving her alone on the ranch. Or else Rio had taken the truck.

Not that it mattered to her either way. She had no reason to make a long ride into town. What did matter, and what she reluctantly admitted to herself, was that she had been looking forward to seeing Rio this morning, to sharing coffee and breakfast and conversation with a dark stranger who seemed more familiar to her than most people she had known for years.

Carrying the fresh eggs, Hope hurried across the dusty, gravel-strewn yard between the barn and the ranch house. She hesitated at the back-porch door. A quick glance told her what she already suspected. Rio was gone. He hadn't even left a trace of his presence. The daybed was made up with military crispness and the braided rag rug lay smoothly in place on the uneven floor. Not only was the wash-basin empty, it had been wiped dry until the old metal gleamed.

It was as though she had dreamed yesterday after-noon at the stock tank, the unexpected luxury of a hot bath, and the compelling man with night-black hair and gentle hands.

With an unconscious sigh she went into the kitchen. Normally Mason would have been up and making cof-fee strong enough to float horseshoes. But the kitchen was as clean and empty as the washbasin had been. A note on the scarred table explained that Mason had taken Rio to the Turner ranch to pick up his truck. Rio would come back after work. Mason would turn up sometime before noon.

Hope fixed breakfast and ate quickly, hardly taking the time to admire the color and freshness of the eggs. She poured coffee into a large thermos, tucked it under her arm, and hurried toward the water truck. She had three other stock tanks to fill, one of them even larger than the tank she had trucked water to yesterday. Twice.

She wouldn't get every stock tank completely full. There simply wasn't enough time. All she could do was haul enough water to each tank to keep the cattle from drifting off into wild country in a futile search for something to drink.

With a deep, unconscious sigh Hope opened the heavy truck door and swung up into the cab. The engine grumbled and coughed and backfired and grumbled some more, but finally ran. She let out the clutch, turned the wheel, and discovered that the truck was ungodly heavy. The only explanation was that its tank was already brimful of water.

Not only had Rio filled the trough in the Angus pasture, he had driven all the way back to the Turner well, filled up again, and driven all the way home. All that, after a full day of work with Turner's horses, and another full day ahead of him.

Hope blinked rapidly, trying not to burst into tears at this new evidence of Rio's thoughtfulness.

"Oh, wonderful," she muttered to herself, swallowing hard. "You stand to lose everything you ever had or wanted and you don't even sniffle. But let somebody be kind to you and you spring a leak. Get a grip, girl. You're no good to anyone if you snivel."

Despite the bracing lecture, she had to blink several times before she could see well enough to steer the awkward rig out of the yard and onto the dirt road. She drove as quickly as she could to the nearest well. It was the oldest one on the ranch, all but hidden in an unexpected hollow of the land.

The windmill was motionless when she got there, for it was too early in the day for the wind to blow. It wasn't too early for the cattle to be thirsty, yet none were pressed around the trough, eager for water.

Fear squeezed Hope's heart, making it beat harshly. *Why aren't the cattle crowding around to drink? Are they lost? Stolen?*

Dead of thirst?

Then she caught the gunmetal gleam of water brimming in the trough and understood what had happened. This time she couldn't stop the tears from spilling down her cheeks. Rio had filled this trough, let the cattle drink, and filled it again, until the cattle were full, all thirst slaked.

Then he had emptied the last of the truck's water into the trough, gone to the Turner well, and filled up once more, working long hours while she relaxed in a hot bath and slept more soundly than she had in months.

Rio had done all of it without being asked, because he knew she was too stubborn—and too afraid—to admit that she had to cull her herd again, selling off the range cattle she didn't have the time or strength to haul water to.

"Damn you, Rio," she whispered, tasting her own tears on her lips. "You're not fighting fair."

Then she realized that he wasn't fighting at all. He was simply doing what had to be done if she wanted to keep what was left of her range cattle.

And her dream.

"He worked most of the night to give you half a day's start," she told her reflection in the dusty windshield. "Are you going to use it or are you going to sit here and cry enough to fill the trough all over again?"

She wiped her eyes, took a fresh grip on Behemoth's wheel, and drove toward a more distant well. When she got there, she was half-afraid to look. She didn't know what she would do if Rio had somehow managed to be there before her.

He hadn't. Cattle crowded around the useless windmill and the nearly empty stock tank.

She drove the truck in close, wrestled the hose into place, and sat in the cab while the trough filled and the sun climbed out of night's deep well. She loved the pale tremors of peach and rose that preceded dawn, and the incandescent orange and scarlet that silently shouted the arrival of yet another day.

Despite the drought, despite her deep fear of losing everything, despite the exhaustion that would come before sunset, Hope counted each day spent on the ranch as a separate miracle. There was no place on earth for her like the Valley of the Sun.

She rolled down the window of the cab and listened to water rushing into the tank. Cattle bawled and shoved and thrust their dusty white faces eye-deep in the water, drinking lustily. Smiling at the sight, she settled back into Behemoth's rump-sprung seat and dozed to the rich sounds of water pouring.

"I'll expect you for dinner," Mason said to Rio. "Six o'clock sharp. Earlier if you can make it."

"If I'm not there at six, go ahead without me. I'll eat mine cold when I get there."

Mason looked up at the sky. The sun was about a hand's width above the horizon, but he didn't need light to know that today would be another day without a prayer of rain. He could taste the dryness in the air, feel it on his lips, hear it in the crackle of static electricity whenever he slid around on the pickup's vinyl seat.

"You got here at sunup," Mason said calmly. "Even a mean, lazy son of a bitch like Turner can't expect much more than twelve hours a day from a hand, specially when he's only paying for eight and expects you to eat lunch in the saddle."

Rio shrugged and tugged his hat down. Turner was riding him hard, but there wasn't any need to complain to Mason about it. Rio knew, even if Mason didn't, that John Turner came down like a load of stone on any man who showed up at Hope's ranch. Even if she had the money to hire more hands, Turner would have found a way to drive them off the Valley of the Sun. He didn't want any man under sixty within a country mile of Hope Gardener.

A predatory smile curved Rio's mouth. Sooner or later, Turner would stop hiding behind being the boss and start leaning on Rio openly.

Rio was looking forward to it.

"The longer hours I work, the sooner I'm shed of Turner," Rio said easily. "See you tonight."

With a wave, Mason turned the truck around and headed it toward the gate. He was almost halfway to the town of Cottonwood. Might as well go the rest of the way and run a few errands. Seemed like every time he turned around, one ranch machine or another chewed up a hose part or something.

Before he got to the gate, a man on horseback trotted up to the truck. Recognizing Pete Babcock, a man who used to work for the Valley of the Sun, Mason braked and rolled down the window. Babcock was a schoolteacher-turned-cowboy, a gossip, and a hard worker. Mason had hated to let him go, but there hadn't been any choice.

"Morning, Mason. Haven't seen you since calving time. You here to hire some men?"

"Wish I could say so, but it'd be a lie. I was just dropping Rio off."

Pete nodded and squinted toward the east, where the sun was just lifting its burning head above the ragged land. "Heard he was working for Miss Hope. Digging a well or some such."

"You heard right. He's gonna find us some water."

"Sure hope so. Miss Hope could use a break." Pete smiled, showing two rows of gleaming teeth. "It's a day for miracles, sure enough. The boss got up before any of us did and lit out of here like his ass was on fire. Said something to Cook about checking on the south well."

Mason went still. "South well? The one we've been hauling water from?"

"The same. Don't know what got into him. Usually he's the last one in the saddle and the first one back to the corral."

"When did he leave?"

"Oh, 'bout an hour ago. Maybe more. I was just getting up myself."

"Nice talking to you," Mason said quickly. "I'll let you know as soon as we're hiring."

Before the other man could answer, Mason let out the clutch and took off for the gate, tires spitting gravel every inch of the way.

Eight

✿

HOPE SHIFTED SLOWLY out of her half-dozing state and looked around. The canvas hose was flat, the truck's barrel empty of all but a cup or two of water. It was time to head to Turner's well for the first of several trips she would make today.

The road to the well was rough and tiring. Behemoth didn't have anything as modern as power steering, automatic shift, or power brakes. Driving the truck was a test of will and muscle that left her aching. She looked forward to the time when water would be sucked from the well into the truck's big tank. That was when she could rest, gathering her strength for the drive back to the Valley of the Sun. The truck was three times as awkward fully loaded as it was empty.

As soon as Hope turned down into the little valley where the Turner well was, she knew that there wouldn't be any peace and quiet for her while the truck filled with water. John Turner's Jeep was parked just beyond the windmill. The vehicle's bright red paint usually gleamed like a stoplight, but today the color was dulled by a heavy coat of dust, the kind that came from racing over a dirt road.

Her hands tightened on the wheel until her knuckles stood out white. She hissed a word under her breath, hating the sick sinking of her stomach and the clammy sweep of fear over her skin. Turner was quite literally the last man on earth she wanted to see.

Slowly she eased the truck into place by the generator, shut off the ignition, and hopped out with a lightness she was far from feeling. The sight of Turner's six feet four inches of thick-shouldered body didn't do anything for her except make her wish that she was somewhere else. Anywhere else. As long as he wasn't with her.

Since the drought and the second mortgage on her ranch, Turner had been hovering around her like a vulture circling over a downed antelope, waiting for it to give up and die.

"Morning," Hope said as she walked by Turner to get to the hose rack at the rear of the truck. "You're up bright and early."

Turner didn't make a move to help her handle the stiff, heavy canvas hose. "Where's Mason?" he asked.

She didn't bother to stop working and be sociable. She could talk and work at the same time. Especially to John Turner.

"I don't know," she said indifferently. "Do you need him for something?"

As Hope spoke, she wrestled a few coils of stiff canvas hose off the rack and scrambled over to the stock tank, dragging the muddy length of hose behind.

"I don't need that old man," Turner said, "but you sure as hell do."

She didn't glance away from her work.

"Look at you," Turner said in disgust. "Driving a man-sized truck and dragging that dirty old hose around like a drifter working off a handout. If Mason can't haul his own weight, fire him. Only a fool would pay the old fart's wages and then turn around and do his work for him."

Silently Hope pushed the hose into the tank far enough to be sure that the coils wouldn't leap out and flop around when water coursed through canvas. She took an extra amount of time about her work. She was counting on it to help control her anger at Turner's arrogance.

Without even looking at him, she climbed down the stock tank's narrow metal ladder to the muddy ground, caught up the end of the hose that had to be coupled to the generator-driven pump, and dragged the hose into place near the rusty, sunstruck machine.

Turner stalked after her. "Well?" he demanded.

"Well what." Her tone said that she wasn't really asking because she really didn't care.

This was the tricky part of the water-hauling operation. She had to brace the hose so that its weight wouldn't drag the brass coupling apart, while at the same time she struggled to bring the warped threads into alignment.

"I asked you a question," he snapped.

"I answered it. I don't know where Mason is."

"That's not what I meant and you know it." Turner jerked off his pearl-gray hat and slapped it against his thigh impatiently. His men knew it was a warning sign that he was losing his temper. He figured Hope knew it, too.

From the corner of her eye, she saw Turner's wavy chestnut hair gleam richly in the sunlight. His blue eyes were narrow and intent in his cleanly sculpted face. At one time the sight of that movie-star profile and curly hair had made her heart beat faster. But she was no longer young. Turner's shiny hair meant less to her than the dusty red hides of her range cattle.

A lot less.

The threads slipped and jammed. Hope set her teeth, unscrewed the crooked coupling, and tugged the heavy hose back into position.

If Turner had taken his hands out of his pockets and helped, the job would have gone quickly. As it was, Hope wasted several minutes before she succeeded in lining up the threads. She turned the brass ring carefully, always making sure that the threads stayed in the proper position. Holding her breath, she coaxed the coupling into a good mate.

"What the hell's got into you?" he asked finally, his voice harsh.

She reminded herself that she was using Turner's water. It was all that kept her from ignoring him completely. She got up, dusted off her hands, and went back to the truck for the big wrench to tighten the coupling.

"Hope," Turner said in a threatening voice, *"you better answer me."*

"All I heard was a lecture on my stupidity. If you had a question, you'll have to repeat it." Her voice was as even and measured as her motions. She worked the jaws of the heavy pipe wrench until it fitted over the brass ring on the hose.

"What the hell was Rio doing at your ranch last night?" Turner asked baldly.

Anger shot through Hope as hotly as the sunlight pouring over the land. Yet when she spoke, her voice was so carefully controlled that it had no tone at all. "He works for me part-time."

"I told you not to hire him."

The wrench clanged against the ring. She readjusted the jaws, took a better grip, and tightened the coupling with a vicious downward yank.

"Well, baby doll? Didn't I tell you?"

"Do I tell you how to run your ranch?" she asked, shifting her grip for another yank.

"I'm a man."

"The day you run your ranch using nothing but your gonads is the day I'll listen to that argument," she said coldly. "Until then, I'll run my ranch like any normal person would—with my brain and my hands."

She yanked down again. The coupling was so tight that it all but sang with tension.

With practiced motions she loosened the wrench, removed it, and propped it against the generator. Time to prime the pump. She grabbed a bucket and went to the trough.

Turner watched her without moving or speaking.

He didn't have to say a word. She could tell by the color of his face and the set of his jaw that he was furious. His blue eyes looked pale against his flushed cheeks.

"Fire Rio," Turner snarled.

"No."

Hope labored over the pump and generator. Finally she got the crank to turn hard and fast enough to start the balky engine. The pump sputtered, the hose shuddered, and water began sliding through canvas into the empty truck. The muted thunder of water filling the truck normally soothed her. Today she barely heard it for the angry roaring of blood in her own ears.

"You like using my water?" Turner asked.

The fear that leaped inside Hope didn't show in her face. "Are you saying that if I don't fire Rio, you'll shut off the water?"

Turner hesitated. Put that bluntly, it didn't sound reasonable or even particularly rational. As far as he was concerned, Hope's struggle to keep the Valley of the Sun alive was irritating and laughable, but it had attracted more than a little admiration in the closed community of western cattle ranchers. When people found out that he had refused to give her water—water that he didn't need—simply because she had hired a drifter to find a well, Turner would be the butt of hostile gossip and outright contempt among the other ranchers.

"No decent woman would be alone with Rio," Turner said tightly.

"Why?" Hope tried not to show her temper. She failed. She was tired and furious, a combination that loosened her tongue. "Does Rio promise to marry a naive eighteen-year-old, invite her over for birthday champagne, and maul her until she's bruised and screaming? Then does Rio shove a hundred-dollar bill into the girl's blouse and tell her he's engaged, but he'll be around later to collect the rest of what's owed him?"

"That's got nothing to do with—"

"You asked," she shot back, "and I'm telling you." She faced him with hazel eyes that were harder and less feeling than glass. "After the mauling and insulting, does Rio's father drive the girl home, lecturing her the whole way on how she can't expect to marry above herself?"

Turner made a wide gesture with his right hand, sweeping aside her words. "Rio's no goddamn good. He's got women all over the West."

"Are they complaining?"

Turner shrugged impatiently. "Who the hell cares?"

"If the women like it and Rio likes it," Hope said neutrally, "what's the problem?"

"They aren't my women. You are."

"No," she said curtly. "I'm not."

"Bullshit, baby doll. You're mine. You want me. You just don't want to admit it."

"Well, we agree on one thing. *Bullshit.*"

Turner's flush deepened. "Listen, I've had enough of your holier-than-thou act. Your mother was a drunk, your father was a loser, and your sister was a slut with a reputation from here to Los Angeles. Hell, even your grandparents weren't much more than dirt farmers."

"Thank you," she said sardonically. "Always nice to know your friends."

"Hell. It's just the truth. You should be glad I'm offering you more than a hundred dollars a fuck. I want you and I'm going to have you."

"I. Don't. Want. You."

Turner laughed and shook his head. It took more than a few words to puncture his confidence.

"Sure you do, baby doll," he said, reaching for her. "But like I said, you just don't want to admit it. Since you don't believe me, I'll just have to show you what I mean."

She blocked his grab by swinging the heavy wrench between them. He laughed and made another try for her. She leaped to the side and brought the wrench up again.

"That's it," he said, his voice thickening with excitement. "I dream about your little hands clawing and fighting me." He grabbed the wrench and held it despite her struggles. "Yeah. Good. God, it turns me on so hard I can't think when a woman fights me. Remember?"

Hope remembered all too well. She dropped the wrench, twisted out of his reach, and leaped into the cab. Her fist slammed down the lock on the door just as he grabbed the handle.

Laughing, Turner bent to pick up the wrench. It wouldn't take more than a moment to smash out the window. Just as his fingers closed around the cold iron handle, he heard the sound of a vehicle racing down into the valley at a speed too fast for the road.

Assuming that it was one of his own men coming to check on the well, Turner straightened and turned toward the road, still smiling with anticipation of finally having Hope. His smile vanished when he spotted Hope's own beat-up tan truck pulling a rooster tail of dust toward the stock tank. Mason was behind the wheel, driving like a maniac toward Behemoth.

When she recognized the truck, a wave of relief swept through Hope that left her light-headed. Only then did she admit how much Turner frightened her. She was safe now. Mason was here. Mason wouldn't let Turner near her.

In the next heartbeat she knew that she couldn't tell Mason what would have happened if he hadn't arrived. He would lose his temper and jump Turner.

She couldn't let that happen. Mason would be beaten, and beaten badly. Turner liked using his huge strength on weaker people, hitting and hurting them with his thick hands.

She remembered just how much he liked it.

With an effort of will Hope forced her breathing to slow until her body relaxed and her hands stopped trembling.

"Well, old man," Turner said when Mason got out of the truck, "you finally hauled your lazy ass out of bed. I thought I was going to have to do all Hope's work myself."

With eyes that were so narrow they showed almost no color, Mason gave the other man a contemptuous glance. Then Mason saw the wrench lying in the dust and Hope inside the water truck with the window rolled up and the door lock down. Blind rage shot through Mason, shaking him.

"I'm here," he said flatly. "I'm staying. We don't need your help."

Turner smiled amiably. He was sure Hope meant yes even though she was saying no, but he didn't necessarily want witnesses when he made her admit it. Theirs was a private fight. It was going to stay that way.

His word against hers.

"Then I guess I'll get on back to the ranch." Turner looked up at Hope as she opened the truck door. "See you real soon, baby doll. I'm looking forward to it."

"Good-bye." Her voice was like her face, without expression.

When he slammed the door to his Jeep and shot away from the well, Hope swung down from the cab and forced herself to smile at Mason.

"Glad you stopped by," she said casually. "It gets real boring just talking to a bunch of cows while the truck fills with water."

"Did that shit-eating coyote lay a hand on you?"

"Nope," she said honestly.

What she didn't say was that Turner had tried his best. If she had been any slower, she would have been on her back in the dirt.

Mason waited for Hope to say more. He knew he was getting only part of the truth, the part she wanted him to know. He started to say something, then bit it off. His lips flattened into a colorless line.

"I'll do the water hauling from now on," he said.

"No." Her voice was smooth and calm. It left no opening for an argument. "But if you'd like to ride shotgun," she added, smiling widely at him, "I'd love to have the company. Like I said, talking to the cows isn't real stimulating."

He looked at her for another long moment. She was smiling her familiar, heart-warming smile, but her skin was too pale. He was certain that Turner had tried something. It was what Mason had feared since the instant Pete had told him about the boss getting up real early and going to check on the south well.

Though few men spoke aloud about it, Hope wasn't the first woman to find herself on the rough end of Turner's arrogance. Only one girl had gone to the sheriff over it. The humiliation that had followed was a lesson to any other female who thought she had the same rights as Big Jase Turner's son.

Mason knew that no matter what happened, Hope wouldn't say anything to him about Turner. She was trying to protect Mason's pride. Just like she had by taking over the water runs. She knew that Mason's hands were too bad right now to handle the heavy truck and the stubborn couplings. He wouldn't have a chance against a man less than half his age and nearly twice his weight.

Silently, secretly, Mason cursed the fate that had let him live long enough to lose his beloved wife and then grow too old to defend the woman who meant as much to him as any blood daughter could have.

"I'll ride with you from now on," he said quietly.

Hope didn't argue. She was relieved to know that she wouldn't have to face Turner alone again. The man simply didn't understand plain English. To him, *no* was a coy prelude to a wrestling match.

Maybe that was how his other women liked it, but not Hope. The thought of fighting Turner both frightened and sickened her. Like the thought of having his hands all over her again. It made breakfast do a backflip and try to climb right up her throat.

Mason went to the pickup truck and lifted a rifle from the rack that stretched across the rear window. He checked the load, eased the firing pin back into place, and pulled a box of shells out of the glove compartment. When he came back to Hope, he was smiling.

There was something in his smile that made her very glad to be his friend rather than his enemy.

"Snake gun," Mason said laconically. His voice was rough with age and the fury that still turned deep inside his gut at the thought of Turner lying in wait for Hope like a coyote at a water hole. "Drought like this, you git snakes at the wells."

She cleared her throat. "Yes, I've noticed that."

He stopped smiling and looked at her unflinchingly. "If I ain't around and you gotta go to a well, you be goddamn sure you got a snake gun with you. And you keep it real close to hand no matter what you're doing. Hear me, Hope?"

She tried to smile. She couldn't. Instead, she hugged Mason quickly. "I hear you."

He nodded curtly. "I'll watch the pump. You go over that little rise and run some rounds through this here rifle. Been a long time since we done any shooting together."

Hope didn't argue that she would rather have dozed in the cab. She took the gun and the shells and walked over a rise until she came to a place where there would be no chance of a ricochet hitting any cattle. She found a particularly ugly clump of big sage growing against the bank of a dry ravine, mentally labeled the bush *John Turner,* and began trimming it down to size one twig at a time.

When Hope had shot enough rounds to soothe Mason and herself, she walked back over the rise to the well. Mason was tinkering with the generator. Whatever he was doing had an immediate effect; the sound of the engine decreased by about half. He stood up to listen, nodded, and bent over the machinery again. There was a long-spouted oilcan in his hand.

"You're incredible," she said, half-exasperated, half-delighted. "I oiled that blasted machine from one end to the other two days ago and it didn't get a bit less noisy."

He smiled, pleased that there was something he could still do right despite his aching hands. "You done fine, honey, but you don't like this generator and she knows it. Takes a gentle hand to keep her humming."

"Not to mention gas and oil," Hope said beneath her breath. Her fuel bills were a constant drain on her cash. She reached out to unscrew the fuel-reservoir cap and gauge the contents with a pessimistic eye.

"Already checked it. It'll do 'til tomorrow."

Hope hesitated, made sure the cap was on tight, and unconsciously squared her shoulders. "When I get back to the ranch, I'm calling Hawthorne."

It had to be done and Mason knew it. But nobody had to like it.

He took off his hat, rubbed his forehead, and settled his hat back into place with a quick jerk. "How many you selling?"

Closing her eyes, she tried not to think about her range cattle burning like garnets against a sunset ridgeline where piñon grew in ragged lines of black flame.

"I—I don't know. Half." She swallowed. "Yes, half. That should stretch the natural feed enough to last until the rain comes."

"Hawthorne gonna use his own men for the cows?"

"He did the last time." Hope bit back a curse and shrugged instead. Whining never made a job easier. "If he can't use his own men, I'll hire the Johnston boys. They love a roundup."

Mason smiled. "Yeah. Good kids. A mite young, but we all was once."

She remembered her own teenage years and smiled a bittersweet smile. "Yeah. Real young."

He rested his hand on her shoulder and squeezed. The gesture said all that he didn't have the words to tell her: respect, support, love, understanding. He had never been more proud of her than at this moment, when she squared her shoulders and faced what had to be done without complaining.

"You grew into a damned fine woman," he said simply.

"I just do what I have to for the ranch." She smiled crookedly and looked around the dry, mysterious land that was part of her soul. "I spent most of my time after

I was fourteen being homesick for the Valley of the Sun. I hated L.A. Julie and Mom loved it."

Hope sighed and fell silent. If her father hadn't had to pay for two homes, he would have had enough cash to look for more wells. But her mother had insisted on having her daughters go to high school in a "civilized place." So her father had taken the ranch's small profits and mailed them to L.A. Then he had prayed that the Hope well would keep on running sweet and pure until he had saved enough money to dig a deeper well.

"Poor Dad," she said softly, not realizing that she had spoken aloud.

Mason put his arm around her shoulder. "Don't go feeling sorry for him. He done what he wanted and let hell take the rest."

Her throat ached with tears she wouldn't cry. "But he worked so hard."

"He didn't grudge a bit of it. He lived for the summers when you and your ma came home."

Mason didn't mention Julie. Hope's sister had always been a beautiful butterfly child, barely able to stand up to the heat of a simple summer day. The hard work and isolation of the Valley of the Sun had defeated her as much as they had bored her.

Hope had been the opposite. She loved the heat, the isolation, the silence, and the sight of cattle moving through the piñons. She had been born for this land in a way that her mother had never understood.

Mason smiled, remembering the good times. "Having you following him around with bright eyes and bushels of questions made your dad feel taller than God and smarter than Satan."

Hope smiled sadly. She had loved her father very much.

So had her mother, something that Hope hadn't realized until her mother was dead and a grieving daughter found the letters that her parents had written while they were separated.

"Mom loved him," she said.

Mason sighed. "Love. Hate. Coins have two sides. Your ma's passions ran deep. Deeper than the wells we never drilled."

Hazel eyes looked up at Mason, seeing the past in his lined face, hearing it in his familiar voice.

"You're like her in that, honey, when you let yourself be. You got your dad's grit, though. His and then some. You musta got Julie's, too." Mason shook his head at the memories welling up like a clear, unexpected spring. "She was pretty as a Christmas calf, and just as sure to die young."

A familiar tightness settled in Hope's throat. She had loved her older but not wiser sister, had held her hand through wrongheaded affairs and brutal rejections. Hope had tried to talk with Julie, to help her understand and cope with a world that simply did not care whether one Julie Gardener had champagne and roses or vinegar and skunkweed.

Julie had never accepted the basic truth of the world's indifference. Her self-absorption had been both innocent and soul-deep. After their mother had died, Julie discovered drugs.

She had died within two years.

"Don't look so down in the mouth, honey." Mason tugged gently on a handful of Hope's dark curls. "Julie just wasn't made for this world. It happens that way, time to time. So you bury the ones that can't make it and you wipe your eyes and you get on with living. Because you was made for this world, Hope. No mistake about it. You're strong and straight and giving. You was made to love a good man and raise strong sons and daughters with staying power. You and your children will heal the Valley of the Sun. And then the past will all be worth it, all the dying and the tears and the pain."

Looking at Mason's seamed face and clear eyes, she felt his certainty like a benediction. She stood on tiptoe and kissed his gray-stubbled cheek. "You're a good man," she whispered, her voice catching. "The best."

He smiled gently at her and handed her a faded scarlet bandanna to catch the tears that were welling from her wide hazel eyes.

"Thanks." She laughed oddly as she wiped her eyes. "Lately I seem to have more water than my namesake well."

"You're tired, honey. You're doing the work of two men."

Hope's only answer was a long, ragged sigh and a shrug. "Not of two men like Rio. Did he get any sleep at all last night?"

"He's a tough son." Approval warmed Mason's laconic statement.

"But it isn't fair for him to—"

"Fair don't water no cows," Mason interrupted bluntly. "You git to worryin' about fair and you won't have no time left to smile. Take my word for it, gal. I been there."

"The least I can do is fix up the other bunkhouse for him to use."

"Don't bother. Rio liked the porch just fine. If it gits too cold," Mason added matter-of-factly, "he can take one of the upstairs bedrooms."

Hope knew her shock showed on her face. She had expected Mason to object to any arrangement that ended up with Rio and the unmarried boss lady sharing the house.

"Something wrong?" Mason asked.

"I don't know."

"Speak plain, honey. I'm an old man."

She snorted. "As long as I've been at the ranch, you've been standing over cowhands with a shotgun if they so much as said hello to me. But Rio—Rio moves into the house with me and you don't turn a hair."

"He's different."

"Are you saying he likes men better?" she asked baldly.

Mason laughed and shook his head at the things she had learned during her modeling career. Then he looked at Hope with eyes that were faded by age and made wise by experience. "Nope. He's not married, neither. But that's not why Rio won't touch you."

She made a wry face and swiped her hand down her blouse, brushing out dust. "I'm not real happy about touching myself right now."

Mason didn't smile. "Oh, you tempt him sure enough. He ain't blind. But he won't do nothing about it."

"Why?" she asked, her voice tight with the surprising pain she felt. "Is something wrong with me?"

"You know better, honey. Rio's just got too much respect for you—and for hisself—to bite off something he ain't got no mind to chew."

"What does that mean?"

"Rio knows you're a permanent sort of woman. And Rio . . ." Mason rubbed his neck and shrugged. "Rio's a temporary sort of man. He never stays nowhere for more than a few months at a time. Just the way he is. Footloose as the wind."

Hope said nothing for the simple reason that her throat was closed tight. She didn't doubt the truth of what Mason was saying. In the deepest part of her mind she knew that he was absolutely right.

And in the deepest part of her heart she wished that he was absolutely wrong.

Nine

❧

BECAUSE THERE WAS no one around to notice, Hope climbed slowly, almost painfully, down from Behemoth's cab. Stretching helped, but not much. Her arms were cramped and aching from the effort of manhandling the heavy vehicle out of ruts and through tight curves.

Even with only half the range cattle left to take care of, she still had barely enough hours in the day to make the necessary water runs. Since Hawthorne's men had trucked away her cattle last week, she had worked constantly while dry winds churned dust devils out of an empty sky.

In the past week the temperature had dropped into the low sixties for several days. The nights had edged down toward freezing. Rain had been predicted yesterday and the day before, part of a northern storm front sweeping down from Alaska and Canada.

So far, no rain had fallen.

Half-eager, half-dreading what she would see, Hope looked toward the Perdidas rising tall and hard from the dry land. Thin clouds shimmered and swirled around the rugged peaks. Other patches of clouds floated randomly in the deep blue sky.

Not enough.

Not nearly enough.

Although the air was no longer so dry that it burned against Hope's skin, rain hadn't fallen in the high desert. Only the mountains had been blessed with water. Clouds had condensed in the cold air high up the Perdidas. After a day, moisture thickened into a black veil stitched with glittering threads of lightning. Wind carried the sound of thunder to the desert below like a distant sigh, bringing with it a scent of rain that was as thin as a shadow.

Some of the temporary creeks that drained the Perdidas' rugged slopes carried small streams of water again. There wasn't much, but it was enough so that the most adventurous cattle could spread out from the wells. Every cow that moved out into the countryside eased the strain on the natural feed around the troughs. The animals were on the edge of dangerously overgrazing the land around the wells, damaging it beyond repair or recovery.

Yet the small pools in the creek beds and ravines were already drying up. The parched land and dry air sucked up water much faster than it could be replaced by mountain runoff. If it didn't rain again soon, there wouldn't be any more surface water around than there had been a week ago.

If it didn't rain soon, she would have to haul feed as well as water to her remaining range cattle.

"You're borrowing trouble again," she told herself. "No need to do that. God knows you have enough without going looking for more."

Nearby an Angus mooed and walked with heavy grace toward her. The cow's eyes were huge, dark, and had lashes as long as Hope's little finger. The animal's coat was thick, slightly curly, and had a black satin richness that begged to be stroked. Butting gently against Hope's arm, the cow demanded attention.

"Hello, Sweetheart." Smiling, she rubbed her palms vigorously over the cow's long, solid back. Automatically she looked for any cuts or scratches that might need a swipe from the bottle of gentian violet that she always kept in the truck. "Where's your Sweet Midnight?"

Sweetheart snuffled.

"Out running around again, huh?" she said sympathetically, scratching the base of the cow's blunt ears. "Well, what do you expect of a half-grown bull calf?"

Sweetheart butted Hope less gently this time. The cow knew there was a handful of grain somewhere nearby.

Laughing, Hope shoved against the cow's muscular neck. She might as well have shoved on the Perdidas. Sweetheart stood pat on her four sturdy legs, demanding her due as Hope's first and most favored Angus.

"Sweetheart, if I'd known eight years ago that such a cute little 'kivver' would grow into twelve hundred stubborn pounds of confident cow, I'd have sold you for steaks."

The Angus blinked her incredibly long-lashed eyelids. Her moist muzzle prodded Hope's stomach again.

Giving up the game, Hope went back to the truck's cab. She untied the grain bag, picked up a battered cake pan, and scooped out some grain.

"Here you go, girl."

Sweetheart cleaned the pan with more enthusiasm than manners. Her long, thick, surprisingly agile tongue slicked over the metal until nothing was left but a vague scent of oats. The cow lifted her head and looked patiently at Hope.

"Nope," she said. "Just one pan for you."

She threw the pan back in the truck and started to pull the hose off the back. As she dragged the ragged canvas tube toward the well, Sweetheart backed off a bit and watched with what could have been interest, confusion, or amusement.

None of the more than thirty black cattle crowded in around the trough as Hope filled it. She was careful not to let the water get so low in the Angus trough that there would be shoving matches and trampling hooves around the big tank. Her breeding animals were too valuable to risk in a free-for-all among thirsty cows.

To Hope, the Angus were the very core of her dream of building the Valley of the Sun into a productive ranch. For that—and for their massive, muscular beauty—Hope loved the Angus. Sweetheart was more a pet than the lean cats that kept the barn from being taken over by mice.

Sweetheart was also a valuable breeder. Hope had kept four of Sweetheart's calves for the breeding herd. Sweet Midnight, the most recent of her calves, showed promise of being a prizewinning bull. Several ranchers had offered to buy the robust yearling. Hope had turned them down, even though the money would have helped her out. She was saving for the future.

Sweet Midnight would be the founding sire of the Valley of the Sun's Angus herd. The cows he would breed were as carefully researched and chosen by Hope as Sweetheart had been. Their bloodlines were the finest. It showed in their bulky grace, surprisingly gentle temperaments, and their vigorous, muscular offspring.

Relaxing against Sweetheart's massive warmth, Hope listened to cattle suck cool water from the trough she had filled. Other cows came up and snuffled over her shirt as if to say hello. Then they moved off to bury their noses in the fragrant hay Mason had brought to the pasture earlier in the day.

Hope watched each cow, each calf. She knew them individually, their strengths and weaknesses, their quirks of temperament. She was alert for any signs of disease or injury, no matter how small.

There weren't any. With a wry smile she admitted that the cattle were in better shape than she was.

The wind stirred, shifted, blew more strongly.

Sweetheart turned and watched beyond the truck. Her blunt, furry ears were cocked forward, but she wasn't nervous.

Hope glanced over her shoulder and saw Rio walking toward her. Sweetheart mooed softly as she wandered over to the tall man. Hope saw the sudden flash of Rio's smile as he held out one hand and ran the other down the cow's neck. Sweetheart's long tongue curled out, swiped across his extended palm, and vanished.

When Rio walked up to Hope, the cow followed like a pet dog.

"What's your secret?" she asked.

"Salt," he admitted, grinning.

He shoved hard on the persistent cow's neck. She heaved a barn-sized sigh and ambled back to join the other Angus.

"Must be time to put out more salt licks," Hope said.

"I'll do it tomorrow."

"I can do it."

"I'm sure you can." He had seen her handle the heavy blocks of mineral salt once, and had promised himself he would take over that job.

"But you're going to do it anyway."

"How'd you guess?"

Laughing, she shook her head, pushed off her hat, and let it hang from its rawhide thong down her back. She shook out her hair and combed her fingers through it. She loved the feel of the wind lifting the heavy mass of hair away from her face.

Rio wondered if the sudden, hungry speeding of his pulse showed against his neck or temple. Deliberately he looked away from Hope's unintentional seduction and stared at the cattle instead.

"Good herd," he said after a moment or two. "One of the best I've ever seen."

"Thank you. I won't pretend I'm not proud of them. I bought some, culled calves, and raised the rest. They're my gift to the Valley of the Sun."

Rio's black eyebrows rose in surprise. To him, Hope was as unexpected as water in a stone desert. "Your family didn't raise Angus?"

"No, but Dad always wanted to. The first thing I bought him with my modeling money was Sweetheart. He didn't live to see her bred."

"You were a model?" Rio asked, surprised again.

Hope thought of the picture she must make—dirty boots and stained blue work shirt, faded jeans and a beat-up cowboy hat. She smiled crookedly. "Long ago, far away, in another country."

Not all that long or that far, Rio thought hungrily. He didn't say it aloud. He was trying not to look at her the way a man looks at a woman he wants. Badly.

Yet he couldn't always force himself to look away. His uncanny eyes had memorized the purity of Hope's profile, her shining hair, the womanly lift of her breasts, and the long, achingly lovely line of her legs.

He had known more beautiful women in his wanderings, women who could make men stop and stare in hunger and disbelief. He had never known a woman who called to his mind and senses the way Hope did. He wanted to talk with her, laugh with her, help her, protect her, stand close to the shimmering radiance of her dream.

And he wanted to touch her, to learn the hot, secret textures of her body, to know the sweet demands of her mouth and the heat of her response, to hear her cry out his name when the pleasure he brought her consumed her to her soul.

Grimly Rio called himself a goddamned idiot.

Hope wasn't for him. His mind knew it, but his body was fighting that knowledge every bit of the way. All Hope had to do was breathe and he wanted her with a force that was different from anything he had ever known with another woman.

Despite the heat coiling in his gut, making him ache, Rio wouldn't make a move to touch Hope. He had nothing to give her but the well he wanted to find for her, for her dream. When he found it, when the dream was truth, then his brother the wind would call to him. And he would leave.

Hope deserved better than that.

He looked away from the woman he shouldn't touch and said quietly, "I'll bet you were good at it."

"Modeling?"

He nodded.

Hope smiled and dismissed her career with a wave of her hand. "I made a lot of money, but I wasn't an international cover girl, if that's what you mean."

"Did you want to be?"

"No."

"Why not?"

"All I ever wanted was the Valley of the Sun. After Mom and Julie died, I was free to come back home."

"You don't model anymore?"

Hope gave Rio a sideways glance out of hazel eyes that were haunted by shadows and lit by flecks of gold.

"No. When I'm in L.A. . . ." She shrugged. "I'm not a city girl. I can live there, but I don't like it."

"The money is good."

"That's why I stayed as long as I did. I had to pay off the inheritance taxes or sell the ranch. After I paid off the taxes, I worked until I thought I had enough money to keep the Valley of the Sun going while I built up the herds and put the ranch on a paying basis."

"Is there ever enough money on a ranch?" he asked dryly.

She gave him a bittersweet smile. "In some ways, I was as green as grass. I didn't know that there's no such animal as 'enough money' when you're talking about a desert ranch."

"Could you go back to modeling?"

"Could you live in a city?" she asked.

"I have."

"And now you don't."

Rio didn't answer. He didn't have to. He was here rather than in a city. So was she.

Hope looked at her beautiful black cattle and the brilliant currents of water welling silently up from the hose at the bottom of the tank.

"I could exist in the city," she said slowly, trying to make him understand what she barely understood herself. "I can only *live* here. This is my past, my present, my future. No matter where I live, the Valley of the Sun is the only home I'll ever have. I've always felt that way. I always will. The ranch is part of me."

He wanted to put his arms around Hope, to fold her gently against his body and hold her, to promise her that he would find the well that would allow her to live forever on the land she loved.

But he couldn't do it. Not the holding. Not the promising.

As a child he had learned that promises were only words, and that the unspoken promise of a comforting hug could be the biggest lie of all.

Not that his parents had meant to be cruel. It just had turned out that way. They had been more interested in fleeing the Indian part of their heritage than they had been in anything else, even their black-haired son.

Silently Hope and Rio watched the cattle glisten blackly beneath the clear light of morning. The fact that it was Friday morning—and early morning at that—suddenly registered on Hope.

Rio shouldn't be on the Valley of the Sun. He should be at Turner's ranch.

"Did you finish with Turner's horses?" she asked.

"After a fashion."

She turned and looked at Rio, caught by something buried in his western drawl. "What does that mean?"

He smiled sardonically. "Turner gave me a choice—work for him at triple my present wages, or work for you full-time." Rio's drawl deepened. "I allowed as how I'd rather dig wells in bedrock with a toothpick than work for him."

"*Damn him,*" Hope said savagely, furious. Turner knew she couldn't afford to pay a hand full-time wages. He had counted on squeezing Rio, who needed a paying job. "I'll make it up to you somehow."

"Like hell you will," Rio said coolly, no drawl left. "Any problems I have with Turner are mine, not yours."

"Not this time. Turner doesn't want you working for me. He threatened to cut off my water unless I fired you."

Rio said something beneath his breath that Hope was just as glad not to quite hear.

"When?" he demanded.

"A little more than a week ago. It was just a bluff. I called it and that was the end of it."

"Well, that explains something."

"What?"

"Why Turner suddenly found twenty hours a day of work for me to do at his ranch. He was making sure I was too dog-tired to sweet-talk you into anything he wouldn't like."

"Too tired? He doesn't know you very well."

Rio gave her a sidelong glance. "You hinting that I'm a tomcat who's never too tired for a quick one?"

She laughed almost bitterly. "I'm saying you have better things to do than screw around with me."

"Turner says you're engaged to him."

Anger sent scarlet rising in Hope's cheeks. "He's lying."

Rio measured the truth and fury in her and nodded with a satisfaction he didn't show. "Is that why you're carrying a rifle in the water truck these days?"

She gave a casual, on-cue shrug that was worthy of her best modeling days. "Mason said there were a lot of snakes around the wells."

"Smart man," Rio said. Then with deadly calm he asked, "Did Turner make a try for you at his well?"

She looked at Rio's eyes and saw the promise of violence in their cold blue-black depths. She looked away and said nothing, not wanting to lie to him.

"Hope?" he asked softly.

"It wasn't anything serious," she said finally. "It just takes a while for the word *no* to sink into Turner's thick skull."

Rio hooked a thumb toward the heavy cast-iron pipe wrench that was propped against the truck's rear tire. "Try using that to drive home your point."

"I did."

He glanced sideways, saw that she meant it, and smiled like a wolf. Silently he added one more to the list of things he would do on the Valley of the Sun: if he had to leave the ranch for any reason, he would be certain that Hope wasn't alone.

Then Rio remembered that he wouldn't always be around to protect her.

Hope saw his sudden frown. "I have enough money to pay wages," she said. "Not as much as Turner, but—"

"No," Rio cut in. "Our deal hasn't changed. Room and board for me, range and a stud for my mares."

" 'For as long as the water flows.' "

He raked his hat from his head, holding on to the Stetson's dusty black curves with fingers that were weathered and lean. Eyes that were used to focusing on distant, wild places measured the surrounding lands. He didn't see whatever he was looking for. With a disgusted word he replaced his hat and yanked on the rim.

"I have to find the damn stuff first."

What Rio didn't say was that he had been looking. He had come up as dry as the land itself.

Ten

🌿

"A FEW DAYS ago some of the slopes got rain down toward Turner's ranch," Hope said, watching Rio from the corner of her eye, wondering why he looked so grim. "Maybe it will rain here. Anything would help."

Reluctantly Rio focused his attention on the sky instead of the water he sensed was somewhere beneath the dry land, waiting to be found, waiting as it had for a thousand thousand years. Squinting against the sun, he measured the day on an inner, instinctive scale he had learned to trust.

A haze had formed above the peaks. Within the haze, thicker streamers of clouds were condensing as he watched. Instead of being painfully clear or brassy with dust, the air had a silver shimmer to it.

Moisture.

Well, that's something, Rio thought. Not the end of the drought, but better than a kick in the butt with a dusty boot, which was all they had gotten up to now.

"Rain by tonight." His voice was deep and certain. "A decent rain. Not enough to bring up the water table a whole lot, but it should revive a few of the seeps."

Hope let out a sigh that was almost a groan.

He smiled slightly. "Don't let down yet. We're not off water-hauling duty. But for a week or so we'll only have to make one trip a day, twice at most. We'll have to start hauling feed, though."

"I'll do the hauling. I hired you to find a well, not to be a ranch hand."

"That's right," he said agreeably. "You didn't hire me. I volunteered."

"I can't let you—"

He cut off her words with a dark blue glance that told her he was every bit as determined as she was. He was bigger, too, with a masculine power she couldn't hope to match.

But Rio wasn't like John Turner. Rio would settle disagreements with words, not raw physical strength.

"If we share the water hauling, you'll have time to ride the land with me," he continued.

The words surprised Rio even as he spoke them. He had been doing his best not to be alone with Hope. Yet, as he heard his own words, he admitted to himself that she was a big part of the reason he had offered to find a new well for the Valley of the Sun. The thought of riding the land with Hope had flowed deeply beneath his offer, like artesian water beneath a layer of unyielding slate.

He couldn't be her lover, but he could share her dream for a time, filling the emptiness that had come to him long ago, when he had stopped believing in his own dreams.

"I'll bet there are parts of the ranch that you've never seen," he said softly. "It's your land, Hope. Your future. Your dream. You should know every hard, beautiful inch of it."

Caught by his words, she looked at him with a longing she didn't know how to conceal or control. Like the land she loved, Rio could be grim and seductive by turns. His eyes were as deeply blue as twilight condensing into night. And like the night, he was alone.

She sensed very clearly the isolation in him, the darkness that lay beneath his smile, the long times of silence when he saw no one, heard nothing but the wind, and spoke only in the depths of his own mind. She felt a driving need to know the secrets hidden in his depths, the riches and sweetness that lay beneath a hard surface that no one had ever breached.

And because she wasn't a fool, she also wondered what dangers were waiting beneath his rugged surface, fault lines where reality could shift suddenly, crushing the unwary.

Yet danger, too, was part of why Hope loved the land. The Valley of the Sun accepted few people, and none of them easily. The children of the land knew how to survive. They also knew how to *live,* how to take a single moment and find in it an incandescent joy that few people ever knew.

The land had given her the incredible, silky coolness of water in the midst of drought. She had known the shimmering flash of light as the sun sank behind a stark, blue-black ridge, and she had tasted the piñon-scented breeze that flowed out of canyon mouths when everywhere else the air was still. She had shared the terrible power and beauty of an eagle swooping down on its prey, and savored the lush, secret perfume of a night-blooming cactus.

And always, always, there was the land itself, a silent symphony in every tone of gold and brown, moonrise and night.

These were just a few of the moments of intense pleasure, of soul-deep awareness of being *alive*, that the Valley of the Sun gave to those who understood the land. Hope wanted to share those moments with Rio, and to discover what other moments he had found to share with her.

"Yes," she said quietly. "I'd like to ride the land with you."

Rio's midnight-blue eyes memorized Hope. He saw both the darkness and the light in her hazel glance. The darkness he understood.

The light fascinated him as much as it made him wary.

"I'll unload my gear at the house," he said neutrally. "If it's all right with you, I'll take the east bedroom up-stairs. That way you and Mason won't feel like you have to tiptoe through my territory every time you use the back porch."

"Sounds good."

Hope ignored the flash of sensual awareness that came at the thought of Rio sleeping in the room next to hers. Even if he was sleeping on the floor in her bedroom, she wouldn't have to lie awake waiting for him to crawl into bed with her. Not by so much as a gesture had he showed any real sexual interest in her.

He liked her, though. She was sure of it. Even Mason had noticed it. He said that he had never seen Rio smile so much as he did when Hope was around.

"You going to fill the Hope's tank next?" he asked, referring to her slowly failing well.

"Yes."

"I'll be ready."

"Have you eaten yet?" she asked.

He shrugged.

Hope looked at the level of the tank she was filling. "I'll be finished here in about twenty minutes. Breakfast in thirty-five."

"You don't have to make—"

"Better hustle," she said, cutting across his objection. "If your boots aren't under the table when the eggs are finished, I'll feed every bit of your food to the pigs we don't have. That would be a terrible waste of fresh eggs."

His smile flashed, a hard curve of white against his dark face. He touched his hat brim in a brief salute. "Yes, *ma'am*," he drawled, his tone both soft and suitably awed.

She tried not to smile at his gentle teasing and ended up laughing out loud. Rio's response was that of a polite, slightly backward boy, yet he radiated a seasoned masculinity that was as unmistakable as it was fascinating. It was impossible not to be amused by the difference between the bashful words and the confident reality of the man.

He saw her struggle not to smile, heard her laughter, and winked at her just before he turned to go back to the house.

He didn't know who was more surprised by the wink, Hope or himself. He couldn't remember the last time he had felt so lighthearted, as if the day ahead was full of new places and possibilities to explore. There was something revitalizing about being in the presence of Hope, whether it was the woman or the simple fact of hope itself.

The memory of Rio's teasing kept Hope's mood light even when the brass coupling on the hose proved unusually stubborn. She whacked it apart with the heavy wrench, put everything back in its proper place, and drove the truck out of the pasture.

After she washed up outside, she let herself into the kitchen through the back porch. A single glance told her that Rio hadn't taken any chances on missing breakfast. He had set a place for himself—plate, silverware, coffee mug, napkin.

And his boots were tucked neatly under the table.

Hope laughed, feeling like a teenager again. She had expected many things after hearing Mason's description of Rio, but a dry sense of the ridiculous wasn't one of them.

Still smiling, she lit the oven, turned it as low as it would go, and put Rio's plate and a big platter inside. With no wasted motions, she took thick slices of bacon out of the refrigerator and draped them in a heavy cast-iron pan to cook. While the bacon sizzled she cut up potatoes into another black pan to fry.

When the bacon and potatoes were crisp and ready, she moved them onto the platter and tucked it into the oven again. Four slices of bread disappeared into the toaster. They popped up after a minute, transformed into crunchy brown squares. She buttered the toast and stashed it in the oven to stay warm.

As soon as she heard Rio's soft footsteps on the stairs, she reached up to the open cupboard shelf where she kept fresh eggs in an unglazed pottery bowl. When she brought the bowl down to eye level, she made a sound of surprise. A scattering of golden blossoms were tucked among the smooth, creamy curves of the eggs. The tiny wildflowers had bloomed out of season following a desert shower.

Rio must have picked the flowers on his way off of Turner's ranch. It was the only place around that had known rain in months.

The scent of the flowers was a delicate caress and a silent promise of life renewing itself despite the harshest drought. She closed her eyes and breathed deeply, filling herself with both the fragrance and the promise.

Emotion twisted through Rio as he watched Hope from the doorway. He would have given away everything he owned for the right to hold her, to inhale her promise as deeply as she was breathing in the fragrance of flowers.

But to do that would be to make promises of his own, promises he couldn't keep. *Brother-to-the-wind.*

When Hope opened her eyes, she saw Rio watching her with an expression that was close to hunger and even closer to regret. She smiled at him, wishing that he wasn't a temporary kind of man, wanting him anyway, wanting him even though she knew that he wouldn't take her.

She didn't know that her smile was an echo of his own expression, hunger and regret mingling into a yearning too deep for words.

"Thank you," she said huskily.

He watched her fingertip stroke a soft petal. He wished that it was his skin being touched so gently by her.

"My grandmother called them rain flowers," he said. His voice was almost rough with the beat of his blood, his hunger, the rushing need he refused to give in to. "She said they were the only gold that mattered in this land."

"What did your grandfather call them?" Hope asked, remembering Mason saying that one of Rio's grandfathers had been a Zuni shaman.

Rio's eyes narrowed as he tried to remember rituals from deep in his past. Slowly knowledge condensed like clouds across an inner sky, bringing a rain of childhood memories. The soft golden blossoms were medicine flowers, revered for their survival in the face of the harshest conditions.

Softly he spoke in phrases that had odd rhythms, ritual intonations, sacred sounds from a time and a place and a culture that had never been truly his, for his only culture and solace was the land.

He didn't translate the words into English for Hope. There was no translation that anyone would understand. His grandfather's spiritual center had been a blending of Zuni and Navajo, Apache and missionary Christian rituals. It had worked for his grandfather in ways that Rio understood but couldn't explain, one man's balancing of the ageless animism of Indian heritage with the overwhelming reality of modern European man.

"There's no real translation for the flower's name," Rio said. Then, softly, he added, "I've always called these flowers *hope,* for they bloom at times and in places where nothing else can survive."

Silence stretched between Hope and Rio, a silence that shivered with unspoken words and hungers. As she looked away from the midnight-blue depths of his eyes, she realized that for the first time in her life she wanted a man, truly wanted him.

And then she knew it was deeper than mere wanting. It was *need,* a raw emptiness that she had never known before. The thought of not having Rio, of never having him, was a pain so intense she had to fight back a cry of protest.

Hope's hands trembled as she filled a shallow earthenware saucer with a thin layer of water. Carefully she picked the small blossoms out of the bowl of eggs and floated the flowers on the transparent shimmer of liquid. She placed the saucer gently on the table between her place and Rio's.

The blossoms shivered with each movement of the water, as though they were alive and taking quick, tiny breaths.

"How do you like your eggs?" she asked, her voice

husky with all the things she wanted to say, and knew she shouldn't.

"Over easy."

Rio reached past Hope to pick up the huge black coffeepot that was warming on the back of the stove. His arm brushed over hers. It was an accident, but the brief sliding contact sent heat surging through him. He remembered the instant weeks ago when her breasts had pressed against him while she wrestled with the stubborn coupling on the canvas hose. The tactile memory was as clear and hot as the flame burning beneath the cast-iron pan.

The intensity of his response to a memory and a casual touch both surprised and unsettled him. Nothing had gotten underneath his skin like this for a long, long time.

He had thought that nothing could.

None of his turmoil showed in his face as he poured himself a cup of strong coffee. Life had taught him to show no more expression than that of an eagle arrowing out of the sky to claim its prey.

As he replaced the coffeepot, Hope reached for an egg. Her hand bumped into his arm. She felt resilience, heat, and strength as his biceps shifted beneath her fingers. The temptation to prolong the contact by running her palm over his arm almost overwhelmed her. She wanted to feel the warm satin of his flesh, the flex of his strength, the heat of his life beneath her palm.

The intensity of her need to touch him shocked her. She snatched back her hand as though she had touched burning metal.

"Excuse me," she said quickly. "How many eggs do you want?"

"Four."

His voice was absent. He was watching the very fine trembling of her fingers as she blindly reached for an egg. The evidence of her response to a casual touch set off a soundless explosion of hunger deep inside him that he could neither control nor deny.

Angry, needing, yearning, he watched her over the rim of his steaming coffee mug. A lock of her bittersweet-chocolate hair had crept free of the clip at her nape. The tendril of hair slid forward to curl softly against her neck.

He wanted to capture the dark curl in his fingers, to lift it to his lips, and then to kiss the golden skin of her unclothed neck.

Rio didn't know how desperately he wanted it until he saw his own hand reaching for the silky curl of hair. Cursing silently, he made his fingers into a fist and he turned his back on Hope's endless, innocent temptations.

As he pulled out a chair to sit down at the table, he saw his boots beneath and remembered Hope's delicious laughter floating up the stairway when she discovered the empty boots. He looked back at her silently cooking his breakfast and he . . . *hungered*. Automatically he kicked his stocking feet into the cowboy boots and adjusted his pant legs.

Then he realized he hadn't stopped watching the delicate curve of her neck, hadn't stopped wanting to taste her skin, hadn't stopped needing her in ways that shocked him even more than the unruly, insistent beat of his arousal. The direct response of a teenage boy combined with the complex needs of an adult male swept over him like wind over the open land.

And like the land, he had no defenses, only emptiness.

Grimly he reined his thoughts. There was only one way he could touch Hope that wouldn't destroy both of them, and that was by finding water for her, fulfilling her dream. It had always been enough for him in the past. It would have to be enough now. He had no more to give her except emptiness and pain.

"I've been looking over the papers your last hydrologist left," Rio said. He sipped at the hot coffee and added dryly, "Educated man, no doubt about it. But he didn't know a hell of a lot about this country on a first-hand basis."

"He was just out of school." Hope turned eggs with easy motions of her wrist. "City boy through and through. Nice kid. Earnest and real sorry there wasn't any water on my ranch."

Hope slid the eggs onto Rio's warm plate and retrieved the platter with its load of bacon, potatoes, and toast. She put it all in front of him. After adding honey and a jar of cherry preserves to the table, she left him to eat in peace.

Silently she poured herself a cup of coffee and began making sandwiches for lunch on the trail. Between sips of coffee she deftly assembled slices of beef and slabs of yeasty homemade bread. Several apples, plus a double handful of oatmeal and raisin cookies, joined the growing heap of food on the counter.

When it was all tightly wrapped and ready to go, she poured herself some more coffee and sat opposite Rio, not at all bothered by his silence. She had grown up around ranch men. Their work was hard and endless. No one had time for conversation until after his belly was full. Then the men would lean back and talk until their food settled or their consciences got the better of them and prodded them back to work once more.

Rio sensed Hope's relaxation and relaxed completely himself, grateful for her acceptance of silence. It left him free to savor each bite of the crisp fried potatoes, country bacon, homemade bread, and perfectly cooked eggs. He ate every bit of breakfast, mopped his plate neatly with a last crust of toast, and sighed with real pleasure.

"I'll take my wages in your cooking any day," he said, meaning every word.

She shrugged and smiled slightly. She had been raised cooking. She had always loved it, the colors and the textures and the smells, the pure sensual reward of creating a good meal. Her mother and older sister had never understood how she felt. To them, the kitchen was a punishment for being born female on a ranch.

"It's hard to go wrong cooking breakfast when you have fresh eggs in the cupboard and your neighbor's best pig in the freezer," Hope said.

Rio made a sound of disgust. "Tell that to the hundred bunkhouse cooks I've known."

Her smile widened. "That's how I learned. The

hands threw the cook in the corral trough and threatened to quit. I was only ten, but I'd been cooking since I was seven."

"What about your mother?"

"She hated cooking."

Rio heard more than the words. He heard the sadness and the acceptance and the loss that never went away but simply became part of life. He understood those things, and respected the fact that Hope faced what life gave her with a smile and the quiet strength that came from accepting what would never change.

"Did you spend much time in the drink?" Rio asked, smiling in spite of his thoughts. The image of a young Hope dumped into the horse trough was beguiling. She would have taken it with a splash and a smile, pulled herself out, and dripped all over the nearest cowboy.

"Just once. Thank God it was summer. The dunking felt real good."

"What did you do to earn the trough?"

"I made chocolate cake, but I mixed up the sugar and the salt. It was so awful even the dog wouldn't eat it."

Rio threw back his head and laughed.

The deep sound was as much a reward to Hope as his enjoyment of breakfast had been. She laughed softly with him, shaking her head at the memory of her mistake.

"Even today when I make a chocolate cake, Mason takes a very tiny first bite," she admitted. She smiled into her coffee cup. "Nothing obvious, mind you. Just a cautious little taste to make sure the sugar and the salt didn't get swapped around."

"I'll remember that."

He drained his coffee cup with a long swallow, then stood up with a smooth determination that Hope remembered from her childhood. *Man of the house, fed and ready to go back to work.*

The thought of what it would be like to have Rio as the man of her house leaped into her mind, burning with an intensity that stopped her heart. She forced herself to breathe, to push the idea of Rio aside, to ignore it. Impossible dreams had killed her mother and her sister. Hope had vowed that they wouldn't kill her.

She didn't have the strength or the emotion to spare for destructive dreaming. She knew it as surely as she knew that the man called Rio was as rootless as the wind keening across the land, always searching for something, never finding it, always moving on.

She hadn't needed Mason to tell her. It was there in Rio's eyes, in his silences, in his memories of a hundred bunkhouse cooks.

Rio's long fingers tightened around his coffee mug as he saw darkness veil the humor that had made Hope's eyes brilliant just a moment before. He wondered what memory or fear had come to her, stealing her laughter.

Suddenly, savagely, he wanted to know what haunted her. Then he wanted to smooth the downward curve of regret from her mouth with his own lips. But if he did, in the end they both would have more regrets, more sadness, the unending bitterness of betrayal.

She couldn't leave the Valley of the Sun.

He couldn't stay.

Brother-to-the-wind.

For the first time, Rio understood the tears in his grandfather's eyes when he told his grandson his true name.

Eleven

AFTER BREAKFAST, Hope and Rio walked beneath an empty, cloudless sky to the horse pasture just beyond the barn. The lunch she had just packed was in the saddlebags over his shoulder. So was a canteen of coffee. It would lose its heat soon enough, but people who worked the land learned to take coffee at whatever temperature they could get it.

"Where do you want to start?" Hope asked.

"We'll ride the boundaries first."

"High or low?"

He gestured toward the Perdidas rising in stark grandeur above the rumpled land. "Up there at the northern end of the ranch."

"Then you better take a good horse," she said. "The Valley of the Sun goes as low as two thousand feet here in the south and as high as seven up along the northern boundaries."

"You have timberland?" Surprise was clear in Rio's voice and in the dark line of his eyebrows.

She gave him a wry, sideways glance. "Timberland? Are you kidding? If it's a tree, it's on government-lease land. The part of the ranch that's above seven thousand feet is all on northwest-facing slopes."

"Northwest facing," he repeated, shaking his head. "That means nothing grows but big sage, mountain mahogany, piñon, and juniper."

"You got it. Not a decent board foot in the lot."

His mouth turned down in a sardonic curl. "It's the same way all over Nevada. The best land is government, the worst is Indian, and the rest of the Basin and Range country belongs to anyone tough and smart enough to hammer a living out of it."

"But it's beautiful land," Hope said.

"Most people don't think so. They look at the sagebrush and the bare mountains and they can't drive through the state fast enough. Maybe you have to be born here to appreciate it."

"My mother was born here. She hated it."

"So did mine," Rio admitted. "Being raised on a reservation was no treat for anyone, especially a part-Indian girl who looked like she got off at the wrong bus stop. She couldn't get off the res fast enough."

"Did your father like it?"

Rio made a sound that could have been laughter, but was too hard. "He hated this land more than she did. He was part Athabascan, born to northern forests and lakes. He hated them, too. But most of all he hated

being called Indian when his father was a renegade
Scotsman and his mother was a quarter Dutch."

Hope glanced sideways at Rio. She wondered if his
father had been like him, strong bones and easy
strength, raven-black hair and quick mind, silences as
deep as the night.

He hated being called Indian.

She wondered if Rio did.

As though hearing her silent question, Rio moved
his wide shoulders in a casual shrug that belied the
dark memories in his eyes. "My father never grew up.
He never accepted the fact that there's no such thing as
mostly white. People look at you and see only *not*
white."

There was a cynicism in Rio's words that made
Hope ache. She wanted to say he was wrong. She knew
he was right.

But not when it came to her. "When I look at you,"
she said calmly, "I see a man. A good one. Period."

He glanced quickly aside at Hope. Her voice was
like her expression, matter-of-fact. He could take it or
leave it, but it wouldn't change the truth of how she
saw the world.

How she saw him.

Without knowing what he was doing, he lifted his
hand to touch her cheek. Before he could, a drumroll
of approaching hooves drew his attention away from
Hope.

Storm Walker was cantering toward the fence, making rhythmic thunder roll from his dark hooves. In the
center of the pasture, two of Hope's four remaining

mares watched the Appaloosa stallion rush to meet the humans.

The stud was worth watching. Black except for a white stocking and the black-spotted white "blanket" that covered his powerful rump, Storm Walker moved with a muscular grace that made Rio want to climb on the strong black back and ride forever.

With a horseman's knowing, appreciative eye, he watched the stallion mince up to the fence and nicker a greeting. Quietly he stroked Storm Walker's warm, glossy neck.

Neither the man nor the stud was wary of the other. They had made friends the first time Rio leaned against the fence and talked Storm Walker over to him in low, soothing tones. Since then Rio had come to the horse pasture at least once a day, bringing a reassuring touch, a sprinkle of salt, and an admiration that grew every time the stallion moved over the ground with long, liquid strides.

Storm Walker blew on Rio's hat and shirt collar. Smiling, he pushed away the velvety muzzle.

"You're an old softie, aren't you," he said in a low voice.

Hope snorted. "Only until you get in the saddle. Then he'll shake the change right out of your pockets."

"Rough-gaited?" Rio asked, surprised. "He sure doesn't look it."

"Oh, once he settles down he's as smooth as deep water." She paused, then added dryly, "But settling this bad boy down is a bone-shaking proposition, kind of like riding a landslide. He needs a lot more work than he's gotten lately. He's spring-loaded and looking for fun."

"Hauling water hasn't left you any time to give him exercise," Rio said, understanding.

"Even if I had time, I can't risk getting thrown. If I break an arm or a leg trying to settle Storm Walker down, I'd have to sell my cattle or let them die of thirst." She shrugged. "My prancing bad boy will just have to wait until the rains come. Then I'll ride his spotted tail right into the ground."

Rio's smile faded at the thought of Hope climbing up on the big stud and being bucked off into a corral fence. Not that he thought she was a bad rider. He knew she wasn't. When he had put her up on Dusk, Hope had been as graceful and confident in the saddle as she was on the ground.

But Storm Walker was big, hard, and had a stallion's aggressive temperament.

"Is he a good rough-country horse?" Rio asked.

"He was born in the foothills east of here and ran free for the first three years of his life."

"Like Dusk. She lived wild until two years ago."

"Did you catch her?"

He nodded. "She led me on one hell of a chase, too." His eyes focused on an inner landscape of memory. "Her mama was a ranch horse gone wild, an Arab–quarter horse mix that was tougher than an old boot. Her daddy was part Morgan, part Arab, and ninety percent cougar, near as I could tell."

Hope remembered how her father had hated it when the wild horse herds grew beyond the land's ability to renew itself and still feed the herds. Then the meat hunters would come, chasing the wild horses with airplanes and driving them lathered and terrified into funnel-shaped corrals concealed by brush.

The hunts had been necessary to cull the herds back from the brink of starvation and to return feral horses to their owners. Necessary, but brutal. The alternative—starvation, disease, and a lingering death—was even more brutal.

Hope sighed. "How did you catch Dusk? Airplane?"

"I used the oldest method, the one the Indians invented centuries ago, when the Spanish horses were so new to America that the Cheyenne called them 'big dogs.' "

She smiled. "What method is that?"

"I walked Dusk down."

Turning, Hope stared at Rio. Mason had told her of men walking down wild horses more than a century ago. They followed the wild herds from water hole to water hole, never allowing them to rest. At first the horses ran at the sight and smell of man. Then they cantered. Then they trotted. Then they walked. Finally they were too tired to move at all.

It, too, could be a brutal method of capture, but at least it was almost as hard on the men as it was on the horses.

"It wasn't that bad," Rio said, understanding the expression on Hope's face. "I wore out Dusk's flight response as much as her feet. I just hung around the fringes of the herd, leaving bits of salt and grain, following the mustangs everywhere until I kind of grew on her. By the time I walked up to her with a rope, she simply wasn't afraid of me anymore. I was a member of the herd." He grinned suddenly. "A strange, slow, small, awkward kind of horse, but one of the herd just the same."

"How long did it take you?"

"Eight weeks. Ten. Maybe more. I lost track of time. This country's good for that."

"Losing track of time?"

Rio nodded absently. His attention was once again on the glossy Appaloosa stallion. "Mind if I ride him today?"

"Only if you break something," Hope said wryly.

"I wouldn't hurt a hair on his spotted hide."

"It wasn't Storm Walker's hide I was worried about," she retorted. "He's only been ridden a few times in the last year."

"He looks it. Just full of himself, isn't he? Don't worry, we'll do fine together."

Hope smiled. "Forget I said anything, just like I forgot that you make your living as a horse trainer when you aren't drilling wells for dirt-poor dreamers."

He looked at her, curious about the complex emotions in her voice when she described herself as a dirt-poor dreamer.

"I'd love for you to ride Storm Walker," she said. "The longer he goes without work, the harder he'll be for me to handle. And he never was easy. Not for the first few minutes, anyway."

Rio didn't waste any more time talking about it. He flipped the saddlebags he was carrying over the corral rail and went after Storm Walker. He had the stallion caught, curried, bridled, saddled, and inside the corral before Hope could change her mind.

Storm Walker knew what was coming. He was dancing and snorting, bristling with energy and eager for some fun.

"You sure you want to ride him?" she asked Rio. "You don't have to. I need a well more than I need a well-behaved stud."

Rio grinned like a boy. "You're doing me a favor. I've wanted to climb on Storm Walker since the first time I saw his glossy hide across the pasture."

"Okay, but don't say I didn't warn you." With one hand wrapped around the bridle just above the bit, she held the stallion still for Rio to mount. "Tell me when you're ready."

Rio gathered the reins tightly and sprang into the saddle with catlike ease. His feet settled into the stirrups as Storm Walker's body bunched into a hard knot of protest.

"Turn him loose," Rio said softly.

Expecting Storm Walker to explode, Hope let go of the bridle and climbed the corral fence in two seconds flat.

Rio didn't allow the stallion to buck. He held the horse's head up and let him fight a useless battle with the bit. The stud's powerful hindquarters rippled as he alternately lashed out with his heels and spun on his hocks. Sudden spins and jerks were the only way he could try to unload his rider, short of scraping Rio off on the fence or rolling over on him. Storm Walker was basically too good-tempered a horse to resort to those tactics.

Bucking, on the other hand, was just good clean fun.

Smiling slightly, Hope watched the man and the horse test each other, probing for weaknesses. Storm Walker backed up constantly, as though to say if he couldn't buck, he wasn't going to go forward, either. Rio's long, powerful legs closed around the stud's black barrel, urging him forward with relentless pressure. Rio could have used the small, blunt spurs he always wore on his boots, but he didn't.

After a few backward circuits of the corral, Storm Walker stood still and chewed the bit resentfully.

"Round one to you," Hope said.

Rio glanced sideways and said dryly, "Something tells me I can either let this son buck here or I can let him buck out there when my mind is on something else."

"You've got it. Storm Walker just won't settle down until he's had his fun."

"Yeah, I was afraid of that. Had a horse like him once."

"What happened to it?"

"I swapped it for a dog and shot the dog," Rio drawled. "Course, it was a gelding and ugly as sin."

She laughed, not believing a word of it.

With a sigh Rio tugged his hat down hard, eased his grip on the reins, and touched Storm Walker lightly with his spurs. The stud's head shot down, his heels shot up, and for the next few minutes he did his best to turn inside out. Rio rode the whirlwind with a skill that made it look easy.

Hope wasn't fooled. She had ridden that same whirlwind more than once. She knew there was nothing easy about Storm Walker working off a head of steam.

After the first few moments she let out her breath, confident that neither horse nor man would be hurt. She relaxed on the top railing, hooked her feet around the next railing down, and simply enjoyed the man and the stallion as they tore up the corral, two healthy animals perfectly matched, enjoying the test of power against skill.

Without warning, Storm Walker's head came up. He snorted deeply, then pricked his ears and looked over his shoulder at the man who hadn't come unstuck.

"Finished?" Rio drawled.

Storm Walker rubbed his nose on Rio's boot and then stood as placidly as a cow, waiting for instructions from his rider.

"That's it," Hope said, jumping down from the fence. "He won't buck again this ride."

"Thank God for small favors."

Rio stretched his back and shoulders, feeling the stallion's unleashed power in every muscle of his body. Then he looked at Hope's slender form and wondered how she had managed to stay on top of Storm Walker. It wasn't raw strength, that was for sure.

"My hat's off to you," Rio said simply. "You must be one hell of a rider."

Hope grinned. "I've eaten my share of dirt. And that spotted stud fed me most of it."

He chuckled and shook his head, enjoying her matter-of-fact acceptance of getting thrown. At the same time he quietly promised himself that if Storm Walker unloaded anyone for a while, it would be him. There was just a whole lot of power in that stud's spotted body. He could hurt a rider and never mean to.

"Want to ride Dusk," Rio asked, "or does one of your mares need work?"

"I'll ride Aces. She's Storm Walker's favorite. He'll be less anxious to get home if she's along."

Rio moved to dismount, then stopped and looked dubiously at Storm Walker.

Hope hid her smile. "Don't worry. You're okay as long as you don't take off the saddle. That's how Storm Walker knows a ride is finished—when the saddle comes off."

"One bucking session per saddling, huh?"

"That's it."

"Makes a man consider the joys of sleeping in the saddle," he said dryly.

Hope stopped trying to hide her amusement. She leaned against Storm Walker and let laughter bubble up like pure spring water. It had been a long time since she had simply given herself to any emotion except determination. When the last laughter finally rippled into silence, she took a deep breath and looked up at Rio.

"You're good for me," she said, her lips still curving in a deep smile.

"Keep you from breaking your neck?" he guessed.

"No. You teach me to laugh again. I'd almost forgotten how."

Her words sank into Rio like water into thirsty land, renewing him. Without stopping to think, he smiled gently and touched her cheek with his fingertips.

"It's you who teach me," he said, his voice warm and deep.

"What?" she whispered.

"Beautiful dreamer," he said softly. "You don't know, do you? You don't know what your dreams do to me. And your laughter."

Abruptly he closed his eyes, shutting out the vision of Hope watching him, eyes luminous with dreams, deep with promises that shouldn't be made and couldn't be kept. The fingers that had touched her so gently retreated and clenched into a fist on his thigh.

"I wish to Christ I was a different kind of man," he said bitterly.

"I don't." She trembled from his brief touch and from the savage emotions that had made his voice harsh. "I wouldn't change you any more than I would trade the Valley of the Sun for the green Perdidas. I was made for this land, Rio."

And I'm afraid I was made for you, too.

She didn't say the words aloud. She didn't have to. He heard them clearly in his own mind, as clearly as though he had spoken them himself.

And then he was afraid that he had.

Twelve

❧

SITTING ASTRIDE STORM WALKER, Rio didn't open his eyes again until he sensed Hope moving away. Brooding, he watched her go to the horse pasture. A clear whistle floated through the air. One of the horses whickered and trotted over to her. Like Storm Walker, the mare's stride was leggy and elegant.

A minute later, using nothing more than her fingers twisted lightly into the slate-colored mane, Hope led the dark gray mare into the corral where Storm Walker and Rio waited. The mare was big, clean-limbed, and powerful. She moved with the calm assurance of a domestic animal that had never been mistreated.

Hope shut the corral gate behind Aces and went into the barn. She returned almost immediately with a saddle, blanket, bridle, and a bucket of grooming tools.

Rio dismounted as smoothly as he had gone into the saddle in the first place. One-handed, he took Aces' saddle from Hope and flipped it expertly over the top rail of the corral. The blanket followed.

Together, working in silence, they groomed the mare. Before Hope could, Rio checked the mare's steel shoes carefully, knowing they would be going over some rugged, stony land. He checked the saddle cinch with equal care, looking for any weakness that could make the strap give way at the very instant it was most needed. A fall in rough country could easily be fatal.

While Hope watched, bemused at having the familiar tasks taken from her hands, Rio saddled Aces with the same automatic ease that he had done everything else. He had spent his life around horses. It showed in every smooth motion he made.

When Aces was ready, Rio pulled his oversized saddlebags off the corral rail and tied them in place behind Storm Walker's saddle. Not quite trusting the stallion to behave, he mounted in a single catlike motion. If the stud bucked, Rio would be ready.

As though the thought of bucking had never crossed his well-bred mind, the stallion turned eagerly toward the corral gate. With a wry smile at his own expense, Rio opened the wooden gate, let the horses out, and then refastened the gate without getting out of the saddle.

"How did the last hydrologist get around?" he asked.

"Truck," Hope said succinctly,

Beneath the shield of hat brim and eyelashes, she glanced aside at Rio. The harsh lines on his face had relaxed and his voice was calm, neutral, wholly controlled. It was as though he had never touched her, never regretted the kind of man he was, never heard her response, never shut her out so finally behind his closed eyes.

But he had done all of those things.

Hope turned Aces onto a dirt ranch road that went a short way into the foothills.

Rio followed. "Just a truck? He must have missed a lot of your land."

"He had a fistful of survey maps."

"Good thing, maps. Save a man a lot of saddle and boot leather. Not worth much for finding wells, though."

She let out a long breath. "That's what I hoped. I just don't see how he could spread out a piece of paper on the kitchen table and then tell me that if there was any artesian water on my ranch, it was three miles down and hotter than hell."

Rio's mouth turned in a sardonic curve that was a long way from his earlier smiles. "He was half-right. Three miles down it is hotter than hell."

With a light touch of spurs, he lifted Storm Walker into a lope on the dirt road. He held that pace until the horses began to breathe deeply and their coats took on a satin sheen that was just short of sweat. Then he alternated between a trot and a lope, eating up the miles without wearing down the horses.

When he reined Storm Walker back down to a walk, Aces was still alongside, her gunmetal legs easily keeping pace with the more powerful stallion. Rio nodded approvingly.

"Good animal," he said.

Hope smiled. "Thanks. I picked her out when she was two days old."

"You have a good eye."

"Right now I'd rather have a good well."

"If it's here to find, you'll get it. According to my map, the road ends two miles up from here. Is there a trail to the ranch boundary?"

"The road ends a mile up," she corrected. "Landslide."

He smiled slightly. "That's the problem with maps. The land keeps changing."

"There's a trail to Piñon Camp. Dad used to hunt deer there. That's only a few hundred yards from the ranch boundary, I think." She shrugged. "Close enough. It's hard to tell without an expensive, full-blown formal survey."

"It's hard to tell with one," Rio said wryly. "Sometimes it seems like each new surveyor has a new opinion. Besides, a surprising amount of the Basin and Range country has never been surveyed. Hell, it's hardly even been settled. Two or three cities and a whole lot of sagebrush and mountains in between."

"That's why I love it. Plenty of room to just . . . *be*."

"Yes," he said. "A lot of people don't understand that."

"Good. Leaves more room for the rest of us."

Smiling, Rio looked down at the road. There hadn't been enough rain to wipe out the tracks of the last vehicle to pass over the gritty surface. In places that were protected from the wind, tire marks still showed clearly. He noted that the tread patterns weren't those of either ranch truck.

"Hunters?" he asked, gesturing toward the tire tracks.

"The hydrologist. He came up here to get an overview of the whole ranch."

"Well, at least he wasn't entirely a fool. That's one of the things we're going to do."

The hydrologist's tire tracks went up to the landslide, stopped, crossed over themselves, and headed back down the mountain. Rio guided Storm Walker carefully around the tracks, looking for boot marks or any other sign that the hydrologist had gotten out of his truck and walked around.

There weren't any tracks.

Rio turned in the saddle and looked back over the trail. The road had climbed steeply in the last mile. There was a clear view of the tiny ranch buildings, the low desert basin beyond, and the next mountain range beyond that.

"This is as far as he went," Hope said. "I told him that Piñon Camp had a better view. He said he could see more than enough from here."

She looked beyond the landslide to the Perdidas rising darkly above the dry foothills. Then she turned as Rio had, toward the west.

The ranch boundaries sprawled invisibly along the rugged foothills like a carelessly thrown blanket. The basin between the Perdidas and the next mountain range fifteen miles to the west was low desert, a place of alkali flats in the summer and temporary, brackish lakes during the season of winter rain and mountain runoff.

The foothills were rugged, but not as steep as the east-facing foothills of the Perdidas. Small valleys thick with grass lay in the creases of the hills, guarded by rocky ridges where big sage and piñon and mahogany grew nearly twenty feet tall. They were shrubs rather than true trees, but so tall they were often called pygmy forests.

The endless changes of elevation fascinated Hope, basins alternating with mountain ranges that looked like tawny velvet waves frozen forever in the moment of breaking. A thin silver haze of heat shimmered above the basins, blending invisibly into the blue-white haze of extreme distance. There was nothing to stop the eye but range after range of mountains falling away to the far curve of the earth.

"How much do you know about the geological history of this land?" Rio asked quietly.

"Not much more than the name 'Basin and Range,' and that's self-explanatory," she said, gesturing toward the view. "Basin followed by mountain range followed by basin, world without end."

His clear eyes narrowed slightly as he focused on the distant horizon. *World without end.*

"You live in a rare place, Hope. It's almost unique on earth. Its closest cousins are the Baikal region of Siberia and the African Rift Valley. Those are places where the crust of the earth is being stretched by the force of molten basalt pressing up from below, literally tearing the continent apart. The crust thins and breaks apart under the pressure in a process called rifting."

Hope turned toward Rio, drawn by the near-reverence in his deep voice.

"In Africa the process has gone so far that parts of the rift are below sea level, just waiting for the south end of the rift to split the edge of the African continent and let in the ocean. Then a new sea will be born. Like the Red Sea, where the Arabian peninsula slowly split away from Africa and salt water bled into the gap, concealing the rift."

He watched the horizon for a moment longer, but his eyes saw only the compelling, massive, surpassingly slow movements of continental plates over spans of time so immense that they could only be named, not understood. Geological time. Deep time.

"A similar kind of crustal spreading is happening all the way down the center of the Atlantic Ocean," he added.

Just listening to Rio made Hope ache with all that couldn't be. His words were alive with a subtle excitement, the voice of a man who saw things few other people could, a man who was intellectually, spiritually, and sensually alive to the world around him.

"I'll show you maps of it tonight," he said. "The Atlantic rift is really something, all the frozen ridges of basalt and the flat intermediary basins being pushed east and west from a great central seam at the bottom of the ocean."

"I'd like to see that."

Slowly Rio's focus returned to the rugged land in front of him instead of the images in his mind. "The Basin and Range country is pulling itself apart, just like the Atlantic. Basalt wells up deep below the surface, fracturing the crust in thousands of fault zones. Some of the land rises along the faults, some drops, and then huge blocks of land tilt up and back like a dog pushing up on its haunches after sleeping in the sun."

Hope smiled at the image of blocks of land changing positions like a pack of great, shaggy dogs.

"That's what makes our mountain ranges," he said. "The tilting. Look over there. See it?"

She followed his glance from the Perdidas to the distant basin shimmering with heat.

"Tilting is why the west side of the mountains isn't as steep as the east side," he explained. "The uplift is sharper on the east face of the blocks. If you look with your mind as well as your eyes, you can see the blocks of land shearing apart, rocking back, rising, mountains growing up into the sky. And the higher the mountains go, the more clouds are combed out of the sky, and the less rain falls on the eastern side. The dry side."

"Valley of the Sun."

"Yes. And a lot of other valleys. That's where part of your water problem comes from. The Basin and Range country is in the rain shadow of the Sierra Nevada mountains. Young mountains, tall and growing taller. They block the clouds coming off the Pacific Ocean, milk them, and very little rain escapes to the other side. It's as though the mountains cast a shadow where it rarely rains."

He shifted slightly in the saddle, putting his palm flat on the saddle horn, and studied the land he sensed in his soul as much as saw with his eyes.

"Okay, living in a rain shadow is part of my problem," Hope said. "What's the rest?"

"There just isn't as much water in the atmosphere as there used to be," he said simply. "We're in a dry cycle. And I don't mean only the last few decades or generations. A hundred thousand years ago, if we looked over the Basin and Range country, we would have seen water, not sagebrush."

At first she thought Rio was joking. A look at his face told her that he wasn't. He was watching the land with eyes that saw through the surface of reality to the shifting forces beneath—shaman's eyes, darker than twilight, as hypnotic as his voice sinking into her, wrapping her in visions of an earth she had never dreamed.

"A lot of little lakes and two big ones covered this land," he said. "One of the lakes was nearly nine thousand square miles of water. The other was twenty thousand square miles." As though he was remembering, his eyes looked inward. "They were deep lakes. Hundreds of feet deep. They filled the rift in the land where the crust was being pulled apart."

"How? Was there really that much more rain back then?"

"Partly it was more rain. Mostly it was runoff and meltwater from the Sierras. The mountains got a lot more rain and snow then. Rivers that only run part of the time now were a year-round torrent racing down to fill the crustal rift."

"What about evaporation? Why didn't the runoff lakes dry up then the way they do now?"

"It wasn't as hot, which meant less evaporation. The water that came to the Great Basin stayed and created lakes. Men lived along the lakes, fished there, explored island mountain peaks covered with pines and glaciers, hunted animals that are now extinct, and saw vast fields of wildflowers bloom."

Hope listened without moving, enthralled by the words and the man who spoke them. While Rio talked she saw her land change before her eyes—and she saw him change, too. His country drawl was overlaid with words and phrases and concepts that should have been utterly alien to a drifting cowhand.

"But the last ice age ended, the weather warmed, and rivers stopped running year-round," he said. "Less moisture to evaporate. Less moisture to gentle the climate. More evaporation and then more, until the rains couldn't keep up." His voice was low, intense, seeing today's drought foreshadowed in the climatic shifts of fifteen thousand years ago. "The vast lakes began to evaporate. They shrank and shrank and shrank until nothing is left today but what we call Great Salt Lake and Pyramid Lake on the California-Nevada border."

He closed his eyes for a moment, seeing it happen, vast lakes becoming a desert. "All that immensity of water. Gone."

Hope saw, too, and mourned.

When Rio's eyes opened, he looked out on today's land, a dry land layered with fossil life forms from long-dead lakes.

"Today almost no water flows out of the Basin and Range country to any sea," he said simply. "Think of it, Hope. Thousands upon thousands of square miles of land drained by rivers that run into the desert and vanish. Mountain runoff goes down to the playas, the sinks, the basins between the ranges. And there the water stays. There are no networks of ponds and lakes, no rills and creeks and rivers running down to a waiting sea. There is only a blazing sun and an empty sky. And the wind, always the wind, blowing over the changing face of the land, touching all of its secrets."

Hope heard both Rio's words and the hissing whisper of a dry wind blowing over the Valley of the Sun. She had a thousand questions to ask him, a lifetime of questions aching for answers. Yet she didn't speak because she wanted him to keep talking, wanted to see the world as he saw it, an endless process of change and renewal, seas and mountains rising and falling, continents shifting.

And through it all there were rivers and clouds pregnant with rain, the recurring miracle of water.

As though Rio sensed her silent plea, he began talking again. "In the rare cases where there's still enough runoff to keep a low spot covered with water year-round, the lakes evaporate at a fantastic rate, up to one hundred fifty inches a year."

Hope winced. "God. It barely rains a tenth of that most years."

"That's how fresh becomes salt, over time. All water, even so-called fresh water, contains tiny amounts of dissolved salts. When the water evaporates, what goes into the air is truly fresh, no salts allowed.

The salts stay behind. Each year the fresh water goes and the salts remain."

Her saddle creaked as she moved slightly, as though she would hold back the flight of water from the dry land.

"Without enough new, fresh water, evaporation slowly turns a freshwater lake into a saltwater lake, useless to animals or plants," Rio said simply. "The Great Salt Lake is what's left of one of the huge Pleistocene lakes. Mono Lake is the remainder of another. Salt and little water." He shrugged. "That's how it went from the Sierra Nevada to western Utah and even beyond. All that land. All that water stolen by the sun and the thirsty sky."

Hope waited, watching him with an intensity that made her eyes almost dark. "Then the hydrologist was right? There's no hope for my ranch?"

Rio shifted in the saddle, wanting to promise and knowing he couldn't. All he could do was offer a fighting chance.

And that was all she had asked for. A fighting chance.

"Not all of the water evaporates," he said. "Some of it slides down into the land itself. It gathers between fist-sized rocks and pebbles no bigger than my thumb. It hides between grains of sand and oozes between particles of silt so fine you have to use a microscope to see them. It sinks down into some of the rock layers of the mountains themselves, limestone and sandstone and shale."

Suddenly Rio turned and pinned Hope with a vivid,

midnight-blue glance. "And the water stays there. There's water all through this country. Some of it is old water, fossil water, rains that fell when men hunted mammoths by the shores of ancient lakes."

Wind like a long exhalation from the past moved over Hope's skin, stirring her in a primal response. She looked at her ranch with new eyes, seeing beyond the drought of today to the water of a million yesterdays. When she turned back to Rio, her eyes were radiant with the vision he had shared.

He saw the beauty of her eyes, green and gold and brown, a mixture of colors that changed with each shift of light. He saw his own vision of time and the country reflected in her eyes and in the primal shiver of awareness that rippled through her.

And then he knew that she had understood his words as few people would have, or could. She had *listened* with her soul as well as her mind. She had seen time and the great land as he saw them, sharing his vision in an intimacy that he had never known with anyone.

At that moment he wanted nothing more than to lift Hope from the saddle and let her flow over his skin and he over hers like a rain-sweetened wind, touching all the secret places, bringing a passionate storm, sharing his flesh with her as deeply as he had shared his mind.

Silently cursing his unruly body, Rio reined Storm Walker around the landslide. After a moment he heard the long-legged gray mare follow. A shod hoof made a distinctive sound as steel rang on a stone buried just beneath the surface of the landslide.

When Aces moved alongside the stallion, Rio didn't

look at Hope. He couldn't. He was afraid that she would read the hunger in his eyes, afraid that her eyes would be hungry, too. Then he would reach for her, lift her into his arms, know her as deeply as he knew the land.

And in time the wind would blow and he would leave her as surely as water had left the land.

Rio rode on, wondering if the Great Basin's long-vanished rains hated themselves for leaving a hungry, hurting land behind.

Thirteen

HOPE AND RIO rode in silence until he could look at the bleak mountains without seeing a far more gentle flesh, could focus his thoughts on the slabs of differing rock strata broken and canted up to the sky instead of on the hunger that clawed through both his body and his mind.

He could deal with the passionate needs of his body. But the passionate hunger of his mind for Hope was new to him, as deeply disturbing to him as the up-welling of molten basalt was to the thick crust of the earth. He knew that their shared silence, like the shared vision before it, held an intimacy that he could neither describe nor deny.

Rio didn't speak until he was in control of himself again. It took a long time. Much too long.

"Most of the boundaries marked on my map of the ranch go something like 'one hundred and twenty paces on a Montana horse' or 'twelve degrees northwest of Black Rock Wash,' " Rio said. His voice was practical, empty of visions, offering no more than the dictionary meaning of his words.

"Homesteaders' measurements," Hope said. "Dad called them horseback estimates."

"They're not a hell of a lot of use when you're trying to figure out how to avoid drilling a well on someone else's land. When was the most recent survey of your ranch done?"

"Oh, about 1865, shortly after Nevada became a state. That was when one of Mom's great-greats decided to file on land that we'd been squatting on for twenty years," Hope added with a small curve of a smile.

Rio sighed and tugged his hat into place. "That explains it," he drawled. "Some rawhide ancestor of yours took a notion and filed on about thirty square miles of sagebrush and foothills. Damn shame he didn't take a cut of the high-country watershed while he was at it."

"Oh, he tried, but we could only show improvements in the foothills—spreader dams we'd built to slow the flow of the runoff streams, water holes deepened and cleaned out, wells dug, that sort of thing. Because we didn't need anything like that for stock in the high country, where there is water year-round, we didn't make any improvements."

"So the government kept the high country and you kept as much of the foothills as you could," Rio summarized. It was an old, familiar story around the Basin and Range.

"Plus all the government land we could sneak cows

onto," she added wryly. "We've never been real big on fences here in Nevada."

He smiled. That, too, was an old, familiar story. "How deep were the wells in those days?"

"It's hard to say. You know how it is. The 'good old days' were always better. The truth is they had droughts then, too." She hesitated, fighting to keep her voice neutral. "It's also true that the water table is dropping gradually, and has been for years. Some of the drop comes from too much pumping for local irrigation. Some of it comes from pumping water out and selling it to cities like Las Vegas. And some of it," she said bleakly, "comes from the simple fact that less rain is falling. This is a dry land and it seems to be getting drier every year."

Rio heard the hollowness in Hope's voice that she couldn't hide. He didn't ask any more questions.

Side by side they rode in silence until the dirt track dwindled to a trail winding up toward a ridgeline covered with piñon and juniper. Higher up, far beyond the point where foothills blended into the mountains themselves, stands of aspens touched by frost blazed like golden embers burning against a green and gray backdrop of pine and sage.

Saddles creaked and the horses began to breathe deeply as they leaned into the steep climb that led to Piñon Camp. Finally the trail took them to a gently sloping piece of land where piñon and pine grew thickly. A sun-cured meadow made a tawny contrast with the black rocks of the mountainside and the dense green of the piñon.

To one side of the trail there was a fire-blackened ring of stones, a rack for hanging game, and faint old footpaths leading from the camp to the meadow. Overhead a hawk soared in transparent circles, watching for movement below. Ravens and scrub jays called from nearby perches, warning other animals of the intruders that had appeared from the dry lands below.

Rio took in everything with the quick, comprehensive glance of a man who has spent most of his life in wild country. Then he looked again, seeing beyond the superficial clothing of plants and animals to the geological history beneath.

The meadow and the camp were part of a bench, a small block of land that a minor fault zone had caused to break away from the larger mountain block. The mountain had continued to rise on the far side of the local fault, while on this side the bench had continued to rise, too, but more slowly. The result was a sloping land surface that was higher than the surrounding foothills but lower than the mountain it had sheared away from.

Rio reined Storm Walker across the open land. Ahead of him the mountain rose suddenly, its side bare of all but the most determined sagebrush. The various steeply tilted layers of rock that made up part of the mountain showed in the changing colors and textures of the cliff, looking like thick stone ribbons that had been pushed and pulled by unimaginable forces.

Though worn by time and weather, twisted and broken by the movements of the earth, the stone layers had a story to tell to anyone who could read them.

Some ribbons of stone were relatively young sedimentary rocks. But the majority of the stone layers were old, dense, so darkened and changed by time and the movements of the earth that they were all but impervious to the elements now. Storm, wind, water, sun, nothing changed them. They were the spent, blackened bones of a younger time, a different world.

Somewhere, tilted at a steep angle and buried from sight, Rio believed there would be at least one thick layer of limestone, legacy of the great sea that had covered the land long, long before man arrived forty million years ago, when the Basin and Range country lay beneath a wealth of water that could hardly be imagined now. Since then, continental plates had oozed over the earth's surface, their passage lubricated by molten rock. The movement of the plates changed everything, making mountains rise and dragging other lands down beneath the surface of the earth until it became so hot that rock melted and ran like water.

"What are you looking for?" Hope asked.

"Potential aquifers." Rio's eyes were intent on the mountainside as he visually traced various twists and turns of stone. "An aquifer is a layer of rock that can absorb water."

She looked at the mountainside and then at him, then back at the flint-dry slope. Though she said nothing, it wasn't hard to read doubt in her silence.

"I know it's hard to believe," he said, reaching back into his saddlebag without taking his eyes off the mountain, "but some kinds of rock layers are nothing but big stone sponges. Given time and the right conditions, those strata will soak up incredible amounts of water."

"If you say so," she muttered. Her tone was as full of doubt as her expression.

By touch alone, he pulled a worn map and a pencil out of his saddlebag. "Sandstone is an aquifer, a stone sponge. So is limestone. Buried alluvial fans make great sponges. Most of your wells are drawing on buried beds of sand and gravel washed down from the mountains millions of years ago."

She looked at his hands. He was sketching as he talked.

"The water your wells brought up came from recent rains," he continued, "this year's water and the last, water soaking down into the land and renewing the wells with every rainy season."

He tipped his hat back on his head and studied the map. A lock of hair, straight and black as night, fell over his forehead. He didn't notice. His attention was on the tiny symbols he was adding to the worn map.

Hope ached to push the lock of hair back into place, to feel its texture and the heat of the man who wasn't even looking at her.

"In most places on earth," he said, squinting up at the mountain, "the groundwater would just ooze slowly downhill until it reached a river or a lake or the sea itself. But this isn't most places. Here the water just sinks down and down until it reaches a layer of rock it can't penetrate or until the heat of the basalt welling up from the mantle turns water into steam and sends it pushing back to the surface as hot springs and geysers."

She remembered, and in remembering, wanted to weep. Turner's land had such hot springs today. The Valley of the Sun had once had them, but they had dried up in her childhood, leaving behind a crust of colorful minerals and the memory of unearthly turquoise water that had pulsed with the earth's own heartbeat.

"Most people think of this land as desolate, sterile, and uninteresting," Rio said, his voice vibrant with his pleasure in the wild landscape. "It isn't. In many ways it's the richest, most exciting, and rarest of all the lands on earth."

Hope heard the emotion in his voice and felt even more drawn to him. She, too, loved this lean and difficult land. She, too, had learned the subtle, sweet, extraordinary rewards that the land gave to those who understood it. Her mother had never found those rewards.

Her father had, and had given up his wife and family rather than leave the land.

A quick movement of Rio's head caught Hope's attention, but it was the mountain he looked toward, not her. She remembered his words, watched his confidence as he reduced his observations to mysterious symbols.

And she wondered who Rio really was, and how someone of his obvious education had become a man who drifted through the country like the wind, leaving little to mark his passage but enigmatic symbols made upon the softer surfaces of the land.

What set him to living with the wind? What would it take to hold him in one place?

Hope heard her silent questions and smiled a bittersweet smile. Nothing held the wind. Nothing.

Certainly not a woman's dreams.

"What are you looking for?" she asked.

If he heard the sadness in her voice, he didn't show it. He wedged the notebook under his thigh and reached back into the saddlebag again.

"I'm looking for a layer of sandstone or limestone that's sandwiched between strata of rock that won't let water leak away. Sort of like a solid river flowing between waterproof banks."

It wasn't the answer Hope had asked for, but she knew it was the only one she would get. She shook off the sadness that clung to her like dust to the dry land. Her ranch needed water. Rio was a man who could find water. That was all that mattered.

It had to be.

"How does water get into the limestone if it's sandwiched between waterproof layers of rock?" she asked after a moment.

Rio glanced aside and couldn't help smiling with approval. She not only listened, she thought about what she heard. Other people he had helped had listened to him without understanding. They had been focused on only one thing. Water.

He knew that Hope needed water as much as the others had. Yet she was able to see the land as something more than a way to make a living. She sensed that in some indescribable way the land was alive, growing and changing with its own rhythms, its own inevitable movements, its own awesome beauty.

Hope saw that you could share the land's life if you had enough room in your soul for the sound of coyotes calling to a moon they had always known and would never understand, and for the sheen of a rainbow stretching between drought and water, and for the tiny, fleeting perfection of a medicine flower blooming against rocks a billion years old.

With a feeling of inevitability as deep as time, Rio understood that Hope had room in her soul for all that and more, much more, things he had always hungered for and never touched.

Does she know my hunger as deeply as I know her beauty?

With an odd feeling of sadness he turned his mind to Hope's question rather than his own. Her question was the only one that he would allow himself to answer.

"If the sandwich is lying flat," he said, demonstrating with one palm on top of the other, "the rain will just roll off the top piece of bread, the waterproof layer. But if you break the sandwich in several places and tilt the pieces up toward the sky, the aquifer—that's the softer center of the sandwich—will be open to the rain."

"So the center, the sponge, just soaks up everything?" she asked.

"I wish," he said wryly. "It would make my job a lot easier. Most of what falls still vanishes as runoff in mountain streams. But not all of it. Some of that water sinks into the aquifer itself. Pulled by gravity and pushed by the weight of new rain sinking in, the water seeps down through the aquifer."

Rio dismounted, rummaged in his saddlebags, and pulled out a hinged black box no bigger than a pack of cigarettes. He handled it with the same ease that he handled reins or boots, silently telling Hope that the box was very familiar to him. When he opened it, she caught a glimpse of a mirror on one side and what appeared to be a complex compass on the other.

She watched with growing curiosity as he held the box up, tilted it until it roughly matched the line of the rock layer that interested him, fiddled with a small lever on the back of the box, and then wrote something on the map. He repeated the process several times, using different strata of rock.

"Is that a compass?" she asked.

"A special kind, yes. It's called a Brunton compass." He showed it to her. "The built-in clinometer measures the dip of a rock stratum. Of course, you're supposed to lay it right on the stratum you're working with." He glanced toward the huge, nearly vertical chunk of land in front of him. "Since I left my mountain goat at the ranch, I'm doing it the easy way. For now, a guesstimate is good enough."

"What did you learn from the compass?"

"That the dip of the rock layer is steep, but not steep enough to put an aquifer totally out of reach if you drilled down on the flats. That's assuming there's an aquifer in that broken mess," he added, studying the rugged mountains. "And also assuming the aquifer runs beneath the mountain all the way down to your ranch without being interrupted by fault zones. Big assumptions."

"What happens if it's faulted?"

Rio mounted Storm Walker in an easy motion and

settled into the saddle. "Sometimes the water leaks away at the fault zones. Sometimes the aquifer is offset so much by faults that you can't find it again. Sometimes it just slips down so far that you can't get to it."

Hope gestured toward the steep mountain slope he had been measuring. "Is there an aquifer?"

"No. The sandstone is dry, or there would be a seep right here, maybe even a spring."

It was absurd to feel disappointed, but she felt it just the same. "Oh."

He replaced the Brunton compass in his saddlebag. "Don't worry. This is just one small piece of the mountain. Not even a representative part. It's a transition between Turner land and your own."

"What do you mean? We're both bounded by the Perdidas on one side."

"The mountains near his place are almost entirely made of Precambrian rock a billion and a half years old, stone so hard it makes a steel hammer ring. There's no way for water to sink into that kind of dense rock. Everything runs off in streams or gathers on the surface in lakes. Even where little pieces of the mountain have washed down to the plains and built up rough soil, the groundwater stays close to the surface because of the impermeable roots of the mountain beneath."

She squinted, imagining a relatively thin layer of sand and gravel covering the much more solid rock layer beneath. "That's why Turner has so much water, isn't it? The water can't sink down and get away from his wells. It's all there, waiting to be tapped."

"For a while, yes. If he doubles his cropland as he talks about doing, he'll be living off the future. Sooner or later he'll suck it all dry."

At least he has a future.

Though Hope didn't say it aloud, she might as well have. Rio knew how desperate the Valley of the Sun was for water. It was there in the empty sky, in the dry land, and in Hope watching him, eyes filled with fears and dreams.

Fourteen

WHEN HOPE COULDN'T bear the silence any longer, she looked away from the land's innocent betrayal and asked Rio, "What's different about my mountains?"

"The rocks are much younger, more porous. They erode much more quickly. That's why your mountains are lower than Turner's, even though they're part of the same block fault. Your outwash plains are thick, deep. Water soaks down into them almost as soon as it falls."

"Then the land should hold more water, not less."

"But it's out of reach," he said simply. "There are many places on your ranch where you could go down a thousand feet and then keep on going for thousands more and get nothing for your time and money but dry gravel."

Hope took a ragged breath at the thought of drilling that far down and finding no water, a dry hole draining away her slender reserves of money, turning her dreams to dust.

When Rio saw the fear darkening her eyes, he cursed his thoughtless words. With gentle, relentless fingertips he turned her face toward his. For the first time since he had seen his visions reflected in her eyes, he allowed emotion back into his voice, the deep certainty that came from a knowledge that had nothing to do with diplomas and schools.

"That's why you hired me," he said simply. "I won't waste your money drilling where there isn't any chance of water. Do you believe me?"

His words and his touch took away the fear that had chilled Hope. She put her hand over his fingers and pressed, not speaking for fear that her voice would break.

Her eyes spoke for her. They said that she trusted him with her dreams, and that she was quickly, inevitably, coming to the point where she would trust him with herself. That was something she had never done with any man. She had held herself aloof, knowing from the example of her parents' lives and her sister's life that loving someone wasn't enough to ensure peace, much less a dream of love returned.

So Hope had loved only the land.

Now Rio was sliding through the hard layers that had protected the life-giving core of her. Each day with him, each conversation, each touch, he sank more deeply into her, coming closer to the instant when he would break through the last layer of her reserve and touch the flowing wealth of love concealed deeply inside her.

The thought terrified her.

And the thought that he might not break through,

might not touch her, might not release her love, also terrified her.

"Hope?"

"Yes," she said in a husky voice, "I believe you."

With an effort of will, Rio forced himself to release the silky warmth of her. Even after he removed his hand, his fingertips tingled with shared warmth, the energy of two lives touching.

Without a word he turned Storm Walker toward the edge of Piñon Camp and forced himself to think only of finding water in a dry land.

"Are there other benches like this farther south toward the ranch house?" he asked.

Caught in her own thoughts, she didn't answer. *His fingers no longer touched her skin.*

She was shocked by the loss she felt at such a simple thing as the absence of his touch. Shaken, she reined Aces to follow the stallion.

"Piñon Camp," she said finally. "It's a landmark around here simply because it's different."

"How about cliffs? Old mining or timber roads? Deep canyons or ravines? I'm looking for places where I can see layers of rock that are buried out of sight in other areas."

Frowning, Hope recalled details of the land she had ridden over since she was old enough to sit upright in a saddle. "Just on the ranchland, or on the lease lands, too?"

"If the lease is above your watershed, I'll be glad to look at it, although I've already seen most of the government land. Whatever you have on your own property should come first."

She urged Aces to the edge of the bench until she could see the country falling steeply away below. Storm Walker came up alongside the mare, standing so close that Hope's stirrup rubbed against Rio's.

"Over there," she said. Pointing, she touched his sleeve. Even that light brush of her fingertips against cloth reminded her of his vitality. The heat of him demanded a deeper touch, a longer sharing. "See that bald spot just beyond the ranch house?"

"Yes."

"Straight up from there, hidden behind the shoulder of the mountain, there's an old road. A hundred years ago there was some kind of mining operation up there. Silver or gold, I forget which. It didn't amount to a hill of beans, but they cut a wagon road up above Wind Canyon, into the high country where there was another mine."

"Any luck?"

"Just the bad kind. The mine caved in long ago, but some of the road is still there. It's a scary piece of real estate. It hangs by its toenails to the edge of Wind Canyon. The canyon itself is thousands of feet deep. The land is different there. Crumbly rather than solid. Even sagebrush has a hard time clinging to the mountainside."

"Perfect," Rio said, satisfaction obvious in his tone.

"If you say so," she muttered. "I remember that road scaring the hell out of me."

"You don't have to go."

She gave him a level look.

He knew she wouldn't be staying behind.

"There are a few other places between here and there that have bare rock," she said.

"We'll see them on the way."

She shook her head. "Not unless we plan to be gone for a few days. Each one of the sites is up a long, blind canyon."

His eyes narrowed as he considered the possibilities. "Any signs of water?"

"Do you mean springs?" she asked in disbelief. "If there were springs, I'd be laying pipe instead of hauling water by truck."

"Nothing as obvious as a spring. I'm looking for unusually big brush, grass that stays greener longer than in other places at the same elevation and exposure, that sort of thing."

"Oh. Well, maybe in Stirrup Canyon. Dead Man's Boot might be a possibility. Then there's always Silver Rock Basin," she added, gesturing toward the lower part of the ranch. "Jackass Leap, too. That's up above the head of Wind Canyon."

"Hold it." Rio began unfolding more of his map.

The basic map was the result of a USGS survey. It showed each contour of the thirty sections of land that made up the Valley of the Sun. The paper was nearly four feet by four feet, more suited to a kitchen table than to a saddle. The map showed deep creases and frayed edges from being handled a lot.

Hope wondered how many times Rio had studied the map. And why. Surely the time since she had hired him hadn't been enough to make that much wear on a map. Yet what she could see of the map covered her ranch and little else.

"Silver Rock Basin is no problem," Rio said, "but where is Dead Man's Boot?"

She laughed. "That's a family name, not an official one. So are the other ones."

Smiling, he refolded the map. "Where do you think most of the names on maps came from? Place names are one of the richest oral traditions in the West." He handed her the pencil and the map. "Mark them in."

She took the pencil, unfolded a panel of the awkward map, and was promptly lost.

The amount of detail already on the paper was both staggering and absolutely unlike any map she had ever used. In addition to contour lines showing the changing elevations of the land, there were many other lines whose purpose was a mystery to her. Most of those lines had been drawn in after the fact. Indecipherable symbols—both printed and handwritten—appeared in odd places on the map. Even more enigmatic notes appeared in the margin. Formulas, Greek letters, cryptic comments; all had been added by hand.

Hope had only to glance at the map to know that Rio already had put in a lot of time studying her land, much more than he could have in the less than two weeks since she had hired him. She looked up, puzzled.

"Lost?" he asked, expecting it.

"Yes, but it's not just the map."

"What else, then?"

"You," she said quietly.

He stared at her.

"Nothing adds up," she said. "You're a drifting horsebreaker who knows more about this land than the highly educated, highly recommended hydrologist who was out here six weeks ago. You've worked for me for less than two weeks, but this map is worn thin in the creases and has enough notes on it for some kind of textbook."

She wanted to go on, to say, You have only one name, and it's neither Scandinavian nor Zuni nor Scots. Nobody knows where you came from or where you're going, but Mason trusts you more than he trusts anybody except me. You have a reputation as a bad man to cross, but you've been so gentle with me that it's all I can do not to crawl into your arms and never let go.

She wanted to say those things, but she didn't, for Rio was already talking, answering the questions she had asked and a few more that she hadn't.

"I heard about you all over the West," he said simply. "A drifter in Idaho told me there was a woman who needed help in a place called Valley of the Sun, Nevada. In Utah a farmer I helped said his wife's sister had heard from her brother in Nevada that a woman called Hope needed a well and nobody would dig it for her. A cattle breeder I once found water for said he'd sold one of his best Angus to a woman with beautiful eyes and a mind like a steel trap, and that she was going to lose her ranch unless the rains came or she found water."

Hope's throat closed with tears she fought not to shed. But the thought of strangers knowing her need, and caring enough to help in the only way they could, made it very hard for her to hold back. She wanted to tell Rio to stop talking, that he would make her cry and she didn't want to, but she couldn't get any words past the emotion filling her throat.

"So I drifted south," Rio said quietly, watching Hope with eyes that saw everything, the vulnerability and the tears, the determination and the strength. "And I listened. Every time the wind blew, it whispered your name and your need and your dreams."

Silent tears slid past her dark lashes to leave shining trails on her cheeks.

"The closer I came to the Valley of the Sun," he said, "the more people talked about you. People I had helped in the past left messages for me in every country store and café in the West. The messages all said the same thing: *This is a good woman, Rio. Can you help her the way you helped us?*"

The midnight blue of Rio's eyes was so intense that it was like crystal burning in the sun. She watched him with equal intensity, feeling his words sinking into her, sliding through the protective layers she had built up to guard the vulnerable woman beneath.

"I didn't know if I could help you, and I wasn't going to come to you until I did know," he said.

Then he looked out over the land again, freeing her from the blue blaze of his eyes.

"This country isn't a stranger to me," he said quietly. "I've found water in some damned unlikely places. And I've seen a few places where there isn't any water to be found anywhere by anyone. I didn't know if the Valley of the Sun was one of those places."

She held her breathing, waiting, hoping not to hear the end of her dream.

I've seen a few places where there isn't any water to be found anywhere by anyone.

"I went over all the USGS maps, got the latest satellite photos, talked to university experts and to Indians whose ancestors had hunted along the shores of long-ago lakes. I flew over the steep parts of your ranch with a photo recon camera and a pilot who wasn't afraid of God, the devil, or gravity." Rio's mouth turned up wryly. "Hell of a flyer, though. He saved me weeks of rough-country riding and hiking."

Hope looked at Rio, but tears prevented her from seeing more than the powerful outline of his body against the sky. "Why?" she asked huskily. "Why did you go to all that trouble for someone you didn't even know?"

It was a question that no one had ever asked him. In the past, people had been more than happy to take what he offered. They had never stopped to wonder why he wanted to help.

But Rio had asked himself that question for as many years as he had drifted through people's lives and through the bright, colorful shadows cast by their dreams.

He didn't have an answer.

He had helped many people, touched the luminous edges of their dreams, and moved on. Those people remembered him with gratitude and sometimes even affection. They always had a meal and a bed and a handshake for him whenever he went back.

But they didn't know him. He was as much a mys-

tery to them as their ability to dream in the face of brutal odds was a mystery to him.

He found water for those special dreamers. And
each time, each place, each well, he wondered if he
would also find the ability to put down roots and dream
for himself.

He hadn't found any dream to equal the whispering
seduction of the wind moving over the face of the land.
He no longer believed that such a dream existed.

"I admire people who are strong enough to dream,"
Rio said finally. His long fingers caressed Hope's face,
feeling the warmth of her tears sliding beneath his fingertips. "Like you."

"You're strong," she whispered. Then, even more
softly, she asked, "What are your dreams?"

"I don't have any. I stopped dreaming the day I
really understood what half-breed meant."

Her eyes darkened. Slowly she shook her head,
denying both the pain of Rio's long-ago discovery and
the ache of her own realization that she was falling in
love with a man who had no dreams.

She closed her eyes and tried not to cry anymore.
Tears kept falling in spite of it.

He bent slowly toward her, brushed his lips over her
eyelashes, tasted the warmth and salt of her tears. He
wanted to do more, much more. She called to his
senses and his soul in a way that nothing ever had,
even the wind.

"It's all right," he murmured.

He kissed her softly, aching to turn the world inside
out and make everything right for her, the past and the

present and the future rich with water and dreams. But he couldn't do that, and unless he stopped touching her, he wouldn't be able to remember why he shouldn't touch her at all.

He was the wrong man for her.

It was that simple and that final.

Slowly, feeling like he was pulling off his own skin, he straightened in the saddle again until he no longer touched Hope.

"I'll help you find your well, your dream," he said quietly.

It was the only promise he could give to her. The only promise he could keep.

She opened her eyes. Her tears were shining on Rio's lips. The sight pierced her, coming so close to her core that she almost cried out in fear and hope.

"But what about you?" she asked.

"I'll share your dream for a time. Then the wind will call my name and I'll go."

Hope looked away from him. She bit her lip, trying not to rage against the truth of his words, wanting to deny the pain stabbing through her as his need reached down past her barriers to the reservoir of love that she had protected so long and so well. She blinked slowly, releasing tears from beneath her burning eyelids.

It was Rio she cried for, not herself. It was too late to protect herself. He had touched her too deeply. Whether or not he found water on the Valley of the Sun, she would love the man who had no dreams.

"I'll dream for you, Rio," she promised in a soft,

husky voice. "I'll dream for you until you can dream for yourself."

Hope brushed her arm over her eyes, clearing them of tears. Then she calmly began to puzzle out the mysteries of the map that he had given her, matching place names with contour lines until she could orient herself. With increasing confidence, she began to fill in the old family names that Rio had asked for.

Motionless but for the occasional small stirrings of his horse, Rio watched her work over the map. He would have leaned closer, pointing out contour lines and explaining symbols to her, but he didn't trust his hand not to tremble with the aftershocks of the emotion that had gone through him when he had heard her husky voice promising to dream for him.

In the past women had sometimes cried over him, when the wind blew and they knew he would be going soon. But that wasn't why Hope cried. She was the first woman to look deeply inside him and cry when she saw the void where his dreams had been. She had wept, knowing his emptiness and pain. She had wept for him rather than for herself.

And she would dream for him.

"I'll put in the rest of the names tonight," she said, refolding the map along its telltale creases. "Dead Man's Boot is closest to us. It has a clump of big sage that has to be seen to be believed. Nothing else like it on the ranch."

Hope didn't look at Rio when she spoke. She didn't trust herself to. If she saw again the soul-deep hunger in his eyes when he talked of dreams, she wouldn't be able to control her tears or her need to hold him.

With a touch of the reins she sent Aces over the lip of the bench and onto the steep trail.

Holding Storm Walker in check, Rio watched until Hope disappeared into a steep fold in the mountainside. He had never felt so alone as he did at that instant, with her words still echoing through him.

I'll dream for you until you can dream for yourself. I'll dream for you. I'll dream. For you.

The echoes were like the wind blowing through emptiness, defining it.

"Don't do it, Hope," he said softly, achingly, her husky words echoing through him, defining him. "You'll waste your dreams until the mountains are nothing but sand at the bottom of a nameless sea. I've forgotten how to dream. Don't dream for me."

Yet Hope's promise kept echoing in his mind, sending fine tremors of emotion through him. He couldn't have been more shocked if she had said she loved him.

And then he realized that she had said just that.

He bowed his head, staring sightlessly at his fingers wrapped around the reins. Storm Walker tugged at the bit, wanting to follow the other horse. His rider didn't notice.

Finally Rio yielded his iron grip on the reins, allowing the stallion to plunge over the edge onto the narrow trail. The shrill cry of a hawk followed him, carried by the wind.

The hawk's cry became a word repeated endlessly, falling from the empty sky.

Hope.

Fifteen

❧

"NOW, ARE YOU SURE, HONEY?" Mason asked. His faded yet still clear eyes measured the lines of worry on Hope's face. "I ain't all in a lather to drive to Salt Lake just to eat turkey and trimmings. We got real fine turkey right here in Nevada." Then he remembered. "Hell, tonight's your birthday. I can't go."

"Of course you can," she said. "I won't be alone here, and even if I was, it wouldn't be any big deal. I've had birthdays before."

"But—"

"No buts," she cut in firmly. "You're barely going to make Thanksgiving with your sister-in-law as it is. Get going."

"I don't like it. Rio's out poking around most of the time, looking for a place to drill. You'll be lonely."

The wind gusted suddenly, stirring up dust. The sky was blue and cold, devoid of clouds.

"Mason, if you don't go to Utah, I swear I'll saddle

Aces and ride to Piñon Camp and not come back until December first. You haven't had a vacation for years. You deserve a few weeks with your nieces and nephews."

He watched her with anxious eyes. "You sure?"

"You can set your watch by it," she said firmly, using a favorite phrase of his.

Mason sighed, shifted his battered suitcase to his other hand, and followed her out to the tan pickup. "I don't feel right taking the truck."

"Rio said I could use his truck if I needed to go to town," she said patiently, ready to go over every argument one more time. "In fact, he insisted."

Mason hesitated before he opened the truck door and tossed in his suitcase. "All right, no need to put your hand on my back and shove. I know when I ain't wanted."

"Mason!" she said, shocked. Then she saw the mischief in his eyes. "That's right," she said quickly, putting her hand on his back and shoving gently, "you're not wanted. Go away."

Then she spoiled it by throwing her arms around him and hugging him from behind. He turned around and hugged her for a long moment, savoring the love she gave so freely to an old man whose only relationship to her was bittersweet, overlapping memories of her parents.

The wind flexed again, pushing against Mason as though hurrying him on his way. Hope's hair flew up, tickling his nose. He smoothed her hair with a gnarled hand, holding the soft strands away from the wind.

"I'll be home by the end of the month," he said, resting his gray-stubbled chin on her dark hair. "Sooner if Rio finds a place to start drilling. Keep that rifle handy. The bit of rain we been getting the last week or two ain't put all the snakes down."

She nodded her head, agreeing without arguing. She didn't want to open the subject of John Turner. Other than a few calls at odd times of the night, Turner hadn't bothered her. Maybe he had thought over the scene at his well and decided that she wasn't just being coy. Maybe he had finally gotten the point: she wasn't interested in him sexually.

The truck door slammed, the engine revved, and Mason let out the clutch.

"Take care," she said.

"You, too, honey. Don't be lonely, now."

"How could I be?" She smiled. "I've got the whole Valley of the Sun for company."

He winked, rolled up the window, and headed out of the ranch yard.

Hope's smile held a melancholy that she wasn't aware of. Even with Rio around, she was lonely. That was new.

She was still trying to get used to it.

Before Rio came she had been alone but not lonely. He had changed that. Despite her efforts to withdraw from any emotional connection with him, despite his own blunt withdrawal since their ride up to Piñon Camp, despite knowing she would be hurt more the closer she got, Hope longed to spend time with Rio, to talk with him. To touch him.

Yet she knew she couldn't. Not really. Not deeply.

He was like a rain-sweet wind blowing through her life, washing away the dust of years, revealing the living spirit beneath. She was the land, unmoving.

And the wind was always moving, always leaving the land behind. Leaving her.

In time, the wind would come again to the Valley of the Sun, bringing Rio once more, if only to claim the colts Storm Walker sired on his mares. Rio would return . . . and then he would leave again, called by the wind.

She wondered how many women around the West waited in an agony of hope for Rio's return, aching for him, holding their breath as they watched the road like ranchers scanning the desert sky for the first signs of life-giving rain. She didn't want to be one of those women.

Yet she was, and Rio hadn't even touched her.

Hope was both sad and grateful that he had left her alone since Piñon Camp. He talked with her on the water runs, but his talk dealt with weather and cattle, feed prices and the cost of fuel. Ranch talk. His voice was no longer rich with visions. His eyes were no longer dark with a hunger that went deeper than the night, as deep as his soul.

He hadn't touched her at all in the five days since Piñon Camp. Not even in the most casual way.

Not once.

Mason was right. Rio had too much respect for himself and for her to begin something that would end with his leaving and her crying.

It made Hope want to laugh bitterly, to lash out at the irony of life. As a child she had heard her parents argue about whether to live on the Valley of the Sun with its endless, brutal demands, or to sell the ranch. Silently the child she had been assumed that if her parents just loved each other, everything would work out. Love was all that mattered.

And then the child had watched her mother and father tear each other apart in the name of love.

Hope had sworn then that she would never love a man. The cost was too high. The destruction too great. The grief too endless. It was all there in her parents' lives, in their arguments, in their letters, the words and phrases burned into Hope's mind, a warning of love's limitations that was branded on her soul:

I love you, Debbie. Come home to me. I need you. I need you with me at the end of the day when I'm so tired that nothing seems worth it.

And the reply, always the same.

Sell the ranch. I can't bear watching you kill yourself for that damned land. For nothing. I love you too much. Wayne, I love you!

In the end, the Valley of the Sun had killed Hope's father, just as her mother had predicted. It had killed Hope's mother, too. She had lived less than a year after burying the man she loved.

Yes, her parents had loved each other. Passionately, bitterly, hopelessly, helplessly.

It hadn't been enough.

Hope had learned the hard way that there were practical limitations on the thing called love. She had watched her mother, her father, and her poor broken sister try to make love carry more burden than it could.

Love didn't magically change people.

Hope had seen that simple fact demonstrated time and again. Her mother had loved her father with every bit of passion in her soul. It had been the same for him. But it hadn't changed them.

Her mother still couldn't live with the land.

Her father still couldn't live without it.

Love hadn't been able to bridge that fundamental difference between her parents.

Hope wasn't fool enough to forget love's limitations. She accepted the fact that she was falling in love with Rio. She also knew that it didn't make a damn bit of difference. It wouldn't change him. Or her. Rio was rootless, like the wind. And like the wind, he would leave her behind.

She had put down roots in the Valley of the Sun. Even if she could tear out those roots and survive, it wouldn't be enough.

Rio was what he was—a rain-sweet wind moving over the face of the land. Alone. As inevitably and as finally as the wild wind was alone. It was the life he had chosen. It was the life he had lived. It had made him what he was.

And she loved what he was, for better or for worse.

The knowledge expanded through Hope like the shock waves of an earthquake focused deep within her. She swayed, wrapping her arms around herself while old certainties shattered and fell away, leaving her vulnerable and raw and alone in a new world.

Is this how Mother felt when she realized that she had to leave the man she loved?

Is this how Father felt when he knew that the woman he loved would leave him?

Did they see the future coming down on them like a terrible desert storm, see it and know that there was nothing to do but to hang on and hope to survive until the storm passed?

They couldn't change each other.

They couldn't stop loving each other.

And they hadn't survived the storm.

"Hope? What's wrong? Is it Mason? Is he sick?"

It was Rio's voice, deep and worried, calling to her as though from a distance.

She opened her eyes and saw that he was close, close enough that she could see his concern in the intensity of his glance, the hard line of his mouth, his hands reaching for her in the instant before he controlled them.

At that moment she understood that he cared for her as much as he could, and he was protecting her in the only way he could. He was leaving her alone. He must have seen the clouds massing on their personal horizon. He was trying to protect her from that future storm, to keep her from being consumed. He was doing all that he could for her short of turning and walking away.

That he couldn't do, for it would have been even more cruel to her than staying. She had a ranch that was dying for lack of water, and he was a man who could find water in hell itself.

"Hope?" Rio's voice was soft yet harsh. "What is it? Is there anything I can do? How long have you been standing here?"

She answered the only question she could, for she

didn't know how long she had been standing in the yard. Long enough for her skin to feel dry and for a fine shimmer of dust to coat her arms. Long enough to learn more about love and herself and the future than she wanted to know.

"Mason's fine. He's on his way to Salt Lake," she said. She watched Rio with eyes that were dark, shadowed by understanding and regret. Her voice was soft, as shattered as her past certainty that she could never love a man the way she had come to love Rio.

Passionately. Helplessly. Hopelessly.

But not bitterly.

Not that. There was no room in Hope's soul for bitterness, because she had accepted what she was, and what he was, and that neither could change.

"How did it go today?" she asked. "Did you find a place to drill?"

"Tell me what's wrong."

"Nothing that can be changed," she said calmly.

She understood her own limitations and his. If she had been different, he wouldn't care about her. If he had been different, she wouldn't love him as she did.

"What do you mean?"

"There's nothing that I would change even if I could. I am who I am, and . . . *you're Rio*. I wouldn't change what you are even if it meant a river flowing forever through the Valley of the Sun."

Her sad, accepting smile made the small lines at either edge of Rio's mouth deepen into brackets of pain. He saw all that she hadn't said in the darkness of her beautiful eyes.

"I didn't want this!" His breath came in roughly and he said no more. His fingertips touched her cheek in the instant before he balled up his hand into a fist and stepped back. "I'm going into town. Some of my equipment just came in. Don't wait dinner for me. I'll get a room and stay over for a few days, until I get everything I need."

She didn't answer, didn't move, didn't react in any way.

"Hope, are you listening?"

She nodded. She was listening, hearing everything he didn't say, the pain and the anger and the frustration, as relentless as the wind. "Yes. I'm listening."

The wind swirled around her, blowing over the land with a long, low wail that was so familiar she didn't even hear it. The same wind curled around Rio, pressing his shirt against his chest, riffling through his hair like a lover's fingers.

Abruptly Hope turned away and went into the house.

Rio didn't follow.

As she closed the front door behind her, she knew it was good that he was leaving. She was too vulnerable to him right now, still caught in the aftershocks of her own realization. She didn't think she would be able to sit across from him in the intimacy of the kitchen and not tell him the simple truths that she had just discovered.

I love you.

I wish you loved me.

But it doesn't matter. Even if you loved me, you'd

*still have to leave. I understand you, Rio. I know you'll
hate yourself if you hurt me.*

And I'm already hurting.

Hell of a mess, isn't it, love?

The wind paused long enough for her to hear Rio's
pickup truck leave the ranch yard in a rush of gravel
and grit. Then the wind swept on, blotting out every
sound but its own endless sigh.

When she was certain that nothing remained of Rio,
not even dust hanging in the air, she went out again,
climbed into Behemoth, and began the chore of hauling water. The loaded rifle kept her company in its rack
behind her head.

When she drove over the ridge and down to the
emerald oasis of the well, there wasn't any other vehicle in sight. As far as she knew, Turner hadn't come
here since the day he had made a grab and she had
locked herself in the truck.

Yet each day, every day, she watched for him at the
well.

Squinting against the strong wind, Hope jumped out
of the cab and set up the water hose. The job wasn't as
difficult as it had been before Rio replaced the worn
coupling and Mason did something to the generator
that made it start more easily. Also, she wasn't as tired
as she had been before Rio came to the Valley of the
Sun. He had quietly, systematically taken much of the
hard physical work from her shoulders. If she objected,
he simply ignored her.

In truth, she hadn't protested much. There was
enough work for five more ranch hands.

Behemoth's tank filled with sweet water until it couldn't hold any more. Hope stowed the hose and drove back to her forlorn wells, where some of her cattle stood hunched against the brash, dry wind. They welcomed the truck with low bawls, as though asking what had taken so long.

Enough rain had fallen so that all of the range animals weren't completely dependent on the various wells. It was a good thing, because the wells weren't dependable. There hadn't been enough rain to bring up the water table or the natural feed. If real rain didn't come quickly, the minor seeps and holes would dry up again, forcing all the cattle back to the area around the wells.

Then Hope would have to start hauling food as well as water. Or she would have to sell more cattle.

When the truck was empty, she racked the hose again and headed back to the ranch. There was enough water that she didn't have to make a second run today. There was even water to spare for a bath if she was feeling a little reckless.

The thought tantalized her all the way back to the house. She argued with herself over using water that could go for cooking or drinking or watering cows. Then she decided that the bath was almost medicinal. She needed it to soak away the weariness that she had felt since she understood more than she wanted to about herself and Rio and love.

Besides, it was her birthday.

As a kind of penance for the water she was going to use, Hope forced herself to go through the ranch accounts before she went upstairs. Feeling too tired for five o'clock in the afternoon, she sat in the straight-backed walnut chair that was paired with the old oak desk her father had used.

The first thing she saw was the note she had written to herself ten months ago and pinned to the cubbyhole: *Second mortgage due 1/15.*

Though it didn't really worry her, for a moment she stared at the note. Despite the many temptations, she hadn't touched the money she had set aside for the balloon payment. Selling half of her remaining range cattle had been an emotional wrench, but it had given her enough cash to keep the ranch going for a while longer without nibbling away at the money she had set aside for the mortgage and for drilling a well.

Sighing, she pulled out the ranch account books and began to catch up on the bills.

"An hour of this," she promised herself, "and then a lovely, long, hot bath. A happy birthday present to me."

She kept her promises, even to herself. Especially to herself.

After an hour at the books and an hour in a steaming bath, she felt less . . . brittle. With languid movements she toweled her body dry, then her hair. Almost defiantly she smoothed a perfumed cream into her skin before she walked to her bedroom. The clean clothes she had set out on the way to her bath lay on the bed.

She looked at them and felt something close to rebellion. Abruptly she decided that she didn't want to put on jeans and a work shirt and boots again. She wanted to feel soft fabric caressing her, to look down and see her long legs bare of everything but silky skin. She wanted to look like a woman, to feel like one.

"Why shouldn't I?" she asked the silence. "No one is in the house but me."

Mason wouldn't be here to smile at the first instant of seeing her, and then sigh sadly when he realized that there was so little opportunity for Hope to laugh and dance and flirt with admiring men.

Rio wouldn't be here to look at her and wonder if she was trying to seduce him with feminine clothes and a perfume that could be enjoyed only by a man who was close enough to brush against her skin.

Tonight she was a woman alone. She could dress to please her own needs.

With hands that had almost forgotten how, Hope put on delicate touches of makeup that brought out the beauty of her slightly tilted eyes and generous mouth. Then she went to her closet and pulled out a floor-length caftan cut from a French velvet so fine and soft that it was almost impossible to tell apart from brushed silk. The rich forest green of the cloth brought out the elusive green of her eyes.

After a moment of hesitation, she put her hair up in one of the sophisticated styles that had once been a daily part of her life. The golden nugget earrings she put on had belonged to her great-grandmother, a present from a man who had come home from the Klondike gold rush.

The slippers Hope chose were very high heeled mules, made to accent the long, elegantly curved legs that had been her fortune. The legs themselves were revealed by a tantalizing slit that was just off-center of the deceptively casual lines of the caftan. It had been one of the most successful outfits she had ever worn in her modeling career.

Despite the caftan's impressive price tag, she had never regretted buying it. More than once the caressing velvet had picked up her sagging spirits. Like tonight.

When Hope looked in the mirror, she saw someone who had become a stranger to her. The reflection showed an elegant woman who would be at home anywhere in the world of glamour and cities, but had chosen to live in the Valley of the Sun and had never looked back.

Not even now, when she was alone on a dying ranch.

"I hope my birthday dinner appreciates me," she said, smiling with amusement at her image in the mirror. "Not every meal gets eaten by someone in pajamas as fancy as mine."

It was crazy even to think of fixing dinner in the elegant caftan, but Hope was feeling a little crazy at the moment. She had pushed herself too long, too hard, in too many ways. She needed a rest from the relentless pressures of her ranch and her foolish heart.

She went to the kitchen and opened the bottle of Chardonnay that she had put in the refrigerator for the day that Rio found a place to drill for water—a day that hadn't yet come.

A day that might never come.

That was something she wouldn't think about now. Worrying about what she couldn't change wouldn't do anything but wear her out.

She poured herself a glass of wine and inhaled the

heady scent of fine Chardonnay. She breathed in again, savoring the moment with the intensity that was as much a part of her as the love waiting deep within her for the exquisite instant of release. A release that might never come.

And she wouldn't think about that, either.

Beyond the house, the wind wailed as though unhappy at being shut out of the kitchen's warmth. Humming in quiet counterpoint to the long cry of the wind, Hope pulled a chicken out of the refrigerator. Using a knife that Rio had honed to a glittering edge, she cut away the breast and boned it with quick strokes.

The blade moved smoothly, slicing flesh as easily as butter. Even Mason had been impressed by the edge on the old knife. He had threatened to use it in place of his usual straight razor. Rio had offered to shave Mason with a butter knife instead. A very dull one.

Smiling, remembering, Hope set the knife aside, rinsed off her hands, and reached for the crystal wineglass. The wind's cry climbed higher, then dropped into a temporary silence. As the wine touched her lips she heard the muffled sound of a vehicle pulling up outside.

Rio! He must have come back early.

The glass dipped alarmingly in her hand, almost spilling wine onto the velvet caftan. She heard a door slam, heard booted feet coming up the front steps, heard the front door opening. A wave of longing swept through her, shaking her.

And then John Turner walked into the kitchen as though he owned the house and everything in it.

Especially her.

Sixteen

HOPE'S FIRST REACTION on seeing Turner was anger and a disappointment so deep that it made her dizzy.

"Haven't you ever heard of knocking on doors?" she asked coldly.

The wind gusted back up to its full strength, making the house tremble with its endless power. Wind whispered grittily against windows and walls in a long exhalation that became a low wail masking all sound from outside the walls, increasing the isolation inside.

Turner smiled with a predatory anticipation he didn't bother to conceal. "Baby doll, I'm hurt. Is that any way to welcome your fiancé on your birthday, especially when he's got a present for you?"

Hope remembered the night eight years ago, when he had grabbed her and taught her just how careless a strong man could be.

Turner noticed the elegant green dress, the shadowed invitation of her long, long legs, the heightening of her eyes, the fullness of her mouth. She was a woman dressed for a lover.

And she hadn't known he was coming.

"Who are you all tarted up for?" he snarled.

"No one."

"Bullshit. No woman dresses up like that except for a man."

"I do."

She went to the refrigerator, pulled out a ham, and sliced off a chunk. Swiss cheese came next. Deliberately ignoring Turner, she cut the ham and cheese into neat strips.

Turner watched her every motion with brooding eyes. He hadn't dressed up for her. He was wearing the same spotless, ironed jeans, shiny boots, and crisp white shirt he wore every day on his ranch.

"It's Rio," Turner said. His voice was like his eyes— flat, ugly, threatening. "The bunkhouse gossips are right. That half-breed's fucking you."

Hope's fingers tightened around the knife handle. Her hands wanted to shake with anger and a wave of fear. Turner was a man who had never understood a woman's refusal. Never accepted it.

Never permitted it.

I should have known he would wait until I was truly alone. That's his style. No witnesses. No word but his against mine. And who would believe a dirt-poor ranch girl turned down the richest bachelor around?

No one believed me before. No one would now. What are a few bruises against a few million dollars?

Coolly Hope went through her options.

There weren't many. Assuming she could stay away from Turner long enough to get to a phone and call the sheriff—which she doubted—help was almost an hour away. There were two exits from the kitchen. Turner was standing in one and closer to the second than she was.

But somehow she had to get out of the kitchen. Given a chance, she was certain she could outrun him.

Ignoring him, she made small pockets in the chicken breast with the knife's gleaming tip. She tucked strips of ham and cheese into the pockets, along with a sprinkling of herbs.

There was no sound in the kitchen but the rough cry of the wind.

"You answer me when I talk to you," Turner said harshly.

"Nobody is my lover," she said, her voice as cool and precise as the blade Rio had sharpened. "Nobody is fucking me, either. Thank you for your neighborly concern, but you made a long drive for nothing."

Turner listened to her, measured the anger in the stiff line of her shoulders and acknowledged the only part of her words that he wanted to hear.

"I told you if you hired Rio, people would talk."

She shrugged with a casual ease she was far from feeling.

Mason was gone. Rio was gone. John Turner was here, standing between her and the nearest door.

"People talk all the time," she said calmly. "It's like the wind. Sound without meaning."

"Not when they're talking about my future wife."

The wind's keening rose until it was just short of a scream.

Hope wanted to scream with it, to curse Turner's thick indifference to anything but his own desires. Her sister Julie had been like that, totally self-absorbed. But Julie hadn't been consciously cruel.

Julie's selfishness had puzzled and saddened Hope. Turner's self-absorption frightened her.

She took a slow, inconspicuous breath. Defying him verbally was risky, but not nearly as risky as cowering. If she showed fear, Turner would be all over her in an instant, dragging her down to the hard floor, raping her no matter how much she screamed at him to stop.

"What makes you think I'm going to marry you?" she asked in a tone of simple curiosity.

"Because I'm the only one who will have you. I made sure of it," he said with calm satisfaction. "Every man within a hundred miles who can get a hard-on knows if he comes near you, I'll beat him to bloody rags with my bare fists. So nobody's been scratching that itch between your legs. Getting hungry, baby doll? I sure as hell am."

Hope wanted to point out that Rio had been the exception to Turner's rule of driving men away, but she held her tongue. She sensed that bringing up Rio would change a frightening situation into a desperate one.

"See," Turner continued, "two years ago, when you came back here to live, you ignored me, so I knew you were still mad because of that hundred-dollar bill I stuffed down your blouse. That's why you went away to the big city and turned into a real classy piece of ass, something worth a lot more than a hundred bucks. You were real mad at me."

Hope kept on fixing her dinner even though the churning of her stomach told her she wouldn't be eating anything for a while.

"You looked better than ever when you came back, but you wouldn't give me the time of day." Turner shrugged massively. "Hey, fine. I had lots of time and lots of women to play with. I could wait." He smiled widely. "You know, I kind of liked waiting. Most women bore me after I fuck them. But with you I could lie in bed and think of how many ways I'd do it to you. I never got bored."

The shudder of revulsion that went through Hope didn't escape Turner. He smiled, misreading her now as he had always misunderstood her in the past.

"Turns you on, huh?" he said, hooking his thumbs through his belt loops. "Yeah, me, too. Come here, baby doll. I've got something in my pants for you."

"No."

"Hey." He smiled hugely and held up his hands as though she had a gun on him. "My intentions are strictly honorable. I won't touch you until we're married, if that's the way you want it."

"That's the way I want it," she said instantly.

"Then move your ass, baby doll. There's a man in town who'll have us married before you can say—"

"No," she cut in.

"What do you mean?" he said, exasperated.

"Just that. N. O. No." Hope looked at Turner and spoke calmly despite the fear prowling through her, shaking her as the wind shook the house, howling. "Don't you understand yet?" she asked with a calmness that was balanced on the brittle edge of desperation. "You only want me because you can't have me. You said it yourself. Women bore you. I'll bore you, too."

"No, you won't. You're the only woman who ever said no to me and made it stick. C'mon," he said impatiently, holding out his thick hand to her. "Let's go to town."

"No."

The hand became a big fist. "Listen, I'm getting real goddamn tired of hearing *no* from you. The game is over. Rio's sniffing around, and he's got too damn many women hot for him. He'll get you to spread your legs, too. I've thought it over real careful. I was going to come here and beat that son of a bitch until he can't ever get it up again. Then I saw him in town and decided to settle some things with you first. I'm going to fuck you until you can't even think of saying no anymore. Got that, baby doll?"

Hope looked from Turner's flushed face to the fist he had unconsciously made of the hand he had held out to her. She wondered if he had been drinking, then decided it didn't matter. He hadn't had enough alcohol to slow him down, which was all that mattered to her.

For an instant she thought longingly of the rifle in the water truck. No one had guessed that she would be cornered by a snake in her own kitchen. But then, no one had guessed that she would be so alone, so vulnerable.

The back door had never looked farther away. All that was left was to go along with Turner's "offer" of marriage until they got to town, where she would run for the first open door she saw.

Then Hope measured the flat light in Turner's eyes and realized that he wouldn't wait until town to rape her. He had been content with his coarse fantasies as long as he knew that she wasn't interested in any man. But now Rio was around.

Turner wasn't going to let her get away. Not tonight.

Hope's hazel glance flickered again to the back door.

"You start running and you aren't going to like it when I catch you," Turner said, following her glance. "I'll like it, though. I'll like it a whole lot."

The chill wind moaned and blew over the land, buffeting the house.

Hope wanted nothing more than to be as wild and free as that wind. And as safe.

Mentally she went over the drop from her bedroom window to the sloping roof of the back porch and from there to the ground. The wind would cover any sounds she made. She could be in the pasture, up on Aces, and over the back fence before Turner caught on.

"I'll need to change my clothes before we get married in town," she said calmly.

Turner cocked his head as though listening to the wind. His opaque eyes looked her over, seeing through the soft caftan to the curving, softer flesh beneath.

"Sure thing, babe. I'll just come along and watch.

Sort of an appetizer, see? I'll even get in a bite or two," he added, surging forward and reaching for the slit in her caftan. "Right about *here*."

She twisted away to keep her legs beyond the reach of his clutching hand, but she wasn't quite fast enough. His fingers grabbed the caftan below her waist. The lush green material bunched in his fist.

Hands braced on the counter behind her, Hope stood very still. If she moved, she would arouse his predatory instincts even more. He liked women to fight him. They were so easy to defeat, so soft, and their smooth skin showed every mark of his victory.

"Is this what your word is worth?" she asked with a calm that went no deeper than her cold skin. "You said you wouldn't touch me until we were married."

"Does that mean you finally decided to marry me?" he asked carelessly.

Slowly, as though in a nightmare, Hope felt the handle of the boning knife pressing against the edge of her palm.

"It's about time," Turner continued. Almost absently his huge fist crushed the velvet fabric, pulling on it, playing with her. He was strong enough to have her in an instant, but then the game would be over. "I'm tired of jumping through hoops for you. First the mortgage, then the water, and you still keep saying no."

She spoke carefully, trying to bring reason to a situation that was unraveling into terror. "I borrowed the money from Cottonwood Savings and Trust. One year, interest only, the land and buildings as collateral. Nothing was said about you."

"The bank is owned by my aunt, and I'm her favorite nephew. If it hadn't been for me, you'd have been turned down flat." The big fist twisted very slowly, wrapping the green velvet more tightly around his fingers, dragging Hope closer. "I didn't figure you'd make more than one or two payments before you went belly-up. I was going to step in and buy your ranch. Then you were going to earn it back one trick at a time, like any other whore."

"I've made every payment." Her voice was so controlled that it was almost toneless.

"Yeah," he said in disgust. His fist twisted harder, tightening more fabric around his fingers, pulling her closer. "You sure as hell did. Bill Worth says you've got money saved up for the balloon, too."

Unable to force sound past the fear closing her throat, Hope let the wind speak for her in a low, endless cry of despair.

"Well, shit, baby doll," he said in exasperation. "You don't leave a man enough room to swing his cock, do you? You won't even spread your legs for the water you've been taking. So I'm going to collect what's coming to me, starting *now*."

Turner yanked the fabric, throwing Hope off-balance, jerking her away from the counter before she could grab the knife. His thick arms pinned hers against her sides while his teeth ground against her lips. He backed up, dragging her with him, until the kitchen table pressed against his thighs. Then he lifted his head and grinned, humping his hips against her fast and hard.

"How about right here, baby doll. Just you and me and the big hard table."

Nausea turned over in Hope's stomach and clogged her throat. Her mind raced with frantic speed. She wanted nothing but to be free of Turner's touch, his smell, his obscene strength. With an effort of will that left her shaking, she smiled and lowered her eyelashes to keep him from seeing her revulsion. Deliberately she kicked off her fragile mules, getting ready to run at her first chance.

"How about in my bed?" she asked, her voice hoarse with fear rather than husky with desire. She doubted he would tell the difference. "I'd hate to get your fancy jeans all greasy."

He hesitated, surprised and disappointed by her unexpected surrender. On the other hand, it was what he had been waiting for. His arms loosened. "Well, if—"

She threw herself away from him with a strength that came from desperation. He staggered against the table, off-balance. Her right hand closed over the boning knife as she sprinted between the counter and the table, heading for the back door.

Turner moved with surprising speed for such a big man. He didn't manage to catch her, but he did cut off her escape.

She backed up rapidly, retreating from him. He didn't bother to follow. He simply stood with his legs braced far apart, admiring her flushed face and dark hair. He smiled with cruel anticipation.

"That's more like it, baby doll. I like a good run for my money." Then he saw the boning knife glittering in her hand. "Put it down. Fun's fun, but I'm not into knives."

"Then get the hell out of my kitchen."

Hope's voice was cold and empty, like the wind wrapping around the house in a sustained wail.

Turner hesitated before he smiled again, an ugly smile. With small movements of his body, he began closing the distance between them. "You won't do it."

She simply waited, knife in hand. She would do whatever she had to.

The expression on his face said that he was finally figuring that out.

"Last chance," he snapped. "Put it down."

She waited, watching. She knew just where she was going to put the knife.

So did he.

"*Bitch*. When I catch you, you'll wish to God you'd never even thought of it!"

The cry of the wind masked the heavy sound of Turner's boots against the floor as he closed in on Hope.

Seventeen

"I'M TEMPTED TO watch her castrate you."

Rio's voice was as cold and empty as the wind, as cold as his eyes watching Turner from just beyond the kitchen doorway.

The interruption was so unexpected that the big rancher simply stood and stared for a moment. Then he shook his head like a dog coming out of an icy rain.

Relief surged through Hope with a power that made her light-headed.

"But Hope isn't used to drawing blood," Rio drawled. "I am. I'm going to see what color yours is, Turner. I'm betting it's yellow."

With a smooth, predatory stride, Rio walked toward Turner, nakedly stalking him. There was strength and control in each clean movement of Rio's body.

And violence.

It radiated from the coiled perfection of each stride.

Hope backed away from Turner in a rush that took her beyond Rio to the living room.

"Go outside," Rio said calmly, not looking at her, watching Turner with eyes that were both savage and utterly controlled. "This won't take but a minute."

Before she could answer, Turner charged into the living room with his arms spread wide to drag everyone down. She threw herself to the side even as Rio gave her a hard shove, removing her from Turner's reach. Her knees hit the couch and she fell on it in a sprawl that sent the knife flying out of her hand. The blade slid hilt-deep into a cushion.

The instant it had taken to push Hope to safety left Rio at Turner's mercy. He was knocked off-balance by the rancher's massive tackle. They crashed to the floor with a force that shook the room.

As Turner had in so many bar brawls with smaller men, he used his superior weight and muscle to flatten his opponent. Straddling Rio, he smiled and cocked a huge fist, preparing to beat the man beneath him into a bloody rag.

Hope struggled upright and looked frantically around for the knife. She spotted the handle, grabbed it, and turned around just in time to see Turner's fist start down.

It never reached Rio.

With an upward sweep of his left arm, Rio knocked aside the blow. His right hand made an unusual fist, middle knuckle extended. With a deadly, twisting movement at the moment of impact, he rammed a shot straight to Turner's heart.

Before the rancher went white at the pain exploding through his chest, the callused edge of Rio's open left hand connected with Turner's thick neck in a short, brutal chopping motion. With a low sound, the big man slipped sideways and flopped facedown on the living room floor.

Rio came to his feet in a flowing, catlike movement. "Hope? Are you all right?"

"I—Rio?" she asked, disbelief in her wide eyes.

The violence had happened so fast that she was having trouble understanding that it was over. Rio had moved so quickly, so lethally, no more than a handful of seconds from the moment Turner tackled them. Even with what Mason had told her, she hadn't expected Rio to be so deadly against the much bigger rancher. Turner had earned his reputation as a brutal, boots-and-bare-knuckle brawler.

Rio took the knife from Hope's slack fingers and set it on the lamp table. He knelt in front of her, searching her face with blue eyes so dark they were almost black.

"Are you all right?" he asked urgently. "He didn't have time to hurt you, did he? I saw him drive out of town. He turned toward the Valley of the Sun, not his own ranch. I got here as fast as I could."

Abruptly reaction hit Hope. She began to tremble violently. Tears spilled out of her eyes. Her skin went pale. Her breath came in short gasps that couldn't get enough oxygen into her lungs.

Rio saw blood welling from a cut on her lip and knew that Turner had caused it.

Hope saw the change in Rio's eyes, the blackness of

violence wholly unleashed. With a guttural sound he turned toward the man lying unconscious on the floor.

"No," she said quickly. Her cold fingers closed over Rio's arm. The bunched hardness of his muscles shocked her. It was like grabbing a steel fence post. "He didn't—do anything."

Rio searched her face, hearing both the truth and the desperation in her broken words. He looked away from the tiny drops of blood on her pale lips. A fierce emotion went through him, cutting him, making him bleed even as she bled.

"Hope," he said softly.

He ached to touch her and knew he shouldn't. If he touched her, he would make love to her, kissing away even the memory of brutality, caressing her with his lips and his tongue and his body until she trembled and wept with ecstasy instead of fear.

Turner's low groan echoed the sound of the wind, rough and empty of meaning.

Rio slanted the man a single feral look. Then he closed his eyes and fought to keep himself from curling his long fingers around Turner's throat and squeezing until there was nothing left of the rancher but a mound of cooling meat.

Violence had never tempted Rio so much.

Flexing his fingers, fighting a savage need to destroy, he turned away from the man who would have raped Hope. For a few terrible moments, Rio wasn't sure he could let Turner live.

Self-control had never been so hard before, not even when he was young and as wild as a winter storm.

Hope whispered his name.

"It's all right." Rio forced calm into his voice instead of the violence that coiled within him, straining to be free. "I won't kill him."

Yet, Rio added silently.

Hope looked at him and heard what he hadn't said aloud. "No, Rio. Don't. Turner's not worth going to jail for."

"You are."

Before she could say anything more, Turner groaned again.

Rio moved with shocking speed. His fingers clamped around a thick arm. With an impatient jerk he rolled Turner over onto his back.

"Can you hear me?" Rio asked indifferently.

The other man's groan didn't tell Rio anything new. His palm smacked the bigger man's face with measured force.

Turner's eyes flew open. The instant his vision cleared enough to make out Rio, he lunged upward at him.

Rio wrapped his hands around the rancher's arms just above the elbows and used the bigger man's momentum to yank him to his feet. Steel fingers flexed and dug in like talons.

Waves of pain slammed up Turner's arms. He sagged and almost blacked out. The next time he looked at Rio, it was with dawning fear instead of rage.

Rio saw the change and nodded. "We're going to reach an understanding, you and me," he drawled, his voice mild and his eyes promising hell everlasting. His fingers dug deeply into Turner's muscular flesh, grinding nerve against bone in a gesture that was punishment, warning, and promise in one. "You touch Hope again and I'll hurt you. Hear me?"

"All I hear is the wind, *drifter*," Turner said hoarsely.

He didn't say any more. He didn't have to. The knowledge that Rio wouldn't always be around to protect Hope was there in Turner's eyes.

It was there in Hope's, too, raw fear and regret.

"That's right," Rio said softly. "I'm the wind. I'm everywhere. I see everything. I hear everything. Nothing happens that I don't know. You touch Hope just once and you better start looking over your shoulder, living in your rearview mirror, locking your doors at night, and checking the locks again before you go to sleep. You better start going to church every Sunday and praying to God that you never see me again."

Turner's eyes widened. He stared at Rio through waves of pain and began to understand more than mere words could say. Rio's smile was as much a warning as the agonizing grip that was making the world go gray around the edges.

"But if you touch her, no locks and no God will save you," Rio said almost gently. "One day you'll hear the wind and you'll turn around and I'll be there. That's the day you die."

The unlatched front door banged open, pushed by a cold shout of wind.

Pivoting, Rio released Turner with a hard motion that sent the rancher smashing into the doorframe. He pulled himself upright, took one look at Rio's face, and stumbled down the front steps and into his Jeep.

Cold fingers of wind raked through Rio's hair. He didn't feel it. He stood in the doorway, watching while the Jeep's headlights made a sweep of the yard and sped down the road until there was nothing left but a pinpoint of brightness.

Coils of wind hummed around and through the house, making the walls shiver.

Rio shut the door, turned, and saw that Hope was shivering, too. She came to her feet slowly, looking at him with eyes that were wide and very dark.

"I know you don't—" Her voice broke and she tried again. "I know you don't want to, but would you hold me, please?" She swayed, holding on to herself because there was no one else. "Please," she said desperately, scrubbing her face and arms with her hands. "I can't stand the feel of him on my skin any longer!"

With a hoarse sound Rio went to Hope, wrapped his arms around her, rocked her gently against his body.

He held her for long, long minutes, until her skin was warm beneath his hands and her body no longer shuddered with vicious memories. He felt her take a deep, ragged breath, and then felt her lean against his strength with a trust that made him want to cry out in despair.

"I would have used the knife," she said bleakly.

"I know." His voice was soft and certain as he smoothed his cheek against the dark satin of her hair.

"Do you?" she asked, tilting her face up to his.

"Yes. You're a one-man woman," Rio said, bending down to Hope. "And God help us both, *I'm that man.*"

He lowered his mouth to her trembling lips, kissing her with melting gentleness, cherishing her. The tip of his tongue caressed the cut on her lip.

"Even your blood is sweet," he whispered.

She made a low sound and swayed against him.

"Does that hurt?" he asked softly against her mouth, not lifting his head at all.

"No," she said in a low voice, watching him through half-closed eyes. "It feels . . ."

Her voice died. She shivered and moved her head very slowly from side to side, offering more of her mouth to him in a silent plea.

With tiny, hot movements of his tongue he caressed her lips, licking away every last bit of Turner's ugly embrace. She moaned and clung to Rio, letting his warmth and his tenderness fill her senses.

Her lips parted in a helpless invitation that he accepted with a deep sound of pleasure and need. His tongue stroked the inner softness of her mouth, tasting her while tiny shudders of desire rippled through his powerful body, passion surging hotly, threatening to strip away his control.

He shouldn't be holding her, touching her, tasting her on his tongue like a wild, sweet rain.

"Hope," he breathed against her mouth. And then again, urgently, "Hope, tell me to stop."

Her eyes opened, luminous with emotion. "I love you," she whispered, and her breath flowed warmly over his lips.

"God," Rio groaned, and he buried his face against her neck, unable to bear the radiant truth of her eyes. "I didn't want to hurt you," he said harshly.

"I know." Her voice was like her eyes, serene, certain.

"I don't have any past, any future, any present. *I am the wind.*"

"Yes," she said, turning to caress his cheek with her lips. "I know."

He straightened and confronted the extraordinary beauty of Hope's eyes. His hard, warm hands shaped her face.

"Then tell me to go," he said in a hoarse voice.

She smiled sadly. "Never, my love."

"Hope—"

"Kiss me," she interrupted, standing on tiptoe to reach his mouth.

"Hope, I don't—"

The soft heat of her lips, her tongue, drove every word from Rio's mind. He made a rough, low sound and took her mouth even as she took his. The gliding pressure of tongue over tongue became a wildness shaking him. He couldn't hold her close enough, taste her deeply enough, or control the hunger sweeping through him like a violent desert storm.

Before the kiss ended he was fully aroused, needing her as he had never needed a woman before. With an effort that left him shaking, he lifted his mouth from hers.

"No more," he said hoarsely.

Her luminous eyes searched his. "Why?"

His laugh was short, rough. He felt her warmth over every inch of his body, but most of all in the rigid flesh straining against his jeans. Against her. He moved his hips once, slowly. The blunt, unmistakable ridge of male passion caressed her.

"That's why," he said almost angrily.

Hope's smile was like her body, invitation and incitement at once. "That's the best reason I can think of *not* to stop," she murmured, kissing the corners of his mouth, moving her hips against him in return.

"Hope—"

"I'm not asking you to stay with me forever," she interrupted, breathing her warmth into his mouth. "I'm not even asking you to say you love me. All I'm asking is to feel your life inside me. That's all, Rio. Just that. You. Inside me."

Her words wrenched a cry from him that was both harsh and infinitely sweet. He could no more resist the outpouring of her love than the land could resist a silver fall of rain. Without stopping to think or argue or deny, he lifted her into his arms. Her weight was as feminine and heady as her smile.

"You don't have to carry me off to the bedroom," she said. "I won't change my mind or run away."

"You sure?"

Smiling, savoring, she rubbed the palm of her hand over the hard muscles of his chest, the strong tendons of his neck, the line of his jaw. His head turned swiftly. Lovingly, his teeth captured the flesh at the base of her thumb. With sensuous finesse he bit down.

Desire lanced through her with a force that dragged a hoarse, surprised cry from her throat.

He repeated the caress, then sucked on the tender flesh.

"Run away? My God, I'd be lucky to stand up," she said raggedly. "You make me weak."

He heard the surprise in her voice, felt the quivers of need that coursed through her body. Smiling rather fiercely, he started up the stairs. Then he stopped without warning and looked down at Hope. His pupils were fully dilated, leaving only a crystal rim of midnight blue. He took her mouth with a hard thrust of his tongue and laughed aloud to feel the passion shaking her.

"Beautiful dreamer," he said huskily, and thrust into her again. "*God, how I want you.*" He lifted his head finally, all but crying out in protest at having to end the kiss. "I'm carrying you because I'm trying to slow myself down."

She searched his face, reading his hunger in every taut line, every harshly drawn breath. "Is it working?"

"What do you think?"

Hope smiled slowly. "I think your bedroom is closer than mine," she murmured, tracing the line of his jaw with the tip of her tongue.

His eyes closed for an instant while desire raged through him. "I think you're right."

He stopped and kissed her again, searching the hot textures of her mouth with slow strokes of his tongue. When he heard the sounds welling from deep in her throat, and from his, he wondered if he would be able to get enough of her even when he was buried in her.

Then he wondered if he would be able to wait to find out, or if he would take her right here, right now, on the stairway.

He was certain that she wouldn't protest if he turned

her in his arms and fitted her body over his, sheathing himself in her slick, passionate heat. Her willingness was plain in her hazel eyes dilated and dazed with hunger, in the way her lips opened beneath his kiss, wanting his tongue deep within her mouth.

Wanting him.

All I'm asking is to feel your life inside me. That's all, Rio. Just that. You. Inside me.

With a hoarse sound that could have been Hope's name, he dragged his mouth away from hers and went up the stairway with long, powerful strides. The door to his room was open. He kicked it shut behind him and carried her over to the bed. Then he stopped, still holding her, but not kissing her, not even looking at her.

Hope was afraid that he had changed his mind. She didn't want that. She wanted to belong to him in a way that she had belonged to no other man. Urgently she slid her fingers between the snaps on his shirt. The heat of his body was like a furnace burning her with the promise of strength and passionate need. Shivering with pleasure and hunger, she caressed him and felt the answering quiver of his body.

"You want me," she said huskily. "I can feel it. Why did you stop?"

He gave her a crooked smile that made her ache. "You've driven me crazy."

"What do you mean?"

"I can't even let go of you long enough to undress you."

Hope would have smiled, but the hunger she felt for Rio was too close to pain. Her fingers shook as she reached for the long zipper that lay hidden beneath a front fold of the caftan. The zipper made a soft, secret sound as she opened it.

He watched with dark, hungry eyes while green fabric fell away from skin that was both softer and hotter than velvet. She shrugged away some of the cloth, revealing the creamy curves and dark rose peak of one breast. The nipple pouted and grew tighter as he looked, begging for his tongue, his teeth, his mouth.

Slowly, with an aching kind of control, he turned Hope in his arms and allowed her legs to slide down over him. The changing pressure of her body against his arousal made him shiver with raw pleasure.

He didn't let go of her. He couldn't. He lifted her until her breast was level with his mouth. With small, slow movements of his head, he brushed his lips over her nipple and felt the passionate trembling of her response. Even as she cried out his name, asking for him, he drew her deeply into his mouth, caressing her as though he was drawing life itself from her. Then he lost himself in the taste of her and she lost herself in the feel of his mouth so hot and knowing on her breast.

It was a long time before he released her, long enough for her to be shuddering, long enough for her skin to become as hot as his, as misted with passion.

He wanted to open his jeans and bury himself in her right where they stood.

He wanted to lie down with her, take her so slowly she would be crying and wild before they were halfway joined.

He wanted it fast and hard, slow and sweet, violent

and serene. He wanted everything with her, more than he had ever wanted from any woman. The depth of his need would have frightened him if he had room in his mind for anything but Hope.

When he put her on the bed, the caftan fell open at the slit. One slender leg gleamed between green velvet folds. Her exposed breast quivered as she breathed, its tip taut and glistening from his hungry mouth. She smiled up at him with lips still hot from his kisses, wanting him.

He had never seen anything more beautiful, not even the land itself.

Eighteen

※

WITH HANDS THAT ached to touch Hope, Rio tore impatiently at his own shirt, undoing the steel snaps in a single ripping sound. His leather belt hissed as he jerked it through denim loops. The rest of his clothes quickly dropped to the floor until he stood naked before her, fighting to slow himself down yet unable to control the hunger that made his breath short and his arousal pulse hotly with every rapid heartbeat.

He saw her look at him, all of him, accepting him without hesitation or fear. When he heard her murmuring sound of admiration he thought he would lose control right there. She was destroying him and she didn't even know it.

Her trembling fingers traced a line from his waist to his thigh. Curiously she touched the thrusting evidence of his desire. He clenched his hands and groaned with pleasure. When her fingers curled softly, sweetly around him, sweat gathered and ran down his spine.

"You're killing me," he said hoarsely.

She gave him a startled look. "Am I too rough?"

He gave a crack of laughter. "My beautiful dreamer. Don't you know? Right now you could skin me with a dull knife and I'd beg for more."

He lifted her fingers to his mouth, biting them sweetly and then rubbing them across his chest, his nipples, his belly. But he couldn't bear being without her taste for more than a few seconds. He lifted her hands and bit them again, groaning with raw hunger. He had just enough restraint not to leave more than fleeting marks of passion on her skin. But he wanted to.

And she wanted him to.

She wanted him with an intensity that made her twist and tremble and utter small, wild sounds that ate at the core of his control.

"I want to be gentle," he said through his teeth. "Help me."

Gracefully she shrugged away the green velvet folds of her caftan. When he saw that she wore nothing beneath the cloth but a flush of desire spreading across her smooth, pale skin, he nearly went to his knees.

His dark hands stroked from her lips to her toes, wanting all of her, shaking with the wanting. Finally his fingers tangled in the dark curls between her thighs. Gently he slid one finger partway between her soft, hot folds, silently asking if she was as ready for him as he was for her.

She was slick, hot, wet, and very tight.

He knew then that she wanted him—and that it had been a long, long time since she had been with a man.

The knowledge both excited and chastened him. With two fingers he delicately, teasingly, moved within her. He went just far enough that she knew he was there, just enough to stretch her, but not nearly deep enough for either one of them.

Her hips lifted, following his touch as she had followed his kiss. He laughed softly and circled the hot nub that was no longer hidden, but begging openly for his caress. She gasped, shivered, and watched him with smoldering eyes. He watched her the same way, burning, as he bent down and kissed her, caressed her, teased her, tasted her until she cried out and melted for him.

"Sweet," he said in a low voice, watching her, tasting her. "So damned sweet. No woman has ever burned for me like you."

He took a deep, racking breath and forced himself to look away from the heat welling out of her in gentle pulses.

She breathed his name and opened even more, needing him.

Abruptly he knew he couldn't wait any longer. He turned and grabbed blindly for his jeans.

"Rio?" She watched him with hungry eyes, afraid that he was going to pull on his clothes and leave her lonely and aching.

He saw her fear, and her need. He kissed her in swift, steamy reassurance.

"It's all right, dreamer," he said, biting her lips softly while he tore open the tiny package he had found in his jeans. "I'll take care of it."

When Hope realized what he was unwrapping, she shook her head. She didn't want that. She wanted him. All of him. Everything he could give. If that meant his baby, too, she would be the luckiest woman on earth.

"No," she said quickly, covering his fingers with her own. "You don't need to. It's all right. Please. I don't want anything between us. *Nothing.*"

He looked into eyes that were both burning and clear. A shudder of raw pleasure went down his spine at the thought of being truly naked within her. She hadn't been with any man for so long that she was as tight as a virgin, yet she had wanted him enough to protect herself in advance, freeing both of them from the sensual restrictions of a condom. That kind of freedom was something he had never permitted himself with any woman.

"Are you sure?" he asked. "I'm used to it. I always . . ."

His voice faded as he watched her lean toward him until her lips brushed over the heartbeat that pulsed visibly through his thick, rigid sex.

"I want you," she said. "I want this. Naked."

The touch of her tongue made him jerk. The foil packet fell from his shaking fingers to the floor. He uncoiled with a powerful movement that pressed her back onto the bed.

"Woman," he said thickly, "so much woman."

His whole body was hard with the force of restraining the hunger that shot through him with every motion of her lips brushing over him. His need of her raged like lightning through his body.

She trembled and opened to him, yielding a hot rain of pleasure as his fingers again found the secrets hidden within her softness. He had never wanted anything as much as he wanted to take her in that searing, endless instant when pleasure melted her.

Yet he was sure he would hurt her if he did. For all her heat, for all her need, she was still so tight he could barely ease two fingers into her.

He rolled over onto his back, pulling her with him, lifting her until her beautiful legs were pressed alongside his. Hard hands caressed from her shoulders down her back, kneading her hips, rubbing her softly against him until she shivered and shared her passion with him in a rain of hot silk. Need raked through him, white-hot, violent.

"Take me, Hope," he said hoarsely, easing just a small part of himself inside her. "Take as much or as little as you want. It's the only way I won't hurt you."

She looked down at his rigid flesh pressing gently into her. Pleasure swept through her in expanding, liquid pulses. She shared them with him, moving against his arousal, making him as slick and hot as she was.

"I can't imagine anything hurting with you," she said, watching him with eyes that knew only love.

"Dreamer," he said hoarsely, "beautiful dreamer."

His breath broke in a groan as her soft, passionate heat caressed him again. Involuntarily he closed his eyes, giving himself to her, losing himself in her.

Then he opened his eyes and moved in return, watching her with eyes that had no blue, only the dark glitter of desire. He felt her begin to ease more of herself onto him, more and then more. But still she was tight, a sweet, slick fist squeezing him. Small, too small. It had been too long for her since her last man.

"I'll hurt you," he said through clenched teeth.

"Not much. I'm told it's a very fragile piece of skin."

Sweat broke out all over Rio's body as he realized that he had been wrong. It hadn't been a long time since Hope had been with a man. It had been forever.

She had never given herself before, to any man.

Ecstasy swept through him in a searing silver rain.

"My God," he groaned, "I wonder which one of us is dreaming now."

The only answer was her heat closing over him, retreating, then advancing again, more deeply with each motion.

He wanted to put his hands on her hips and thrust into her, burying himself completely in her tight satin heat, ending the exquisite torment. All that prevented him was the intense pleasure that transformed her face each time she moved over him. Eyes closed, generous mouth taut, she came to him with the same abandoned grace he had seen when she'd arched herself to the sky and let water pour from her cupped hands.

"I want all of you," she whispered against his lips, straining to be as close to him as a woman could be to a man. "Help me, Rio. Help *us*."

He looked at her flushed face and saw no fear, no hesitation. The simple truth of her words broke over him, shaking him. He felt her softness straining against the last barrier between them.

"Gently," he murmured. "Gently, my dreamer."

His fingers caught her hard nipples, caressing her, sending exquisite lightning through her. He let the storm build, piling caress upon caress until he felt pleasure burst inside her. At that instant he thrust once, deeply, sweeping away the barrier between them. Then he retreated again, fearful of hurting her any more.

Hope followed his retreat, sliding over him, sheathing him deeply in her body. They both cried out in fierce pleasure, wanting it to last forever, to live and die feeling only the unbearably sweet instant when she first measured his full power.

He was no longer the wind. He was as hard and as hot and as hungry for rain as the desert itself. He could feel the storm coming now, feel it sweeping out from him, feel himself on the brink of—

His hands clamped over her hips, holding her absolutely still.

"Don't move," he said hoarsely, fighting for control of the storm they had created. "It's too soon. You aren't ready."

Slowly she opened her eyes and looked down at the man she loved. Every muscle in his body was rigid, hot, gleaming with sweat. He filled her mind, her heart, her body, and she wanted nothing more than to bring him a pleasure as wild and as true as her love for him.

He could hold her hips prisoner, but there was nothing he could do about the deep, involuntary movements of her body as she looked down at him with love in her eyes.

He groaned. "Don't—"

And then he could say no more. Hope was all around him, tugging sleekly at him, and he gave himself to her as though she was the wind calling his name.

She closed her eyes, savoring Rio's release, feeling the most intense pleasure of her life as the man she loved pulsed within her. She kissed his hot skin, breathed in his unique male scent, tasted the salt of passion. Smiling dreamily, she lay on his chest, content to listen to his heart beating wildly beneath her cheek.

When Rio could breathe again his hands slowly traveled from Hope's tangled hair down her spine to the warm curve of her hips, and from there to the secret cleft between. His fingertips brushed over sultry flesh, making her breath catch.

The sensitivity of her own body surprised her. She lifted her head and looked into his midnight-blue eyes. He moved against her, within her, smiling up at her with male intent.

"Rio?" she asked, not understanding. She had felt his climax. She was certain that he was satisfied.

"Did you think I would leave you hungry?"

Hope could only shake her head. "You haven't," she said simply, still not understanding. "I've never felt more pleasure than I did with you just now."

As Hope's words sank in, a hot shudder of desire stitched down the length of Rio's body. She had never had more pleasure—and he hadn't even begun to make love to her. The thought tore at him with the honeyed claws of ecstasy barely restrained.

"I've never lost control with a woman before," he said in a gritty, rueful voice, "and damned if you aren't taking me right up to the edge all over again."

"I don't understand."

"You will," he promised.

Without separating their bodies, he rolled her over onto her back and fitted his mouth to hers.

And then he loved her.

It was like being caught in a hot, gentle whirlwind. Hope felt his tongue thrusting sensually into her mouth even as his hands found the satin weight of her breasts. He caught her nipples between his fingers and tugged. Lightning streaked through her. She moaned and her body moved reflexively, tightening around him.

He laughed with sheer male pleasure.

The sound was another stroke of lightning taking her body by storm. She twisted up against him, needing the feel of his flesh buried inside her. He laughed again before he bent his head and drank the sounds that rippled from her. His fingertips closed on her hard nipples and tugged while hot waves of pleasure washed through her to him, a sensual yielding that was also a feminine demand.

He shifted one hand to the lush curve of her bottom, flexing his fingers against her resilient hip. His words were a dark wind surrounding her, telling her what she felt like, tasted like, what he wanted from her, what he would give to her in return; and through it all his hands stroked and tugged and burned over her, teaching her more than she had ever dreamed about sensual hunger and response.

"Rio," she said breathlessly, "I—"

The word became a cry as his hand slid between their joined bodies, finding and caressing the slick, pouting knot. He felt her sudden tension, her breath stopping within her, her nails digging into his back. He laughed softly, hotly, confidently, like his fingers stroking her, taking her to the edge and then holding her there poised and shivering on the brink of release.

She made a ragged sound that was his name and a question, surprise and something close to fear. She felt her own body being seduced from her control, a storm at the instant of breaking, her nerves a violent network of lightning straining to be free. Instinctively she held back, uncertain.

"Dreamer," he said huskily, caressing Hope, "come to me."

She cried aloud and she gave herself to the storm, to Rio, holding nothing back, knowing ecstasy for the first time in her life. It swept through her like a long, wild wind, shaking her to her soul.

She held on to him, crying, and he held her, kissing away the sweet rain of tears. Blindly she clung to him while her lips caressed his neck, his chest, the hard nub of his nipple. She was drowning in ecstasy, in him, and she whispered her love with each breath she took.

He heard her words, felt the tiny wild movements of her body, and control began slipping away from him again. He fought the whirlwind of desire spiraling up from their joined bodies, making him fill her until each of her breaths was a separate caress over him. He wanted to hold himself back, to protest that he wasn't like this, that no woman had ever aroused him until he wanted to scream with it, but even that primitive release was denied because his throat was as tight around his words as she was around him.

"I wondered on the stairway if I could get enough of you," he said finally, his voice low and gritty, as intimate as his movements deep within her body. He bit her shoulder with fierce restraint. "I don't think I can. Have you had enough of me?"

Her only answer was a sharp cry as anticipation coiled impossibly, hotly, within her again. Lightning strokes of new pleasure ripped through her before the aftershocks of her first ecstasy had fully stilled. She tried to say his name but couldn't. She could only feel his presence inside her.

He filled her, all of her, leaving room for nothing except the hot silver rains sweeping over her once again. This time she didn't hesitate in surprise or fear. She knew that he was waiting for her within that torrential passion. And then she was with him, holding him hard and close while ecstasy broke around them, consuming them.

It was a long time before the sensual storm passed, leaving them spent, gleaming with moisture, their bodies tightly intertwined.

Rio kissed and caressed Hope gently, cherishing her. He had never known such wild, intense pleasure with a woman. He hadn't even believed it was possible. She was like a new land opening before him, a new wind calling his name.

"Hope," he whispered.

He wanted to say more, but was able only to say her

name again and again. His mouth opened on her lips, asking for a greater intimacy. When she answered with a gliding pressure of her tongue, he caught it almost hungrily.

Rio didn't understand his need, for it wasn't sexual hunger driving him. He felt like a man racing to catch the wind, to hold it, to absorb it so completely into himself that he would never be separate again.

So he held her, surrounding her, letting her drift asleep within the cradle of his arms.

He didn't sleep. He couldn't. He lay and watched moonlight bathe Hope in unearthly silver beauty. And when he could control himself no longer, he began touching her with his hands and his lips and his tongue.

She woke slowly, languidly, murmuring Rio's name and her love while his mouth caressed her lips, her neck, her breasts, her body, moving over her like his brother the wind, learning each of her soft secrets. Long before he came to her she was crying and twisting against his unbearably knowing mouth, lost in the ecstasy shaking her.

Even then he didn't take her. He simply, hungrily, began all over again, memorizing her, leaving none of her hot skin untasted, knowing all of her, cherishing her with a primal sensuality that shattered her.

That was when he took her, when his name was a wild cry on her lips.

It was her name, too, his broken cry against her mouth, their voices intertwined as deeply as their moonlit bodies.

Nineteen

THE NEXT DAY Hope awoke to the fragrance of rain flowers drifting softly over her skin. She opened her eyes and saw bright yellow blossoms falling from Rio's hand.

His smile was as warm as the sunrise flooding the room with shades of gold and rose. Kissing her lips gently, he pulled the covers back up to her neck, concealing the womanly allure of her body. His hands curved around the blanket and her breasts.

"Last night taught me that I have no willpower where you're concerned, so I'm going to put all your temptations out of my sight."

"Why?" she asked sleepily, winding her arms around his neck. "If you give in, I won't be nearly so tempting to you afterward, will I?"

Laughing almost roughly, he disentangled her arms, kissing every inch of them along the way. He bit her palms and touched the sensitive skin between her fingers with the tip of his tongue.

"The more I have you," he said, closing his teeth over each of her fingertips in turn, "the more I want you. If I give in, the only explorations that get done on the ranch today will be done in this bed."

Hope's hazel eyes kindled. "What a lovely thought," she murmured, curling her fingers around his, tugging him down toward her.

"Does that mean you don't want to go riding with me?"

Amusement curved her lips.

"Let me rephrase that," he said quickly. "I've got a very interesting prospect for a well site. Do you want to go over it with me?"

Her sleepy, sensual humor evaporated. "Do you mean that? Have you really found a place to drill for water?"

"I don't know. So far things look good. I was going to check it out yesterday, but I went into town instead." He watched her with searching, intense eyes, wondering how she felt toward him in the clear light of another day.

Hope's smile faded as she remembered why Rio had left yesterday. He hadn't wanted to be her lover.

And now he was.

"Hope," he began, seeing shadows in her eyes.

"No," she cut in, her fingers over his lips. "I know you didn't want to be my lover. But it happened. I don't expect you to change. Don't expect me to change, either. I love you, Rio. Nothing will change that."

He gave her a swift, fierce kiss, then left the room

like it was on fire. He didn't trust himself to touch her anymore without sweeping away the blankets and knowing again the searing ecstasy of her body joined with his, her cries rippling through all of his silences.

Yesterday she had been a virgin. Today she was his woman. Tomorrow . . .

Tomorrow belonged to the wind. He would face it when he had to. Until then, today beckoned, radiant with Hope.

"Your bath is two feet deep and steaming," Rio called as he went down the stairs. "By the time you're dressed, I'll have breakfast ready."

"Where are we going?" Hope asked as she got out of bed. She shivered when her warm bare feet hit the cold bare floor.

"Ain't telling," he drawled.

She laughed at his laconic imitation of Mason. Then she raced for the hot welcome of a bath. She lingered, soaking out every small ache of the body she and Rio had so thoroughly enjoyed.

Finally she couldn't resist the smell of breakfast. Without looking, she stood and reached for a towel. The rack was empty. The nearest towel supply was in the linen closet down the hall. The cold hall.

Just as she nerved herself up for a chilly dash to the linen closet, the bathroom door opened. Rio's hand appeared. A thick, soft towel dangled from his fist.

"Missing something?" he asked.

"Brrr," she answered.

He came in and closed the door behind him so that the steamy warmth couldn't escape. Then he held the towel wide in silent invitation. She stepped into it, and his arms. He kissed her until it was impossible to know whether her flushed skin came from the hot bath or from the even hotter passion he called from her.

"That's what *I* was missing," he said huskily. Then he lifted his head and put her away from his hungry, insistent body. "If I don't stop right now, neither one of us is going to be in any shape to get on a horse."

"Especially if the horse is Storm Walker," she said, smiling at him with trembling lips.

"I think I'll leave that tough old son in the corral today," Rio admitted. "I suspect he has more hard in him this morning than I do."

When Hope looked down Rio's body, she saw the unmistakable bulge pushing against his jeans. A shiver of pleasure coursed through her when she remembered the beauty of his body beneath her hands. In the wake of memory came the rushing, liquid heat that had become familiar last night. Slowly, murmuring approval, she moved her hand over the length of his arousal.

His breath broke. "I thought you would be sore."

She shook her head.

His hand slid up between her legs. The hungry, molten silk that waited for him was a revelation. His breath broke as his heartbeat doubled.

"You sure?" he asked, stroking her, watching for any sign that she was flinching away.

She shifted, opening to his touch. The hot pulse of her response on his fingers said that she was ready for him.

"I want you to be able to ride," he said.

Yet even as he spoke, he caressed her, drawing more of her liquid silk to him.

Her eyelids trembled down as an exquisite thrill of pleasure rippled through her. "I'll tie a pillow to the saddle."

He laughed and sank to his knees. "That won't be necessary."

The sultry, wild whirlwind of his mouth closed over her. When she was trembling and crying, he pulled her down and let the storm take them both. By the time it was spent, he lay fully clothed on the cold floor with her over him like a blanket. Smiling, he stroked her back.

"I must be crushing you," Hope said.

He laughed, and in laughing moved inside her.

"Mmm," she purred. "That feels good."

His heartbeat quickened again. "Better get up, dreamer. We have a well to find."

She kissed his jaw, sighed, and struggled into a sitting position astride him.

His breath caught. "Hope?"

"Mmm?"

He lifted her off his quickening flesh. "Get out of here or neither one of us will be able to walk, much less ride."

She looked at Rio, saw that he was still hard, and said, "Why don't I just drag you fully dressed into that tub? It's still hot."

For an instant Hope thought he was going to let her—and so did he.

With a wrench that was almost painful, he stood and tucked himself back into his jeans. He started to say something, shook his head ruefully, and got out of the steamy intimacy of the bathroom.

"Breakfast is ready," he said from the safety of the hallway. *And so am I.*

Again.

His response to Hope kept taking Rio by surprise, like finding an artesian spring in the middle of a vast desert waste. The spring shouldn't be there. All logic and experience were against it. But there it was just the same, pure and sweet and inexhaustible, pulsing with rhythms that were deeper than logic and experience, as deep as life itself.

By the time Hope dressed and walked into the kitchen, Rio had filled two plates with mounds of hotcakes, ham, and eggs. She measured the huge breakfast and looked at him in silent protest.

"You'll be glad for every bite by lunchtime," he said.

She ate without arguing. She knew he was right. Besides, she was unusually hungry. When she tucked the last morsel of hotcake neatly into her mouth and looked up from her plate, he was smiling at her.

Rio touched the fullness of her lower lip, licked his fingertip, and said, "Sweet."

"Syrup always is," she pointed out reasonably, smiling at him with love in her eyes.

He shook his head slowly. "Not syrup. You." He sighed and pushed his chair back from the table. "Let's go before my good intentions hitch a ride on the wind. Again."

"You never told me where we were going."

"You distracted me."

"Good for me. Was it good for you?"

He laughed. "You know it was. Wind Canyon."

Smiling, Rio poured the rest of the coffee into a canteen, tossed a paper bag full of sandwiches to Hope, put his arm around her shoulders, and walked out into the sun-filled morning. Leaning lightly against him, she slid her arm around his waist. Her long legs kept pace with clean, graceful movements.

"I'm not a bit sore," she said, grinning. "Must be all those years of riding."

He gave a crack of laughter, kissed her swiftly on the lips, and lifted her over the pasture fence. He watched while she caught Aces, swung up bareback on the mare, and rode to the fence. The elegance of Hope's legs was clear even when they were covered by worn jeans and scuffed cowboy boots. He kept remembering how it felt when those long legs had wrapped around him, holding him tightly within her silky heat.

"You have beautiful legs," he said when she rode close.

She looked at him, startled. Then she smiled, slid off Aces, and picked up a curry comb.

"My legs are how I got the money to keep the ranch alive," Hope said as she worked. "Shoes, hosiery, and slit-to-midthigh bedroom stuff was my specialty. The green caftan came from one of my last modeling assignments. I love the way it makes me feel."

Rio half-closed his eyes. The memory of her silky, beautiful body glowing against the deep green velvet was a pleasure so acute it was almost pain.

"So you take it out and wear it when nobody is around," he said huskily.

"Except for last night." Hope shuddered. "Turner knew I'd be here alone. He saw you in town."

"I know. One of the clerks in the hardware store told me that John Turner took one look at me through the window, reversed direction, and set off out of town like the hounds of hell were after him." Rio's eyes changed, becoming as hard as blue-black stone.

"I'm glad you came back," she said simply.

"Not half as glad as I am." Emotions vibrated in his voice, a volatile mixture of rage at Turner, anger at himself, and a hunger for Hope so intense that it still could shake him.

With a muttered word, Rio went to the barn. He emerged in a few minutes, leading Dusk. The mare headed toward the horse trailer that had been un-hitched from Rio's pickup and parked beside the barn. Dusk's movements were the automatic reaction of a horse accustomed to being trailered all over the West as her owner went from town to town, ranch to ranch, horizon to horizon.

"Not yet, girl," Rio said, draping the roping rein over the corral railing. "First we've got a well to find."

Hope had watched the horse turn toward the trailer, heard Rio's casual words, and now a cold wind was keening through her soul.

Not yet.

But it would happen. There was no question, no doubt, nothing in Rio's voice but a calm certainty that he would leave.

Leaning against Aces, Hope struggled to control the storm of grief shaking her. *You knew he was going to leave,* she told herself fiercely. *Last night didn't change that. Tonight won't change it.*

Nothing will change it.

You've fallen in love with the wind, and you knew it even while you were falling.

She had no complaints coming, and accepted it. The choice had been hers every step of the way. Rio hadn't wanted to be her lover.

Hope. Tell me to stop. I didn't want to hurt you! I don't have any past, any future, any present. Hope, I don't—

Then she had kissed him, wanted him, and he had given her all he could. It was more than any other man had given her: tenderness and fierce passion, serenity and wild ecstasy. She wouldn't throw Rio's gift in his face and say that it wasn't enough. He would blame himself. She knew it as certainly as she knew she loved him.

Are you cruel enough to make him hate himself? Hope asked herself harshly. *Is that your idea of loving him?*

After a few moments Hope straightened her shoulders and went back to grooming Aces with smooth motions of her arm. It wasn't long before she saddled the mare, led her out of the corral, and mounted swiftly, before Rio could help her, touch her.

Side by side the two horses loped along the dirt road. The wind blew fitfully, tearing puffs of dust from the land.

Rio kept glancing over at Hope, quick looks that were hidden within the shadow of his hat brim. Back at the corral he had seen intense unhappiness on her face. He had wanted to go to her, to hold her, to assure her that everything would be all right, that he would protect her from whatever she feared.

And then he had seen her gather herself, shaking off whatever had clawed at her.

He didn't know what had happened, or why. He only knew that for a moment Hope had been sliced open all the way to her soul.

He understood what that kind of pain was like, how unexpected it could be, how devastating. So he watched her, reassuring himself that she was truly all right.

Hope caught the indigo flash of Rio's glance and turned, smiling at him for a moment before she looked back over the velvet-shadowed hills glowing in the early sunlight. The peace of the morning and the rhythmic beat of hooves were like a benediction to her grieving soul.

Rio's eyes followed her glance. He was accustomed to such sunrises, such silence—but this time Hope was with him, sharing the quiet and the compelling land. Like the dawn itself, she had a quiet that pleasured him. Other women he had known were hurt or frightened by his silence. They had demanded that he take their emotional temperature with constant conversation. He had hated that, hated being with someone so shallow that she changed temperature with each of his silences.

Leaning over, Rio ran his fingertip down the line of

Hope's jaw. She looked at him and smiled, her eyes almost golden in the rich morning light.

Hunger and something more powerful moved through him, something indescribable, as though a spring was pushing up from his soul and lapping gently outward, sweet water bringing life to everything that thirsted. Gently he touched Hope again, as though to reassure himself that she was real and he was real and the moment itself was real.

The two horses walked into the thick shadows slanting from Wind Canyon's broad mouth. In this place there was a long exhalation of air, an almost intangible stirring of the atmosphere that was always more apparent here than at any other canyon mouth on the ranch. It was as though something immense slept, and in sleeping, sighed deeply.

Hope glanced up the canyon where the old wagon road began to snake up into the heights. She grimaced and looked away, grateful that Rio hadn't wanted to go all the way to the abandoned mine.

"What are we looking for?" she asked.

"Nothing we can see."

She gave him a sideways glance. "That's going to make it difficult, isn't it?"

Rio tugged his hat more firmly around his head and almost smiled. "Look at Eagle Peak."

Dutifully Hope looked at the ragged mountain that had dominated the skyline of all her childhood mornings.

"What do you see?" he asked.

"Rock. Lots of it."

"Close your eyes. You'll see more that way."

She looked at him for an instant. Then she closed her eyes.

"Remember that sandwich we talked about?" he asked.

"The torn-up one with waterproof bread?"

"That's the one. Now, imagine the sandwich is whole. Imagine that it's slanted up toward the sky at a fairly shallow angle."

"Umm."

Rio looked at Hope. Her eyes were closed, her lashes almost black against her golden skin. He remembered the intriguing softness of her eyelashes against his lips, the scent of her when he rested his cheek between her breasts, and the heady taste of her passion.

Impatiently he yanked his wandering thoughts back to aquifers and Eagle Peak.

"Now, that peak is like a party sandwich with all kinds of fancy layers," he said. "Rocks like granite, quartzite, and slate are the waterproof strata. The meat of the sandwich is limestone laid down in ancient seas. The limestone doesn't vary much in thickness here, but the surrounding layers do. Granite intrusions can be only a few inches thick in some places, and hundreds or thousands of feet deep in others."

Hope frowned, eyes still closed as she visualized a rather lumpy, disorganized sandwich. "Then how do you know where to sink the well? If you start where granite is thousands of feet thick, you'll never get anything but worn-out drill bits and dry holes."

"That's why you go to the Colorado School of Mines and get a master's degree in hydrology," he said dryly. "It gives you a fighting chance of guessing right."

Her eyes flew open as she understood what he was saying. At some time in his past he had earned a master's degree from one of the foremost centers for the study of applied geology in the United States.

Hope watched Rio intently, hoping he would tell her more about himself, but he didn't seem to notice. He was looking at Eagle Peak with trained eyes that saw through the mixed layers of rock to the chance of water beneath.

"Not much limestone shows through on this side of the mountains," he said. "That's probably why your geologist gave up."

Silently Rio added, *That and the fact that his grandfather wasn't a Zuni shaman who taught a wild kid to be so still that he could feel clouds condensing around distant peaks and water flowing in the earth far beneath his feet.*

"He was real sure there wasn't any water," Hope said.

"He might be right. But there's limestone in those mountains. It shows high up in the most deeply eroded peaks over on the dry side of the Perdidas. Because limestone weathers away faster than other strata, it undermines the layers of rock that cover it. They crumble and collapse until the exposed limestone is all but buried by slides of harder stone."

Though Rio was looking up at the rugged mountains, she sensed that his focus was inward, deep down where knowledge, experience, and instinct arranged and rearranged the possibilities of the layers of rock.

"The limestone I saw could be just fragments of a stratum that has long since dissolved away," he said. "Or it could be the tip of an aquifer that's thousands of feet thick and has been soaking up water for millions of years."

Her breath came in quickly and stayed, filling her until she ached. The thought of so much water waiting beneath her feet was almost unbearable.

"Is it?" she asked, her voice hungry, yearning. "Is there a layer of limestone filled with water for the Valley of the Sun, just waiting to be discovered?"

Twenty

❦

RIO DISMOUNTED AND looked up at Hope. "That's why we rode to Wind Canyon," he said simply. "To decide if it's worth the gamble of drilling here."

"How will you do that?"

He hesitated, not wanting to explain what he didn't understand himself; he simply accepted. He had already done everything he could using conventional knowledge of geology and hydrology. He had narrowed the search to three possible sites. Of the three, Wind Canyon was by far the most likely.

Now he would walk the land, letting its silent messages seep into him. He would wait deep within himself, hoping to feel the rippling echo of water flowing beneath his feet. It was like tiny currents of electricity whispering through him, telling him that *something different* lay beneath his feet. Often the feeling was so subtle that it was easy to miss. Silence was required, silence and an inner stillness that had to come from his whole mind.

White men called what he was doing water witching or dowsing, and claimed not to believe in it. Despite that, many western wells had been found by men or women carrying peeled forked sticks that quivered and dipped in the presence of hidden water. His grandfather had called Rio's gift the breath of the Great Spirit.

Rio didn't call it anything at all. He accepted it, just as he accepted the color of his hair and the number of his fingers.

"Experience," he said finally, handing Dusk's rein to Hope. He loosened the saddle cinch with a few expert tugs. "That's how I decide. If the land feels right, I drill."

"And if it doesn't?"

"I move on until I find water or there's nowhere left to look."

He unbuckled the deep saddlebags he always brought with him and reached inside. After a moment he pulled out a pair of scarred hiking boots. Sitting on a convenient rock, he kicked off his cowboy boots and pulled on the others.

"I learned when I was young to trust my instincts," Rio said, quickly lacing up and tying the boots. "My grandfather was a good teacher."

She wanted to ask more questions, but Rio was already walking slowly away. He moved over the rocky canyon floor like a man looking for a faded trail. She sensed that it wasn't the dry surface of the ground he was concentrating on, but something else, something indescribable.

I learned when I was young to trust my instincts.

Silently Hope dismounted and loosened the cinch on her saddle. After a short search she found a flat, sun-washed rock to sit on. She didn't know how long he would be walking the land, but she sensed he didn't want any distractions.

In the cool hours of early morning, the sun felt good. Knees tucked under her chin, arms wrapped around her legs, Hope watched the man she loved move over the land like an intelligent wind.

With slow strides Rio quartered the mouth of the canyon. Several miles wide, jumbled at the center with debris from thousands of flash floods, the canyon mouth was more like the lip of an outwash plain than a true canyon. The soil was so coarse and stony that little grew there. Water coming down from the heights simply sank into the millions of spaces between the rocks and disappeared before the thirsty roots of plants could soak it up.

Hope watched Rio and remembered that her father had tried drilling a well in a canyon mouth similar to this one. He had drilled down hundreds of feet deeper than his deepest existing well before he gave up and admitted that there was no end to the dry, loose, rocky soil.

That was when he had decided to drill where her namesake well was now. He had struck groundwater and had prayed that his water worries were over.

It hadn't turned out that way.

With a weary gesture Hope readjusted her hat to shade her eyes against the changing angle of the sun. Thinking about her father scraped at her emotions, yet every time she thought of water she couldn't help thinking of him.

She loved the land.

She had loved her father.

And the land she loved had killed him. He had worked himself to death trying to get around the stony reality of a retreating water table. It was as though he believed if he just worked hard enough, long enough, faithfully enough, water would return to the land.

With each summer's visit to the ranch, Hope had seen her father grow older, more tired, more unbending in his determination to make the ranch become what it once had been—alive.

Within a year of her eighteenth birthday he had a stroke, followed by pneumonia. Hope, her mother, and her sister had visited him in the small hospital, sitting beside his bed, listening to him fight for breath. At least Hope and her mother had sat and listened; Julie had been terrified of the broken, white-haired old man who had taken the place of the strong father of her memories.

His death had increased Julie's terror and her mother's hatred of the land. Only the fact that her father had willed his half of the ranch to Hope kept her mother from selling it.

Instead, her mother had abandoned the Valley of the Sun, leaving Mason to live alone amid the wreckage of so many dreams.

Hope had come back as often as she could, but the demands of providing for her mother, her sister, herself, and the ranch had meant long hours of modeling.

Rarely could she afford to leave Los Angeles to come home to the land she missed with an intensity that would have shocked the people she worked with, people who thought she was cold because she didn't share their zest for weekend romances and frequent lovers.

Before Hope was twenty her mother had died. According to the accident report, she lost control of her car and crashed into a cement freeway overpass.

Hope knew the explanation wasn't that neat, that easy. Her mother hadn't wanted to live. Even Julie's iridescent smile and feverish pursuit of the perfect lover hadn't been able to sink through her mother's grief for her dead husband.

In the end only Hope's silent, enduring love of the land had touched her mother. She left the ranch to Hope, asking only that Julie receive half of the profits.

There hadn't been any profits. Not during the two years that it took for Julie to kill herself with drugs and despair, not in the four years since then. The only money that came to the Valley of the Sun came by way of Los Angeles and the Sharon Morningstar Modeling Agency.

Hope had lived in L.A. until she couldn't stand it any longer. Then she had packed up and returned to the land she loved more than anything else. She had told herself that she had saved enough money to do everything—meet daily ranch expenses, pay off back taxes, and even drill a new well if it came to that.

She hadn't thought it would. There had been dry years before. They had always passed before all the wells failed. It would be the same this time.

It hadn't been the same.

In January of this year she had been forced to take out a second mortgage at high interest rates. She had told herself that it would be all right, that once she found a good well, the second mortgage could be renegotiated on the basis of the ranch's greatly increased production.

But she hadn't found a well. She had spent thousands of dollars on surveys and geologists. They had told her there wasn't any water to be found on the Valley of the Sun.

She hadn't believed them.

She couldn't. It would be the end of her dream.

Stiffly Hope shifted on the unyielding surface of her rock and wondered how long she had sat there, thinking of a past she couldn't change and a future she couldn't control. She was all but numb.

Gingerly she slid off the rock and stretched. Dusk flicked an ear in her direction, snorted softly, and returned to her three-legged doze. Aces had her head up, ears pricked forward, watching something. Hope turned to see what had caught the mare's interest.

After a moment she saw Rio walking along the southern edge of the canyon, where rock crumbled and rattled down the slopes onto the dry, furrowed land below. As she watched, he began yet another zigzag across the mile-wide canyon floor. Soon a small fold in the land hid him as he worked his way up the broad canyon.

Hope tightened the cinch on Aces, mounted, and grabbed Dusk's rein. She rode farther into the canyon, passing Rio far enough away not to disturb him, and chose a piece of higher ground to wait on. Up here nothing would get in the way of watching him while he zigzagged slowly toward her, searching for water hidden deep beneath the dry surface of the land.

As morning blended seamlessly into afternoon, Hope shifted position many times, riding Aces and leading the patient Dusk on a slow retreat up the canyon. Rio followed silently, quartering the land with extraordinary patience.

The climbing sun brought first warmth, then a surprising autumn heat to the canyon floor. Drowsiness turned Hope's bones to sand. She found a wide, shallow bowl of land set apart from the canyon floor. Quickly she took out the obvious rocks, spread an old quilt, and fell asleep beneath the sun's golden caress.

She dreamed of Rio, a river flowing through the landscape of her love. She awoke to a kiss as sweet as spring water, as warm as sunlight.

"Wake up, my beautiful dreamer," Rio murmured against her lips.

"But the dream was so lovely."

"What was it?"

"It was you, Rio. You and a well and water flowing. All of life in a single dream."

Unable to speak, he held her face between his hands.

She watched as sunlight struck his eyes, turning them into blue-black gems. His eyelashes were thick, utterly black, like his hair burning darkly beneath the sun. She looked up at him and knew beyond any doubt that he had been right—she was a one-man woman, and Rio was that man. Whether he was with her or thousands of miles away, she wouldn't change.

When he left he would take her love. While he was here she would take from him what he could give. And she would pray that part of what he gave her was his child.

He kissed her very gently, as though she was a dream he was afraid to awaken. Reluctantly he lifted his head.

"You're so beautiful to me," he said. "Even more beautiful than your name. Hope."

Sunlight brought out both the gold and the green in her hazel eyes, and the love.

He kissed her dark, soft lashes and then stood up swiftly, not trusting himself to touch her any longer. Since he had seen her asleep on the faded quilt, he had thought of nothing but the ecstasy that waited for him deep within her loving body.

"Lunchtime," he said huskily. He went to Aces, pulled the sandwiches and canteen from the saddle-bags, and went back to Hope. "Ham or roast beef?" he asked.

"Yes," she said, stretching.

He hesitated, then smiled crookedly. "You *are* a dreamer if you think you get both sandwiches."

"Two?" she yelped. "You mean you only made two sandwiches?"

"Well, after all that breakfast . . ." He shrugged.

She looked at him in a silence that was broken by her rumbling stomach. He glanced sideways at her, chuckled, and put two sandwiches in front of her.

"No, you need it more than I do," she said hastily, trying to give the lunch back to him. "You're the one who's doing all the work."

He let her put the sandwiches in front of him. Then he pulled two more sandwiches from the lunch bag and waited. It didn't take two seconds. With an indignant sound she snatched back her sandwiches and ignored his laughter. Muttering about men who had been out in the sun too long, she bit into the yeasty bread.

Both of them ate quickly, sipping coffee from a shared canteen. In the end she could eat only half of what Rio had given to her. Smiling to himself, he wrapped up half of the remaining sandwich and put it back into the bag. He ate the other half.

Despite the coffee and the nap, Hope felt sleepy. She yawned and stretched.

"Bored?" he asked quietly.

Startled, she blinked. Bored? With Rio so close and the ranch she loved all around her? She shook her head. "Just content."

"Sure?"

"Have I missed something?" she asked, puzzled.

"It seems like every time you come with me, either I talk your ear off about geology or I don't say much at all about anything." He watched her intently. "I just thought you might be bored."

Speechless, she simply stared at him for a moment, thinking that he must be teasing her the way he had with the sandwiches. Then she realized that he was serious.

"Up at Piñon Camp," she said, "you shared your visions of this land with me. I saw miracles. Continents moved and range after range of mountains rose from beneath the sea. There was water everywhere, good water, lakes gleaming beneath the sky, forests growing tall and thick against the mountains, snowfields and glaciers blazing on the rocky heights."

She smiled helplessly, unable to explain what she was feeling. He was so silent, watching her. *Doesn't he believe me? Didn't he hear when I said I loved him?* Slowly, deliberately, she framed his tanned face with her hands.

"Rio, I've never been more excited and yet at peace with anyone or anything, not even the Valley of the Sun. Today I watched you move over the land, searching, *listening.*" She hesitated, then continued softly, sadly. "You're like a . . . a brother to the wind. Belonging to nothing, seeing everything, knowing things about the land that no one else does."

The words struck Rio with the force of an explosion, shaking him. Somehow Hope knew the name that no one else had ever spoken aloud but his grandfather, and then only once, when he gave Rio his name during a ceremony conducted in a place few men had ever seen.

"You see too much," Rio said savagely.

He felt naked before the clarity of Hope's vision. He surged to his feet and strode away from her, farther up the narrowing canyon, shutting her out. Then he realized the unfairness of what he had done and struggled to control the emotions that were reducing him to reflex and impulse. His grandfather had always told him to *listen,* to hold himself utterly still and *listen* with every bit of himself. In time, understanding would come.

So Rio stood motionless, *listening* as he never had before.

He heard only Hope's love for him in every word, every gesture, every look. There was nothing else, no desire to cage the wind, to break him like a wild horse, to change him into a man who would be more comfortable to love.

Like the wind itself, she asked nothing of him.

And like the land itself, she gave everything in return.

Tension flowed out of Rio, leaving him both at peace and alive in a way he had never known before. He turned and walked back toward Hope. With each step he sensed the warm fall of sunlight, the subtle murmuring of the wind, the power of his own body, and the gritty whisper of the land beneath his feet.

It was a hard land, an honest land, a miraculous land with a million million yesterdays and more tomorrows than a man could count, a land where rains came and sank into stone until strange rivers seeped through the fossil remains of ancient seas.

The years peeled away until he was thirteen again, light-headed from ceremonial fasting and shivering with cold. It hadn't mattered. Nothing had been real to him then but the presence of buried water like gentle electric shocks against the soles of his bare feet.

It was the same here, now.

Water within the stone, water's ghostly presence tingling up through him with each step until he stood transfixed, not able to take another step. Incredible currents sang through him, making him want to throw back his head to the sky and shout, but he had no voice. He had only the certainty of ancient water running black and sweet and deep beneath his feet.

Hope had seen Rio turn and walk back toward her, had seen him slow, then stop. The absolute stillness of his body screamed that something was wrong.

"Rio!" she called, scrambling to her feet.

He didn't answer.

She ran across the canyon bottom toward him until she could see the expression on his face. She stopped as though she had run up against a cliff.

"Rio?" she asked softly.

His eyes opened. They were almost as black as the water buried deep beneath the earth.

She walked toward him, touched him, and trembled. It was as though the ground had shifted beneath her feet.

He saw her knees buckle and his arms swept out, pulling her close, supporting her. He kissed her while the land whispered its secrets to him, to her, water singing to both of them from deep within the earth.

Then he gave to her what he had given to no other person.

"My true name is Brother-to-the-wind."

Twenty-one

MASON SLAMMED THE truck door and held out his arms to Hope. "Honey, you should have called me sooner! I'd have come back right after Thanksgiving instead of sitting around on my dead end stuffing my face with leftovers."

Laughing, Hope ran down the front steps and hugged him, burying her face in his red flannel shirt. He smelled of wool and cold and the awful pipe he never smoked around her. She loved all of it, for it meant that he was here again, ready to laugh and tease and share the Valley of the Sun with her.

"I wanted you to have a real vacation," she said. "You haven't had one in years."

"But the well—"

"You came back in time to help me set up the rig," Rio interrupted. "I didn't really need you until now."

Mason looked over Hope's shoulder at the tall, dark man filling the doorway to the house. As Mason and Hope climbed up the steps, he gave Rio a sideways look.

"Heard in town you had some trouble with Turner," Mason muttered.

Hope stiffened, remembering the ugly look on Turner's face when he stalked her through her kitchen.

Gently Rio's hand stroked over her hair, reassuring her with his touch. Without thinking, she turned her head so that her lips brushed against his palm.

Mason saw the gesture, understood everything that hadn't been said, and frowned.

Deliberately Rio put his arm around Hope and drew her against his side. "Turner won't be back. He knows that Hope is my woman."

Mason's faded green eyes focused on Hope. "Honey?"

"Yes, I'm Rio's woman." She searched Mason's eyes, remembering what he had said about Rio. *Temporary man.* "Don't be angry."

"Angry? Shoot!" Grinning, Mason held out his hand to Rio. "Welcome home, son. It's about time you found a good woman and settled down. And God never made no better woman than Hope."

She started to protest, to explain that Rio hadn't meant that kind of belonging, home and children and forever.

Rio tilted her face up to his and kissed her lightly on the lips, stilling the protest he saw forming.

"I know," he said softly.

The words could have been an answer to Mason's praise of Hope or to her silent protest.

"This calls for a drink," Mason said happily.

He strode into the house and went directly to the old-fashioned walnut bar cabinet that stood at one end of the living room.

"None of that city bubbly, neither. Rye," Mason announced.

Hope and Rio smiled as the old man pulled a bottle out of the bar, opened it, and inhaled with appreciation. He pulled out three cut-crystal whiskey glasses, examined them critically for dust, and poured a splash of amber liquid into each. He handed out two glasses and held the third high.

"To the both of you," Mason said, his voice husky.

Hope touched her glass against Mason's, making crystal ring triumphantly. She turned to Rio—and the searching intensity of his look made her knees buckle as they had in Wind Canyon when she had sensed the certainty of water coursing through him. Through her. Her hand trembled, sending tiny shivers through the potent whiskey.

Rio's glass rang sweetly against hers, then against Mason's.

She wanted to reassure Rio that he didn't have to worry about her, that what had happened between them was her choice, her joy, her dream. But Mason was there, smiling like a man who had just stumbled onto the golden end of a rainbow. So she simply looked at Rio, telling him silently what she couldn't say in front of Mason.

Brother-to-the-wind, I love you. All of you. The easy and the difficult and everything in between.

Watching Rio over the brilliant crystal rim of her glass, she sipped the potent whiskey.

He watched her in turn, open to every shift of emotion across her face. The taste of rye swept across his tongue, exploded in his mouth, but it wasn't nearly as potent as the love he saw in Hope's eyes. He touched his glass to hers again. Then he bent and kissed her slowly, *listening* to her as though she was an unknown country whose secrets he was only beginning to explore.

"Guess I better dust off my go-to-town suit," Mason said smugly. "How much time I got?"

Hope smiled up at him from within the curve of Rio's arm. "For what?" she asked.

"To git geared up for your wedding." His tone of voice said that he thought she had better sense than to ask such a silly question.

"There's no rush." Hope's voice was calm and very final, an unmistakable verbal NO TRESPASSING sign.

Mason had considered himself Hope's honorary father for too long to pay any attention to the warning. His heavy gray eyebrows levered up almost to his hairline.

"What are you talking about, gal? I want my grandkids born proper!"

Hope felt Rio's tension in the sudden hardness of his arm around her shoulders.

"Mason," he said in a soft, inflexible voice, "leave it alone."

For a moment there was an electric tension in the room. The old man's mouth opened, then closed hard and tight. The narrowing of Rio's dark eyes and the flat line of his mouth were as much a warning as his voice had been. Only a foolish man would ignore the signals of Rio's anger, and Mason's mama hadn't raised any fools.

The old man looked at Hope with swift concern. Being Rio's woman was not the same as being Rio's future wife. The shadows in her beautiful eyes told him that she knew it, and had accepted it.

Anger surged through Mason, shaking him. *She's giving herself to a man that don't appreciate her.*

On the heels of rage came a tumble of confused thoughts. Mason shook his head as though to settle his mind.

It don't make sense. Rio ain't no drunken buck that can't keep his pants zipped. Rio wouldn't touch a woman like Hope unless he cared about her in a permanent sort of way.

He just don't know it yet, that's all. He'll smarten up quick enough.

Mason sighed and hoped it would be soon.

Real soon.

"You be right careful of Hope," he said quietly, looking Rio straight in the eye. "That woman's worth more than you and me put together."

In silence Mason tossed back the rest of his rye, put the bottle away, and went out to the truck to bring in the supplies he had picked up in town.

"Don't be angry," she said quickly, softly, to Rio. "He's all the family I have."

Rio bit back on the emotions that had exploded when Mason turned on Hope: *I want my grandkids born proper.*

He wondered if Mason would feel better knowing that Hope had gone into the affair with her eyes wide open. There wouldn't be any children. No matter how much she thought she loved him, she didn't want her children born not white.

"I'm not angry," Rio said.

And he wasn't. He understood. He had understood before he turned eleven.

Together Rio and Hope helped Mason carry in the sacks and boxes of food he had picked up in town. Without hampering Hope in any way, Rio made it clear that she wasn't to lift, drag, shove, or otherwise disturb the heavy burlap bags of potatoes and rice, flour and beans, sugar and dried apples, and all the boxes of canned goods.

Though she eyed the closed cartons, sacks of the drilling lubricant everyone called "mud," and bags of hardware that Rio had ordered for the drilling rig, she didn't touch anything. He was ignoring them as though they didn't exist. Mentally she shrugged and reached for a big sack of flour.

Rio beat her to it. He hefted the sack over one shoulder, gathered up a fifty-pound sack of potatoes with his other arm, and headed for the kitchen. She grabbed a bag of milk, butter, and cheese that was teetering on the edge of falling over and started after him. When she got back to the truck, she reached for a burlap bag of rice.

"I'll get it," he said, lifting the slithery weight of the rice bag to his shoulder. Then, when she reached for more potatoes, he added, "Mason's going to drop one of those grocery bags."

She looked up, saw that he was indeed close to losing a bag full of fresh vegetables, and snatched it from him.

The next time she reached for something heavy, Rio picked it up before she could, even though he already had one bulging sack riding on his shoulder.

"Rio," she said in a reasonable tone, "I've been playing tug-of-war with fifty- and hundred-pound bags of food since I was twelve."

"Bet you lost, too."

She smiled reluctantly. "Well, my style leaves something to be desired, but the job gets done just the same."

Rio shifted the heavy bags so that their weight was comfortably balanced on his shoulders. "Stand on tiptoe so I can kiss you."

As soon as Hope's lips brushed his, he said, "We have a deal, woman. You dream for me and I'll haul mountains into the pantry for you."

Mason cleared his throat loudly from the doorway. "You know, them that don't work don't eat."

Laughing, Rio stole another kiss from Hope.

Mason tried not to smile. Then he gave in and grinned as broadly as a kid. He had never seen Rio so open, so . . . free. And Hope, well, Hope looked like she had swallowed the sun.

Mason decided that he would stop worrying about wedding dates and Rio's wandering past and Hope's generous, vulnerable heart. A man would have to be stump-dumb and mule-stubborn to walk away from a woman like Hope. Rio was neither.

While Hope sorted out vegetables at the kitchen counter, she listened to the good-natured ribbing Mason was giving Rio over some incident from his past. Relief swept through her, and a rushing gratitude. She had been afraid that Mason wouldn't accept the fact that she was Rio's woman, period. No rings, no ceremony, no until-death-do-us-part. Mason hadn't liked it, but he wasn't holding a grudge. He loved both Rio and Hope.

If she was lucky, she could give Mason one of his heart's desires. She could have a baby for him to fuss and worry over, a child who would call him grandpa and pester him with endless questions about the past.

If she was lucky.

She hadn't been lucky this month. After almost two weeks with Rio, her period had come with the regularity of the moon's own cycle. But December would be coming soon. It would be different then. It had to be. She wouldn't get many more chances.

When the well came in, Rio would leave.

She knew it as deeply as she knew that she wanted his child. Yet within her acceptance part of her cried: *Why does he have to leave? What can he find out there that he can't find on the Valley of the Sun?*

The questions had no answer, and no end to the asking. They were still quivering in her mind when Rio shut the bedroom door behind him that night and took her in his arms.

"I'm sorry, little dreamer," he said, stroking his hands down the line of her back.

For a moment she stiffened, wondering if he had read her mind and knew that she was crying in silence over the future when he would leave.

"Mason won't lean on you again," Rio said. "He understands how it is between us."

How can he? she asked silently. *I don't understand myself.* But all she said aloud was, "I'm glad. Maybe he can explain it to me."

"What?"

"You."

"What don't you understand?"

"Why you'll leave."

Before Rio could speak, Hope kissed him long and hard, filling herself with his taste.

"Never mind," she whispered against his lips. "It doesn't matter. Understanding why won't change anything, not really. I'll still love you and you'll still leave me."

"Hope, I—"

"Brother-to-the-wind," she said over his words. "Love me while you're here." Her hands moved over his arms, his shoulders, his chest, and she shook with sudden hunger for him. "Love me now."

His hands tangled in her dark hair, tilting her head back so that she had to meet his eyes. What he saw shook him to his soul: grief and acceptance, passion and love.

Most of all, love. She loved him as no one ever had, more than he had believed anyone could love.

"Hope," he said hoarsely, "I don't want to hurt you. Please, don't let me hurt you."

Her hands moved over his body, savoring the heat and power and arousal of him. She bit his lower lip with an exquisite sensuality she had learned from him.

"I'm hurting now," she said huskily. "I want you so much I'm shaking. Can't you feel it? I—"

The rest of her words were lost as his mouth came down on hers with a power that would have been painful if she hadn't wanted him so badly. She shivered as his salt-sweet taste filled her mouth. Her hands kneaded down his back to his waist and then his hips, loving the lithe, flexed strength of him. Wanting to feel the smooth heat of his skin beneath her palms, she slid her fingers inside the waistband of his jeans.

It wasn't enough.

He said something hot and dark as her fingers moved over his silver belt buckle, tugging on it. It didn't open. She made a broken sound of frustration and pulled harder. The buckle stayed closed.

"Damned stubborn thing," she muttered. "Reminds me of a certain water witch I know."

He laughed low in his throat and stepped back, peeling away his clothes until he stood naked before her.

"Is this what you want?" he asked. "Is this—"

His words broke off as she came to him, licking his lips with tiny strokes of her tongue, teasing him when he tried to capture her mouth. She moved against him, gently pushing him backward, inciting him with her sultry caresses and silky retreats.

When he felt the bed against his legs, he sank down, pulling her after him. She slipped from his arms as her hands and mouth moved over his face, his shoulders, his chest. The hot, wet caress of her tongue made him wild. Hungrily he tried to unbutton her blouse, but she slid away again.

"No," she murmured, biting his nipple with exquisite care. She sat up and her hands moved quickly, taking off her clothes, throwing them aside. "Let me dream you," she whispered, coming down beside him in a warm rush. "Let me. Dream."

At first Rio didn't understand. Then she began to move over him like sunrise, warming everything she touched. And like sunrise, she touched everything. The pleasure of her hands was a sweet violence. The pleasure of her mouth taking him was an ecstasy so great he couldn't breathe.

And still she dreamed him, creating him with each hot touch of her tongue, each shivering instant that she held him, dreaming and loving him equally, suspending both of them in a timeless sensuality that ended only when he looked at her dreaming him and knew that he had to share both the dreaming and the dream or he would die.

He reached for her, saying her name again and again, his voice as rough as his breathing.

Her only answer was the intimate glide of her tongue over his aching flesh, her murmur as she tasted his hot essence.

Suddenly the world spun and Hope found herself flattened beneath Rio's weight. Her smile became a blaze of sensual anticipation. His smile was narrow and taut. Her elegant legs rubbed caressingly against him in mute demand that he fill her until she overflowed.

But it was his turn to dream, and hers to be dreamed, and he wouldn't be denied one single instant of it. His hands and mouth moved over her like the wind, wrapping her in a sensual storm, taking her to the edge of breaking and holding her there, shaking, holding himself there with her, dreaming with a consuming passion he had never known before.

When he finally sank into her, he drank her scream of pleasure with a deep kiss. They moved together as one, dream and dreamer, and neither knew who was dreamer or dream.

Hope fell asleep locked tightly in Rio's arms, her questions abandoned because the answers no longer mattered. She was the land and he was a rain-bearing wind. Against that truth, no question or retreat was possible.

She would stay, he would go, and love would be the empty sky stretched between them.

Twenty-two

"WAKE UP, DREAMER," Rio said, nuzzling against the satin weight of Hope's breast. "We've got a well to dig."

Her eyes opened. The first pale radiance of dawn was filling the room. She smiled at the hard-faced man who lay naked beside her. Sighing, she eased her hands into his thick, collar-length hair, savoring the feel of it against her sensitive skin.

Deliberately he moved his head against her palms, increasing the pressure of her caress. The frank sensuality of his response sent visible shivers through her. Her breasts tightened and peaked, tempting him. She shifted her legs until they were tangled with his, asking for the gift of his body.

He kissed the dark rose tip of one breast and sank deeply into her, loving the feel of her sultry, welcoming heat. He moved slowly, slowly, nudging her from sleepiness into dreamlike arousal until she lifted and twisted against him, but still he pushed her slowly, tenderly, irresistibly over the sensual edge. He savored his nakedness inside her, shared the shivering, tugging, pulsing of her ecstasy, and then he put his face against her neck and gave himself to her in a long, unraveling release that was like nothing he had ever known with a woman before.

For a time there was only silence and dawn and the warmth of their intimacy. Then Rio sighed and reluctantly separated himself from Hope.

"I'll wait in the shower for you," he said.

After a few lazy minutes of wishing that Rio was still in bed with her, Hope went down the hall still half-asleep, lured by the sound of running water. When she stepped into the bathroom, he leaned out of the bathtub shower and watched while she wrapped her hair in a towel. He kissed her nose, nibbled on her lips, and pulled her into the shower with him.

She yelped. The water had just barely begun to warm the pipes. "How can you stand it?" she asked through clenched teeth.

"Keeps me out of trouble."

She slanted him a remembering kind of look. "Are you calling me trouble?"

"Real quick this morning, aren't you?"

He gave her a kiss that made her forget the temperature of the water, handed her the soap, and got out of the shower before he started something they didn't have time or privacy to finish properly. Mason had just come in downstairs and was banging pots in a wordless warning of his presence.

Hope didn't linger even though the water was getting

hotter with each passing second. She knew how eager Mason was to get out to the well site. And so was she.

Today was the first day of December. More important, it was the first day of drilling.

Part of her was like a kid at Christmas, half-wild to unwrap the biggest present and end the suspense. The rest of her was adult. She wanted the well. She must have it for the Valley of the Sun to survive. But when the well was dug, Rio would leave.

She pushed the thought aside and soaped herself quickly. There was nothing she could do about the future except let it ruin the time she did have with him. She wasn't going to do that.

The smell of bacon and coffee drifted up the stairs to Hope. She pulled on clothes in a rush and went downstairs with the heedless speed of a child.

"Morning, Mason," she said when she got to the kitchen. "What's for breakfast?"

"What does your nose tell you?"

"That you've been sucking on that horrible pipe."

He snickered as though they hadn't said the same thing every morning for as long as he could remember.

Rio handed her a steaming cup of coffee that was as black as his hair. Automatically she went to the screened porch and looked out at the dawn sky.

Pure air, shimmering with light and color, absolutely empty of clouds. It was cold, too, the kind of dry cold that made the air shine like polished crystal.

"No rain," Mason said without looking up from the bacon. "This here drought is shaping up to be a real doozy." He dragged a few crisp strips of bacon onto a paper plate to drain. "How are the troughs holding out?"

"Filled them yesterday," Rio said.

He snitched a piece of bacon as soon as Mason's back was turned. He took a big bite and fed the remaining half to Hope.

"Saw that," Mason said without heat. "May be old, but I ain't blind. You doing the eggs this morning, gal, or are you gonna eat whatever I take a notion to fry?"

Hastily she put down her cup of coffee and began cracking eggs into a pan. Very quickly everyone was sitting down to breakfast. As usual, silence reigned until the last bit of food was eaten.

While Mason and Rio loaded lengths of pipe and five-gallon cans of water and fuel into the pickup, Hope raced through the kitchen, setting up everything for dinner. The three of them climbed into the front seat of the truck and headed for Wind Canyon.

As soon as they turned off the main ranch road, the truck started shaking like a rough-gaited horse. The side road was nothing more than twin ruts that snaked over and around natural obstacles. It was better suited to horses than to vehicles, but as long as it didn't rain, the four-wheel-drive pickup was more efficient for hauling people and supplies than a horse and wagon.

Both excited and content, Hope sat quietly between the two men she loved. From time to time she watched Rio from under her eyelashes, admiring the strong masculine lines of his face and the midnight-blue clarity of his eyes.

He caught one of her looks, took his hand off the

wheel long enough to trace the line of her cheek with a gentle knuckle, and then concentrated on the rugged road again.

Mason smiled to himself. Rio had never been an outgoing and affectionate kind of man, yet he rarely had his hands off Hope for more than a few minutes. It wasn't just her female parts he was after, either. He touched her hair, her cheek, her hand, her arm. It was a man's way of saying without words that he liked being with a woman. And she sure liked being with him. It showed in her smile, her eyes watching him, her complete ease with a man that lots of folks were uncomfortable around.

In all, Mason was planning on a January wedding. February at the latest.

Blissfully unaware of Mason's thoughts, Hope leaned lightly against Rio and watched the land unfold. Wind Canyon looked different to her now. Instead of being a dry, nearly useless piece of the ranch's history, it was the leading edge of the Valley of the Sun's future. To Hope, in Wind Canyon the air was cleaner, the sun brighter, the sage more silver, and the mountains a beautiful, jumbled treasure house whose riddle her lover had solved.

Rio saw the excitement on Hope's face and wanted to warn her again that he couldn't guarantee a successful well.

There was water here, no doubt about it. Water that had fallen on the mountaintops and transformed limestone into a huge, unlikely sponge. Water that had sunk gradually into the limestone and moved through it at a pace that made a glacier look like a racehorse. Water pulled by gravity and pushed by the increasing weight of each season's rain sinking down until the aquifer became a solid river under tremendous pressure, millions upon millions of acre-feet of pure cold liquid waiting to pour out once the waterproof stratum over it was broken by a drill bit.

Water that had flowed for a million years and would flow for a million years more.

Yes, the water was here. He could still remember its presence tingling up through his body. But how far down? And how much hard rock was between the limestone and the surface of the earth?

How much hard *luck* waited, too?

He knew very well the kinds of incidents that plagued drilling. Broken drill bits and tools dropped into the drilling hole. Injury caused by carelessness or exhaustion or both. Water discovered, but too little to do any good.

Then there was the weather. Wells, especially in the West, rarely came in convenient places. Wind Canyon was no different. Remote. Rough. Unforgiving. If it rained too much, it would be almost impossible to supply the drilling site. Then Rio would have to shut down until it dried out.

Hope didn't have enough money to carry the ranch through those kinds of delays.

At least rain didn't seem to be a problem for a while, but the rest of the hard-luck list couldn't be shrugged off. The only way to find out how far down the water lay was to drill until you hit it. If you ran out of time, money, luck, or guts before you brought in a well, you had your answer—the water was too damned far down.

It was the time factor that ate most deeply into Rio's confidence. He had worked as little as a week drilling a successful well and he had worked for months on hard-luck, hard-rock holes.

Though Hope hadn't said anything herself, Mason had quietly told Rio that the second mortgage was due January fifteenth. She insisted that she had the money to pay off the second mortgage and still keep the ranch alive, but Rio knew that Hope's resources were very limited.

He was haunted by the idea of her pouring everything she had into a useless hole in the ground, a hole he had chosen and encouraged her to dig.

Rio hoped that the aquifer was close to the surface, but every bit of his education and instinct told him that the water was down, way down, right at the breaking point of money, luck, and nerve.

The pickup bucked and slithered and crabbed up Wind Canyon's rocky bottom. Before Mason had come back from his sister-in-law's home, Rio had used the pickup's winch to pull out sage clumps, piñon, and juniper. In the end he had managed to hammer out a rough track that allowed the pickup truck to get up into the canyon. The track would turn to glue and quicksand with the first real rains, but there wasn't time or money to build a better road.

If Rio had to, he would camp out here and bring supplies in on horseback. He had slept in worse places in the past. He would sleep in worse places in the future.

When you were drilling wells, comfort wasn't on the list of necessary supplies.

He parked the pickup beside the stark angles of the old derrick he would use as a drilling tower. Small, battered, rusted, the derrick wasn't much to look at. But it was sturdy. He had used it at some god-awful sites, places where even a professional optimist would have laughed at the thought of water.

That ugly old derrick had brought in well after well.

The other drilling machinery he had to work with wasn't any more impressive than the derrick. He had built this rig from cannibalized parts of other rigs that had been tossed away and forgotten in Hope's barn, plus equipment he had scrounged in countless other barns during his travels around the West. The new pieces Hope had bought to make it all fit together stood out like dimes on a dirt floor, making everything else look even more shabby by comparison.

"Good thing this ain't no beauty contest," Mason said, climbing down out of the truck. "We'd lose sure as God made little green apples."

Rio's only answer was a grunt as he carried supplies out of the truck and over to the drill site.

Even though the three of them worked quickly, it seemed like forever to Hope before everything was in place and Rio was ready to start drilling. She all but danced with impatience when he started up the engine that would drive the drill. The sudden explosion of sound was shocking in the canyon's sunny silence.

When Rio saw Hope flinch at the racket, he went over to her and said loudly, "You get used to it after a while."

"Yes," she retorted. "It's called going deaf."

He laughed and his long arms reached out, lifting her up level with him. "Give me a kiss for luck and then go over to the board and throw the number-one switch."

Eyes sparkling with excitement, Hope wrapped her arms around Rio and gave him a kiss that made him ache to be alone with her. Everything about her called out to him—her sensual riches, her serene silences, her determination, her intelligence.

Hope felt the same way about Rio. She loved being close to him, talking with him, being silent with him. He was a river flowing through her, bringing life to everything he touched.

Slowly, hungrily, Rio let Hope slide down his body. Reluctantly he opened his arms and let go of her.

She took a broken breath, feeling almost disoriented. Then she shook herself and went to the board attached to the derrick. Lights, dials, switches, gauges, and a tangle of wires took the pulse and temperature of the drilling equipment. She located the number-one switch and looked over her shoulder at Rio.

He was standing braced, leather-gloved hands steadying the mechanism that controlled the alloy drill bit. He looked up at her and nodded.

Her hand swept down and power surged into the drill.

The bit turned rapidly, making an odd, high noise. Then it touched the ground, biting into it with a grating sound. The soil was alluvial, loose. It wasn't long before the drill vanished, pulling pipe after it.

Rio looked up from the drill, smiled quickly, and gave the board a swift, casual glance. He didn't really need to look at gauges and dials to know that everything was working properly. He went by the sound of the engine, the vibration of the drill, the feel of the equipment.

He knew that the first part of drilling would be the fastest, the easiest, and the most rewarding work right up until the instant water was struck. Other than the occasional huge boulder, the bit wouldn't have to chew through anything hefty until it reached an underlying layer of hard rock.

Out on the plains, bedrock could be thousands of feet down, buried under millions of years of debris from the highlands. But here, in the canyon, gravity and regular flash floods carried away much of the loose soil.

The well itself would be beyond the reach of those seasonal floods. Rio had begun drilling in a shallow bowl above the canyon floor. Forty extra feet of drilling was a small price to pay for a well that would survive the winter floods.

After an hour or two, Hope told herself that it was foolish for her to stand around and watch pipe disappear. She should go back to the ranch, get on Aces, and check on the range cattle that were depending on scarce natural water instead of the wells.

There was also Sweet Dreams, another of Sweetheart's calves, to check on in particular. Hope thought she had seen a slight hesitation in the heifer's gait, but it had been too dark to be certain. After she looked over

Sweet Dreams, she had to wire up the hole a coyote had dug to get to the chickens. Then there were the bills to pay and the latest tax assessment to protest.

And the drill bits—she couldn't forget them. Some old ones had been sent off for sharpening. They were ready to be picked up in town. She also had to order two special hard-rock bits. The expense involved had shocked her, but she hadn't protested. If Rio needed titanium alloy drills with diamond-studded teeth to find her water, that was what he would get.

Uneasiness snaked through her as she remembered Rio's expression when he had asked for the special drill bits. He said that he might be able to get the job done with the bits he had, but it would take much too long. Though he hadn't said anything else, she wondered if he was already getting restless, if the wind was calling his name.

The thought made her ache, even though she had to admit that she didn't have a lot of time, either. Not when it came to the well. It was proving much more expensive to drill than she had expected. She had based her estimate on what it had cost to drill her namesake, and then had doubled it, adding a ten percent margin for error.

The margin hadn't been big enough. A lot had changed since her namesake well had been drilled more than a quarter of a century ago. A combination of inflation and more advanced technology had sent the cost of drilling a well soaring like a moon rocket.

Just buying the parts to make Rio's old equipment work had cost more than she had budgeted to buy an entire secondhand rig. The endless bags of "mud" used to grease the drill hole cost nearly as much as an equal weight of grain. As for pipe—you would think from the price that pipe was made of some gem-studded space-age alloy rather than plain old steel.

Though Hope didn't say anything about it to Rio, in order to buy the new drill bits and the extra pipe he had ordered, she would have to dip into the money she had set aside to pay off the second mortgage. She had wanted to ask if he was sure, *really sure,* he would need all that pipe.

She hadn't said a word. If he thought it would be a deep well, she would take his word for it. She had felt water and certainty flowing through him as surely as sunlight through the desert.

"Hope? Hope! You gone deaf, gal?" Mason yelled.

She blinked, startled out of her thoughts. Mason had an oilcan in one hand and was poking at the equipment that ran the drill.

"I asked you three times," he said, "if you're gonna check on the water out at the west end of Silver Basin."

She put away her worries and answered him with a nod. Instantly he went back to nursing the noisy engine.

For a moment she wished she had something as useful to do at the drilling site rather than miles away. But all she could do for now was brood over what the invisible drill bit would find.

Or not find.

It was much too soon for that kind of fretting. The drill bit hadn't even ground down as far as the deepest roots of the hardiest desert plants. If water was that close to the surface, she wouldn't be drilling a new well here or anywhere else on the Valley of the Sun.

"Need anything?" Hope asked loudly, catching Rio's eye.

To her surprise he nodded and gestured her over to him. Wondering what they could have forgotten at the ranch, she stepped up to the drilling area.

Rio took off his leather gloves, framed her face with his strong hands, and kissed her gently.

"You, Hope," he said against her hair, holding her close. "I need you."

Sudden tears burned in her eyes. She buried her face against his neck and hung on to him with all her strength.

"I'm here," she said fiercely. "I'll always be here for you."

She felt his arms tighten until she could hardly breathe.

"Watch that third turn on the way out," he said, when he finally released her. "The wheel will buck like a steer halfway through." Then, quickly, he added, "Be careful, my beautiful dreamer. Keep that snake gun loaded and handy."

Hope's eyes widened. "Do you think Turner will come back?"

"No." Rio's voice was flat, harsh. "If I thought he'd touch you again, ever, I'd take him up in the mountains and lose him. It's just that I . . ."

She waited, wanting him so much she ached.

He made a helpless, almost angry sound and kissed

her suddenly, searchingly. He lifted his head and looked at her with eyes the color and radiance of indigo twilight. "You're so damned precious to me. The thought of anything happening to you makes me want to grab you and hide you in the safest place on earth."

She smiled and brushed her lips over his. "I'm fine."

"I know. But . . ." He took her hand, peeled back her work glove, and saw again the bruise that he had noticed this morning, a mark no bigger than his fingertip. "Even a little thing like this." His lips and tongue gently touched the bruise. "I can't explain it. I don't even understand it. I just know that the thought of you being hurt makes me bleed."

She saw the intensity of his emotion in his eyes and felt it in the powerful, taut muscles beneath her hands. For the first time she had the tiniest stirring of hope that perhaps he wouldn't leave after the well was drilled.

The possibility quivered through her, making her tremble.

It was like the possibility of an artesian well, an endless upwelling of life itself transforming everything it touched. She and Rio could live on a renewed Valley of the Sun, raising cattle and children and loving each other until the last sun had set—and still the land would go on, the water would flow, and their children would sow their own crop of dreams and know the bittersweet joys of harvest.

Rio's breath caught at the emotion radiating from Hope. She had never been more beautiful to him, more alive, incandescent with love for him. The thought of anything dimming that joy was a tearing agony deep in his soul.

Hope—my beautiful dreamer—don't let anything hurt you. Even me.

Especially me.

But he would hurt her, and he knew it as surely as he knew she loved him.

Twenty-three

THE DRILLING WENT SLOWLY.

Day by day, December slid toward Christmas. Day by day, one piece of equipment after another gave out, protesting its burden and the patchwork nature of the rig. The delays lasted from a few minutes to much longer, depending on how soon a replacement part could be brought in.

When the bit finally reached hard rock, the pace of the drilling slowed to inches, then to fractions of inches. The special, and very expensive, bits Rio used could have gone faster, but not when they were driven by an old, cranky engine that couldn't go for long hours at high output.

The layer of rock the drill hit was thick and ungiving. The rock didn't hold water. There was no place within the dense crystalline stone for liquid to hide. Everything soft had been cooked out when the rock was deep within the earth's mantle, where the heat and

311

pressure were so great that solid rock strata melted and bent like great layers of wax.

If there was water to be found, it was farther down, beyond the dry, dense layer of stone.

Rio changed bits, drilled, changed bits again, and drilled again. The relentless work and hammering noise were numbing. Progress slowed to tiny inches that were measured in frustration and increasing incidents of mechanical breakdown.

At the end of each day, Hope no longer asked how the work was coming. The lines on Rio's face, and on Mason's, told her more than she wanted to know. She drove the men to Wind Canyon at dawn, picked them up at dark, and ran the ranch in between.

The rains still weren't heavy enough to free the cattle from depending on the troughs. She hauled water from the Turner ranch. Although Turner hadn't turned up again, she kept the rifle loaded.

Even before the first week of drilling passed, people from town and from Turner's ranch had started showing up at the Gardener ranch house. They always had an excuse—a saddle to sell or to buy, a mare to be bred, invitations to Christmas barbecues. Invariably the conversation circled around to what was really on the visitor's mind.

How's the well doing, Hope? Strike anything promising yet?

Hell of a place to drill, clear up in a canyon. Everybody knows that water goes down, not up.

You lookin' for artesian water? Ain't never heard of no artesian well around here, and my granny was born just the other side of your ranch.

Don't envy you none. Drilling wells is expensive as hell these days, and the price of beef just ain't worth mentioning.

Those were the most tactful people. The others, including a few of Turner's men, began looking at Hope like she had put a FOR RENT sign around her neck when she became Rio's lover. None of the men said or did anything out of line, because none of them wanted the kind of grief Rio would give them. But they looked at Hope with a lecherous speculation that made her quietly furious.

Hear Mason went up to Salt Lake for Thanksgiving. Musta been lonely for you, huh? Oh, yeah, Rio was there, wasn't he?

Gotta hand it to him. That drifter has a good eye for how the land lays.

Hear he tried to buy a ranch around here a time back. Didn't have no money, though. Bet your little ranch looks real good to him.

Hope ignored the men's insinuations and sideways looks, staring them coolly in the eye until they shifted uneasily and allowed as how it was time for them to be getting back to town or to Turner's ranch or to whatever rock they had crawled out from under.

She turned down all holiday invitations. She didn't have the time or the energy for parties. There was nothing in her life but cattle, drilling, and Rio.

Hope bumped along the last hundred yards of road and shut off the truck's engine. The derrick looked like a child's toy against the soaring walls of the Wind Canyon.

"Good timing," Rio said as Hope got out of the truck.

"Why? Did you run out of coffee?"

He grinned. "Nope. We finally broke through the hard rock. I took a core sample of what was below. I was just getting ready to look at it."

Is there water?

But Hope didn't say it out loud. She didn't want to add to the pressure that showed in the tight lines around Rio's mouth. So she waited in hungry silence while he opened the special pipe that held the core sample.

A single look at his face told her everything she needed to know.

"Dry," he said neutrally. "Dry as the rock above it. No aquifer at this depth. But the stratum is softer than the one I just went through. The drilling will go faster now."

And it did. Days flew by as expensive pipe and lubricant vanished down the hole in the earth as though there was no end short of China.

Rio didn't say anything about the cores he took from time to time, or the changing layers of rock. With Mason at his side, he simply drilled and kept on drilling down through compacted soils older than man, layers of stone that had been laid down long before true mammals walked the earth, drilling down and down and down, pouring money and dreams into the dry land and getting nothing back but dulled or broken drill bits and blistered hands.

*   *   *

"Damn slippery damned coffeepot!" Mason growled.

Hope said, steadying the pot before it dropped, "Must be time to scour the grease off it again."

But she knew that the problem wasn't the pot. It was Mason's hands. He had used them too hard, for too many hours, working alongside Rio for twelve and fourteen hours a day.

A sideways glance told Hope that Rio knew what was wrong. Mason's hands wouldn't heal until he rested them, but he was too proud and too stubborn to admit it. His pain showed in the deeply cut lines of his face and the dark circles beneath his eyes.

"I have to go into town this morning," she said casually. "Mason, I want you to stay at the house. There have been too many people coming through here lately, and some of them I've never seen before." She turned to Rio. "You can get along without him for a day, can't you?"

"I'll manage." He had just the right mixture of reluctance and acceptance in his voice to ease Mason's pride.

She thanked Rio with her eyes.

"Do you need anything up at the well?" she asked Rio, ignoring Mason's mutterings that he didn't want to "baby-sit no damn house" when there was real work to be done.

Reluctantly Rio reached into his pocket. He avoided drawing on Hope's reserves of cash until he absolutely had to. But it was time.

"We barely have enough pipe and mud left to cover the normal lead time in ordering," he said. "There's only one hard-rock bit that's still sharp for when we hit another solid stratum. The other bits are in the pickup."

Trying not to show any emotion, she nodded and took the list. She had already dipped into the money that had been earmarked for paying the balloon on the second mortgage. Now she would have to take even more out of the special money market account.

She had known it was coming. That was why she was going to town today. She had an appointment with the bank. She was determined to renegotiate the second mortgage for another year. Or six months. Or two months.

Even one.

She had to buy enough time for Rio to drill down to the artesian water that lay beneath the dry land, waiting for the silver moment of release. She knew the water was there. She knew that he wanted to find it with the same intensity she did. Maybe even more.

He called himself a man without dreams, yet she knew that this well was Rio's dream in everything but name.

No matter how many people had told Hope it was impossible, she hadn't flinched away from her own dream of living on the Valley of the Sun. She wouldn't flinch in the face of Rio's dream, his need. She would give him all the time she had, all the pipe she could buy, all the drill bits, all of it, and never regret anything but that she had so little to give.

"Aren't you even going to ask me how close we are to water?" he said, watching her with shadowed blue-black eyes.

"Do you know?"

"No."

"Then," she said with a gentle smile, "there's no point in asking, is there?"

He caught her hand, rubbed his cheek against her palm, kissed it in silent thanks. "After weeks of drilling and nothing to show but dry rock, most people would be all over me like a bad smell."

"Most people don't have enough sense to come in out of the rain," she retorted.

"Dreamer." His voice was husky. He kissed her palm again, lingering. "My beautiful dreamer."

The warmth of that moment stayed with Hope all through the long drive to town. She ordered the drilling supplies first, paying a hefty charge for a rush delivery. Then she went to the small brick building that had a freshly painted sign out front: COTTONWOOD SAVINGS AND TRUST.

William Worth, the loan officer, was expecting her. He had been expecting her since loan payment checks had started coming through her money market account, eating into the funds that he knew she had reserved for the balloon payment on the second mortgage.

Worth was a patient man. He let her go through her entire speech with barely a frown to wrinkle the loose skin of his forehead.

Then he said no.

"But I'm digging a well," Hope said as though she hadn't mentioned it before.

"Ms. Gardener, excuse me for speaking so bluntly, but you're basing your request for a loan extension on a fool's dream. Your well is being dug in a godforsaken dry canyon by a half-breed troublemaker who has nothing to his name but a five-year-old pickup truck and a fine Arab mare he claims he caught running loose."

Hope bit back hot words.

The telephone on Worth's small, fake-wood desk started ringing, interrupting his prepared speech.

"The only way the bank could grant an extension," he said, reaching for the phone, "would be if you found a cosigner for the note."

Before she could say anything, he picked up the telephone, listened, and said, "Yes, sir." He replaced the phone, stood, and went to the office door. "I have to leave for a few minutes. I'm sorry we couldn't help you. Please keep the cosigner possibility in mind."

The door closed behind Worth with a distinct, final sound.

Hope felt as though an icy northern wind had blown over her, sapping her strength. The refusal hadn't been unexpected, but it was rock-solid. There was nothing in Worth's manner that gave her any grounds for thinking that he might change his mind in the few weeks between now and the day that the note was due.

For a moment she simply sat and gathered herself for the long drive back to the ranch. As she reached for her purse, she heard the door opening and closing behind her. She turned, expecting to see the loan officer again.

What she saw was John Turner.

"Now, what kind of look is that for the man who's going to save your ranch?" he asked, smiling thinly. "We're going to make a deal, you and me. I co-sign that note and you come to heel when I snap my fingers. No more giving away to drifters what I'm paying good money for. You cross your expensive legs and you cross them tight or I'll beat the living hell out of you."

His words buzzed around Hope like flies, noisy and meaningless.

Turner pulled a sheaf of papers out of his hip pocket and tossed them down in front of her. "Take your choice, baby doll. Me and your ranch or nothing at all. And don't kid yourself. Nothing is all you'll have. That blankethead won't hang around once we foreclose on the Valley of the Sun."

All the pressures Hope had been under bit into her with steel talons. All the disappointments, the fears, the endless quest for water, the knowledge that Rio would leave when water was found—everything. Rage swept through her, burning away the despair she felt, replacing it with a firestorm of adrenaline. She shot to her feet and looked at Turner through narrowed, glittering eyes.

"Go to hell." Her voice was soft, low, vibrating with anger.

He laughed. "Don't be a sore loser."

He walked toward her, stopping just short of her, so close that he could smell the subtle perfume she used. So close that when he reached inside his jacket pocket for a pen, the back of his arm almost brushed over her breasts.

"What kind of flowers do you want?" she asked coldly.

"Flowers?" He frowned. "What are you talking about?"

"Your funeral."

He flushed with anger and the memory of how easily Rio had brought him down. "I haven't laid a finger on you, and if you tell Rio any different, you're lying."

"You won't have to wait for Rio to catch up with you," she said, her voice brittle with contempt. "I'm not your victim to bully or to crawl all over in your bathroom fantasies. If you touch me, I'll come after you myself. And I won't use a kitchen knife this time. I'll use my father's shotgun."

For a moment there was only silence and the thick sound of air being drawn into Turner's lungs through nostrils pinched by rage. His lips twisted into a cruel smile.

"I'll see you the morning after the loan comes due. Mark it on your calendar, baby doll. January sixteenth, at your ranch house, and the sheriff will be right with me. That's the day you'll beg to suck my cock. I'm going to enjoy hearing every word of it."

"It won't happen. I'm not like the other women you've hounded and bought and bullied into bed. I'm not like the men you've dangled money in front of and leaned on until it was easier for them to sell you their stock or real estate or mistress than it was to make you angry by continuing to say no."

"Like I said, baby doll. I get what I want."

"Have you ever wanted something that didn't belong to someone else? Ever? Even once in your spoiled life?"

Turner's only answer was the red flush crawling up his face.

"That's what I thought," she said coolly. "You're still a baby. You're buried in toys, but the only one you want is the one you see someone else holding. You're obsessed with what you don't have. Until you get it. Then you drop the new toy and look around to see what other people are playing with. You've never grown up."

"Listen, you—"

"But that's your problem," she said, ignoring his attempt to talk over her. "It's not mine. Not anymore. No matter what happens with the ranch, with Rio, with anything at all, *I will never be your whore.*"

With an ugly sound, Turner spun around and slammed out of the room. As much as he wanted to put his hands on her, there were too many witnesses in the bank.

And there was Rio.

Always.

Slowly the adrenaline seeped out of Hope, leaving her face pale and her muscles like sand. When her hands no longer trembled she picked up her purse and let herself out of the small office. Other than a few curious stares from tellers who knew her, no one seemed interested in what had happened in the tiny office.

A few miles out of town, she took a detour to a small house where a silversmith lived. There she picked up the presents she had had made for Mason and Rio. She couldn't believe that Christmas was only a few days away.

She had never felt less like celebrating. There was too much to be done. Some of it was bitter and hard.

Yet it had to be done just the same.

"How was town?" Mason called from the porch.

Though Hope hadn't said anything, he suspected that she had gone to ask for an extension on the second mortgage.

"Same as always."

He heard the anger and weariness beneath her carefully neutral tone and sighed. "I'll unload them supplies and go pick up Rio. You go talk to your black cows. They been mooing up a storm for you."

Hope turned the truck over to Mason and went to the home pasture to check on her Angus. Sweetheart came walking over, radiating muscular health with every stride. Her eyes were clear and deep, like pools of liquid darkness shining out from the midnight sea of her winter-thickened coat.

"Sweetheart, you're so beautiful you make me feel like a burlap bag," she said.

Sweetheart sighed as though to say, *Of course I'm beautiful. I'm perfect.*

Hope rubbed the cow lovingly, gave her a pan of grain, then shook the feed sack until the other Angus started ambling over. Quickly she poured out a long, thin line of grain. As the black cattle lined up for their treat, she watched their movements critically. None of them appeared lame now.

For a few moments she simply stood and looked at her cattle. They had a solid, earthy reality that renewed her belief in her dream of a thriving ranch. Without realizing it, she smiled, feeling better just for being with her healthy, handsome herd.

She was seeing more than beautiful animals when she looked at her Angus. She was seeing the future of the Valley of the Sun.

"Good night, Sweetheart," she whispered. "And you, too, Sweet Dreams. Grow big and strong and gorgeous, just like your mom."

When Mason and Rio drove into the yard, there was just enough time for Rio to shower before dinner. With steps that he felt in every bone in his body, Rio dragged himself up the stairs and let steaming water pour over him, washing away the dust and grit of another dry day.

But nothing could wash away the bitter taste in his mouth.

He pulled on clean clothes and went downstairs. The thought of Hope's smile was as much a lure as the cooking scents that had his stomach growling impatiently.

"Come and get it or I'll feed it to the pigs," Hope said cheerfully when she heard Rio's footsteps on the stairs.

It was her standard greeting at the end of the day. Usually he responded by grabbing her and kissing her soundly. This time he simply wrapped his arms around her, lowered his cheek to her hair, and held her as though she needed comfort.

Or he did.

"Long day?" she asked softly.

His arms tightened around her.

"Hit more stone," he said at last. "Finally got through it." Then, "It's dry on the other side, too."

Cold spread through Hope. She put her lips against his neck and counted the beats of his heart for a long, silent moment. Then she stirred and smiled up at him.

"Come on," she said. "You'll feel better after you eat."

Gently Rio moved his thumbs over her cheekbones and lips. He started to speak, but instead kissed her with a tenderness that brought a sheen of tears to her eyes.

"There is no one like you," he said simply.

That night Rio told her again, differently, wordlessly, taking her and being taken in turn, giving himself to the endless passion and shattering release that only Hope had ever called from him. He no longer questioned the urgent upwelling of her need and his own, the hot perfection of their fused bodies, the sense of rightness he felt all the way to his soul when he held her asleep in his arms.

There were times when he wished that he could drill for water in Wind Canyon forever, finding nothing but the unbelievable joys of this one woman's love.

Yet Rio knew he must find water, ending this dream and beginning another, Hope's dream of a Valley of the Sun that lived again. He had to find water, and find it soon. The longer he stayed, the more he would hurt her when he left.

And the thought of hurting her was like hot metal drilling through his flesh and bone to his soul.

*   *   *

"I'm going to start drilling around-the-clock," Rio told Hope the next morning. "We're running out of time. The well has to be in by January fifteenth. Otherwise you'll never get the bank to extend your loan."

The darkness in his eyes was more than she could bear.

"No," she said calmly. "I can pay off the second mortgage. There's no need for you to kill yourself working double and triple shifts. We have as much time as you need."

Rio gave her a look that shook Hope to her soul, as though he sensed that she was talking about more than the well being drilled through layers of rock and time into an undiscovered past and an even more mysterious future.

"One of Mason's grandnephews is coming in after Christmas," Rio said. "I'll start around-the-clock drilling then."

She wanted to argue but didn't. He was right. Whether it was time or money or both, it didn't matter.

They didn't have enough of either.

Twenty-four

❧

HOPE, RIO, AND MASON spent Christmas Eve out at the well site. She decorated the derrick with colored lights and piñon boughs, hung popcorn and cranberry strings over nearby sagebrush, and cooked turkey over a spit that Rio and Mason had rigged. They sang all the old carols, Hope's true alto mixing with Rio's bass while Mason played a scarred harmonica with surprising skill.

Tears ran down both Hope's and Mason's cheeks as the music brought back people and Christmases past, Hope's parents and Mason's beloved wife, memories of laughter and holiday surprises.

When there were no more carols to sing, they toasted Christmas and the well and one another with cut-crystal glasses of rye that caught and multiplied every colorful light Hope had strung from the derrick. For a time they sipped potent whiskey, savoring the silence and the wind and the special peace that came with the season.

Finally Mason stood, stretched, and went to the truck. He returned quickly, carrying two presents.

"Here you go," he said to Rio.

Surprised, Rio took the package and slowly pulled off the wrapping that Mason had taped until there was almost no paper showing. When Rio finally managed to open the long, flat box, he made a sound of amusement and pleasure.

A handmade snakeskin hatband gleamed up at him from the box, reflecting firelight from the pale, diamond-patterned scales. The size of the scales told him that the rattlesnake had been a big one.

"Don't I recognize this hide?" he asked wryly.

"Sure do," Mason said with satisfaction. "That's a chunk of the big son that thought he could live near Hope's Angus herd. I showed him otherwise."

"He's a beauty," Rio said, running his fingertips down the supple hatband.

"He'll look a damn sight better on your head than he did under the rocks by the trough."

Rio laughed.

Grinning, Mason gave Hope another package. She opened it and found a strip of the foolish snake made into a belt.

"Same for you, gal," Mason said, smiling. "The snake will look right pretty wrapped around your waist."

"Thank you," she said huskily. "I wondered what you were doing in the barn workshop all those early mornings. Now I know."

The thought of how the cold must have bitten into

his hands as he worked on the gifts made her want to smile and cry at the same time. She settled for giving him a big hug and a kiss on his scratchy cheek.

"This isn't as fancy as rattlesnake," Rio warned, handing a soft package to Mason.

Eager as a kid, Mason tore into the wrapping and found a new pair of leather work gloves. He pulled them on and admired them. They were tough and yet flexible enough not to bind knuckles that were swollen and sore from arthritis.

While Mason thanked Rio, Hope went to the box of kitchen supplies that she had brought up from the ranch for dinner. Inside, buried beneath the potato sack, she had hidden two small presents. She gave Mason his package first.

He opened the little box and his breath went out with a whoosh. "Damn, honey, I can't say when I seen something so pretty."

Gently he lifted out the silver buckle. It was a hammered oval with a running horse made of mother-of-pearl painstakingly inlaid in the center. He held the buckle in his gloved, gnarled hands, admiring the play of firelight across the silver and pearl surface.

"Can't wait to put it on," he said, winking at her.

He walked quickly over to the bright work light in the shed on the far side of the derrick, pulled off his belt, and began replacing his old brass buckle with the new silver.

While he worked, Hope handed Rio his present. He looked at her for a long moment, holding the small package in his hands before he began unwrapping it.

Inside the box, nested within layers of tissue paper, lay a heavy bracelet made of a single piece of cast silver. There was just enough of a gap in the oval form to allow it to fit over a man's wrist.

Rio whistled softly.

The curved surface of the bracelet was inlaid with pieces of polished turquoise in a rippling wave pattern that was a common Native American symbol for Rio's name.

The cool perfection of the silver caressed his fingertips. Then he felt an irregularity on the inner side and tilted the bracelet so that he could see the hidden surface. Inscribed on the thick silver were the words: *For as long as the water flows.*

Emotion wrenched through him, pleasure and pain at once.

With a smooth twist of his right hand, he fitted the bracelet on his left arm. The silver glowed against his dark skin. The wavy lines of the river symbol seemed to flow with each shift of wind and firelight.

When Rio looked at Hope, light and emotion gleamed in his eyes. He couldn't remember the last time that someone had given him a present, much less one that was so perfectly suited to him. He eased her down into his lap and kissed her gently, repeatedly, as though he was afraid that she would slide through his fingers like the wind if he tried to hold her too tightly.

"Thank you," he said almost roughly. "It's like you. Unexpected. Beautiful." He opened his collar and reached inside his shirt. "There's no fancy wrapping on your gift. I wanted to give it to you the same way I got it long ago, warm with the giver's own life."

She watched as he lifted a Southwest Indian necklace from around his neck.

"This was my great-grandmother's, my grandmother's, and my mother's," he said quietly. "Mother gave it to me when she left me with my grandfather and went back to the city."

The necklace shimmering in Rio's hands was in a traditional squash-blossom pattern, but instead of hammered-silver crescents and turquoise stones, the blossoms were made from dimes more than a century old. It was a compelling blend of white and Indian cultures. Its stately beauty and history made chills move over her skin.

"Rio, I can't take—"

He kissed her until she forgot what she had been trying to say. While he kissed her, his fingers unbuttoned her blouse until his hands could circle her neck freely.

She felt the smooth, oddly reassuring weight of the necklace against her breasts. The silver was like a caress, radiating back the heat it had absorbed from his body.

Helplessly she whispered his name.

He kissed her again. Then he lifted his head and looked at her with eyes darker than the night, deeper.

"My grandmother told me that one day I would find the right woman to wear this necklace," he said. "I never believed her until I saw you by Turner's well with laughter in your eyes and water running like liquid silver from your cupped hands."

Hope blinked against the tears that burned her eyelids.

"Maybe, someday," he said, brushing his lips over hers, "your daughter will wear this necklace and you'll tell her about the man who gave it to you. I can't think of any better gift than that this silver be warmed by a child born of your body."

"What about your children?" she asked, her throat aching.

His gentle smile was like a knife turning in Hope.

It was just as painful for him.

"Once, I wanted a woman to have my baby. It was in the city, before I accepted that I was what my grandfather had named me. Brother-to-the-wind. The woman loved me, but she was pure white. She didn't want to have mixed children."

"Then she didn't love you," Hope said starkly.

He shook his head. "No, dreamer. She was just being honest. I've always been grateful to her for that. Another kind of woman wouldn't have told me until we were married. It happened to one of my cousins."

"I'm not like that," Hope said, her voice shaking. "I want—"

But Rio was still speaking, refusing to hear her, and his words were talons sinking deeply into her, making her soul bleed. "I'll never again ask a woman to bear my child."

Hearing Rio's lifetime of isolation summarized in his gentle, relentless words almost destroyed Hope. She tried to speak, to tell him that she would have given even the Valley of the Sun if she could have his love and his children. But she couldn't speak. Words and emotions clogged her throat, defeating her.

"Rio, I—"

"Let it go, dreamer," he said against her lips. "My beautiful dreamer. Accept it. I have."

Head bowed, she fought the tears that were choking her.

And she wondered if she might be carrying Rio's baby now, if after he was gone she would one day give a warm silver necklace to a child he had never known.

The wind keened down the canyon, covering the small sounds Hope made as she struggled for self-control. Rio's hand moved slowly, repeatedly, over her hair, and with each motion the silver band on his wrist shimmered with unearthly light. Yet even more brilliant than hammered silver were the cascading stars and the glittering, ghostly river of the Milky Way overhead.

Mason returned to the campfire proudly wearing his new buckle. If he saw the gleam of tears on Hope's face, he didn't mention it. He just joined the intimate silence by the fire until only embers remained.

Coyotes began singing their own carols. Ancient harmonies shivered through the darkness with an eerie beauty that made it easy to believe in spirits and gods walking across the face of the night.

"My Zuni grandfather loved Christmas," Rio said quietly.

Hope turned her head against his shoulder and looked at his profile outlined by stars.

"He told me Christmas was the only time that the

white-eyes gathered in family clans and sang the songs of power with their souls in their voices. He said he could feel the Great Spirit flowing through the churches like a rain-bearing wind, sweeping away the dust of the previous year."

"Then why didn't he become a Christian?" Hope asked softly.

"He did."

"I thought he was a shaman."

"He was."

She looked over her shoulder at Rio. Smiling, he pulled her even closer between his knees, brushed his lips over her sage-scented hair, and tried to explain.

"My grandfather knew there were other gods, but he was convinced that the white man's God was stronger. For my ancestors, the proof of power was in day-to-day living. His children spoke a European language, learned European history, and worshipped a European God. That was power."

Rio hesitated, then added softly, "But the coyotes still sing harmonies older than man, the rain still can be called from a cloudless sky, and the wind still is brother to a few men. For Grandfather, that, too, was power."

Soft laughter breathed into Hope's hair, Rio's laughter as he remembered.

"But he had a hell of a time convincing Grandmother that there were other spirits as valid as the Holy Ghost. She prayed for his half-heathen soul until the day she died."

Hope ran her hand caressingly over Rio's arm. She

lingered to feel the silver bracelet, already warm with his life. His hand closed over hers, holding her between silver and his palm.

"Is your grandfather still alive?" she asked.

"Yes." Rio brushed his lips over her hair. "He's part of the coyote's song and the long cry of the wind. He's a phrase from a white man's carol and a breath of the power pouring through a Christmas church. There was room in his soul for all of them. I like to think there's room for him now in all of them."

Mason's soft "amen" came from across the campfire.

The wind gusted, sending a shower of sparks upward in an incandescent spiral.

After a moment Mason stretched and stood up. "Well, I'm gonna take these old bones back to a soft bed."

"I'll bring Hope to the ranch in a while," Rio said.

"Suit yourself. I'm too old to need baby-sitting."

Mason walked beyond the range of the campfire's wavering light and climbed stiffly into Hope's truck. The engine turned over, the headlights swept across the sky, and the tires grumbled over the makeshift road.

"What about you?" she asked when it was quiet again. "Aren't you going to stay at the house?"

"I brought up a bedroll and mattress earlier."

Turning, she slid her fingers beneath his denim jacket until she found the warm flesh between the snaps on his shirt. "Is it big enough for two?"

His whole body tightened at her touch, as though her fingers were molten silver instead of flesh. Without a word he stood, pulling her with him, and led her to his bed behind a big clump of sage.

Then he made exquisite, consuming love to her. Like a passionate wind he whispered her beauty and her sensuality, sang of his own need to fill every hollow of her, and then he came to her and moved within her, telling her with his touch those secrets only the wind knew. Again and again he brought her to shivering completion, knowing her with an intimacy that was greater with each touch, each instant, each movement of his powerful body over hers.

When she wept his name in her ecstasy, he gave himself to her and to the silver rains he had called from the desert of his own need.

Long before dawn the drill was turning again, chewing down through solid rock, dragging a long steel straw behind, drilling down to the point where dreams came true or died.

Twenty-five

AS THE DAYS passed and Hope's money poured in an unending stream down the drilling hole, softer rock gave way to harder and then to softer again. When Rio took a core of the new layer and opened it, his heart leaped when he felt the gritty texture of the sandstone. It was damp, tantalizing with a whisper of water.

He went back to drilling with renewed energy. The layer of sandstone stayed damp but no more, as though the years had leached all except a shadow of water from the rock.

When he drilled through to a new layer, it was dry.

No matter how many times the engine broke down or how many cores came up dry, Rio said nothing, did nothing except work even harder. His eyes were black and his mouth was bracketed by grim lines of exhaustion and determination.

The teenager who had come from Salt Lake to help

him worked with the tireless strength of youth. Mason worked with the unflinching endurance of a man who knew his own limits and hadn't yet reached them.

Every afternoon Hope came to them, bringing supplies and a smile. Except once. One day she couldn't smile.

That was the day she watched men load up every last head of stock on the ranch except Storm Walker. She only kept the stallion because she had promised him to Rio as a sire. She had sold the remaining range cattle the first week of January. They had already been trucked off to new pastures, places where water wasn't more precious than diamonds.

Mason didn't know about any of the sales. Hope made sure of it. No trucks came or went from the ranch except during the long hours when Mason was at the drill site.

As for Rio finding out . . . Rio was always up in Wind Canyon, always working, always watching with eyes that got darker and grimmer with each day. When he tried to talk about the deadline for the second mortgage, Hope always said, *You worry about the well. I'll worry about the rest. That was the deal.*

Today she had done everything she could to keep her part of the deal.

The door to the expensive black cattle truck shut with a final sound. Inside the trailer, Sweetheart bawled uneasily. Sweet Midnight answered her.

McNally sighed and turned toward Hope. He was a big, ruddy-faced man dressed in jeans, scuffed cowboy boots, and a leather jacket that was worth three thousand dollars. His pale blue eyes could be kind or wintry, depending on his mood. Right now he wanted to bawl like the fine Angus he had just bought back from Hope.

"You sure you won't think about it?" he pressed. "I could co-sign a note or—"

"No," she cut in swiftly. "But thank you." She managed half of a smile. "Don't look so grim. You're thrilled to get Sweetheart back and you know it."

"Hell," he muttered. "If it was anyone else but you, I'd be laughing like a coyote right now." He sighed and looked at the relentlessly empty sky. "Damnation. Dry as a ninety-year-old virgin." He smacked his hat against his hand. "Let me help, honey."

"You have." She waited until he looked at her. "You paid what my Angus herd was worth rather than what you thought you could get me to agree to because I was desperate. Thanks to you, I'll keep the ranch. Your integrity made the difference."

McNally started to say something but thought better of it. Instead, he tugged his expensive fawn-colored Stetson into place and signaled for his driver to get ready.

"If you change your mind," McNally began.

"I won't," she said quickly.

"Yeah, I can see that. *Hell.*" He stared at the bleak sky for a long moment, then sighed again. "Well, it's a long drive back. Better be going."

"Good-bye," she said. "And thank you. I mean it."

"Hell, honey. I'm the one should be doing the thanking. You have the finest little herd I've ever seen. You ever decide to take on a partner, put me at the top of your list. I could use someone with your eye for blood-lines and calves."

McNally stepped up into the big cab, ran down the passenger-side window, and called out as the truck moved away. "I transferred the money yesterday. You have any problems with your one-horse bank, let me know. I'll fix it real quick."

She managed a smile and a wave as the big black rig moved slowly out of her yard and down the road, leav-ing behind nothing but sun, dust, and the memory of what it had been like to look in the home pasture and see her beautiful black Angus.

Instead of going to the drilling site as had become her habit, Hope drove her truck to town. Worth was waiting for her at the bank. The expression on his face told her that he expected an unpleasant scene.

The bright pickup in the parking lot told her that Turner was somewhere nearby, waiting to buy the ranch at a bargain price. Waiting to hear her beg.

The second mortgage was due today.

"Good afternoon, Ms. Gardener," Worth said, clos-ing the door to his office behind her. "I know this is difficult for you, but you're young yet. There's plenty of time to—"

"Writing a check isn't difficult," she interrupted coldly. "I've had lots of practice."

While he watched in disbelief, she sat down, pulled out her money-market checkbook, and wrote a draft that would pay off the second mortgage to the last penny.

Worth took it without a word. Then he went to his

computer and called up the amount in her money-market fund.

"Well, goodness," he said, staring at the screen. "How did you, uh, manage?"

"The money is there," she said. "That's all you and your bank have a right to know."

"Er, of course. I'll have one of the girls draw up the paperwork. It will take a few minutes. We weren't expecting this."

"I have other errands. I'll be back in an hour. The paperwork will be ready by then, correct?"

Worth blinked. Hope was wearing faded blue jeans, an equally faded pink work shirt, and boots that were dusty and scarred. Yet her crisp tone would have done credit to a duchess.

"Yes, of course. We'll be ready," he said.

With a curt nod, Hope left the bank and went to pay off the rest of her bills and pick up more supplies. More drills. More pipe. More mud. More of everything that she needed for Rio to pursue her dream.

She drove back to an empty ranch. Storm Walker paced the huge horse pasture with endless, wild whinnies, searching for his four mares.

He wouldn't find them. They had been loaded up and shipped out that morning, before McNally arrived.

As Hope looked out over a pasture empty of black Angus, her own emotions echoed the stallion's desolate calls. Yet if she had it all to do over again, she wouldn't have changed one thing. Cattle, even her Angus, could be replaced. A dream could not.

Dry-eyed, she stood and watched the sunset mirrored in the half-full, utterly useless water trough. When she finally turned away, Rio was there.

"The Angus," he said. "Where are they."

But there was no question in his voice. He knew what had happened just as surely as he knew the date: January fifteenth.

"McNally in Utah bought them." She smiled sadly. "He was delighted when I called. Said he'd regretted selling Sweetheart to me ever since he heard about her calves."

"And Storm Walker's mares." Rio's mouth was a flat line. "Did you sell them, too?"

"Yes. The Angus. The mares. The range cattle. Everything but Storm Walker. I paid off the second mortgage and bought enough supplies to drill for at least a month more."

"*Christ.*"

Rio closed his eyes like a man who had seen too much, none of it comforting. His hands became fists that strained the leather of his work gloves.

"My degree in hydrology doesn't guarantee a well," he said harshly. "The money from the cattle should have gone for a new life for you somewhere else, not for a goddamned useless hole in the ground!"

"I didn't sell my cattle because I had faith in your degree." Hope went to Rio and put her hands on the coiled power of his biceps. Her voice was as strong as the muscles beneath her fingers. "I've seen you move over the land. I've seen your uncanny communication with it. I've seen you feel the presence of water beneath your feet. Your gift is as mysterious, as inde-scribable, and as *real* as my love for you."

She watched his eyes slowly open. They were the eyes of a man in torment.

"Rio, listen to me," Hope said urgently. "I know the water is there. If it's possible to drill down to it, you will. If it's possible to pay for the drilling, I will. And if it isn't possible, then we'll at least live the rest of our lives knowing that we did everything we could, no bets hedged, nothing held back. There's no shame or regret in losing that way. There's only shame and regret in not trying!"

He stared at her with sudden raw intensity. He didn't know that he made a choked sound as he reached out and crushed her against him. He only knew that no one had understood and accepted so much of what was hid-den beneath his rough surface. He tilted her face back and looked into her beautiful hazel eyes.

"I'll find water for you even if I have to drill down to hell itself."

First Mason and then his grandnephew gave way to the exhaustion of working around-the-clock. That was when Hope came to Wind Canyon and stayed, working alongside Rio, blistering her hands and scraping her-self raw on the unfamiliar equipment.

At night she lay down with him, falling asleep in his arms even as she felt their warmth and strength closing around her. Then she awakened beneath a glittering canopy of stars and felt Rio's mouth and hands caressing her until she couldn't breathe for wanting him. She opened for him, cried for him, and he gave himself with an intensity that shook her to her soul.

That was when Hope dreamed that the search for water could go on forever, keeping Rio here with her on the Valley of the Sun. But she knew the dream couldn't come true.

And she couldn't stop dreaming.

In the icy chill of desert just before daybreak, Hope stood in front of the board, watching dials as Rio started drilling. The pressure gauge kept stuttering as though it was going to quit. It had happened before, but not with that particular gauge.

"Rio, can you come over here? I'm having trouble with the—"

The rest of her words were drowned out as daylight broke over Wind Canyon with a rumble and a drawn-out, wrenching groan of thunder. Hope made a startled sound and looked around for the source of the noise.

Rio didn't. He dropped the huge pipe wrench he was holding and sprinted to her. He snatched her from her station by the derrick board, all but yanking her out of her boots.

"Run!" he yelled.

She couldn't hear him, but it didn't matter. He didn't let go of her, so she had to run or fall. When he finally stopped running and half-dragging her along with him, she fought for breath.

"What's wrong?" she gasped.

"It's going to rain, beautiful dreamer," he said, grinning down at her. "It's going to rain for a thousand years."

She looked at the dry, cloudless sky and thought that he had gone mad.

Thunder rumbled again and the derrick groaned.

"Rio? Is it?" Abruptly she stopped speaking, almost afraid to believe.

"Yes," he answered, laughing exultantly. "We did it!"

Water jetted up out of the drill hole like a bright silver spear. It shot above the derrick and fanned out into a jeweled curtain of moisture that glittered with every color of the dawn.

After the initial, almost explosive release, the artesian fountain gradually shrank to half its former height. Slowly, elegantly, it began dancing in graceful spurts and pulses that reflected the massive, hidden rhythms of the earth.

Hand in hand, laughing, Hope and Rio ran back down the canyon. They didn't stop until the brilliant, transparent drops of water rained down over them. She held up her arms as though she would embrace the dancing fountain, but it was Rio she reached for. She licked cold silver drops from his eyebrows, his cheeks, his lips.

"Sweet," she said, laughing and crying at once.

He kissed drops from her eyelashes and lips. "Very sweet."

"I meant the water." She nuzzled against him. "I was afraid it might be a saltwater well. But it isn't. It's sweet."

"Not as sweet as you," he whispered.

She threaded her fingers into his straight black hair, feeling the warmth of him welling up beneath the cool veil of artesian water. "Thank you."

She repeated it again and again and again until the words blended into kisses. Passion raced through her and she arched hungrily up to him.

Rio felt her passion, tasted it, and pain drenched him more deeply than the pulsing water of the well he had drilled. Instead of responding to her searching, shimmering kiss, he gently lowered Hope until her feet were on the ground again.

The dawn wind blew through the canyon, whispering the secrets of the land.

"We should tell Mason," Rio said.

He dipped his head for a kiss so fiercely yearning that she trembled even as she returned it. He released her quickly, yet his fingers slid down her arms as though he couldn't bear to end the contact. His eyes were as dark as a night with no stars, as empty as the wind curling through the canyon, calling his name.

"Rio?" she asked, knowing that something was wrong but not knowing what.

Then she heard the long cry of the wind and knew. She started shaking.

"No," she said in a raw voice. "Not yet. Not now!"

She turned away from him and jammed her fist against her mouth, stopping the flow of words she had promised herself she would never speak. With every bit of strength left in her, she fought to control her emotions.

If she came apart now, it would destroy everything that she and Rio had, even memories.

She must not make him feel guilty for giving her what she had asked—*demanded*—of him. She had been strong so many times in her life. She had to be strong once more.

Just for a few minutes.

Just long enough to say good-bye to the man she loved.

Looking at her rigid back made Rio feel as though he had taken a punch to the gut. He tried to speak, failed, tried again. His voice was so tight it sounded like a stranger's.

"Hope, if I don't go now, it will just be worse when I do leave. And I will leave. I have to." Then, with a self-hatred that clawed at both of them, he added bitterly, "I knew I never should have touched you."

After a long moment Hope turned back to him, her face desperately calm.

"You gave me as much as you could," she said in a husky voice, "and that was much more than I ever expected from any man. Don't be angry with yourself for that. I'm not. I love you. *And I know that my love isn't enough for you.* I knew it even before I fell in love."

He made a rough, anguished sound.

Hope held her hand out to the brilliant dance of water, letting it wash over her fingers like the kisses she would never again share with him.

"You gave me my dream," she said. "I would give you your dream, but you don't have one, and the one I dreamed for you wasn't strong enough. So I'll give you all I can, all you want. The freedom of the wind."

"Hope." Rio's voice fragmented in a harsh kind of silence. His hands clenched again. "Oh, God, I wish I were a different man!"

"No!"

She closed her eyes, not trusting herself to look at or touch him. She heard his anger at himself twisting viciously through every word, destroying him, destroying her, destroying love.

"Don't hate yourself, Rio. If you do that, you'll hate me, too. I couldn't bear that." She took a ragged breath. "If you think of me at all after you leave, remember that I love you. All of you. Even the wind."

For an instant Hope thought she felt the warmth of his breath against her lips. Then the wind blew, taking everything away, the warmth and the man.

When her eyes finally opened again, she was alone except for the long sigh of air through the canyon.

"I love you, Brother-to-the-wind," she whispered.

Nothing answered her but the silver dance of artesian water.

Twenty-six

❦

IN THE RESTRAINED silence that had become second nature to Hope in the weeks since Rio left, she drove Behemoth over the rough road leading into Wind Canyon. She made no attempt to talk to J. L. Hunsaker, the hydrologist who was going to pass judgment on the quality of Rio's well.

Hunsaker looked like he was on the downhill side of forty. He was lean as rawhide and burned dark from the sun. His clothes were those of a field engineer—sturdy and thick, like his lace-up boots. Even the wedding band on his left hand looked solid enough to take a beating. Streaks of silver shot through his dark brown hair, suggesting that the man himself had been hard used for his age.

But there was nothing worn about his eyes. They were a pure brown, narrowed, and penetrating as he studied the dry, harsh land. He glanced up at the looming Perdidas and the steep, eroded foothills that bordered the canyon. Nowhere was there any sign of water, not so much as a seep with a handful of green grass around it.

Shifting in the seat, J. L. Hunsaker shook his head. "If you'd told me there was water here before we set out, I'd have said you were crazy."

Hope gave her passenger a quick glance and concentrated again on the road. No matter how many times she drove it, the road always managed to give her a few bumpy surprises.

"A lot of people thought I was crazy," she said in a matter-of-fact voice. "Including the Reno bank that hired you. That's why they're demanding a survey of the well before they even consider a loan."

She hadn't bothered to ask for another loan from Cottonwood Savings and Trust, even after the well came in. She would never again put herself in debt to anyone related to John Turner.

"Who brought the well in for you?" Hunsaker asked.

"A man called Rio."

"Rio?" Hunsaker turned toward her suddenly, his face alive with interest. "Big man? Black hair?"

"Yes." Her voice was clipped, almost curt.

"Well, hell, if the bank had told me that, I'd have saved us all a trip. If Rio brought in your well, it's as good as gold. Better," Hunsaker added, chuckling. "Cattle can't drink gold."

Hope tried not to ask, but her hunger for news was greater than her pride. Maybe Hunsaker had seen or heard from Rio.

"Do you know Rio?" she asked as casually as she could.

Hunsaker shrugged. "Can't say as anyone really *knows* Rio. We went to school together. Colorado School of Mines."

Again Hope looked quickly at the hydrologist.

"Yeah, I know. I look older than him," Hunsaker said. "I am. I did a stint in the military and Rio was barely sixteen when he started at the School of Mines. He had his master's degree before he was twenty. Most brilliant man I've ever met."

Her hands clenched hard on the wheel. Too hard. The truck jerked and swerved as though protesting. Automatically she brought the heavy vehicle back into line.

Hunsaker braced himself when the water truck lurched over a particularly rough patch of road. He didn't say anything about the hard ride. He was used to worse. At least this truck had a seat for passengers. He had been in some that had wooden benches just like a buckboard.

"In college at sixteen?" she managed finally. "That must have been hard for Rio."

"Not the school part. Like I said, he was brilliant. But the people . . ." Hunsaker shrugged. "Rio was alone a lot. Being part Indian is no picnic in some places around the West. A lot of men would have grown up real mean if they'd been treated like him."

She remembered how Rio had fought Turner, swift and skilled and ruthless. She had wondered who taught Rio to fight, but she had never wondered why he had learned. She had known.

"But Rio was different," Hunsaker said. "When he

had a bellyful, he'd just go out into the mountains for a while and then come back . . . soothed, I guess. Yeah. Soothed." He smiled rather grimly. "Course, the fact that he beat the hell out of more than one loudmouth son of a bitch soothed him from time to time, too, I imagine."

Hope's hands tightened on Behemoth's steering wheel until her knuckles were white. She couldn't bear the thought of Rio being hurt for no better reason than an accident of birth.

Like the woman who had been so blind and so stupid that she refused to have Rio's child. The thought of it enraged Hope.

She would give up even the well if she could have Rio's baby.

Maybe this time. Maybe February is the month my period won't come.

"How'd you meet Rio?" Hunsaker asked.

He had to repeat the question twice before Hope heard him. She was lost in her memories and the yearning that never left her, the dream that she couldn't help dreaming no matter how little chance it had to come true.

One impossible dream had become real. Why not two?

"People told him I needed a well," she said. "Desperately."

Hunsaker nodded. "Yeah. That's Rio. Always ready to give a hand."

Hope remembered those hands, long-fingered and lean and strong. Skilled with machinery. Skilled with horses. Skilled with her. So much to give and take and share. So little time.

"Funny thing," Hunsaker continued. "Rio was good, real good, at his work. He could have been rich ten times over. He could have taken that money and crammed it down the throat of every bigot he ever met."

"That wouldn't be like him."

Hunsaker nodded. "Instead, he just drifted until he found someone that life had really dumped on. If they had the grit to fight, he'd help them. He didn't ask for cash. They paid him in crops or cattle or a place to sleep, whatever they could afford. Bet he's got stock pastured all over the West as part of his pay. But never money. No way."

"People paid him in dreams," she said.

"What?"

"Rio is a man without dreams. When he finds people who can dream, he helps them, sharing their dream for a while."

There was a long silence while Hunsaker watched the land and quietly reassessed the woman who sat beside him.

"Never thought of it that way, but you're dead right," he said finally. "You must have gotten closer to him than most."

She didn't respond.

Hunsaker opened the window, lit up a cigarette, and blew smoke out. Cold air poured in, but neither he nor she cared. Both of them were dressed for a winter hike.

"Damn shame someone didn't help Rio when he was still young enough to dream," Hunsaker muttered.

"What do you mean?"

"He had a hell of a childhood. Mother and father drank and he ran loose in the streets. When he got too wild they dumped him on the res with his grandparents and took off."

"How old was he?"

"Twelve, thirteen." Hunsaker took a hard drag on the cigarette and sighed. "Don't know what his grandfather did to straighten Rio out. That was one tough old Indian, from all I hear. Had about as much give in him as a rock."

Hope concentrated on the road, but it was Rio she saw, a younger Rio, defiant and lonely. "Are his parents still alive?"

"Not hardly. They wrapped their car around a telephone pole on the way home from a bar. Rio must have been about fifteen then."

She flinched and gripped the wheel until her hands ached. Love for Rio poured through her like a molten river, painful and beautiful at once. If she could have, she would have taken every one of his hurts on herself, healing him, freeing him to love. But that was even more impossible than her dream of sharing her life with him.

"Rough road," Hunsaker said. He grabbed the armrest as the truck jolted and bucked over a mound of rocks and loose sand. "Must be hard work for you coming out here, hauling water for your house and your stud."

Hope shrugged. It wasn't the road that had brought the grim lines to her face, it was the loss of the man she loved. She wanted Hunsaker to keep talking, to share with her his memories of Rio, every one of them. Maybe if she could collect enough memories, enough pieces of him, he would be whole again—and so would she.

Hunsaker smoked in silence.

"You must be a friend of Rio's," she said at last. "You know a lot about him."

Smiling, he drew on the cigarette again. "More like a fan. Rio's kind of a hobby with me."

Startled, she glanced quickly at the hydrologist. "A hobby? What do you mean?"

"I did my thesis on dowsing. Thought it was a crock of shit, no two ways about it."

"You aren't the only one."

"Yeah. Well, Rio heard about my thesis. He looked me up and told me I was dead wrong. I didn't take real kindly to it."

Hope wasn't surprised. For all his slow western drawl, Hunsaker was a hard man.

"What happened?" she asked. "Fists and boots at dawn?"

Hunsaker laughed. "No, ma'am. Even back then, I wasn't a fool. Rio was maybe seventeen, but you forgot that when you looked him in the eye. He was one tough son of a bitch. I kept the argument to words and theories and formulas."

"You didn't convince him."

"Nope. And I wouldn't listen to him. So we went head to head on a piece of desert west of here. I had my compasses, survey maps, satellite photos, laser-sighting devices, the whole damned shooting match."

"I wish I'd seen it."

Hunsaker smiled ruefully, remembering. "Not much to see. Rio found water before I'd finished my preliminary survey."

"Really?"

"As ever was. Made the hair on my neck stand straight up."

A shiver of memory went over Hope, soft electrical shocks flowing, Rio's eyes black and deep with uncanny knowledge.

Hunsaker shifted on the bouncing seat and stared out the window at the unpromising land. "Finding water is my profession, and I'm damned if I can figure out how water witching works." He stubbed out his cigarette in his traveling ashtray, folded it up, and put it back in the rucksack between his feet. "So I collect stories about dowsing while I'm out doing hydrological surveys. Rio's name comes up regular as the sun. He's been finding water since he was thirteen."

Hope made a startled sound.

"It's true," Hunsaker said. "Like dowsing. Odd but still true. You see, I know a lot of facts about Rio—his parents, grandparents, the wells he's found, the people he's helped, the horses he's tamed, the men he's fought, the women he could have had and didn't."

For a moment Hope felt light-headed, almost dizzy.

"But I don't know anything about him, not really," Hunsaker said. "Not even his name. No one does. A real private kind of man. Never shared his secrets with anyone."

My true name is Brother-to-the-wind.

Rio's words echoed in Hope's mind, making her throat ache and her eyes burn with unshed tears. He had shared so much with her, given so much to her, taken so much less from her than she wanted to give.

Behemoth slithered over the last sandy patch in the road, breasted a small rise, and stopped. Ahead lay a rippling silver bowl of water. A small artesian fountain danced above the surface of the new pond.

As though in a trance, Hunsaker got out of the truck. He walked to the edge of the pond without looking away from the silver transformations of the water.

Hope followed. The surprise of seeing water dancing in the midst of stone was new each time. So was the pain of remembering. She took off her hat and stood while the wind caressed her with restless, transparent fingers.

"I will be damned," Hunsaker said reverently.

After a few more minutes, he shook himself and hauled out some forms. His questions came in a rapid stream. As she answered, he filled in blanks with a mechanical pencil. When she told him how deep they had gone to get water, the pencil lifted. He looked straight at her.

"You got guts, lady. Anyone else would have given up halfway down."

Instead of answering, she simply watched the miracle of water in a dry land.

"No wonder you're broke," he said. "That's a hell of a lot of pipe, mud, and supplies." He paused. "Heard you sold everything but your stud to pay for the well."

She closed her eyes, haunted by memories of beautiful black Angus waiting patiently for grain.

"Yes," she said simply.

Hunsaker measured the height of the artesian fountain falling into the pond that filled the hollow where the well had been drilled. "How much has the fountain gone down since it first came in?"

"After the first few minutes it didn't diminish at all."

His eyebrows rose. "Good solid flow. Going to put a lid on it?"

"Not right away. I know I should, but . . ." Her voice faded.

"Yeah, I know what you mean. That pulsing water is something to see, isn't it? You know, you could put a small dam down in that crease."

Slowly she focused on Hunsaker. "What?"

He pointed toward a dip in the rim of land surrounding the pond. There, water rippled out toward the canyon floor below, creating a stream where none had ever before flowed.

"Drill a pipe through the base of the rim and let gravity do the rest," he said. "If that's not enough punch, install a wind-driven pump. That way you could have piped water and your artesian fountain, too."

She smiled, pleased by the idea.

For a moment Hunsaker simply stared at her. It was the first time she had smiled in all the hours that he had been with her.

"Don't worry about your ranch, ma'am. When the bank gets my recommendations, they'll lend you enough to get started again. It won't be a quarter what you need," he added bluntly, "because wells are dicey things. But you've got plenty of guts. You'll make it."

"Thank you."

"Don't thank me." He watched the rippling water with something close to awe. "Thank Rio. For a man without dreams, he sure as hell has made a lot of them come true."

Robert Moran's ranch was even more remote than the Valley of the Sun. Colorado's high, snow-covered mountains rose in jagged crowns against the cobalt-blue sky, but where Rio stood, the land was flat, dry, a frozen February landscape that offered no hint of the summer ahead.

"That you, Rio?" Moran asked, rushing out of his new barn. His breath was a silver burst in the instants before the wind swept it away. "Thought I recognized the truck. Coming to check on your cattle and the well?"

Rio didn't know why he was there. He only knew that, like the wind, he had to keep moving. He shook Moran's hand.

"No, I'm just . . ." Rio's voice died. *Restless, angry, hungry.* "Moving around, like always. How have you been?"

"Marti will be smiling to see your truck in the yard. She's in town right now. One of the kids had an ear infection. Other than that, all of us are healthy as horses and fat as pigs, thanks to the well you found for us."

"My pleasure," Rio said simply.

And it had been.

"You should see your cattle," Moran said enthusiastically. "They're multiplying like flies. I'm thinking you'll want to cull some. That's why I left word down to Rimrock for you to come see me. I didn't want to sell any of yours without you okaying it."

"Our deal was that you would treat my cattle just like yours. Nothing has changed."

Moran smiled. "Fine. I'll put the money in your account or in better bloodlines, whichever you choose."

"Better cattle."

"You got it. Come on to the house and put your gear in the spare room. Marti must have known you were coming, because she baked enough cookies to bury us chin-deep. After dinner, we'll—"

"I won't be staying," Rio interrupted softly.

"Of course you are. Marti would have my hide if I let you get away."

"Maybe next time."

Moran started to say something else, then looked at Rio, really looked at him, for the first time. Rio was drawn, filed down, honed to the kind of edge that could cut everything in reach.

"Well, sure," Moran said. "Maybe you'll see Marti on the road back."

"Maybe. Say hello to her for me."

"Sure. Where you going in such a rush?"

Rio didn't answer. He didn't know. He only knew that he must leave.

As he went back to his truck, the wind blew restlessly, freely. It combed his hair, tugged at his sheepskin jacket, and whispered to him about the woman who had looked at him, *seen* him, and loved everything she saw.

Even the wind.

Twenty-seven

GRINNING, MASON PUT a final twist on the connection that would bring water from Rio's well into the old network that had been serviced by the wells that had gone dry. May first was the beginning of a new life for the Valley of the Sun.

"Let 'er rip, honey!"

Hope turned the valve. After a moment, water churned and thundered into the cistern buried beneath her feet.

Behemoth had made its last run to Rio's well to bring water. She had replaced the ancient truck with an expensive, gleaming pipeline that snaked back along the old road starting from the ranch house and ending in Wind Canyon's shadowed depths. Within a week, other pipelines would be finished. Then there would be a network of thick silver straws leading to troughs where range cattle could drink during the dry months of summer. Other lines had been laid so crops could be irrigated.

There weren't any cattle yet. Even with the new loan, she didn't have enough money to replace her herds. She would have to start with calves and go from there. If the crops this year were good, if the alfalfa and oat hay grew thick and rich, there would be enough money and feed to buy and fatten up beef calves in the autumn.

Autumn.

Rio had come to her in the autumn, telling her that he would find water. It had been in autumn that he had first made love to her while a cold wind blew.

The memory shook her even as wind had shaken the house that night.

Her fingers curled around the cold steel valve and she hung on, waiting for the storm of yearning to sweep through her, leaving her spent. Each time it happened, she told herself that her memories of Rio would grow dimmer with each passing day.

They hadn't.

They had grown even as the life in her womb grew, thriving in the secret places of her body, stronger with each hour. She could hardly wait until next autumn, when Rio's baby would be born. She ached to hold it to her breast and hear its tiny cries.

"Prettiest sound I ever did hear," Mason said with satisfaction, listening to the rush of water.

When Hope didn't answer, he glanced at her. The distant, strained look on her face told him that she was somewhere else. He frowned and bit back a curse. She hadn't been the same since Rio left. It wasn't just that she didn't smile easily or laugh at all. She was just different. A woman now, no girl left in her.

The Valley of the Sun had always been important to her, but it was more than that now. It was everything.

In the three months since Rio had left the ranch, other men had come. They had asked Hope to church and to barbecues, to movies and to parties. Her answer was always the same, no matter how handsome or respectable the man was.

No.

Mason had chided her once, telling her that she should go out and enjoy herself. The look she had given him had been enough to make him flinch, but all she had said was, *I'm a one-man woman.*

The sound of a heavy truck driving into the yard between the barn and the house pulled Hope out of her autumn dreams. She looked at Mason. He shook his head.

"Nope," he said. "I didn't order nothing."

Rio! He's come back!

The thought was like lightning—hot, blinding. She didn't know that there was a flash of raw hope on her face as she turned and ran toward the sound. Nor did she know that every bit of light faded from her eyes when she saw that a stranger drove the truck.

"Lost?" she asked evenly as the driver rolled down his window.

The man was at least fifty, as weathered as the hills, and about as talkative. "Yer name Hope?"

"Yes."

"Where ya want it?"

"What?"

"Seed." He jerked a grizzled chin toward the truck bed.

She peered around the cab and saw the bags of oat hay and alfalfa seed. "I didn't order any seed."

He nodded and waited impatiently for her to answer his question so that he could unload his truck and get back to his farm.

"If I didn't order any seed, then that's not my seed in the truck," Hope pointed out reasonably.

"Rio sez bring it. I brung it." He stared at her, waiting to be told where to put the seed.

She stared back, speechless, a single word echoing through her mind and body and soul: *Rio.*

A look of exasperation crossed the stranger's unshaven face. "Where ya want it?"

Mason came up behind Hope. "You say Rio sent you with this seed?"

"Ain't this Hope Gardener's spread?"

"This is her ranch," Mason said.

"So where you want it?"

"I'll show you where to put the seed," Mason said.

" 'Bout time," the man muttered.

Having exhausted his well of small talk, the stranger revved his truck's engine and slowly followed Mason.

Bewildered, Hope watched the man back up to one of the storage sheds and begin unloading bag after bag of seed. He answered no questions, asked none, and refused anything more than a cup of coffee.

After the man left, Hope and Mason stood side by

side in the shed, looking at the unexpected delivery. Silently Mason pulled out a worn folding knife, opened a blade, and slit the top of a bag.

Smooth, rich, plump, the satiny contents cascaded from his hands and whispered back into the sack.

"Prime," he said softly, "really prime seed."

Hope didn't answer. She simply thrust her hands wrist-deep into the seed and lifted. When she poured seeds from one hand to the other, she saw fields green with alfalfa and shimmering gold with oats. There was thousands of dollars worth of seed stacked neatly in the shed, sacks pregnant with future harvests.

With Rio's seed she could begin rebuilding the Valley of the Sun.

When Hope slept that night she dreamed of Rio's child, her child, their child, running through fields thick with grain and sweet with alfalfa flowers. The dream slowly changed, filled with the muted thunder of rain. She woke up in a rush, only to find that it wasn't rain that had awakened her, but trucks.

She ran to the window and simply stared. A convoy of cattle trucks was driving into the ranch yard. Above the roar of diesels came the concerted bawling of yearling steers.

Rio?

Again, like lightning, the thought scored across Hope's emotions.

She yanked on her clothes with fierce speed, kicking into her boots even as she shoved her arms into her jacket.

When she ran into the front yard the sun was barely an incandescent fingernail hooked over Eagle Peak.

A broad-shouldered, bluff-looking man climbed down out of the first cattle truck's high cab. His motions were stiff, those of someone who had been on the road a long time.

"You Hope?" he asked.

She looked up into his ruddy, wind-roughed face. "Yes."

"Name's Martin," he said, holding out his hand.

Hope shook it, feeling as though she was still asleep, still dreaming. The sound and smell of cattle swirled around her on the dawn wind, stirring her. She had missed the earthy smells and plaintive bawls of cattle. She looked at them yearningly.

"Yeah, you're Hope, all right," Martin said, smiling. "He told me, 'Look for a woman with dreams in her eyes.' "

Hope's eyes widened, revealing hazel depths where both gold and shadows turned. "Rio sent you?"

"Sure did. Where do you want the calves?"

"But I didn't order—" Her voice broke. She swallowed and tried again. "Mr. Martin—"

"Just Martin, ma'am."

"Martin," she said somewhat desperately. She didn't know a gentle way to tell this stranger that he had made a long drive for nothing. She hadn't ordered cows because there wasn't enough money to pay for them. Not yet. Not until she harvested and sold a few crops. "I'm sorry. I can't afford to buy your cattle."

Martin shook his head. "Nothing was said about money, ma'am. Didn't Rio tell you we were coming?"

She shook her head mutely.

"Yeah, well, that's Rio. He was edgy as hell when I talked to him. Never saw a man so restless. He came four months early and didn't hardly even stay for a cup of coffee. Just gave me your name and told me to ship whatever I owed him down here."

"Down here?" Hope shook her head and fought for breath. She felt like she was drowning in the soaring dawn and the bawl of cattle. "Where are you from?"

"Montana, way up by the Canadian border. Don't mind telling you, it was some trick to comb these yearling steers out of a storm and ship them through the worst spring I've seen in decades." He smiled suddenly, his dark eyes alive with laughter. "Not that I minded. Not a bit. If Rio had said drive his cows to Hawaii, I'd have loaded them up and driven west until my hat floated."

She just stared at him.

Martin looked over to the pastures opposite the house. "That fence in the bigger pasture strong enough to hold back a few yearlings?"

Closing her eyes, Hope forced herself to breathe. The earthy smell of cattle was more beautiful to her than roses.

"Yes," she said, opening her eyes. "Follow me."

She turned and walked toward the big gate leading into the pasture. She didn't know where she was going to find food for all the cattle—there had to be hundreds of them, and even now another truck was pulling up to the ranch. Although the winter had been mild, there hadn't been much rain. There wasn't much natural food for the cattle.

Then she realized that she could buy hay with the money she had earmarked for seed. Relief made her light-headed. She shook it off. She didn't want to miss one instant of watching cattle streaming back into the Valley of the Sun's empty pastures.

Yearling Herefords crowded down the truck ramps and spread over the pasture in a rich russet tide. Wind sighed and curled through the yard, making dust into a glittering golden veil rising with the dawn. The bawling of cattle rose to meet the cataract of sunrise spilling down the Perdidas' rugged slopes.

Hardly able to believe her eyes, Hope leaned on the pasture fence and simply watched cattle returning to her ranch.

Martin watched Hope for a long time before he walked up to stand beside her. She turned to him with a smile that made him wish she wasn't Rio's woman. But he didn't doubt that she was. It had been in Rio's eyes when he spoke her name—and in hers when she spoke his.

"They're beautiful," she said, emotion thickening in her voice.

Martin laughed as he looked at the wild-eyed, winter-lean yearlings fanning across the pasture. "You're a rancher, all right. Nobody else would think those ragged steers were beautiful."

She hesitated, watching Martin from the corner of

her eye, wanting to know how Rio had looked, if he was happy or sad, well or drawn out to a fine humming wire of tension.

Like her.

Restless. Edgy as hell.

Like Rio.

"I didn't know they were short of water in northern Montana," she said, fishing delicately for information.

Martin gave her an amused look. "Not the part I'm from. I met Rio a different way."

She turned and looked at Martin directly, silently urging him to talk, drinking each word the way thirsty land drinks water.

"Twelve years ago I found three men driving about forty of my cattle into Canada," Martin said simply. "I should have gone for help, but I was so damn mad I just waded right in. You see, those cows were every penny I had in the world back then."

Hope made a sound of sympathy. She knew just how he felt.

Martin shook his head, remembering the younger and much more foolhardy man he had been. He drew out a pipe, packed it with tobacco, and lit it with a special lighter. The pungent fragrance of his pipe mingled with the smell of cattle, dust, and a dry wind.

"Well, to make a long story short," Martin said, "those rustlers beat hell out of me and left me for dead. I would have been, too, if Rio hadn't happened along. He patched me up, got me to a doctor, and disappeared before I could thank him."

She wasn't surprised. "He wouldn't have waited around for thanks."

"No, ma'am. He had bigger fish to fry, and he fried them up real crisp. When I got home again a week later, every last one of my cows was back like nothing had ever happened."

Her breath came in swiftly. "What happened to the rustlers?"

"I didn't ask. Rio didn't say." Martin puffed hard, savored smoke, and continued, "He stayed and ran things until I was on my feet again. I told him that half of everything I owned was his. He refused it, saying even God only took a tenth, and God was a hell of a lot more useful than one crossbreed Indian."

Hope's eyelids flinched in pain for the man she loved, giving so much, taking so little in return.

"Rio never asked a thing from me until now," Martin said. Smiling, he added, "I've done right well for myself and Rio in those years."

Martin and his men left a few hours later. Hope and Mason spent the rest of the day turning on pipelines and putting out the hay that had remained after she had sold her cattle to pay for Rio's well.

Tired but smiling, Mason and Hope finally sat down to dinner. They had barely picked up their forks when two huge hay trucks rumbled up the road. She and Mason looked at each other and got up without a word. As soon as they reached the yard a familiar greeting rang out.

"Where you want it?"

Hope's mouth opened, closed.

Mason walked up to the first truck. The driver was a rail-thin man with a gray mustache that was no wider than the string tie that circled the collar of his pale western shirt.

"You sure you aren't lost?" Mason asked.

"Ranch gate said Valley of the Sun. That's where he sent me."

"He?" Hope stepped forward. "Are you talking about Rio?"

"Yes, ma'am. I'm Tim Webster. My wife Betty is driving the other truck. We brought our boys for the heavy work, because Rio said you didn't have any hands."

"Where are you from?"

"Southern New Mexico."

Hope took a breath. Northern Montana. New Mexico. Rio was everywhere but Nevada. "Show them where to put it, Mason. I'll see about some food for everyone."

The Webster family stayed long enough to unload the hay, eat, and drink quarts of coffee. When Hope offered beds for the night, the Websters refused.

"Thank you, but we need to get back to the ranch," Tim said. "Now, you remember what I told you. This isn't but a handful of what we owe Rio. You ever come up short of feed, you give us a holler. We'll start loading trucks before you hang up."

Their simple generosity moved Hope. "Thank you," she said huskily, "but I hope it won't be needed, now that the ranch has a reliable well for irrigation."

"Just the same, you remember. Without Rio, Betty and me wouldn't have a handful of spit between us. We don't forgot what we owe him. We never will."

The next afternoon two more cattle trucks arrived. Hope watched the dust plumes rise behind the trucks and she thought she couldn't be surprised anymore. She was wrong.

When the lead truck turned, she could see the name on its long black trailer: MCNALLY'S BLACK ANGUS.

Hot and cold chills chased over her skin. She had bought Sweetheart from McNally, and sold her back to him. Dazed, she watched the rig drive up. A big man in worn jeans and an expensive leather jacket climbed down. He walked up to her with a smile as wide as his broad face.

"McNally?" Hope's voice was ragged. "What are you doing here?"

He just kept smiling and looking around at the ranch where late afternoon sunlight flowed like honey across the land. "Didn't really notice it last time, but this is a pretty little place you have. Mite dry, but Rio said he fixed that."

Numb, she just stared at McNally.

Mason walked up and stood beside her, looking at the black trucks.

With a muffled groan, McNally stretched like a man who had spent too many hours behind the wheel. Then he looked at Hope and grinned. "Well, darlin', where do you want your Angus?"

She couldn't have spoken if her life required it.

Next to Hope, Mason laughed and swore softly. He gestured to the other driver, showing him the empty pasture gate where the Angus had been when McNally bought them back.

After the big rig was maneuvered into the opening and the ramp lowered, Hope's voice came back.

"*My* Angus?" she said, turning on McNally. "If they belong to anyone, they belong to Rio."

"That sure isn't what he said." McNally pulled on his Stetson's pale rim, steadying the hat against the playful tugs of the wind. Then he touched the side of the black metal trailer. "These cattle are yours, Hope. Every last hair on their shiny hides."

"I can't take them. I haven't done anything to earn them."

McNally looked at Hope with pale blue eyes that saw through her carefully controlled voice to the unhappy woman beneath. "That's not what Rio told me. He said you sold your cattle, your horses, your future, everything, because you believed in him. When anyone else would have cut their losses and run, you stuck it out. And you did it knowing full well what the odds against you were."

She didn't say anything, just shook her head.

McNally smiled strangely. "That reached Rio down deep, down where nobody ever touched him before. Kind of opened him up and made him bleed. These cattle are yours."

"I can't take them."

"Watch you don't get trampled, ma'am," called the driver as he freed the cattle.

Gently Mason and McNally crowded Hope back out
of the way of the cattle that were coming out of the
truck. She didn't object anymore. She couldn't. She
had recognized the first of the sleek black cows to walk
down the ramp.

"Sweetheart."

The cow's head came up at the familiar voice. She ambled down the ramp and nudged Hope with a broad, damp
muzzle, looking for grain. Her calves followed her, grown
and half-grown, dense black cattle walking down the
ramp and drifting over the familiar pasture to pick at the
new growth that winter rains had called from the land.

The wind followed them, ruffling their thick, glossy
coats.

"I can't take them," Hope said again. She clenched
her hands so that she wouldn't rub them down Sweetheart's solid barrel. "These cows never belonged to
Rio. You bought them from me. They're yours."

McNally tugged on his hat brim. "Without Rio I
wouldn't have a pot to piss in or a window to throw it
out of."

Hope closed her eyes against the temptation of her
Angus just within reach. The future of the Valley of the
Sun had come home.

"Rio was only fifteen when he found water for me,"
McNally continued. "I gave him three Angus heifers
and the use of my best bull. He never came back for
them or their calves until this year."

Hope made a sound of protest.

McNally kept talking. "When it came time to sort
out what was Rio's, we both just kind of decided that

these Angus had his name on them. Now, if you don't agree, you're just going to have to take it up with him. I sure as hell don't plan on crossing him."

Without meaning to, Hope found her hands rubbing through Sweetheart's warm coat. She opened her eyes and saw her fingers curling into the thick, springy mat of black that covered the cow's broad barrel.

"These cattle are Rio's," she said huskily. "For as long as the water flows."

"There's a new one in here," McNally said, going to the back of his own truck. "I'd recommend the barn for this one, but it's your choice."

Hope and Mason followed McNally to his truck. He opened the back and let down a stout ramp.

With ponderous grace, a massive black bull walked out of the truck. Every rippling muscle shouted the animal's fine breeding. Though the bull could have easily crushed the people standing nearby, he stood at the bottom of the ramp, waiting for McNally's signal. When McNally spoke softly, the bull watched him with calm, very dark eyes.

"No." Hope made a choked sound. "That bull is worth more than my whole herd of Angus put together. I can't take him."

"You want me to tell Rio that you couldn't find room in your barn for his bull?" McNally asked blandly.

"Yes. No." Hope's voice broke over the despair settling like ice in her, freezing her. "Damn you, Rio," she cried hoarsely. "I didn't want you to feel guilty about me!"

She turned and ran into the ranch house. The front door slammed behind her.

Mason and McNally exchanged a long look.

Then they led Rio's bull to its new home in the Valley of the Sun.

Twenty-eight

❧

BEFORE DAYBREAK the next morning, Hope lay in bed, her mind a turmoil. Through the open window, wind brought the random scents and sounds of the newly arrived Angus moving through the dawn, snuffling at the hay that had been put out. The scents and sounds of her dream.

Rio's cattle. Rio's hay. Rio's seed.

Rio's well.

But the dream was hers, dreamed for herself and for the man who had no dreams.

Just as the sun rose over Eagle Peak and spilled down into her bedroom, several pickup trucks rattled into the yard. The slam of a truck door and a man's voice hailing the house brought Hope upright in bed, her heart hammering with a sudden wild hope.

Rio?

She pulled on her clothes, kicked into her boots, and raced down the stairs. The yard in front of the barn was alive with pickup trucks hauling horse trailers. Three, four, five trucks, each pulling a four- or six-horse trailer.

Drivers climbed out, stretched, and called back and forth between the trucks with the rough voices of men who had been up all night drinking coffee and smoking cigarettes.

"Mornin', ma'am. You be Hope?" the closest driver asked when he saw her. The man was tall and thin, with a Tennessee accent running like a warm river through his speech.

"Yes."

"Pleasure, ma'am," he said, touching the brim of his hat. He turned his head, whistled shrilly through his teeth, and called, "Yo! Jake! This here is Rio's woman!"

Jake trotted over, shook Hope's hand, and asked, "Where do you want us to put our gear?"

"What?"

"Our gear, ma'am. Rio said you needed help."

"I can't afford to pay you," she said bluntly.

Jake's smile was as gentle as his teeth were crooked. "Makes no never mind, ma'am. We couldn't pay Rio, neither. Didn't stop him none. Won't stop us."

"But—"

"Ma'am," Jake interrupted softly, "I sure do hope you're not going to put us crosswise of Rio. He's got his heart set on us being here."

In the end Mason led everyone to the second bunkhouse, where they all pitched in and started cleaning. Other than Jake and the tall man from Tennessee, the rest of the "men" were hardly more than boys.

But they had handled cattle and horses all their lives, and it showed. Horses began flowing out of the trailers in a calm, multicolored stream. They were sturdy, seasoned ponies that didn't have to be told which end of a cow bit and which kicked.

Hope watched and told herself that she would sort it out later, when she was awake. Right now it was enough just to hear the familiar, rhythmic music of shod hooves in the ranch yard again.

"Ma'am?" Jake called.

"Yes?"

"This one's yours." He led Dusk out of a trailer. "Rio said how you liked to ride at night, and he was worried about you getting on a spooky pony."

Hope didn't know what to say. She hadn't ridden since she sold her mares. She had been afraid to risk her pregnancy on one of Storm Walker's friendly bucking sessions.

"Rio," she whispered to the wind. "How can I forget you when you keep sending me what is yours?"

Cool wind rushed over her face, her throat, her burning eyes.

But she wouldn't cry. She hadn't cried when Rio left. She refused to start now.

Rio stood alone on a high ridge, looking over land that had once been green with forests. The trees had long since turned to stone. The land had been rich with water, water that had sunk down into the earth, water that now was far older than mankind.

The wind moaned around him, tugging at him.

Well, brother, Rio thought wearily, *you've blown me all over the West. Now what? What undiscovered country do you have left? What secrets haven't you showed me?*

Currents of air as solid as hands buffeted him, forcing him to turn his back, close his eyes, and hang on to his hat. Abruptly the wind dropped to a whisper, and that whisper was a name.

Rio got back in his truck and started driving.

Fleeing.

But wherever he went, the wind was always there ahead of him, waiting.

Whispering.

In the days and weeks that followed, by twos and fives and tens, beef and breeding cattle from every state west of the Rockies arrived at the Valley of the Sun. Hope gave up objecting to the men who drove the trucks. Despite differences in age and wealth, the men all were alike in one way: they weren't going to disappoint the man called Rio.

As Hope's fifth month without Rio began, she thought she had accepted it all: the loss of Rio and the gain of the well, the loss of Rio and the gain of the cattle, the loss of Rio and the gain of his child. She thought she was strong enough to see him in every sunrise, hear his name in every wind, taste him in every silver drop of water from his well, remember him with every breath she took; she could take all of that without destroying herself in endless longing for him.

And then one more afternoon came, one more stock truck drove into the yard, and one more man asked her, "Where do you want them?"

In unnatural silence Hope watched him lead horses down the ramp and into the corral. They were magnificent, long-legged mares with clear eyes and powerful haunches and life running through them like leashed lightning. Mares cakewalking across the yard, their heads raised high, nostrils flared to drink the scent of the wind sweeping down from the Perdidas. Wind ruffled silky manes and tails, whispered to pricked ears the secrets of the land, and then sped on.

Hope stood motionless, enthralled by the mares' beauty. A dream swirled within her, a vision of the future when Storm Walker's foals would grow sleek and strong, running through fields where grass never failed and water always flowed.

Rio's stock and her land and their child, and the artesian fountain he had found hidden deep within rock, ancient water flowing, an endless promise of life.

The Valley of the Sun was truly alive again.

Tears flowed silently, helplessly, down Hope's cheeks. She hadn't cried when Rio left or in all the long hours since then. But she couldn't stop crying now. To see her family's dream come true, her father's dream, her own dream, and yet to be alone within that dream . . .

Blindly she turned and made her way to the barn.

Jake and Mason saw her coming, then saw her tears

and her fumbling fingers as she grabbed a familiar bridle. Gently Jake took the bridle from her hands.

"Going for a ride?" Mason asked.

Unable to speak, she nodded.

"Then you'll want Dusk," Jake said.

She nodded again.

The two men went off and quickly returned with Dusk. Though it was a very mild day, Jake took off his big denim jacket and wrapped it around Hope.

"It gets right cool in some of those canyons," he said.

She didn't say anything.

Mason handed her the reins, and both men watched her ride out of the yard.

"She going to be all right?" Jake asked in a low voice.

"She better be," Mason growled, "or I'm gonna skin that thickheaded son of a bitch and use his hide to wipe my boots."

Jake smiled a bit grimly. "Holler if you need help. Me and the boys, well," he said, shrugging, "we owe Rio, but that's one damned fine woman eating her heart out over him."

Mason and Jake went back to their barn chores. They had stalls to muck out, grain to pour, hay and straw to bring, horses to groom, shoes to check: all the small, endless tasks that went into owning horses. After that there were fences to ride, pipelines to check, machinery to repair. The list was as long as it was necessary.

Just as the men finished up in the barn, a pickup

truck pulled into the front yard. A tall, broad-shouldered man climbed out and looked around slowly.

As one, Mason and Jake headed for him.

"Howdy, Rio," Mason said. "Come to check on your stock?"

Reluctantly Rio turned away from the ranch house. He still didn't know why he was here. He only knew that the wind had made it impossible for him to stay away.

"Hello, Mason, Jake," Rio said, shaking hands with each man. "How is . . ." His voice died, but he couldn't keep from watching the door to the house.

"The livestock are fine," Mason said, but it was the house Rio was looking at, his eyes shaded by the brim of his hat. Mason smiled thinly. "Come and take a look at all the changes."

"Not yet."

"Got something else in mind?" Mason prodded.

"Where's Hope?" Rio asked bluntly.

"Riding," Jake said, his voice neutral and his eyes burning.

"Where." It was a demand, not a question.

Jake waved his hand casually. "Out there. She's been real edgy. Spends a lot of time out on the range."

"She should be happy," Rio said in a rough voice. "She has her dream."

Jake shrugged. "She ain't."

"She cried for you," Mason said. "Don't ever hurt her like that again."

Rio hissed a word though his teeth and knew that he

should go. He stared at the house with dark, narrowed eyes.

"Where is she, Mason? And don't give me any crap about 'out there.' She knows better than to ride off alone without telling anyone where she's going. You know better than to let her."

"Who said she was alone?" Mason retorted. "Lots of prime young bucks have come sniffing around since you left."

For an instant something terrible flickered in Rio's eyes. Then he remembered the truth that he had discovered about Hope. She was a one-man woman. He was her man.

That wouldn't change in five months or five years or five hundred.

And he wouldn't change either. Brother-to-the-wind. Nothing had changed except the pain. It was worse every day, every hour, every breath.

"Where is she?" he asked bleakly.

"If you hurt her again—" Mason began.

Then Rio turned away from the house and Mason saw his eyes. However much Hope hurt, she wasn't alone.

"Well, *hell*," Mason muttered.

"Yes," Rio said, turning away again. "Hell."

"If you were hurting, where would you go?" Mason asked.

"The only place I haven't been yet—Wind Canyon."

"Nice place," Jake said blandly.

"One of Hope's favorites," Mason added.

"Is she there?"

The men simply watched Rio with eyes that held both sympathy and anger.

Abruptly Rio turned around and went back to his truck.

Dusk knew where to go without being told. Hope often rode her there. The mare took to the dirt road eagerly, remembering that the grass in Wind Canyon had grown lush and sweet around the new pond.

Hope rode without thinking about it, still lost in the moment when she had realized that she wasn't as strong as she had assumed she was. She was afraid she wasn't strong enough to live on the Valley of the Sun alone within her dream and not destroy herself.

But she couldn't let that happen. She owed it to Rio, to herself, and most of all to the child she carried.

So she rode blindly, tears welling over her cheeks faster than the wind could dry them. She would go to the miracle of Rio's well. Somehow she would find strength again as she had in the past. There was no other choice.

The mare stopped just beyond the rim of the artesian pond, where grass grew in a startling swath of emerald. Wanting freedom to graze, Dusk tugged at the reins.

Hope dismounted, leaving the horse in the patch of grass and finding another for herself. She sat without moving, remembering how it had been to be fully alive within her dream and Rio's arms. With memories came tears the color of artesian water streaming down her face.

Sunlight thickened into the rich orange and molten gold of late afternoon. The wind lifted, keening over the land. She didn't see the sun or hear the wind. She was lost in her memories and her broken dream, groping for the strength she needed to go on.

"Hope?"

His voice was from the broken dream, deep and warm, a richness that was like a caress. A gentle hand smoothed over her hair, calling her from her memories. She blinked.

And saw Rio through her tears.

For a moment her eyes blazed with returning life, a dream made whole again. But even as emotion swept through her, she understood that she was seeing just half of a dream. The wind had blown, bringing him back to her.

And it would blow again, taking him away.

The life that had blazed in Hope faded, taking the dreams from her eyes.

Rio called her name in a raw voice and knelt beside her.

She took his hand and cradled it against her cheek, wondering why half a dream took more strength to survive than a dream that was utterly broken.

He gathered her against his body as though she was more fragile than the dreams that had faded from her eyes.

"I'm sorry, I never meant to hurt you," he whispered. "Hope, please believe me."

He rocked slowly, stroking the cool silk of her hair, repeating his words over and over, hoping if he said them often enough, they would take away her tears and replace them with the incandescent dreams that had once been there.

She put her arms around Rio and let herself drift within half a dream, too emotionally spent to do more than fill her senses with his presence. He eased her down into the grass, cradling her against his warmth, talking to her softly, trying to explain the wind. His husky words wept over her like tears.

"I've spent my life like the wind, roaming the land, looking for . . . *something*," he said. "Like the wind, I never found it. Then I came to the Valley of the Sun and saw you fighting for your dream. I wanted to help you the way I had helped other dreamers."

She lay quietly against him and her tears kept falling.

"Then I began to dream, too," he said. He brushed his lips over her soft hair. "I dreamed of a woman who loved the land more than she loved anything, yet she risked everything she loved on a drifter's belief that he could find water where none had ever been found before. I dreamed of a woman strong enough to stand against drought and soft enough to set my body on fire. I dreamed of a woman who offered me herself and asked nothing in return. I dreamed of a woman who looked at a half-breed and saw a man, and loved what she saw."

Rio's arms tightened even as he felt the emotion that shook Hope's body. He didn't know whether it was joy or rage, love or hate, that made her tremble against him. He only knew that he had taken the dreams from her eyes and had left the emptiness of the wind in their place.

"My dream and your love frightened me," he said, finally understanding. "It was like a beautiful cage closing around me. So I ran and tried to find freedom in all the places I'd found it before. The land was there, but it wasn't the same. It didn't dream. It didn't reach into my soul and make me want to dream with it. There was nothing but the wind mocking me, wind as empty as I was."

With a deep, yearning sound, Rio kissed Hope, trying to say what he didn't have words to describe.

Her hands crept beneath his jacket. When she felt the tension of his muscles and his heat radiating through her, she tried to speak, to tell him that she loved him, but her throat was completely choked with tears. So she simply held him and watched him with eyes that accepted everything, even the wind.

"I came back to the Valley of the Sun," Rio said, trying to explain what he had only begun to understand himself. "The ranch looked beautiful, more beautiful than my dreams—until I found out that you weren't at the house. No one would tell me where you were, when you would come back, *if* you would come back. Even Mason. He just looked me in the eye, said you'd cried for me, and I'd better not hurt you again."

Rio held Hope tight and close, afraid that she would slip away from him as everything else had, even the wind.

He knew now what he had walked away from.

"Marry me, Hope. Dream with me. Love me as much as I love you."

"Rio . . ." Her voice trembled with tears even as she turned her lips to his. "I don't want to cage the wind. You'd hate me."

"Never," he said softly. "The wind taught me that it's empty, not free. Like me without you. You're my freedom."

He straightened for a moment and looked into her eyes, golden with tears and the setting sun.

"You don't—" His voice broke. He kissed her with a gentleness and tasted the tears that ran like molten gold over her lips. "You don't have to have my children," he said simply. "I know that's too much to ask of any woman, even in my dreams."

The words went through Hope like a wild wind, sweeping away everything but her love for Rio. She laughed and cried and whispered her love while she fumbled over the buttons of the denim jacket she wore, until she could open it and then the jeans and blouse beneath.

"Hope?"

Unable to speak, she took Rio's hands and moved them over the warm silver necklace she always wore, his gift to the future. But it was the woman beneath the necklace that stopped his breath. Her breasts were swollen, her waist thickened, her stomach rounded with the promise of future life.

Hope felt the sudden trembling of Rio's hands, saw the disbelief and the incredible hope in his eyes as he looked at her.

"Yes," she whispered. "Ours. Our own dream growing."

Rio bowed his head and touched the dream he had been afraid to believe in.

She trembled as she felt his lips move over her skin, felt the warmth of his breath against her breasts and the unexpected, agonizing heat of his tears as he laid his cheek against their child and whispered his love. His words and his tears and his touch told her that he would always be with her, as close as her heartbeat, as deeply a part of her as the water hidden far beneath them.

And like that water, their love would well forth irresistibly, bringing life to everything it touched.

The wind ruffled the sunset surface of the artesian pond, caressed the two lovers entwined on the grass, and then sang softly down the canyon, blowing over the land, blowing alone.